## THE CONFLAGRATION WAS FREE TO GROW UNHAMPERED

A commercial airline overhead might have spotted the blaze and radioed the alarm, but local flight paths avoided Sierra Grande as a natural hazard it was foolish to mess with, and no sightings occurred.

At last, no longer hidden and secret, large enough now and strong enough to dare the open, like a monster roaring out of its hiding place, the fire burst into view. In the darkness, it threw its lights and contorting shadows into the sky. Bellowing and roaring defiance, it was suddenly alive, and loose!

# WILDFIRE
## RICHARD MARTIN STERN

**ZEBRA BOOKS**
**KENSINGTON PUBLISHING CORP.**

ZEBRA BOOKS

are published by

Kensington Publishing Corp.
475 Park Avenue South
New York, NY 10016

First Zebra Books printing: April 1987

Printed in the United States of America

*TO DAS, with love,*
*as always.*

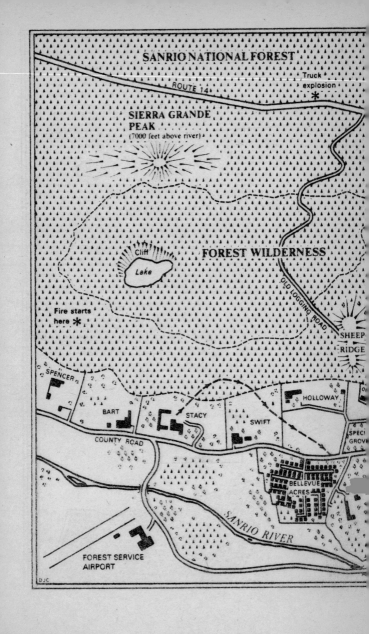

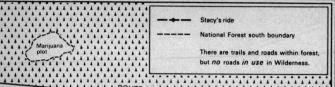

Stacy's ride

National Forest south boundary

There are trails and roads within forest, but *no* roads *in use* in Wilderness.

Marijuana plot

ROUTE 14

SANRIO NATIONAL FOREST

FOREST HEADQUARTERS

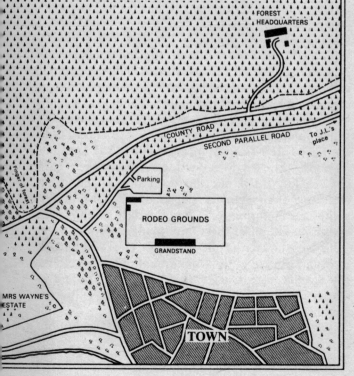

COUNTY ROAD

SECOND PARALLEL ROAD

To J.L.'s place

Finger of forest

Parking

RODEO GROUNDS

GRANDSTAND

MRS WAYNE'S ESTATE

TOWN

This is a work of fiction which neither portrays, nor is intended to portray, any actual person, living or dead. If the characters seem real, I am flattered, because they are purely creatures of invention.

The terrain, however, does exist, although I have taken liberties with geographical placement, and the situations and descriptions are as real as I could make them.

The details of the Forest Service's wildland fire suppression organization — along with others protecting public lands, probably the best in existence — are as I have depicted them, and for the generous help I received in gathering this information and background, I owe debts of gratitude to too many to mention all by name:

To the Forest Service dispatching and administrative personnel of Region 3 (New Mexico and Arizona) both in Santa Fe and at headquarters in Albuquerque; to the administrative personnel of Bandelier National Monument in Los Alamos; to the foreman and crew of smoke jumpers with whom I flew on a practice jump in the Gila Forest (suited up and parachuted and ignominiously hitched to a fuselage stringer by a cargo harness lest I fall out the open door), and to the multitude of anonymous telephone voices always alert, polite and informative when I called with further questions — to all of these, my thanks;

To Ned Jackson of the Forest Service who took the time and trouble to show us through the Boise (Idaho) Interagency Fire Center (BIFC), the heart and research center for all public land fire suppression efforts, our special gratitude;

And, above all, to Don Webb of the Gila National Forest for his unfailing patience in answering my frequently inane questions, and for sharing some of his broad firsthand knowledge as Class A Fire Boss (now, I

8

believe, since the change in nomenclature called Incident Commander) dealing with major conflagrations both inside and outside his own immediate territory, thanks beyond measure.

If the experienced fire-fighter finds errors in facts, they are mine alone. Attribute them, please, to over-enthusiasm.

My own experience with wildland fires goes back over fifty years to the Southern California mountains where, working with axe, shovel, brush hook, or two-man crosscut saw we volunteer amateurs cut fire-breaks where we thought they might do the most good, and by main strength and awkwardness brought the monsters under control, after which, carrying back-pumps, we cold-trailed the perimeters until the danger was past.

That was long ago, but nothing, basically, has changed; despite all modern technology and equipment, it still comes down to the men on the line working with hand tools face to face with the enemy. And the frightening memories of the sights and sounds and the smells of a forest fire in full fury have not faded one iota.

Santa Fe, New Mexico

# PROLOGUE

The wildland fire that came to be known as BACK-SLOPE — the name Jay Paul gave it only because every large fire must have a name — began at 6:12 pm Mountain Daylight Time on Sunday, June 19, when a single bolt of dry lightning struck a towering ponderosa pine tree deep in the Sanrio National Forest.

The electrical charge, following the tree's living inner wood as the most direct path to ground, easily overcame the tree's resistance, in the process generating unimaginably high temperatures and overheating sap to the point of explosion. The force of this reaction, bursting outward like a bomb, opened a great, ugly gash through the tree's heavy, platelike bark.

Smoldering pieces of bark were flung from the tree's wound like shrapnel to fall to the forest floor, some harmlessly on bare ground; but some on twigs, fallen branches, dry grass or trampled brush that for six weeks and more had been ready for a spark.

Match-sized flames appeared, and like matches, some flared briefly, consuming what fuel was at hand before they too died away.

But one large piece lodged in the snug shelter of a recently fallen, but thoroughly dry, dead branch, and there, patiently, began to urge its host closer and closer

11

to the point of combustion.

There was no tell-tale smoke, and no witness to sound the alarm.

# PART I

## 1

Until mid-afternoon on this Sunday, June 19, 1983, it was a lovely, bright, clear, altogether enjoyable southwestern summer day; a day for swimming in the lakes of the Sanrio National Forest—for fishing the Forest streams, for hiking or horseback riding on the scores of hundreds of miles of Forest mountain trails; for home cookouts by the pool in the City of Sanrio, or sunbathing in the patio; for tennis, for golf, for leisurely drinks and talk on the Country Club *portal*.

In a shallow glaciated bowl just beneath the summit of Sierra Grande's near-14,000-foot peak, which rises within the Forest behind the City of Sanrio, there was still snow, reminder of the skiing that had been excellent that season from late November through March. Elsewhere above the 11,000-foot timberline on the mountain slopes, in isolated meadows of alpine tundra, tiny, hardy, dwarf blue forget-me-nots, greenish-to-crimson mountain sorrel, white pussy-toes and yellow meadow cinque-foil clung to rock and what soil there was, defying wind and temperature extremes to bloom in profusion, and welcome hikers staunch enough to reach their elevation.

On the Sanrio, or rain-shadow, side of the mountains, there had been no precipitation for over six weeks, but with the heavy runoff from the winter snowpack, reservoirs were full, and this year water was no worry even in this semi-arid land; no thought at all had been given to watering or car-washing restrictions.

JL Harmon saw it differently, but, then, as Sanrio National Forest Fire Management Officer, that was his job.

"The brow furrowed with concern," Stacy Cummings said, running into him that morning at the Sanrio newsstand. Between them these days there was, not ease, but no longer the kind of wariness that had been present only a few weeks ago. "Problems?"

"Lack of rain," JL said, and then smiled sheepishly, wondering why he was opening himself by even this much to this woman, or, as far as that went, to anyone. He was not a talkative man. "Six weeks without it," he added.

Stacy studied him thoughtfully. "Now why is that so important?" her quick smile flashed. "Assume I really want to know."

JL tried not to sound like a textbook. "All the — stuff on the floor of the Forest, the deadfalls, the fallen needles and twigs, broken branches, brush — all that, we call fuel. And we classify it, 10-hour, 100-hour, 1000-hour, which means how long it will take to dry out after a winter's snow or a heavy, soaking rain. The light stuff dries first, of course, but after about 1000 hours, everything is ready to burn."

"And six weeks is more than 1000 hours," Stacy said. She nodded thoughtfully. "Luck, ranger. We'll pray for rain."

JL watched her go, and had an idea that she was aware of it, although she did nothing so obvious as waggling her bottom in those tight faded jeans. She wore handmade boots, too, polished to a gloss, and a

16

tooled belt with silver-and-turquoise buckle, tip and keepers, along with a light challis shirt—wearing the clothes easily, well used to them.

They had only met how many times—three? Now four? But you didn't tend to forget her, JL thought. Especially not after that first meeting.

That day, six—eight weeks ago, JL had driven the green Forest Service pick-up from the County road, over the cattleguard and past the mailbox that read: Cummings. The graveled drive, probably nearer to half than a quarter mile long, wound in through piñon and juniper carefully pruned and probably sprayed as well. The plat JL had seen showed a full section, one square mile, 640 acres of Cummings property, and nearly as he could make out, the whole thing was enclosed with a split cedar buck-and-rail fence.

Even before he saw the house, low, sprawling, fitting into the scene as if it had grown there, with a superb view of Sierra Grande in all its majesty, JL had decided that you didn't have to be real bright to figure out that these Cummings folks had money, pots of it.

Conscious that his Forest Service uniform presented a picture of Authority, he told the Spanish maid who answered the door that he wished to speak with the head of the house. Throwing his weight around, he told himself, something he disliked doing, but well-heeled newcomers tended to have strangers at their doors sent packing without listening to explanations, so maybe the end justified the means.

The maid hesitated only a moment, and then held the door wide, and JL followed her inside.

The floor was gleaming tile, terra-cotta in color. From the entrance hall, JL could see into a living room with heavy, polished furniture, Indian rugs, oil paintings on the whitewashed adobe walls, and cut flowers in vases adding further color—a huge room, but,

17

somehow, warm, even intimate. Taste, as well as money, JL thought, and felt a twinge of envy, flavored with mild resentment.

"In here, *señor, por favor*," the maid said and indicated a smaller room, office-library. She walked across the tile living room toward muffled sounds of talk and laughter, and opened a frosted sliding glass door at the room's end. The talk and laughter, suddenly louder, were as suddenly stilled.

JL caught a glimpse of water churning in a small tiled pool, of bare bodies and unrecognizable faces turned toward the interruption, and then the sliding door closed again. And he, JL, in his Forest Service uniform, suddenly feeling very much out of place, turned away in what amounted to flight to wait uncomfortably in the office-library the maid had indicated.

And after a bit came Stacy Cummings herself, in a white terry cloth robe, cool, poised, entirely at ease; her feet bare; her black shortcut hair still damp; and her brown eyes with golden flecks in their depths watching him as if he were something impaled on a pin—when he had thought he was asking for, and certainly expected, a male head of the house.

"I am Stacy Cummings," she said. "This is my house. What do you want, ranger?" Probably no more than in her late twenties, but with the kind of assurance she hadn't any right to for another ten—fifteen years.

JL gathered himself. "I make it a point to get acquainted with property owners whose land abuts the Forest." Unorthodox, perhaps, but frequently effective. The words sounded stilted even to his own ears. "But I didn't intend to interrupt—" He stopped, finding nothing further appropriate to say.

Stacy's sudden smile was amused, mocking, still very much at ease. "Shocked, ranger? It is called a spa. It is considered therapeutic. It—"

"I know about them, damn it." It was rare that he allowed annoyance to show. "They are also called jacuzzis and hot tubs, and they're very big in Southern California—"

"You do get around, don't you?"

"I just wasn't aware," JL said, "that the hot tub culture had come to Sanrio along with all the beautiful people." He bore down on that last adjective.

Stacy studied him thoughtfully, the mocking smile no longer showing. "Was that all?"

"Anything else," JL said, "can wait. Have a good spa—or whatever it's called." Exit line, end of their first meeting.

Now, remembering that scene, JL watched Stacy until she turned the corner out of sight. A strange, prickly female, with far more to her than first appeared. Out of curiosity, he had asked questions, and had been astonished to find how easy information about Stacy Cummings was to come by—world champion cowgirl, even with all that Texas oil money, barrel-racer, calf-roper, trying her hand too at bronc-riding and steeple-chasing.

"She's a many-faceted chick," Ken Delacorte had told him, "and don't sell her short on toughness. You don't get to be world champion anything if you've got soft spots."

A little forbidding in a woman, JL thought, but there it was. He walked out to the green pick-up and got in, tossing the Sunday paper to the seat beside him. Automatically, he glanced up at Sierra Grande's pinnacle peak which always reminded him of pictures he had seen of the Matterhorn. Maybe one day he would see for himself. Maybe.

He thought of going home, but aside from the unfinished oil painting on the easel, at which he had glared critically this morning finding multiple flaws, home had little appeal. Nor had it ever drawn him irresistibly, even when Madge was still there.

"Another woman I could understand," Madge had said. "But how can I compete with mountains and pine trees? And at your age still jumping out of airplanes. You could have been killed."

"I was a smoke-jumper for ten years."

"But you're not a kid any more. Or maybe you are. You don't even want a better job."

"There aren't any."

"Then stay here and grow moss like your trees. I'm leaving."

And so on this Sunday morning, as, he supposed, he should have known from the beginning he was going to do, he drove the pick-up through the quiet town, into the Forest and along deserted Forest roads until he reached the boundary of the wilderness and the sign that said No Motorized Vehicles Allowed.

There he stopped and got out just to hear the silence, feel the peace, absorb the flavor of the wildland. Automatically his thoughts went back to his flight with Andy McIlvain weeks ago, his last real overview of the Forest.

They had taken off in Andy's light plane from the Forest Service airport, JL riding co-pilot with a folded topographical map on the clipboard on his lap. He sat quiet and let his eyes wander over the terrain below.

Three-million-plus acres of Forest lay beneath them, five thousand square miles, an area almost as large as the states of Connecticut and Rhode Island together, some of it standing almost on edge, with a thousand square miles of Wilderness area in its center — all of it his, JL's, to care for, to protect. In his opinion, as he had told Madge, no one on the face of the earth had a better job. And it was his private belief that no one was better at it; there was the real source of satisfaction.

He knew the Forest as he knew the contours of his own face that he shaved every morning. From the lakes, river and creek bottoms and the dry arroyos to the pinnacle peaks of Sierra Grande itself, he had walked, ridden or flown over every foot of the terrain, in a sense submerging himself in this vastness that was his responsibility.

The lower edges of the land were in the piñon-juniper stratum, with here and there isolated cholla cactus in colonies or single plants. Scrub oak, which would turn scarlet in autumn, grew on the steeper slopes of arroyos and on sharply contoured hillsides. The big trees, the ponderosa pines, came next in the ascending order, and with them, beginning at 8000 feet, the aspens with their pale chartreuse trunks and their never-still leaves that gave them the name, quaking.

Above timberline were the open talus slopes — scree, as the rock climbers named them — and bare rock faces, these far more prevalent than the alpine tundra meadows, giving the upper mountain slopes in all but deep winter a barren, desolate appearance, hostile, even dangerous to man.

Snow-covered, as they had been that morning, the upper elevations of the Forest had seemed deserted, silent and unmoving, under their white blanket no longer hostile, but at peace. It was illusion.

Looking down from the small plane, JL could make out the tracks of one of the several herds of elk the Forest held, the trampled snow casting odd shadows in the early morning light; there a patch of blood in the snow was what was left of a careless or unwary rabbit and a fox's feast no doubt picked over by ravens or skunks; yonder, peering near-sightedly up at the light plane's sound, was a mother bear, only recently emerged from her winter den, herding her two cubs into the shelter of nearby brush, herself standing tall, ready to fight anything at all if necessary. Ahead, at the plane's own altitude, serene and majestic, a golden eagle soared on broad, flat wings and missed nothing that was happening on the Forest floor.

At times like this, early and alone, JL felt that he was the intruder and the aircraft the single jarring note, their only justification that phrase that damned as it pretended to justify: we mean well.

He glanced at Andy who was pointing down to their left at a minute, clear area beside an open lake. Across the lake, a glaciated wall rose sheer three or four hundred feet. Miraculously, large pine trees clung to the upper slope even to the cliff's edge.

"Nice little place, that," Andy said.

"You'll get wind currents off that cliff face."

"Yep." Andy seemed delighted. "Show you what my new chute will do. Downwind, crosswind, upwind, I told you. Like a modern sailboat."

"And if you miss that open space—" JL began.

"You get your feet wet, or maybe a pine tree up your ass. You asked me, Fire Boss."

"Okay." JL marked his map.

"You still want to try it yourself?" Andy said. "After all this time, and with all those chair-seat calluses?" He nodded, answering his own question. "Yep. You will. What'll Madge say?"

Madge had still been with him then. "She won't know until after."

"And George Jefferson'll know afterward too, and he'll eat your ass out but good." George Jefferson was Sanrio Forest Supervisor, JL's titular boss.

"Could be."

Andy flew for a time in silence, his hands loose on the wheel. He said at last, "Then why?"

"I want to know how good your new chute is so I can

know what kind of terrain I can send you and your smoke-jumpers into."

"I can tell you whether we can go in or not."

JL was silent.

Andy said, "Okay. You want to know for yourself. And that, of course, is just what makes you—I hate to admit it—the best damn fire boss around."

"I don't aim to lose people," JL said. "There isn't any kind of property worth it."

Andy nodded. "Okay," he said again. "When we come down in a month or so, you'll jump. And I'll be your jump mate."

Funny he should think of that now, JL thought, because that morning had been back in the *safe* time when the Forest, snow-covered, was more or less fireproof. Today, in summer, it was different. The Forest was one large tinder box.

On the post beneath the sign forbidding motorized vehicles into the Wilderness was a box and a second, smaller sign reading: Register here. Normally it contained registration cards and a pencil attached to the wood. JL opened it now and found it empty.

The registration cards were not, in JL's opinion, really all that important; the number of visitors here was not critical in the way that it was, say, in Yosemite out in California where they had wall-to-wall people.

But from time to time it was handy to know who was inside the Wilderness and how long they intended to stay. Emergency messages did sometimes come to Forest headquarters, accidents could happen, weather could suddenly close in, visitors could become long overdue and wives could worry. Just knowing what route visitors had taken on entering the Wilderness could be a start in trying to locate them at need. And

23

now, after the middle of June, there would already be a few visitors. JL wondered idly who they were.

## 2

The family's name was Lawry, Les, Cindy Lou and young Tad, and on this Sunday they had driven jolting into the heart of the Wilderness, where no vehicles were allowed, as far as a clear stretch of the upper Sanrio River, where they had stashed their jeep amid some big rocks, covering it with piney boughs against chance discovery from the air.

"This is how you do it, son," Les told the boy, proud to show off his Army knowledge of camouflage. "We always covered our vehicles like this when we bivouacked or set up camp. You never knew when some hostile fixed wing or chopper aircraft might come busting over. There! See?" He pointed suddenly upward as two Air Force fighters on low-level training roared past at little more than tree-top height following the course of the river. "They won't catch your old Dad as easy as that," Les said. His tone was complacent.

Cindy Lou said, "Old Dad hasn't bothered to tell us yet, hon, why we couldn't have walked in like ordinary folks, but maybe he's fixing to explain sooner or later. Or why we had to ride that damn spine-busting jeep all the way from home instead of coming in the nice, comfortable Olds."

"Because most folks don't come this far into the Wilderness," Les said, "so it stands to reason the fishing's better here."

Cindy Lou said, "I didn't even know we had a fishing license."

"We don't. If anybody comes, we'll say we tried to get one in town, but they said they were fresh out."

"Damn it," Cindy Lou said, "do you always have to behave like an operator, a wheeler-dealer, an I-can-get-it-wholesale sharpie? What kind of example is that for the kid?"

"He could do a lot worse than copying his old man," Les said. "I haven't done so bad. Now you two set up the tent, and I'll catch us some trout for dinner. Set it under that tree yonder so it won't be seen from the air."


In another part of the Wilderness on this Sunday, Elsie Edwards undid the belt of her backpack, and gratefully slid off the padded shoulder straps to lower the pack's full weight to the ground. The back of her short-sleeved khaki shirt was wet through with sweat. She stood in silence for a few moments, looking at the blue nylon tent pitched days before beneath the towering ponderosa pine. She listened to the Wilderness in silence. She looked at Don.

"It's not exactly what I had in mind," she said, but she was smiling in that fond, crinkly-eyed way she had, and that was all that mattered. "I was thinking more along the lines of the bridal suite in, say, one of those big hotels along the Promenade des Anglais in Nice, or perhaps the Dorchester in London."

"We'll get to that kind of thing," Don said. "Maybe for our twenty-fifth. Or our fiftieth."

Elsie pulled out her shirttails, unbuttoned her shirt and flapped it vigorously to create a small breeze. She wore no brassiere, and her generous breasts bounced with the effort. "That illustrates one of the differences

26

between us," she said, smiling still, enjoying the sight of his eyes upon her. "You're the patient type, ready to face the long haul. I'm going to speed up your schedule so you get to the top faster. Then we'll take time to enjoy things."

She was a strong young woman in a hurry, this bride of his, Don thought, but he had known that all along, and he was content that it was so. By her very eagerness, she brought to him in many ways an awareness he had lacked, and there was the miracle that overshadowed all else. "And for now?" he said.

Elsie stopped flapping the loose shirt, shrugged it off, and let it drop to the ground. "For now," she said, "first things first." The quality of her smile had changed. "I suggest you get out of your backpack as a starter. I'd say we have all the privacy we need."


Their names were Frank Orwell and Felipe Vigil, and what they had in common was that they had both simply walked away from the New Mexico minimum security facility at nearby Los Ojos, stolen a car they had found on the outskirts of Sanrio with the keys in it, walked into one of the number of sporting goods stores in town, all of them open on summer Sundays, subdued the proprietor with the car's lug wrench, and walked out again with arms, handguns and hunting knives, a backpack each and what cash was in the proprietor's pockets and in the till. $161.11.

At a 7-11 store they bought supplies and managed to shoplift two six-packs of Coor's. Then they drove to the edge of the Wilderness, turned sufficiently law-abiding to leave the car, and headed into the wildland on foot.

"You a damn fool, man," Felipe said as they walked, as he had been saying ever since they had left the state farm. "You got one year, one fucking year left, and you walk out. Now you'll get three more. Maybe more than that."

"They got to catch us first, greaseball. And in the woods there ain't nobody going to catch me. So stop clicking your teeth, and walk, man, walk. We got miles to do before dark."

"You know where we going?"

"I told you. Just walk."

"We walk too fast, we come out the other side."

"Man, you got no idea how big this mother is. You can walk 700 miles in a straight line and still not come out."

With his knowledge of the terrain and the local climatic conditions, JL could almost have predicted the weather progression that Sunday afternoon.

First came merely a faint thickening of haze behind Sierra Grande's lofty peak. Then cloud began to form, rising higher and higher in its ever-changing form, darkening, glowering, gradually emerging through Jekyll-to-Hyde transformation as a truly anvil-shaped thunderhead in which wind currents began to boil, and heated air, rising, was robbed of its heat which turned immediately to pure energy that built in force as pressure builds in a contained vessel, throwing out at last its natural, inevitable product — lightning.

There was no rain. JL, by now back in his studio, brush in hand, watching through the window, swore softly to himself and hoped that all mountain lookouts in this part of the Southwest were also watching. *Carefully, damn it. Keep your eyes peeled.*

Times like this, a man was helpless. Forces far beyond his, or anyone's, control were at work and at their own option or whim either would or would not cause harm. All he could do was wait, his eyes fixed on the big mountain, central feature of the Forest, land-mark dominating the landscape for 100 miles around.

The sky had darkened now. A jagged lightning streak appeared suddenly and seemed to hang quivering, its multiple tendrils reaching down to the forested mountain slopes. Seconds later the thunder reached JL's ears, still sharp rather than muffled, but lacking the whipcrack sound of a strike immediately at hand.

JL watched it, and a second, and a third, unaware that he was holding his paintbrush with his fingers almost in spasm. He waited, and searched the trees, but no tell-tale smoke appeared. That, he thought, would be too easy; the Gods rarely cooperated like that. Nor was there any point in his standing here staring, either. If it happened, it happened, and he would be notified soon enough. He made himself relax as he turned away from the window to face his easel again.

The scene of the half-finished painting was of the Forest, of course, towering ponderosa pines, in partial shade an aspen, its pale trunk marked by an irregular pattern of peeled bark, its quaking leaves already touched by autumn gold. Off-center on the canvas was a patch of sky, deep blue in its infinity of depth. No more than a small craggy outcropping of the big mountain was visible, but awareness of its immense presence filled the picture.

Not bad, JL told himself. Not as good as some could do, of course, but, then, he would never be in their class. On rare visits to Roswell or Santa Fe or Taos, he would go to the galleries and the museums and gaze in wonderment and awe, but without jealousy, at the magnificent illusions some painters were capable of capturing on a piece of canvas. He wondered often what it would be like to spend time in the European exhibits he had read about, the Louvre, the Tate, the

Prado, the National Gallery, Florence, Rome, Amsterdam. Maybe one day.

He picked up his palette, and then set it down again. The hell. With a dry lightning storm going on right over his Forest, it would take a superman to be able to concentrate—and he was no superman.

There was another lightning flash as he left the studio, closed the door and headed for the kitchen and a cold beer. This was the lightning strike that began BACKSLOPE.


Stacy Cummings watched the lightning storm too, and because of it, and the lack of rain, thought again of JL Harmon, that oddly complicated ranger-type. After their first meeting, out at her house, she too had been curious, and asked Ken Delacorte about JL. Ken sold real estate in Sanrio now, and knew all the gossip. Once, not long ago, he had played a lot of tight end for the Houston Oilers, and Stacy felt a kind of athletic kinship for him.

"JL?" Ken said. "He's all right. He's the honcho on what they call wildfire suppression in the whole Sanrio Forest, all three-four million acres of it. Quite a job. And when they get in big trouble other places, he's the fire boss, the head of the team of experts they send out to take over. Quite a guy. Used to jump out of airplanes to put out fires."

He still jumps out of airplanes, Stacy thought, and smiled, remembering.

She had been riding in the heart of the Forest on Sam, her big cutting horse, some weeks after JL's visit to her house; enjoying the true forest coolness, the shade and the almost cathedral hush that surrounded her.

A Steller's jay, his crest saucily raised, bobbed up

30

and down on a low branch and scolded her, telling the forest that an intruder had arrived. Somewhere nearby, probably in a grove of aspens, a woodpecker's drumroll sounded as he drilled for grubs in dead wood. A fat chipmunk paused on a fallen tree to study horse and human before flipping his tail up over his back and scampering off to disappear into the underbrush.

As Stacy rode through a clearing in the trees, a movement overhead caught her attention and she looked up to study the single vulture rocking on dihedral wings in the rising air currents. When a pine needle falls in the forest, she remembered that some-one had told her, the vulture sees it, the deer hears it and the bear smells it. Man is a crude, inefficient creature by comparison.

She rode on without destination, letting Sam pick his sure path through trees and undergrowth. Here and there on bare ground she saw deer tracks and droppings, and in one spot she reined Sam in to stare at a curiously human-like print which could only have been made by a bear. A mountain chickadee inter-rupted his morning foraging to swing upside down on a twig and study her curiously before he too flew off to tell the forest world of the stranger in their midst. Smiling, Stacy watched him as he darted effortlessly among branches and foliage to carry his message.

She came to a stream. It ran clear and boisterous, gurgling to itself as if in high spirits. Sam lowered his head and blew noisily before he had his drink. Then he crossed with careful steps, ears cocked forward, and took the far bank at a single powerful bound to resume his steady, purposeful walk.

The stream emptied into a small glaciated lake beneath a three-hundred-foot cliff above which, incred-ibly, trees had taken root and prospered in the thin soil. In the lake's placid surface the great mountain was faithfully reflected as in a picture postcard. Entirely too much, Stacy thought, smiling; and then the smile turned to a frown of annoyance as the growing sound of an aircraft broke the mountain hush.

It came down the valley, well beneath Sierra Grande's peak, and even beneath the peaks of the lesser mountains nearby, a high-wing, high-tail, twin-engine aircraft, to Stacy's eyes ugly in the extreme. She watched it with distaste as it swept racketing over a tiny meadow among the pine trees on the lake's cliff shore, then her distaste turned to curiosity as three paper streamers of obviously weighted yellow and orange crepe paper dropped from the open doorway of the aircraft and fluttered toward the ground. They landed near the edge of the meadow.

The aircraft banked sharply and came around full circle, losing altitude slightly. Again three paper streamers dropped, to land this time almost precisely in the center of the meadow.

Once more the aircraft made its tight circle, and this time out of the open doorway came one human figure and then a second, and almost instantaneously, it seemed, two multi-colored parachutes blossomed and drifted downward.

Sam snorted at the sight and pawed the ground with a forehoof. "Easy boy," Stacy said. "You're no more baffled than I am."

The lead parachute fluttered in the air, seemed to veer to one side, and then, almost instantly, dipped slanting back to its original path. Stacy guessed correctly that there were wind currents coming from the cliff face.

The second chute fluttered and veered in almost exactly the same spot, and it recovered, but more slowly and with a jerky movement that left the man suspended from the harness swinging like a pendulum.

The first parachute encountered another sideways wind gust, and again recovered smoothly; the second followed suit, once more with less precision that left the parachutist oscillating helplessly.

The first man landed, went down smoothly on bent and yielding knees and rolled easily and lightly on the ground, rising almost instantly to haul on the shrouds and collapse his parachute.

The second man hit the ground on the downswing of an oscillation, went down hard, rolling, and rose quickly on only one leg, the other held free of the ground as he collapsed his parachute too. In the mountain hush, and across the water, the two voices came clearly.

"Not bad for an old man," Andy McIlvain's voice said. "You okay?"

"I over-controlled," JL's voice said. "This chute of yours is so damn sensitive." He was looking back up at the cliff. "But it handles that turbulence well. I'll say that." He lowered the one foot, put a little weight on it, and lifted it again. "Clumsy," he said.

Andy was gathering his parachute. "I'll walk out," he said, "and send a chopper in for you." Neither man wasted time in further comment; it was obvious that they were both accustomed to emergency or mishap, and instantly prepared to deal with it.

Stacy touched Sam's flanks with her spurred heels. They trotted around the edge of the lake to the meadow. She reined Sam in. "We keep running into each other," she said to JL, and took her left foot from the stirrup. "Come on up. Sam can carry two." And to Andy McIlvain in an easy tone of command, "Give him a hand. You won't need a chopper. Just send a car to my place."

Andy was grinning as he helped JL up behind the saddle. "Yes ma'am," he said. "Just treat the old man

33

gently."

They rode for a time in silence, Sam holding to his steady, easy fast walk. Stacy said at last, "Ankle? Bad?"

"It'll do. Plain clumsiness." JL didn't know what to do with his hands. So he kept them on his thighs.

"You came out to the house that day for a reason," Stacy said unexpectedly, her voice coming to him over her shoulder. "Were you going to explain the facts of life near the Forest?"

Talking was good; it kept JL's mind off the bad ankle. "Would you have listened?"

"Probably not very well. But most would have gone through the motions anyway."

There was that between them that tended to draw sparks, JL thought, and wondered why. "Most people waste a lot of time."

"And you don't?"

"I waste as much as anybody. But in my own directions."

Stacy took her time. "For the record," she said at last, "I'm sick and tired of being sniped at. It's my property."

"True."

"I've observed all zoning—what there is of it out where I am."

"True again."

"Then?"

"And you've done a lot of things right."

"Such as?"

"No cedar shake roof to catch fire from a single spark."

"I preferred tile."

"No undergrowth right up against the buildings to compound the fire danger."

"I have horses. I don't want them tangled up in brush."

"That good graveled road all the way in."

"I've lived with mud roads. I don't like them."

"But no road out. Only the one way."

Stacy was silent. She wished she could see his face, but she refused to turn in the saddle. "And you want an escape route."

JL didn't even bother to answer.

"I thought fire people were supposed to come in and put fires out, not run away from them," Stacy said.

With no change of tone, JL said, "Is Stacy your real name, like it says on the plat?"

"It's my name. It was my daddy's."

"He wanted a boy?"

Caught off-balance, midway between resentment and amusement, Stacy chose to smile, and found, astonishingly, that she meant it. "I suppose so. But he took what he got. Me."

"World champion cowgirl," JL said. "Barrel-racer. Calf-roper. I've even heard that you tried your hand at bronc-riding. And steeple-chasing." Ken Delacorte was his source.

"That was then." Stacy frowned faintly. "What is this, *This Is Your Life*?"

"I try to know my neighbors."

"*Your* neighbors?"

"In a manner of speaking." JL looked up at the great mountain. "My forest."

"I thought it belonged to the government."

"I care for it."

Curiosity replaced temper. "And," Stacy said, "on its behalf you resent me, us, with our houses on its fringe. Tell me why. Are we a menace?"

"We have more to fear from lightning."

"Then why not just ignore us?" But it was beginning to dawn upon her that she already knew the answer, and, being Stacy, brought it immediately into the open. "We're your responsibility, is that it? Fire trouble, flash flood trouble, any kind of trouble, and you're the ones to bail us out?" She nodded solemnly. "I hadn't thought of it that way before."

Few do, JL thought, but did not say aloud.

"Is that why the parachutes? All part of the same thing?"

"More or less."

"Not just fun and games." Stacy nodded again, thoughtfully this time. "I think, ranger," she said, "that I'd like to know more about what you do. And why you do it."

"It's a job."

This time the dark head shook in emphatic denial. "I'm beginning to think it's a great deal more than that." Maybe *commitment* was the word, she thought, and how many did she know who were really committed to anything?


As evening came on that BACKSLOPE Sunday, cool dense air began to flow down the flanks of Sierra Grande as liquid flows downhill. Encountering little resistance, it gathered speed, first merely a faint stirring, then a noticeable current, at last becoming a downslope breeze soughing through the evergreens, setting the aspen leaves to whispering as they danced.

Around the base of the stricken ponderosa pine, in response to the moving air, small flames that had died and become mere gray embers, began again to glow, some of them rekindling to reach out for more fuel, dry needles, fallen twigs, small branches, dry brush, a partially rotted log which, heated, began to smolder like a punk. The large piece of bark beneath the fallen branch burst into flame. That was all that was needed to ignite the branch.

At first, one man could have stamped out all the

flames with ease, and with a single green branch as a broom, swept the smoldering fuel into a harmless pile in a patch of bare dirt.

Even by full darkness, that same man working quickly could have contained the threat and snuffed it out with shovelfuls of earth.

## 3

Ken Delacorte came to dinner at Stacy's that Sunday evening. Ken was a comfortable friend from college days. There had never been between them the right chemistry, Stacy had often thought, to produce more than a friendship, which was maybe a pity, but there it was. Stacy said, "I heard that the Brown place next door was for sale." "Next door" was a euphemism; the two properties were contiguous, but the two main houses were more than a mile apart.

"Sold," Ken said. He smiled. "Character who bought it has renamed it El Rancho Costa Mucho, and I can't blame him. The certified check he brought to the closing was well up in seven figures. Fellow named Jones, Bartlemy Jones, goes round in a fancy electric wheelchair." He stopped, watching the sudden change in Stacy's face. "I said what?"

Stacy took her time. Words were not easy to find. "The roof just fell in, is all," she said at last. Her smile was wan. "You couldn't know. An old flame. We parted on something less than a romantic note. Fix yourself another drink."

Ken came back from the wet bar in a thoughtful mood. He sat down slowly. "Jones," he said. "You don't like him? Or maybe you don't trust him? Which?"

38

"Why?"

"Aside from buying the Brown place, he's asking too many questions about Bellevue Acres, my development, not much, but all I could afford to build, where I've bet my shirt." He smiled crookedly. "By your standards, it's not a very expensive shirt, I'll admit."

"I'll ignore that," Stacy said.

Long after Ken had left that evening, Stacy sat on in the office-library staring at nothing. One wall of the room was floor-to-ceiling bookcases filled with much-handled and well-read books—fiction of all kinds both hardcover and paperback, biography, history, animal husbandry, geology, bound horse-breeding records, westerniana, reference works including Black's *Law Dictionary*, Fowler's *Modern English Usage*, the Compact *Oxford Dictionary*, the *Columbia Encyclopedia*, Van Nostrand's *Scientific Encyclopedia* and Bartlett's *Quotations*.

On the remaining walls were photographs of horses, some with Stacy, some by themselves. Stacy could name each one and give place and date. There were times, she thought, when it seemed that her life was there on those walls.

Stacy was then, as JL had guessed closely that first day, in her twenty-ninth year, a woman of medium height, smoothly muscled, lithe in her movements, with high, firm, unbrassiered breasts, slim solid waist, boyish hips and clean straight legs. Of her glossy black hair and brown eyes, "Most likely some Indian in us somewhere," Stacy, her father, had often said, "but, goddamnit, not enough to claim share in any tribe's oil properties, so I've damn well had to find our own."

And he had. He liked to claim that he had tramped and sniffed and dowsed every square foot of Texas, Oklahoma and eastern New Mexico relying on a God-given gift to know where oil was to be found—without bothering to mention that he had an advanced degree in geology, and considerably more than a smattering of geophysics to supplement instinct.

Young Stacy never knew her mother. "Out in the middle of nowhere—" Her father had told her the tale often enough, flagellating himself with the memory. "—and the goddamned well blew in just about the time you began to put in an appearance. I was busier than a birddog in a stubble field, and your mother said she was all right, she'd be fine with Lupe Sanchez who had eight kids of her own and knew all about birthing them." He spread his huge hands in helplessness. "You came through it all right, fine. Your mother didn't. Me, I got another oil well." The last sentence was bitter self-accusation.

It was a strange relationship, father-daughter, no woman in the house other than hired help. There *were* women who tried to take over; the increasing Cummings oil wealth was well-nigh irresistible. But the father saw matters clearly, and refused to be trapped. "If I ever, by God, want another wife," he told young Stacy, "I'll find her myself. She won't find me."

Stacy did not remember when she was first on a horse, but some incidents of her early career remained vivid. There was, for example, the colt she called Boots, her own, hand-raised from a foal. This was back on the old home ranch in central Texas. She was not quite fifteen when she snubbed Boots to a post in the corral, slapped her saddle on him for the first time, and climbed aboard, casting loose the snubbing rope.

Boots was no longer a foal. He now stood something over fifteen hands, and weighed right about a thousand pounds, well over eight times Stacy's own weight. Whether he felt betrayed by someone he had always considered a friend is not a matter of record, but his reactions to the saddle and the girl on his back were anything but friendly. Stacy landed on the hard-packed corral dirt with a resounding thump.

She got to her feet, dusted her bottom, shook her head hard to clear it, and started toward Boots who was standing docilely enough, reins hanging to the ground.

Joe Peakes, the ranch foreman, walked into the corral. "Better let me take a little of the edge off him, girl," he said in his friendly, male-superior way. He reached for the dangling reins.

Stacy's reaction was immediate. "You," she said in a voice that shook, "keep your goddamned hands off him, you hear? He's my horse, and nobody but me's going to break him."

There was silence. Joe Peakes said slowly, "Now, look here, young lady. That's no kind of way—"

"You heard her." This was Stacy the father, and there was that in his voice that forestalled objections. He climbed the corral fence and perched comfortably on the top rail. "Well now," he said in his usual conversational tone, "let the show commence."

It took two more falls, and with each one, young Stacy's chin grew firmer. She limped back for the fourth try, got stiffly into the saddle, and this time stayed there until Boots, tossing his head occasionally but otherwise showing no further resistance, under her guidance walked obediently twice around the corral.

Stacy bent down to pat the sweating neck. "Good boy." Her voice was gentle.

"Good girl," Stacy the father said. "See that he's rubbed down, honey. I think you've got yourself a horse. Now what you'd better think about is a hot bath, and maybe a little liniment here and there."

Schooling presented problems resulting in an inevitable clash of wills. "Your mother," the father said finally, "was well educated in the east. Why she married me, I'm damned if I know. She was too good for me. But she did, and you're the result, and I'm going to

41

see that you turn out to be a goddamned lady too."

"I'm not interested."

"I didn't ask what you thought. I'm telling you. I'm not going to watch, by God, and see you grow up to be a raggedy-assed stablehand or a roughneck out of an oil field. You're going to learn how to behave like a lady if it kills you."

Not all of what young Stacy considered unnecessary airs and graces took, but the product that emerged after three years in Miss Walker's school in Boston was a different article indeed from the one the father had first put on the plane in Dallas.

"Each time you've come home on vacation," he said when he met her final homecoming plane, "you've looked a little better. Now you've turned into a real good looking filly and quite a lady. That one of the outfits that cost more than a good horse and a hand-tooled saddle together?"

"It was your idea."

"I won't deny it, honey. And I think we got our money's worth, not that money matters much any more. Now what do you want to do?"

"The University's got a good rodeo team. I've been reading about it."

"And you're fixing to be part of it?" The father nodded. "I guess you've earned it." He held up an admonitory hand. "One thing, though. I don't want you forgetting all you learned these last three years."

"Fat chance," young Stacy said.

At the University, there were boys and horses, sometimes in one order, sometimes the other. There were also books running a poor third, except in courses having to do with animal husbandry.

"Some folks," Stacy's father said, "like animals better than people. That the way you see it too?"

"People have their uses."

"You mean like that big jock who can't think his way around a revolving door?"

Earl, Stacy admitted, was not too bright. But, she pointed out, like the Budweiser Clydesdales he was good to look at, moved well, and was handy to have around in case there was something heavy to be moved or carried.

"I don't pretend to understand women," her father said. "Seems even the simplest of them has more hummocks and switchbacks than a mountain mule trail. But I'm beginning to believe that you're like the man said, an enigma wrapped in a riddle and tied up with a conundrum. What do you want, anyway, honey?"

"I'm still looking for it," Stacy said. Simple truth.

Stacy was twenty-two when the father died — as he had lived, violently, his neck broken by a falling length of drill pipe.

Stacy showed no tears in public or in private, but the death left an emptiness she doubted would ever be filled. In quiet, waking moments, staring up into the darkness of her room, she would sometimes wonder how it was possible that all the energy and the strength that had been Stacy Cummings could possibly have been wiped away in a single instant leaving not a trace. In one twisted, half-awake moment, she wondered what became of the law of the conservation of energy when such a tragedy happened. At other times, but only to herself, she would think, "God, how I miss him!"

To friends, there was no noticeable change. "She's a tough one," they would say in the smiling, admiring way that one spoke of an athlete who insisted on playing hurt. The result was that no one managed to penetrate the facade.

Bart Jones assumed more importance during this

period than he had before. He was a big man, as Stacy Cummings had been big, and solid, powerful, but with a *macho* streak that was as different from the father's as different could be.

Stacy Cummings the father had always been willing to shoot the works, bet the bundle, go for broke—but only when circumstances demanded that kind of action. Bart Jones would take chances merely to be doing what no one else would dare. To Stacy the daughter, there was a vast difference.

Always she drew a sharp line between risks that were inherent in whatever you did—whether it was barrel-racing, bronc-riding, steeplechasing or just crossing the street—and risks that were purely unnecessary, sheer *machismo*. It was Bart's tendency toward this latter kind that led to a conversational exchange she still remembered.

"You don't have to show off," Stacy had said. "Not to me, not to anybody."

"You've been alone too much, lonely. You get bitter."

It was a moment of relaxed candor. "Lonely? I've never been lonely in my life. I like some people, but I don't have to have them."

"Is that supposed to put me in my place?"

"Oh, come off it," Stacy said. "To you, I'm a few laughs and a roll in the hay. Other people don't matter that much to you."

After what happened on what she thought of as *that night*, she would have given the world to be able to retract those words because, try as she might, she could never entirely shake the sense of guilt they left with her.

Cap and Lucy Meadows were the hosts at the party *that night*, but it could have been any of the many couples back in Texas who now in retrospect had become almost indistinguishable one from the other; all with money, of course, and big houses sometimes on the outskirts of town, sometimes out in the middle of a ranch; most of the men having to do with oil or cattle or maybe the Chicago commodity exchange or maybe all three. Types who traveled much, and entertained often.

The cars in the floodlighted parking area were mostly Mercedes, with a sprinkling of BMWs and even a Cadillac or two. Inside, and out around the pool on the terrace, white-coated waiters took and filled drink orders, and maids in Mexican skirts and off-the-shoulder blouses silently passed canapés. A mariachi band for a wonder played music that was not entirely deafening and conversation punctuated by laughter swirled.

Bart Jones was drunk, not staggering drunk, not even slurred-speech drunk, but wearing his tell-tale grin and the dangerous gleam in his eye. The stage was set for trouble, and Stacy had known it; that was the part that would not go away.

"Suit yourself, sweetie-pie," Bart Jones said, not loud, just conversational, but meaning it, "but I'm headed back to town and a steak so thick." Thumb and forefinger were two inches apart.

"I'll go," Stacy said. "If you'll let me drive."

"No dice. You don't always get your way, you know."

The Cummings temper was never far beneath the surface. "Damn it, you're soused."

"Matter of opinion, and I prefer my opinion to yours."

Old Stacy, her father, had said once, "I read somewhere that a wise man doesn't paint pictures on water, honey. I'll add something else: a wise man doesn't argue with a drunk, either. Pure waste of time."

Still she tried, but she had to admit that she hadn't done it very well. "Look," she said, "will you for once in your silly life be sensible?"

Nothing changed in his face or in his eyes, but a new note came into his voice. "No point starting now," he said with a certain finality, and turned away.

She watched him go, smiling and nodding as he made his way through the guests. He didn't lurch, nor did he walk with the exaggerated care of intoxication. "Old Bart can really hold his liquor." How often had Stacy heard that said? Too damned often, she thought, and was tempted to go after him for one more try. But she didn't.

"Stacy baby." Cap Meadows, her host. "I've got me a new quarterhorse, and I'd admire to have you see him. Cost me a bundle, but just maybe he'll earn it back and then some."

Stacy caught one last glimpse of Bart's broad back disappearing into the house. "Love to," she said. "How about tomorrow?"

Cap had followed her eyes. "Old Bart got the bit in his teeth?" He patted Stacy's arm. "Let it go, honey. He's a big boy. He'll be all right."


At least it was a one-car accident, and nobody else was involved. "He must have tried to take that turn at well over a hundred," one of the state cops said rolling up his tape measure and watching the emergency crew working with an acetylene torch and panel ripper to cut Bart out of the wreck. "Even those foreign jobs with their independent suspension have their limits."

Stacy visited the hospital as soon as she heard the news, but it was three days before she was able to see Bart, and her reception then was less than warm.

"Come to say, 'I told you so?'" were his first words.

Stacy swallowed hard and managed to hold back what was in her mind. Instead, "Anything you need? Books? Magazines?"

"A new spinal cord. Got one?"

It was the first she knew of the seriousness of his trouble, and how she managed to hold back the sudden, unexpected tears that stung her eyelids, she was never to know.

"Hang in there," she said as she left finally, and got in return only a contemptuous snort. It was some time before she psyched herself up to the point of visiting the hospital again, and by then Bart had been shipped off to another place for physical therapy to try to accustom him to his new condition.

Texas soured for Stacy after that, her father gone and now this—thing with Bart. Ken Delacorte, having retired from football and finished his unsuccessful ex-jock assault on Hollywood, was living in Sanrio now, selling real estate, and Sanrio which held no memories seemed as good a place to settle down as any, and so here Stacy was. Not, she told herself, that she needed Ken or anyone else because she was complete within herself, and if, as she knew, that was not wholly true for anybody, it was close enough.

To Sophie Swift, her Sanrio lawyer, she said one day, as she had said to Bart, "I'm never lonely. Not really." And then she had showed the full, brilliant smile that somehow seemed to mock herself. "I talk to my horses. And they talk back. But don't tell anyone."

"The confidentiality of lawyer-client relationship," Sophie said, nodding solemnly, and smiled back.

But now, on this quiet Sunday, hundreds of miles distant from Texas and its memories, here was Bart again, right next door. Too much. Too damn much, she thought as she got up and began to turn out lights on her way to bed. One thing was sure: El Rancho Costa Mucho was no accident, no coincidence, that she knew.

By early morning moonset, urged on by the night breeze, the growing flames had run downslope and fanned out, at last touching a finger of the lower piñon-juniper mesaland, and the pace of the fire's spread then began to quicken.

Dry chamisa and sticky snakeweed, low-growing and in places dense, provided the fuel chain from tree to tree. Juniper burns with a steady, intense heat; piñon, filled with pitch, seems impervious, and then all at once almost explodes; scrub oak too will flame up like a torch.

Hidden in the deep folds of the foothills and the stands of the forest itself, the fire gathered its strength and force. The crackling, sometimes firecracker-exploding sounds became a constant, growing background against which the sights and the acrid smells of combustion were projected.

A commercial airliner overhead might have spotted the blaze and radioed the alarm, but local flight paths avoided Sierra Grande as a natural hazard it was foolish to mess with, and no sightings occurred.

The conflagration was free to grow unhampered.

At last, no longer hidden and secret, large enough now and strong enough to dare the open, like a monster roaring out of its hiding place, the fire burst into view. In the darkness, it threw its lights and contorting shadows into the sky. Bellowing and roaring defiance, it was suddenly alive, and loose.

# 4

Aaron Swift, Attorney-at-Law, P.C., and, out of a deep sense of public duty, also Federal Magistrate, was not sleeping well these nights. At one hyper-religious period in his youth he would have interpreted his insomnia as symptomatic of a deep-seated, perhaps even atavistic sense of guilt. At three o'clock on this Monday morning, a time when, he was quite aware, psychological defenses were substantially lowered, he was not at all sure the guilt diagnosis would have been incorrect.

Debby slept beside him, relaxed as a kitten. In many ways, as a matter of fact, Aaron had occasionally thought, Debby much resembled a cute, cuddly, purring kitten, pink tongue, wide eyes, softness and all.

But having thought that, as Aaron in his judicial way had often reminded himself, in fairness he also had to add that despite her cuddly qualities, Debby possessed accomplishments that contrasted strangely with her cuteness.

Debby was a small-town girl from west Texas who had grown up knowing how to run a house like a taut ship, how to sew a fine seam in the old-fashioned way, how to bake buttermilk biscuits that would almost float off the plate and how without either fuss or advance notice whomp up either a *coq au vin* or a homely meatloaf-and-mashed-potatoes meal, your choice, and charm a grumpy oilman client into smiling agreement in the bargain.

Debby was, in short, the kind of girl who married dear old Dad before Women's Liberation came along.

Sophie, on the other hand, could not be compared to any other creature. Sophie was *sui generis*, strictly one of a kind. Aaron saw her every day in the office, of course, and he had lived with her as her husband for twenty-five years, but he was still not sure that he had ever even begun to understand her. His thoughts kept going back to that one night he would just as soon forget.

"Mr. Bumble," Sophie said without preamble that evening, "said that the law is 'a ass — a idiot'. The law is also a tyrant and a slave master. I have followed its bidding. My fault. That is our problem." As clear, lucid and concise as if she were addressing the bench.

"Damn it, Soph, it isn't — I mean, there isn't any fault. It's — one of those things."

"No-fault? As in insurance? The dispassionate view? But there is contradiction here. Passion is precisely what we're talking about. You have what I believe is called by some the hots for young Debby Winslow. And being the honorable man you are, you have told me about it."

"You make it sound like a — brief."

"That's my failing, Aaron. I don't know how to use the words that demonstrate emotion. They embarrass me. But, believe me, I do have feelings."

"I know."

"Yes. You do. And that is what makes this all the more difficult for both of us. My position is impossible, and yours is no better. What should I do, try to argue you out of this situation? That would be ridiculous, and even if it succeeded, self-defeating. Our relation-

50

ship would never be the same again."

Always she had seen straight to the heart of the matter, Aaron thought, and been able to target clearly the problem to be faced, if not resolved.

"Or should I say, 'good luck and godspeed?' " Sophie said. "What is it you want from me?"

"I guess — understanding."

"You have that. I don't see the world through a man's eyes, but I have read some of the books and I am aware of the susceptibility factor, particularly when it involves a man in early middle age with a wife who is probably no more than — adequate, if that, in the intimate areas of marriage."

"I'm not a lecher, Soph."

"I know that too. But you are flattered by Debby's obvious admiration, and you are susceptible and my only sensible role is that of onlooker. I can't compete with young Debby Winslow. And I am certainly not going to preach to you, or, worse, make myself equally ridiculous by an emotional appeal to the jury. We know each other too well for that kind of nonsense."

"I thought," Aaron said helplessly, "to leave you the ranch and take an apartment in town."

"There is as much of you as of me in every building here, every planting, every wall and fence."

"But it's your home, our home, and I'm the one who's leaving."

"Honorable, *and* generous," Sophie said then. She stood. "I think I'd rather postpone any further discussion. Please?"

"Of course."

After the divorce they retained their joint practice of law, and through it all Sophie maintained her calm, quiet, decisive presence. It was almost as if she and Aaron had never been more than partners, and good friends.

"The quail are back," Sophie said one morning, Aaron was remembering now, "and this year for the first time they've brought their chicks, small, fluffy balls that already know how to scratch and eat the seed I scatter for them."

"I'd like to see them." Simple truth.

"You will be welcome any time. Debby too of course."

And, another time, "We have a new foal. Out of Impatient by Big Red."

"Colt or filly?"

"Colt. And Stacy Cummings says he already looks like a quarterhorse. I'll take Stacy's advice on whether we want to race him later."

"Stacy knows horses. How's your water this year?"

"Sufficient. But we could use a good soaking rain."

"The whole damn county could. If I were JL, I'd worry. He doesn't."

"I'm not sure I agree," Sophie said. "JL isn't as impervious as he seems. I always suspect vulnerability when somebody trades his names for initials."

"I didn't know he had names. Some men don't."

"JL does. Jasper Lightfoot Harmon."

"Well, hell, then can you blame him."

"Not really," Sophie said.

Now, what kind of conversation was that to be remembered in detail at three-four o'clock in the morning? Aaron demanded of himself, and heard no answer. *Was* there some kind of guilt involved, that his mind should keep going over and over scenes with Sophie? Well?

Beside him, Debby, kittenlike, slept on peacefully.

Willard P. Spencer, also awake before dawn this BACKSLOPE Monday morning, felt no sense of guilt, merely annoyance that he should find himself forced to become involved in minor financial details. That it was his own deliberate earlier involvement in other, far from minor financial matters that had brought about this state of affairs, did not even occur to him; and if it had, would merely have indicated to him that those whose function in life was to take care of Willard P. Spencer had fallen down on the job. Add to that annoyance his constant and growing dislike of Sanrio.

The area had been represented to him, by whom or in what manner he could no longer recall, as an idyllic combination of the grandeur of the Swiss Alps, the charm of Old Mexico, the unhurried restfulness of the Greek islands and the growing attractiveness of the southwest sun belt, with the added advantages of being part of the US where English was spoken, the currency was familiar and the plumbing worked. An impulsive man, Spencer had taken immediate steps to make a part of this dreamland his own.

The fact of the matter was that Sanrio with its spectacular scenery and splendid climate was merely on the verge of becoming the kind of Palm Springs-Sun Valley socially attractive locale Spencer had assumed it already was.

By best guess, Sanrio was town of about 25,000, longtime center of an agricultural-mining-ranching region, with a burgeoning ski industry, a few large and expensive estates like Spencer's, and a long tradition of southwestern informality.

Backward, ignorant and lazy would have been Spencer's summation, a place where the citizens, anglo and hispanic alike, had the quaint notion that everyone, regardless of background, breeding or their lack, was as good as anyone else. Spencer had even been called by his given name on occasion on first meeting. It was intolerable.

Three telephone conversations last Friday had brought it all into focus, and he had brooded unhappily all through the weekend.

The first call he had placed himself. "This is Willard P. Spencer," he said, and waited for acknowledgement.

"Yes, sir."

"I have called before and now I find it necessary to call again. The road to my property is the responsibility of the County, is it not?"

"Yes, sir. Is a County road." There was a noticeable Spanish lilt to the words.

"Then why is it not properly maintained?"

"The blade, she was there only five-six weeks ago, after the last snow."

"And now the road is rutted again. I want something done."

"Okay." The Hispanic shrug that accompanied the word came clearly over the wire.

Spencer drew a deep, slow breath. "When?"

"Maybe next week. Maybe week after. Sometime, okay? We're pretty busy."

It was difficult not to slam down the telephone.

And then the call from Aaron Swift. "A couple of things, Willard." And, in a different tone, "Although I'm damned if I know why they come to me instead of you direct."

"Because you are my legal representative here in Sanrio. And you know the local people."

"All right." There was resignation in the voice. "We'll let that go for the moment. Bud Lewis wants to know if you've had your homeowner's insurance invoice for this quarter."

"Certainly I've had it."

Aaron Swift said gently, "What Bud really wants to know, Willard, is are you going to pay it before the grace period expires?"

54

"Of course I am. The question is ridiculous."

There was a short silence. Aaron Swift said, "The second thing is a call from Bert Henry at the bank."

"And what does he want?"

"The last two months' installments on your personal loan. The total is—"

"I am quite aware of what the bank's outrageously high installment payments are. Interest rates have begun to subside, and I intend to see that my loan is re-negotiated. You may tell him that."

The silence this time was a little longer. Aaron Swift said at last in a conversational tone, "You know, Willard, when you really put your mind to it, you can be just about as obnoxious as anyone I know." The line went dead.

Spencer also placed the third call, and to the pleasant female voice that answered, "This is Willard P. Spencer," he said. "I wish to speak with John Walters." And when the new voice came on the line, "What is our situation, Walters?"

They were talking about a property with an asking price of a million-five, Walters thought, seventy-odd fenced and private acres abutting the Forest, with main house (four bedrooms, four baths), pool, four-car garage, an exceptional water supply and stunning views of the mountain range. It was not, repeat *not*, the sort of property you sold over the telephone. "One or two possible leads, Mr. Spencer," he said now, "but nothing definite yet. Interest rates—"

"The buyer you should be looking for," Spencer said in the tone of a teacher lecturing a backward child, "will not care about interest rates. He will make a cash transaction. This is not a tract house."

"I'm afraid we have to be patient—"

"Damn patience. I'm tired of this place, and I want to unload it. It's as simple as that. And you should be thinking of the fat commission you will get if and when. Keep me posted."

"I certainly will, Mr. Spencer," Walters said, and hung up. Unfortunately, the connection was not quite broken by the time he said quietly, but audibly, "You snotty son of a bitch."

Now, lying fully awake in the lightening pre-dawn, Spencer found that he could recall each of these conversations word for word. The experience was roughly analogous to poking a sore tooth with his tongue.

From the other bed, Angela said, as if they had been talking for some time, "I've been thinking. I've heard both good and not so good about the new Orient Express, London to Venice. I think we should try it out, Will. Fly over Concorde, of course. We haven't been in Venice in ages." There was no immediate response, and Angela raised her voice slightly. "Will! Did you hear me, Will?"

"We'll think about it," Spencer said.


JL's ringing telephone brought him instantly awake. "JL here."

"We've got one, JL." The dispatcher's voice, professionally calm. "And it's for real. I sent out two men for initial attack, and they report that it's already out of hand. Deep in the Forest."

"On my way," JL said.


In no more than five minutes he trotted out of the house limping only slightly on that still weak ankle, into the already lightening pre-sunrise, unlocked and started up the green Forest Service pick-up. He switched on the radio as he drove away, handling the microphone with one hand and the wheel with the other.

He would not have admitted it, nor would have been able to explain, but there was a feeling in his mind about this fire, a sense of urgency that did not sound in his voice. "JL here."

"10-4. I read you loud and clear."

"I'm heading for the airport. I want a chopper ready, and a Forest map and clipboard."

"10-4."

"How close can you get a crew in by vehicle?"

Within about a mile, the dispatcher said, and a crew was on the way. In addition—he listed the men and equipment he had on standby.

"Roger," JL said, satisfied, and drove on in silence.

To the limitless east the pre-dawn glow was beginning; the Tetas peaks on the horizon already showed their sharp anatomical outlines. The town-becoming-a-city of Sanrio was dark and silent, only a dog disappearing around a corner and a blinking yellow traffic light gave illusion of life. Beneath the Central Street bridge the Sanrio river showed black—like flowing oil, JL thought, and was conscious that his mind had tucked away another visual scene that might one day find its way into a painting. The mind, as he had noted before, worked in its own way at strange times.

He drove fast, expecting and encountering no other vehicles. He felt keyed-up, eager to come to grips with the emergency. With a wildland fire, as with a fire in a building, time was the critical factor. What could be handled immediately by a few men or a single crew might in only a few minutes require half a dozen crews—120 men—to dig in, establish a fire line, and begin their counter-assault, with perhaps even air tankers guided in by a lead plane to drop their slurry according to ground request. A wildland fire out of control could spread with unbelievable rapidity, its wind-driven and fuel-fed power multiplying in quantum jumps until it could seem, and could even be, that the entire countryside was aflame. Wildfire was the enemy, and sensible men treated it with respect.

The chopper was already rolled out and waiting at the Forest Service airport. A Forest Service lead plane, a light, single-engine aircraft stood off to one side near the high-wing, high-tail chartered Twin Otter from which Andy McIlvain's smoke-jumpers operated, and JL and Andy had jumped. In the distance a World War II vintage twin-engine transport, a C-46, Curtiss Commando, stood ready at need. The illusion, JL thought, was of an airfield in wartime. Well, in a real sense, it was.

"Ready to roll," the chopper pilot said. "Map and clipboard on your seat."

They swung up and over the still sleeping city toward the rising flanks of Sierra Grande. The big mountain's top was now in sunlight, its snow patch colored a deep pink in the low-slanting rays. *Alpenglühe*, the Germans and Austrians had named the phenomenon in their own mountains, JL had read, and had no idea how to pronounce; but to the Spanish coming to this new land, the term became *Sangre de Cristo*, blood of Christ, and was given to the entire range of mountains up behind Santa Fe.

"There she is," the chopper pilot said, and pointed off to their left deep into the Forest. The glow among the trees was unmistakable.

The fire area was midway between the south boundary of the Forest and the large estates that adjoined it, and the edge of the Wilderness, the flames spreading in all directions, in some places rapidly, in others, because of terrain or the type of vegetation, much more slowly. JL estimated the area of the fire at this point to be about 500 acres, what breeze there was coming out of the west-northwest, elongating the burning area to the eastward.

"Take her down for a good look," he said.

"Be bumpy, maybe even a little hairy."

JL did not reply. He had folded the map to show the pertinent area, and was now tucking it carefully beneath the clip of the clipboard. With his pencil he noted date and time, and then began to sketch in the fire's outlines.

It was bumpy, as the pilot had predicted. Currents of heated air rose from the ground, tossing the helicopter like a small boat in a choppy sea. JL ignored the jostling, braced himself against his seat harness, and, with frequent ground sightings to make sure of his points of reference, continued his sketching, applying quick shading to spots of heavy flames.

The feeling he had had was justified, and it was already a bad one; this much he allowed himself to decide while he concentrated on the pencil and the map and the outlines of the flames. But not until he was finished, and the anatomy of the fire, as it now appeared, was plain and clear on paper, did he turn his attention to detail.

Only a portion of the ponderosa stand had so far been affected, which meant, JL guessed accurately, that a single pine, probably a tall one, had been lightning-struck and had started the entire conflagration. But those tall trees that had burst into flame were burning furiously, their lower branches and foliage like so many torches, a sure sign of the temperature and force the downslope night breeze had generated.

By far the larger area aflame was below the ponderosa stand where piñon, juniper, scrub oak and a thorny tangle of undergrowth were sending greasy, sharp, acrid and choking smoke into the sky, reaching them even here in the helicopter.

"Take her up now," he told the pilot. "I want an overview to see if anything else is affected."

Nothing else was—at the moment. But that condition, JL thought grimly, was only temporary.

Movement caught his eye, and through the piñon and juniper growth he could see the twenty-man crew the dispatcher had sent out, all in yellow shirts and hard hats, walking single file, the required six feet apart as they had been taught to avoid accidents from the tools they carried—McClouds, Pulaskis, chain saws, shovels, brush hooks. Their pace was steady and purposeful. The leader, no doubt the crew chief, looked up and waved at the helicopter. JL waved his clipboard in response.

"Okay," he told the pilot, "let's take her home."

His mind was already made up. With the condition of the Forest after six weeks of no rain and constant low humidity, the thirsty air absorbing moisture from the vegetation as a sponge absorbs water in a basin; with the summer swirling winds that would come with full daylight and heated air rising from the sun-baked ground; and most of all with the start this fire already had, hidden as it was and able to consolidate itself before bursting into view, no single twenty-man crew or even two or three or half a dozen crews would be enough. On this one, much better sooner than later, an entire Fire Team was going to be needed.

# 5

JL was Fire Management Officer and Law Enforcement Officer of the Sanrio National Forest, over three million acres, the largest single Forest in Region 3 which includes all of Arizona and New Mexico. Within these two adjoining states lie 20,618,670 acres, 32,000 square miles, of National Forest, much of it connected.

JL's immediate superior was George Jefferson, as Sanrio Forest Supervisor head of the Forest, who was responsible to the Region 3 Forester, who in turn answered to the Chief Forester in Washington, immediately below the Secretary himself in the chain of command.

Whether his call got Jefferson out of bed or not was a matter of complete indifference to JL when he phoned from the Forest Service airport. "It's going to be a big one, George," he told him. "I think we'd better not fool around with a few isolated crews, but put in a Team right off."

This was as far as his recommendation would properly go. A Fire Team consisted of a complete organization of supervisory personnel, designated specialists, their ranks, duties and responsibilities as specific as those of officers and non-commissioned officers of a military unit — perhaps a regiment. The Fire Team supervisory personnel would determine the numbers and kinds required of actual fire-fighting men and equipment, have appropriate numbers of twenty-man crews called up, determine strategy and command the entire fire-suppression operation.

The overall commander of a Fire Team was called the Fire Boss (although in a few years his title would be changed to Incident Commander under the Incident Command System of fire suppression originated in and already in use in California, currently subject of considerable grumbling in other Regions).

There were two levels of Fire Teams constantly available. The Sanrio Forest Fire Team operated only within Sanrio Forest. Its designated Fire Boss was Jay Paul, newly transferred to the area. The Regional Class A Fire Team, the ultimate in experience and capability, of which JL was the designated Fire Boss, operated without geographical limit throughout the entire country whenever and wherever it was needed on massive fires beyond the capacities of local fire authorities. The choice of which Team was up to Jefferson, the Forest Supervisor.

Now, on the phone, "How's your ankle?" George Jefferson said.

"It's fine."

"I saw you limping the other day."

"I told you, it's fine."

"That was a damfool thing," Jefferson said, "jumping with McIlvain."

They had been through all this, at length, and there was no point in even trying to argue.

"You could have been hurt bad," Jefferson said.

That demanded response, "I spent ten years as a smoke-jumper."

"Back in your twenties. You're not a kid any more. You're forty-one."

"George," JL said, "this is going to be a big one. We

need a Fire Team. Now."

"Aren't you supposed to be going to Idaho?"

JL had totally forgotten. Seminar at BIFC — Boise Interagency Fire Center, nerve center, information clearinghouse, discussion center, research center, but not command post, of the nation's total fire-suppression efforts.

Every Federal agency, bureau and service with jurisdiction over public land is represented at BIFC (pronounced biff-see), and the BIFC Situation Room and the Weather Room contain up-to-the-minute data on men and materiel both available and deployed on fires throughout the fifty states, together with current status of fires in progress, weather conditions and forecasts which could affect fire-suppression tactics — a marvel of communication and data gathering accomplished through a nation-wide network of radio, telephones, teletypes and computers.

(A Fire Boss in the Wasatch Mountains of Utah needs additional ground crews with full equipment? BIFC can provide, perhaps from a reservoir of standby crews in Texas or Tennessee. There are no more air tankers available for charter in Minnesota? BIFC can call upon a list of idle aircraft in Wyoming and Colorado, and will do . . . .)

But as far as JL was concerned at the moment, his shaded map in hand, damn the seminar and damn BIFC. "I was."

There was no hesitation. "You still are," Jefferson said. "Call the dispatcher. Tell him to get on it. Forest Team. They can cope."

"Jay Paul's new to the area, George."

"Then he'll have to learn fast."

JL took a deep breath. "George—" Insubordination was the word, he supposed, but right now he could not have cared less. This was *his* Forest, all three million-plus acres of it. "I tell you, this is going to be a big one. Over six weeks without rain. Low humidity. This time of year we'll get winds. And—"

"You want to handle it yourself, is that it?"

"Yes."

"The answer is no. You're due in Idaho. We don't need your Regional Fire Team, and Jay Paul and the Forest Fire Team had damn well better cope. Get on it."

"George—"

"I'm not going to tell you again, JL. Call the dispatcher and tell him to get the Forest Team into action." The line went dead.

JL stood for a moment, indecisive, still holding the phone in his hand. Then, slowly, he hung it up, walked into the radio room and called the dispatcher.

The system worked, and worked well—how often had he told himself, and others, that? The lines of authority were established, guidelines in place, all mechanisms ready to go. You took orders from above and saw to it that your own orders were followed on down the line; simple as that. Period. Into the microphone to the dispatcher he said, "Call the Forest Team. I'm bringing in a map."

"10-4, JL."

He put the mike down very gently and walked to his pick-up.

It would work, he told himself, because it had to. There was too much at stake to allow the system to fail. A fire—he had long thought of it in this way—was a fight to the finish, no-holds-barred, gouging and butting in the clinches all a part of the action with no referee standing by to call foul.

First at hazard, of course, was the Forest itself, and even leaving aside its aesthetic and recreation value, there was its actual dollars-and-cents worth to the nation which owned it, the timber which could be harvested for its variety of uses, lumber only one among them; the grazing land to be leased that the cattle industry might prosper; and, above all, the vegetation that protected the soil, conserved the moisture from snow and rainfall and kept the land from turning into desert waste.

But aside from the Forest, there were the houses, the people who lived in them, the town itself, as vulnerable to destruction from wildfire as a village caught between artillery barrages and aircraft bombing.

Under Jay Paul, as Fire Boss Commander of the Sanrio Forest Fire Team, would be immediately available as required one or more Line Boss over Division Bosses who would command Crew Chiefs, each of these with nineteen men under his or her command. In addition, still under Jay Paul's overall command as specialists and staff, there would be an Air Attack Boss to direct the chartered air tankers which at need would drop their loads of slurry—a liquid combination of fire-extinguishing chemicals far more effective than water—where ground crews could not reach; a Plans Chief; Maps and Records Officer; Intelligence Officer; Fire Behavior Officer to advise the Fire Boss on the probable directions the fire would take; Safety Officer; Equipment Officer; Contracting Officer; Supply Officer; Heliport Air Service Manager; Communications Officer; Finance Officer; Comptroller for Injury Officer; and others, plus trainees where it was deemed advisable.

At need, there would be a Weatherman brought in with his equipment to forecast climatic conditions, and even down from BIFC a special aircraft carrying infra-red photography equipment to provide current temperature maps of the fire area that would air in planning the containment of the fire and its eventual suppression.

At the bottom, the foundation of all this, would be the twenty-man crews on the ground, the troops who would fight the fire face-to-face in shifts, establishing a perimeter and gradually closing it; an army to be maneuvered, fed, transported, provided with sleeping space and rudimentary sanitary facilities and to be looked after, treated precisely like soldiers in battle.

There would be Hotshot Crews (Category 1), smoke-jumpers, SWFFF crews (Southwest Forest Fire Fighters, many of them from Indian tribes and pueblos, many hispanic crews), experienced fire-fighters all, where possible called in from local standby forces, where necessary flown in, sometimes from hundreds of miles away.

The dispatcher summoning all this was, properly, the nerve center of all fire suppression efforts. The Sanrio Forest dispatcher had his office and communications equipment in the Forest Headquarters located within the Forest to the east of the Wilderness, and north of the town. He was constantly in touch, via phone and teletype, with the Region 3 dispatchers in Albuquerque, responsible for communication with all National Forest lands and installations in both New Mexico and Arizona, two states with total area almost five times that of New York State.

The Sanrio dispatcher could call in at need, either directly or through the Regional dispatcher in Albuquerque who in turn had the nationwide facilities of the Forest Service to call upon, standby crews, air tankers, lead planes, helicopters, bulldozers, ground tankers, tools, and supplies of all kinds including food rations; along with multi-channel two-way radios, pagers, automatic telephone dialers, answering services, teletype circuits, telecopier machine and TWX circuits with computer ties to put it all together, and bring men and materiel where needed.

He was a carefully screened and trained man, accustomed to what was called "the hot seat", coping during extreme burning conditions with as many as 200 fires a day within the vast area he was responsible for.

But the plain truth, JL told himself, was that he would rather have kept it all in his own hands, which was ridiculous. Or, was it? He had seen the fire; others had not. And he knew the Forest as no one else.

"Here," he could say, touching a map, "we've got a tangle of clutter and new growth you can't even walk through because they've said no to prescribed burning, and if that catches, as it will, you'll just have to drop your fire line back, probably to here. And over here as soon as the sun is high, you'll have an upslope wind going into all that untouched piñon and juniper, and when it catches, the scrub oak will go next. If it gets into one of these arroyos you'll have the big trees to cope with, and if the fire crowns—"

There was no conclusion to that conditional clause. A fire that "crowned" was one that rose into the tops of the huge trees and spread from treetop to treetop, high above the reach and control of fire-fighters on the ground, its behavior at the mercy of totally unpredictable winds at treetop height. A "crowned fire" could fling burning branches in all directions, jumping laboriously cleared fire breaks with ease. At worst, it could, by expanding the fire's size and fury, turn into the ultimate disaster, a "fire storm" which through the enormous energy of its rising flames and super-heated air could suck in fresh oxygen at ground level, thus feeding itself and turning the entire area into a holocaust which would end only when all fuel was exhausted.

The results of such a fire were awesome and sickening, leaving, when it eventually burned itself out, only charred and worthless skeletons of trees large and small, all ground cover gone, and the land naked and helpless, exposed to erosion from snow run-off or rain flooding and deep scarring from which it might never recover.

Jay Paul, the Forest Team Fire Boss, might be a good man — although that was yet to be demonstrated to JL — but he had not had time to absorb the peculiarities and quirks of these western mountains in the Sanrio, and in a situation such as JL had seen from the chopper, an intimate knowledge of the Forest just could be critical.

JL had a suspicion that George Jefferson, who had never in his life jumped out of an airplane, still harbored a grudge because of his, JL's, test jump with Andy McIlvain. In Jefferson's, and Madge's view, it had been merely a dangerous and unnecessary exercise in sheer juvenile romanticism.

Well, maybe it was, but JL would still do it again, because now he *knew*, and did not have to guess or take others' judgements, just what Andy's newly developed parachute would do. And for that, in JL's opinion, there simply was no substitute.

Andy's own enthusiasm when he talked about the parachute design gave you some kind of hint. "They've accepted it!" were his first words when he saw JL months ago. "Jesus H Jumping Christ, how about that? Two years, and the bastards have finally bent their stiff necks and admitted that we know what we want!"

"Congratulations," JL had said with his enigmatic smile.

"Ice water," Andy said, "goddamned ice water, that's what your heart pumps, I swear. Let's go somewhere I can get a beer in my hand and tell you all about it."

And in the quiet barroom of the Antlers, "Two main

changes, of course," Andy was saying, the words coming so fast they almost ran together. "Thirty-two-foot instead of twenty-eight-foot diameter. That's one. And panels of different porosity nylon. That's the other. Makes all the difference in the world. This baby will go where you want it, down-wind, cross-wind, even up-wind. It—"

That was when JL had made his decision. "When you bring your crew down," he said, "I'm going to try it for myself."

And now, JL was thinking as he turned from the phone, unless he was farther off-base in his judgement that he would have been willing to bet he was, they were going to need Andy and his new parachute and his smoke-jumpers on this fire very damn soon.

On impulse he trotted painfully up the steel stairs to the airport tower where they had the latest weather read-outs which indicated, as JL would have been willing to bet they would, more afternoon thunderstorm activity. "And no rain," he said.

The tower man agreed. "Andy McIlvain's already called in this morning," the tower man said, "and I'll bet he's called the dispatcher too. He says he's tired of sitting on his duff. You going to use him on this one?"

"Not my decision," JL said and went back down the stairs, remembering the keyed-up, eager feelings of his own smoke-jumping days.

The jumpers were an elite group, mostly in their twenties or early thirties, although there was no retirement age and a few, like Andy, forty, kept on and would continue until they could no longer handle the rigors of the job.

They were all experienced wildland fire-fighters, and all in superb physical condition before they were even considered for jump training at centers like Missoula and Redding. Their function was to parachute into terrain too rough for vehicles or helicopter landings; retrieve their "fire boxes" filled with gear they had packed themselves, tools, water, when indicated, explosives, radios, food, shelters, in short, everything necessary for isolated wilderness existence and fire-fighting (the "fire boxes" were also dropped by parachute after the jumpers were on the ground); stay as long as necessary to subdue whatever fire they had been sent in to attack; and walk out, at least as far as the nearest road reachable by vehicle, carrying their gear which weighed about 115 pounds per man.

They were proud of their origins and traditions which dated back to 1940, and proud too that it was their training and techniques that had been copied to organize the first military paratrooper training at Fort Benning, Georgia, during World War II.

During the fire season — in places across the country as early as April or as late as November — teams of smoke-jumpers were moved around the country from Alaska to Florida at need or in anticipation of each area's greatest fire season danger.

That Andy and his crew were already on the ground here and now, JL reflected as he drove back into town, was one more indication of the soundness of the planned routine, the *system*. Still.

He had one more try at George Jefferson, by telephone from his own house. "I've seen this fire, George," he said, "and I don't like it even a little bit. Maybe we don't need the whole Regional Fire Team, but somebody had damned well better be here to look over Jay Paul's shoulder when things start to get rough."

"Namely you," Jefferson said. His voice was heavy with irony, and suppressed anger. "Now I'll do what I said I wasn't going to. I'll go that far, and tell you just once more to get your ass up to Boise where you're scheduled to be, and stop thinking you're the only one around who knows anything about fire suppression. Is that clear?"

JL opened his mouth, and closed it again. "I hear you," he said finally.

"And take your bad ankle with you."


By mid-morning, at the fire base Jay Paul had chosen, well into the Forest, but east of the fire's center and below the Wilderness, communications were still being set up, phone lines strung, radio antennae raised into treetops, and trucks constantly arriving with supplies, but already the fire lines had been established by twenty-man crews with hand tools fanned out in accordance with JL's sketch map.

Out on the fire line the heat was intense, and the smoke. And the crackling of flames punctuated by firecracker-like sounds, as pine pitch-knots exploded, heightened the illusion of battle. Or of hell.

In full sunlight, as JL would have predicted, the bare ground heating the air above it began to produce an upslope wind. In one edge of the tangled brush and scrub oak area, rich with the clutter that JL had wanted to burn out, flames suddenly fish-hooked without warning, out-raced the sweating troops on the fire line and, plunging into unburned piñon and juniper, charged up one of the many narrow gullies called arroyos.

Because of the grueling demands of the job, and the strenuous physical tests to be passed in order to obtain the "red card" all fire-fighters must have, there are not many women within their ranks. But colorful Bessie Wingate, crew chief, big as a big man and as brawny, was a jarring exception. Her crew, twenty fire-fighters in all, was one of eleven crews already deployed, and her position was east of the fire's center on the steepness of Sierra Grande's slopes.

"Maybe I ought to take up mid-wrestling instead," she was fond of saying, "but, hell, it wouldn't be near as much fun."

On this day she wielded her shovel—a No. 2 roundpoint; no lady shovel for Bessie—with grim power and efficiency, nevertheless conscious all the time of the positions and safety of the nineteen crew men under her command.

"I have to figure the bastards have the sense God gave a ground squirrel," she had been known to say after a few beers at the Antlers, "but not a damn bit more. Tim here (or Charlie or Pete, whoever happened to be handy) probably couldn't pour piss out of a boot if the instructions was printed on the heel, but you aim him in the right direction and he'll sure as hell keep right on going until he gets there." Tim or Charlie or Pete would grin hugely, pleased to be so complimented.

The job of Bessie's crew, working with chain saws, axes, brush hooks and shovels, was to maintain a line beyond which their small sector of the fire could not pass, and, if at all possible, drive the flames back upon themselves: hot, dirty, back-breaking and dangerous work.

When the fire began its 180° fishhook turn, Bessie's warning came instantly. "Watch that mother! Gus, Harry, Joe, get after it! But watch that arroyo! There's tangled brush in there, and the goddam mother can turn again! Or start up the sides!"

Worse, although Bessie for the moment did not see it—as JL would have—the upslope wind, compressed in the draw, acted like a blowtorch, intensifying the fire's heat, and driving the flames uphill at an accelerated pace.

Feeding on the tangled ground clutter of brush, the

fire tore into an area of scrub oak, consumed it with a crackling roar and raced on. It swept by a twelve-foot piñon standing alone, leaving the ground blackened and smoking, but the tree itself miraculously whole. The lower level flames were thirty feet beyond when the piñon suddenly became a torch, a twenty-foot pillar of fire. In only moments, it was entirely consumed.

"Jesus wept!" Bessie said, and grabbed the walkie-talkie from her belt. "We've lost our line!" she shouted into it after identifying herself. Her words almost ran together. "The son of a bitch is going up the arroyo right into the big trees!"


Jay Paul, the Forest Team Fire Boss, had attended the National Fire Training Center in Marana, Arizona, had spent fifteen years in fire suppression but was, as JL had said, new to the Sanrio Forest. And right from the start he had an uncomfortable feeling about this fire. It had been too dry for too long, and paradoxically, the fire-suppression efforts in the Sanrio Forest had been just too goddamned successful.

You couldn't say that was anybody's fault, because it really wasn't. JL, as Fire Management Officer, had done the hell of a job, which was exactly what he was supposed to do; as soon as a fire began, he saw to it that it was put out. That made everybody happy clear back to the office of the Secretary of Agriculture in Washington. Well, not everybody; Jay didn't like it, JL didn't like it, and probably George Jefferson the Forest Supervisor didn't like it either, although George kept things like that to himself.

The fact of the matter was that a ponderosa pine forest like this one actually *needed* periodic fires to keep the forest clean, and dangerous ground clutter to a minimum. Every seven or eight years was the optimum

73

timing. But when fires, mostly lightning-caused, were attacked and put out as soon as they began, fallen fuel accumulated faster than natural forces could dispose of it by rot and decay. The result was a build-up of inflammable material just waiting for the inevitable conflagration.

What was called "prescribed burning" was an attempt to do away with this excess of dangerous fuel. Against this was the widespread feeling that *all* wildland fires are bad; Smokey Bear had done his job too well. Worse, on occasion "prescribed fires" had broken free and raged out of control, not many, but some, and the resultant outcry had produced political pressure on the Department to stop all such dangerous practices.

In one of his rare outbursts, "We're damned if we do," JL had said in Jay's hearing "and we're damned if we don't. To Joe Citizen, it just doesn't make sense that we go out and put a match to a forest, so the orders as of now are, 'No prescribed burning.' Tough tit, but there it is."

So now here was JL, who ought to have been in charge, picking this particular time of all times to fly out to Idaho, leaving Jay holding the baby. Bugger it.

"See if we can get aerial tankers in to douse that arroyo with slurry," he told his Air Attack Boss. "If we can't cut it off there, we're going to have the whole goddamned big tree stand of fire."

Despite himself, some of Bessie's excitement had gotten to him, and he found it impossible to keep his voice calm. JL, now, wouldn't even have batted an eye, or raised his voice in the slightest. But, as everybody knew, JL had ice water in his veins.

JL's first stop at the BIFC complex on the outskirts of

Boise was the Situation Room where teletyped reports from each area of the United States — including Alaska and Hawaii — clacked in constantly.

Here was Region 3 and the several situation reports on the Sanrio Forest, specifically the fire named BACKSLOPE. JL read them quickly in reverse order. It seemed to be, he thought, worse than he had feared; the estimated area of the conflagration was now 2000 acres, which put it already in the project fire category.

One of the men at the large horseshoe desk, recognizing him, said, "You've got one going down your way, no?"

JL nodded. "Seems so." His voice was mild, apparently unconcerned. He walked down the hall to the Weather Room.

Here detailed information from the Weather Service — millibar and temperature charts, satellite photos, some infra-red enhanced, and forecasts — were received, digested, scrutinized and passed along to Regional and Forest commands. To one of the meteorologists he knew, "Sanrio," JL said, "what's our forecast?"

"Tourist weather," The meteorologist was smiling. "There's a lovely high sitting right down there, and no nasty storm is going to move in on that. Dry lightning, but no rain. The jet stream is finally behaving itself."

JL made himself smile, nodded his thanks and walked out and back down the hall to the Situation Room.

"What's been committed to BACKSLOPE?" This to the man at the horseshoe desk who had spoken to him.

The information was on the wall chart in the form of lighted, different-colored pins. "Six crews," the man said, looking over his shoulder at the chart, "two helitack crews, two air tankers with lead plane."

"Smoke-jumpers?"

"No."

Jay was going to need them just for starters, JL thought, and said nothing. Six crews—120 troops on the line—was not going to be enough; even from here he could tell them that. And—

"Are you JL Harmon, from Sanrio?" A girl, in neat Forest Service uniform.

JL nodded. Recall? George Jefferson wanted him back? Well, he was sure as hell ready.

Instead, "They're waiting for you," the girl said. "The seminar is about to begin."

# 6

Young Tad Lawry was first out of the tent in the morning, leaving his father and mother still in their double sleeping bag. Home in Texas he was a Boy Scout and had done considerable hiking and some camping, but he had never seen big trees like these, nor a mountain anywhere the size of Sierra Grande which he could just glimpse up through the stands of pines, thrusting its bare peak into the brilliant sky.

And the air tasted strange, too, smelling like the trees and like the pitch that had rubbed off on his hand last night while he was helping his mother put up the tent. And despite what his father had said about their being all alone in here, there had to be somebody camped near because he could smell smoke from their campfire.

His father was a funny guy, and Tad wondered that after all the years they had been married, his mother had never seemed to realize it. "Nobody, but nobody pushes your old man around," Les Lawry had told the boy once. "And don't let them push you, either."

What that worked out to mean, as Tad had discovered early and Mom still didn't understand, was that if you told Pop to do something, he'd turn right around and do the opposite, simple as that.

"Don't drive so fast, Les." And down went the accelerator, almost through the floor. That kind of thing.

It was easy enough to see, but Mom just didn't seem to catch on.

Tad studied the stream. It was clear and fast-running; and it gurgled to itself. He liked that. He followed it a few hundred yards, pleased by its noisy company, he came around a turn that opened to a view and there he stopped. Two deer were drinking, because of the water's sounds oblivious to his presence. He stood quietly, watching.

A new sound obtruded, the staccato chatter of a helicopter overhead. Both deer threw up their heads, ears swivelling, and without even looking up bounded away as if on springs, to disappear into the trees. Tad, remembering his father's caution last night, froze until the sound passed. He felt oddly guilty without knowing why.


Elsie Edwards was up before Don on this Monday morning. She peeked out of the blue nylon tent and looked around at the empty forest. She saw only a Canada jay industriously scratching through their dead fire from last night. He stopped, and cocked his head at her. "You don't really count in the voyeur category," Elsie said, and came naked out into the bright but hazy morning. Don followed, also naked.

The smell of smoke was faint against the scent of the pines. Elsie breathed deep. "You remember my mentioning the bridal suite in the Dorchester?" she said. "Or one of the gingerbread castles on the Promenade des Anglais? Forget them. This is much better." She crinkled her eyes at Don. "I think it may be the company."

"I'm flattered."

"You should be." Elsie sniffed the air. "Smoke. A campfire? Company? No matter. We can't see them, and that's all that counts." She was silent for a moment, a fond half-smile on her lips. "For the record, I don't think I've ever felt so happy in my whole life."

"Wasn't that the idea?"

Frank Orwell waited impatiently for Felipe Vigil, that greaseball, who had wandered off saying he'd be right back. That was a half-hour ago, and it was broad daylight now and time they got the hell on their way. Goddam greaseballs had no sense of time. Right away meant a half-hour; ten minutes probably meant all day. And Orwell was anxious to put as much distance between himself and that Los Ojos place as he could. Goddam.

"Hey, man!" Felipe, breathless, and grinning. "You know what I got? Nooky, man! *Coño*! A bare-ass chick with the biggest *tetas* you ever seen!" He stopped, studying Orwell's expression. "You dig, man? We got us a real live piece of ass right out here in these fucking woods!"

Orwell stood indecisive. His mind said to split just as fast as they could, get the hell out of the area. His loins, after two years of incarceration, refused to listen. He licked his lips. "She's alone?"

"There's a guy with her. He's bare-assed too, and he doesn't look like much. We can take him easy like we took that dude in the store."

Orwell shook his head. "I don't like it."

"You chicken? Nothing to it. We take the dude. You screw the chick. I screw the chick. We on our way. Ten-fifteen minutes, what difference that make? I been saving a load too long, man, too fucking long."

Andy McIlvain, without even waiting for orders, had taken the first eleven men on the jump roster out to the Forest Service airport. They checked their already packed fire boxes into the Twin Otter, lashed them surely, and settled down to wait.

If Andy knew JL, and he damn well did, they'd be thrown into this fire any minute now. That was rough terrain out there, no place for vehicles of any kind, and, if the chopper pilot was to be believed, the leading edge of the fire was already beyond the reach of men on foot.

JL, Andy knew, didn't believe in messing around. He had no patience with fire bosses who committed men and equipment grudgingly—not that JL was profligate, but he did believe in moving fast—and, by holding back and delaying, not infrequently ended by needing far greater resources than they would have had they hit the fire hard right at the start.

But with the sun well up, no orders had come, and Andy, never the most patient of men, got on the horn to find out why. He hung up disgusted. "Jay Paul," he told his men, "he's the fire boss, and he's used to Georgia piney wood fires in rolling country, not this kind of thing. Where the hell's JL?"

Stacy saw and smelled the smoke when she awakened, and noted that the sun had taken on a strange, metallic-orange tinge. The 7:00 local radio news mentioned fire in the Sanrio Forest, but reported that it was under control. *"No hay problema,"* Stacy told Juanita her cook-housekeeper, who agreed that those in charge of the Forest undoubtedly had matters well in hand, and would the *señorita* be home for lunch?

And that, of course, brought up the subject Stacy had been avoiding ever since she awakened — Bart Jones and just what she was going to do about him. In the end, characteristically, she faced the problem head-on and called the number now listed for El Rancho Costa Mucho.

A maid answered, probably young, Stacy thought, shapely and very friendly, unless Bart had changed his spots entirely. And in only a few moments, Bart himself was on the line. "Hi. I wondered when you'd call." His voice sounded normal, friendly, without guile.

"I didn't know until last night that I had a new neighbor."

"I hoped you'd be surprised. When do I see you? Here, I hope. I don't get around much any more."

"I have work to do this morning."

"I heard. You mess around with the sex life of horses, don't you?"

His tongue had not lost its sharpness, Stacy thought. "You might say that. We do go in for artificial insemination."

"Lunch, then? I have a good cook."

"And do you have white wine? I've given up lunch martinis."

"Not a Christer. Not you." His sigh was audible. "Wine it is. One o'clock?"

Stacy hung up and sat for a little time motionless, staring unseeing across the office. Unreal, she thought; unreal that he's here; unreal that he can still get to me; unreal that I carry this sense of guilt around like a curse. Feelings were sometimes like that. She could hear her father.

"Feller named Ben Lugan and I had a kind of feud years back, honey," he had told her once. "It started out over a girl, but it got into all kinds of things like oil

81

leases and drilling rights and whether he'd blocked a loan I wanted from the bank, that kind of thing, a feeling that just kept turning up until I was damn near beginning to think I'd find Ben Lugan under the bed. And the funny part was that he felt it too. I stole an oil lease right out of his hands, he said, and I hadn't had a thing to do with it. That was how it was, and you carry something like that around long enough, a feeling about somebody else, I mean, and it can sour your stomach for damn sure."

"So what did you do?" Stacy said, although, knowing her father, she had an idea she already knew the answer.

"We worked it out, Ben and I. It took only ten-fifteen minutes one afternoon out near an oil rig I had pumping, nobody else around. I lost a couple of teeth, busted a knuckle and cracked two-three ribs. Ben came out about the same way. We agreed it was a stand-off."

"And," Stacy said, "then you drove into town and had a drink together."

Her father nodded. "Something like that. We both felt better. Like after a big thunderstorm."

But how do I settle this thing with Bart? Stacy asked herself, and heard no answer.


Aaron Swift came into the office early as usual that morning. There was already a telephone message from Sophie on his desk saying that she would be in late, if at all. It was unlike her, and Aaron called the familiar ranch number at once. Her voice sounded all right, and he was conscious of a sharp feeling of relief. "You're okay, then?" he said.

"I'm fine."

"I thought maybe a case of the fantods." He tried to keep it light.

"Instead, a case of fire."

"Where?" His voice was sharp now. And then quickly it softened. "Oh. In the Forest? That one? It's way in, deep. Not to worry."

"We're getting ash."

"It's just that the wind is blowing that way."

"Yes. That's what concerns me." Always there was reason, logic behind her words.

Aaron said, "You want me to come out, Soph?"

"Someone has to mind the store."

"That's nonsense. You know it."

"What could you do if you came?" The question was unanswerable, and she knew it. She added, "There isn't anything I can do, either, but I'll feel better just staying here. You can understand that."

Aaron could. More than twenty years of living had gone into that ranch, he was thinking, both hers *and* his. Living and planning, accumulating, revising, working, actual physical work day after day on items like the garden, the special bookshelves in their joint study, his shop, the kitchen; work too precious to be trusted to anyone else.

"Will you call me, Soph, if you want me? Promise me that?"

"You didn't have to ask." Her voice was gentle, and warmly grateful.

Aaron hung up, and instantly the switchboard girl buzzed his phone. Her Spanish-lilted voice emphasized each syllable with carefully unstated contempt as she said, "Mr. Willard P. Spencer is on line Two."

Aaron sighed and punched the button. "You are up early, Willard. I was under the impression that you liked to sleep in."

Spencer did not like to be teased. "When there is a fire —" he began portentously.

"Oh, come now, it's miles away. And we have fires

83

every year."

"Like barbecues and no doubt bullfights as well, one of your barbarous local customs, I'm sure. Nevertheless, I don't like it."

"There's nothing I can do about it, Willard."

Spencer's voice was decisive. "On the contrary, you can find out at once precisely when the grace period of my homeowner's insurance lapses."

Aaron wore his courtroom face. Opposing attorneys had driven themselves to despair trying to figure out what was behind it. "I have a better suggestion, Willard." He paused for emphasis. "It is that you write a check for the amount of your quarterly premium, the invoice for which you told me you had received, and carry the check in to Bud Lewis's office. Then there can be no confusion. Now, if you will excuse me." He hung up, and instantly the buzzer sounded again.

"Mrs. Swift is on line One."

"Debby, honey—" Aaron's voice now held mild protest. The last time he had seen her she had been curled like a kitten, and as relaxed, in a tangle of bedclothes, if not sound asleep, giving a fine imitation of it.

"There's a fire, A. I smell the smoke, and it's on the television. I'm terrified of fire."

You would have told me sooner, Aaron thought, but you didn't think the subject would come up; a gag line, long forgotten. "Tell you what, honey," he said, "you go over to the Club for breakfast, and then stay by the pool in the sun. The fire won't come close, but if you think it does, you can always dive in."

"I thought maybe you and I could drive somewhere. Maybe up to Santa Fe. We haven't been there for ages."

"Sorry." Aaron's voice was gentle, but firm. "Work. You know Sanrio can't get along without me. The whole place would grind to a halt. Nobody would know what to do—"

"Oh, you!" There was a smile in Debby's voice. "All right. I'll be at the Club."

Being married to Aaron was not exactly what Debby had imagined it might be, even though the sense of financial ease and the status as wife of one of Sanrio's — and the State's — leading citizens was even greater than she had anticipated, and at times pleasant beyond words.

But what she sometimes missed was the *spontaneity*, the willingness at a moment's notice to drop everything and rush into some innocuous pleasure like a picnic or an unplanned trip. To be honest, she supposed that kind of freedom could only be a part of irresponsible youth, that the kind of stability Aaron represented, and she so enjoyed, came only with the acceptance of duties and obligations, so it all balanced out. Still.

The Plans Chief, whose name was Phil Sommers, ran his forefinger along the topographical map. "Getting close to the Wilderness," he said, "and unless it's stopped pretty damn soon, we're going to have quite a mess on our hands. Once it reaches this line, it can fan out."

Jay Paul squinted at the map. In places, he had long thought, this country seemed to stand on edge, and it was a wonder to him that any kind of vegetation, let alone big trees, could gain a foothold, but they were there, right where Phil's finger was pointing, and if possible, they damn well had to be protected. "No road in?" he said.

"It's sidehill wampus country." And, seeing the look of puzzlement on Jay Paul's face, who obviously did not comprehend the mythical western analogy, Sommers added, "You know, sidehill wampuses have legs that are longer on one side than the other. That's for walking around steep hills. That's the kind of country it is out there. A jeep would roll over."

"Chopper landing place?"

"Not in that terrain. Andy McIlvain's crew is about the only choice."

"It's not too rough for them?" Jay shook his head decisively. "Damn it, it is. I've been there, on the ground, I remember now, practically on all fours. You can't ask somebody to parachute into that."

Phil Sommers hesitated. "I'm no smoke-jumper," he said, "but those characters seem to think they can go in just about anywhere—"

"No. I won't risk them."

A shrug. "You're the boss."

"I'll see if Tim can get a slurry drop in there."

"A crew on the ground—"

"Damn it, no!"

Phil Sommers nodded. "Like I said, you're the boss. They're predicting wind by noon, by the way."

"I can't help that, either."

Sommers nodded again and turned away, this time in silence.


Felipe Vigil said, whispering, "There they are, see?"

It was impossible not to see, Frank Orwell thought; at that moment in all the world there was only the naked girl in his vision—big, but not overweight, with the kind of breasts you could drool over in a *Playboy* or *Penthouse* centerfold, with a curving waist and full hips and a generous ass that made your hands itch to grab it—

"What'd I tell you?" Felipe whispered. "Some kind of nooky, no?"

Orwell came back to reality. "Okay," he said. "But we make it fast, you hear me, greaseball?"

86

"You got it."

The damn chick was just asking for it, Orwell thought, as they broke cover and began their short, savage charge. Marching around bare-ass, what did she think was going to happen? Well? Her own damn fault.

# 7

Mrs. Tyler Wayne came down to her beloved gardens this Monday morning as usual. Manuel and his assistant, Hilario, were already at work, Hilario on hands and knees weeding one of the rose beds, Manuel with careful skill manicuring the privet hedge that lined the flagstone walk from the big house.

"A lovely morning," Mrs. Wayne said. She was small and slim, with pure white hair beneath the sunshade hat, and eyes of intense blue in her still smooth face. She wore gardening gloves, stout low-cut shoes, an immaculate cream-colored short-sleeve blouse and tailored poplin trousers. "You do such a lovely trimming job, Manuel. And Hilario doesn't miss a single weed. I am very grateful to you both."

In Manuel's experience, anglos did not behave in this graceful manner. He and Hilario had discussed it often as they ate their lunches, sitting on the ground in the shade of one of the great Dutch elms the Senator had had planted long ago in the sweeping lawns. But, then, Mrs. Wayne in many ways was wholly different from all other anglos either man had ever encountered, and although the subject had never been mentioned, both would cheerfully have died for her.

"There is *humo*, smoke, *señora*," Manuel said.

"Perhaps they are doing—I believe it is called prescribed burning in the Forest."

Manuel disliked contradicting Mrs. Wayne, but it was well known that having lived her life, rich and full, she no longer concerned herself overmuch with what happened in the world. "*Lo siento*," Manuel said, "I am sorry, but there is a fire in the Forest. It was caused by lightning."

Mrs. Wayne smiled. "That nice Mr. Harmon will attend to it, I'm sure. Now do you think we might spray the roses again, Manuel? I value your judgement."

These days it was even more important than before, Mrs. Wayne felt, that the property be kept in flawless condition because she was now, in effect, a trustee, and how often had she heard Tyler say that in the eyes of the law, quite properly in his opinion, there existed no more sacred responsibility than that of fiduciary? Vista Hill, Mrs. Wayne's home for nearly fifty years, and Tyler's for a little more than forty, now technically belonged to the State, Mrs. Wayne's gift in her husband's name, hers to live in and care for during her lifetime.

"Spraying is good," Manuel said. "With so many beds is maybe a little expensive, *señora* —"

"That is not important, Manuel. If you think it is good, we will do it. You always know best."

To be chopped into small pieces for her at need, Manuel thought, and not a word of protest would pass his lips.

Bellevue Acres, Ken Delacorte was perfectly willing to concede, did not have the connotation that attached to, say, Beverly Hills or Palm Beach; nor was it intended to. Ken thoroughly approved of the Tyler Wayne estate Vista Hill, along with Stacy Cummings's pad, El Rancho Costa Mucho, the Spencer place, and all the others of that category—for those well-heeled enough to own and enjoy them.

And because after considerable looking around in the uncrowded southwest Ken had picked Sanrio as a coming place, a potential Palm Springs, say, or even a Tucson for growth, a place to attract among other things eastern retired wealth, he would have loved to build luxury condominiums on speculation, but his finances were simply not up to it; hence Bellevue Acres, 135 houses, eight to the acre, because ordinary folks needed places to live too, as Ken could well remember from his wrong-side-of-the-town Waco beginnings before football gave him a hand up.

The houses were not exactly flung together, but they *were* frame, plywood, and insulating board with a skin of stucco rather than solid sun-ripened, hand-laid adobe, or even rebar-reinforced block, filled with pumice, with double-glazed windows, twelve inches of insulation beneath the roof and hand-carved doors.

The houses in Bellevue Acres were crowded together, too, and it was easy enough, impossible not, in fact, to hear your neighbor's TV program or the sporadic arguments over family budgets. There were lots of kids in Bellevue Acres, and dogs, and bicycles, and roller skates; and Sanrio City school buses stopped at almost every intersection.

Ken had no definite idea yet what there was about Bellevue Acres that seemed to be attracting the interest of Bartlemy Jones, who had rolled his fancy wheelchair into the closing when he bought the Brown place he had named El Rancho Costa Mucho, and produced a certified check for seven figures for payment as if it were something he did every afternoon, but the incongruity of that interest was such that Ken didn't think he was being paranoid to wonder about it.

So he did what many folks in Sanrio did when they were in doubt, on this Monday morning he went to see Aaron Swift.

"This Jones dude," Ken began. "You know him, A?"

"I know him."

"Anything wrong with him?"

"I don't know him that well." Then Aaron produced one of his oracular statements, seeming non sequitur. "He banks at the First."

"So?" Ken, puzzled, thought about it. Slowly, as comprehension dawned, he began to nod. "They hold our note on the Bellevue Acres property, is that what you're thinking?"

"I haven't said a word, Ken."

Ken thought about it some more. "If they decided to discount it for cash," he said, "to Jones, say—"

"Happens that way sometimes. Banks these days do like cash."

There was no need to explain the cryptic statement; its meaning was clear enough. With interest rates rising as they had these last years, many financial institutions were delighted to dispose of older, relatively unprofitable mortgages, even at a discount, for cash which could then be lent at higher, far more profitable, and usually flexible interest rates.

"A sharpie in a wheelchair," Ken said. "Is that what we've got?"

"There are slander laws, Ken." Aaron's voice was mild. He looked out the window. "Does it seem to you the smoke's getting heavier?"

Ken stood up. "I hadn't noticed." He nodded again. "Thanks, A."

Aaron waited until Ken had reached the door before he spoke. "Habit dies hard," he said. "It's good to remember that sometimes, Ken."

Ken stopped, turned. "Meaning what?"

"You used to catch footballs." Aaron wore a faint, admiring smile. "You were very good at it." The smile disappeared. "Then, as I remember it, you'd frequently knock down two or three people before they finally pulled you down. You were very good at that too."

"That was then," Ken said, "and this is now?" For the third time he nodded. "I'll try to remember."

But restraint might be uphill work, he thought as he walked down the hall from Aaron's large office, nodded to the cute Spanish chick at the switchboard and went outside into the bright but hazy day. The smoke *was* thickening, he decided, and promptly dismissed the conclusion as unimportant. He had other matters to worry about.

In the off-seasons during his professional football years, unlike many of his colleagues who had spent their leisure time hunting, fishing, or simply enjoying themselves, Ken had put himself through Stanford Business School, emerging with an MBA and a considerable knowledge of the variety of business shenanigans sharp operators have managed to think up over the years. If you had capital, he had long ago decided, the possibilities for shady and profitable, if close to illegal capers were damn near endless.

The Bank, the First, where the Jones dude had his no doubt considerable account, held the underlying note on the Bellevue Corporation. And whoever held that note controlled Bellevue's destiny, and that of the mortgaged homeowners living in Bellevue Acres.

The bank, being a local organization aware that its continued success depended in large part upon the goodwill of the residents of Sanrio, had established and scrupulously maintained a reputation for fair-dealing if not downright compassion.

It tended to view occasional late mortgage payments

with understanding and usually without penalties; it had never been known to invoke the due-on-sale clause in each contract — which called for immediate full payment of the outstanding mortgage balance if a house were sold — but rather had, as was its privilege, allowed a straight mortgage transfer without re-negotiation when one of the Bellevue Acres' residents found it necessary to sell and move elsewhere; and it had never taken full advantage of the leeway that is available to a lending organization when there are fluctuations in the interest standards upon which flexible rate mortgages are based.

The bank had, in short, consistently behaved like a small town institution rather than like the big city giants with computer chips for hearts. In the hands of the bank, the underlying note had never represented a threat to the economic well-being of Bellevue Acres residents with all their kids and all their dogs and their paycheck-to-paycheck lives.

But in the hands of a stranger living in a seven-figure estate, matters might, and in Ken's view very probably would, change drastically.

Ken was not by a nature a crusader. Blessed with both brains and a splendid physique, he had managed to haul himself up by the earpulls of his boots to a comfortable, if not affluent, position in society. He knew others who might have done the same and had not, and for them he had only contempt and total lack of sympathy when they whined.

But the world was also filled with those who had not been blessed with more than average intelligence and whose physiques were no bargain either. The best they could do was struggle through life, marry, have kids and consider themselves lucky if they managed to acquire a house of their own in a development like Bellevue Acres. These were natural prey for the sharpies and the operators, and despite Ken's basic laissez-faire philosophy, letting the cats loose among the penned pigeons did not appeal to him.

He marched into Bert Henry's office at the First and sat down in one of the comfortable leather visitors' chairs. "A dude named Bartlemy Jones," he said, and studied Bert's face as across a poker table. "Making his presence felt in Sanrio, isn't he?"

"You have a point you're working up to, Ken?"

"Our Bellevue Acres note."

"What about it?"

"Are you thinking of discounting it? Maybe to Jones?"

Bert Henry thought about it. "Who told you that?"

"I figured it out for myself."

Bert Henry thought some more. "That's really bank business, Ken, and we don't—"

"Bert, baby." Ken's voice was soft, gentle, but somehow ominous nonetheless. "I'm asking a simple question, and I'd like a simple answer. Are you thinking of discounting the note to Jones? Yes, or no?" He smiled, reminding Bert Henry of a photograph he had seen once of a crocodile smiling from the shallows. It made the skin on the back of Bert's neck crawl.

Bert swallowed hard. He swallowed again. "We're—*thinking* about it." He watched uneasily as Ken got out of the chair and straightened to his full, impressive height. "Was that all you wanted to know?" Bert said.

"For now," Ken said, and walked out.


Stacy drove into the entrance road to Bart Jones's property beneath the hanging sign that read EL RANCHO COSTA MUCHO. In a sense, she thought, it was typical of Bart—brash, assertive, even a trifle boastful and almost guaranteed to affront those in the community who preferred a more muted approach.

Her father had had something of the same tendency, she told herself, but, as with his willingness to dare the world, his flamboyance sprang from a different source than Bart's. The fact of the matter was that Stacy the father simply had not given a good goddam what people thought about him or his behavior, and Bart Jones had always cared excessively. Stacy knew this, because she could recognize the father's tendencies in herself.

There was an incident that had long stuck in her mind, and when she looked back on it now, she was a little ashamed, although then she had scarcely given it a thought because at that time, as Ken had recognized, it was entirely consistent with her character. Strange.

It happened in one of those fancy New York restaurants; she could not now even remember which. Ken Delacorte, still playing football then, was with her as her guest, his birthday or something. Anyway, Stacy ordered a steak, well-done.

The waiter looked like an ambassador from or to the Court of St. James, or at least thought he did. "Madam," he said looking down his nose, "the chef will refuse to ruin good meat by incinerating it."

Ken, Stacy remembered, opened his mouth and then closed it again. There was a hint of a smile around his lips as he relaxed in his chair and waited.

Stacy leaned back and smiled up at the waiter, pleasant as could be. "Buster," she said in a voice she did not bother to modulate, "you go back to the kitchen and tell him that I'm paying for the son of a bitch and I'll have it cooked any goddam way I want it. Is that clear?"

For as long as it might take to count to five, there was silence. The waiter's mouth opened and shut several times, but no sound came out.

"I asked a question," Stacy said, and that broke the spell.

Slowly the waiter nodded. "Yes, madam," he said and turned away, totally, completely, abjectly deflated.

Stacy could almost hear her father if he had witnessed the scene. "I guess," he would have said, amused, "that we can only make a lady of you so far." But that was then. Stacy guessed she had changed.

Now, swinging into the broad parking area by Bart's main house, remembering that restaurant scene and thinking of her father, she suddenly understood at least a part of the impact discovery of Bart's presence here had had upon her. He was a link with the past, with her father and all that her father had meant; he was unlike her father and yet he reminded her constantly, perhaps by the very differences between them, of even the small things that in the old life had been familiar, and now was totally missing.

Again she could almost hear the father's voice. "You're a big girl now, honey, goddamnit. I taught you the best I could, and now you've got to stand on your own feet. You can, you know. You've never failed at anything yet."

She parked the car and got out, self-possessed as always, showing nothing of her thoughts. She noticed that the smoke was heavier in the air, and wondered what that might mean. Maybe she could call JL and ask. Smoke spooked horses if it got too thick; they were scared to death of fire. But that could wait. Right now, she wanted to do what she could to exorcise the ghosts Bart Jones seemed to carry around with him.

At the fire command post within the Forest, Phil Sommers, Plans Chief, was back again bringing bad tidings. Jay Paul thought suddenly that the old custom of putting to death an ambassador who brought bad news may have had its points. "Well?" he said.

"Infra-red photos," Phil said, "superimposed on the grid. Here, here and here we've lost our fire line. It's into the Wilderness now, and it's swinging around here—" His moving forefinger traced the fire's progress.

"Tim's promised another tanker, more slurry drops."

But the words, while not meaningless, held futility in their depths, and Jay knew it. Fighting wildland fires these days was an organized, technical business, with machines and equipment of all kinds, both surface and airborne, and electronic marvels to facilitate communication and even, as with the infra-red airborne photography, to locate and pinpoint danger spots not yet broken into flames. There was state-of-the-art and up-to-date, on-the-spot weather forecasting, and even cloud-seeding had been tried.

But when you got right down to it, fires were still fought, and conquered, by men on the ground, working with hand tools, shovels, axes, brush hooks, Pulaskis, McClouds, chain saws, muscle and sweat. Fire lines were established by grunting, cursing, aching men, breathing smoke and hearing the frightful roaring of flames and the crackling of trees and brush as they perished, seeming sometimes almost to writhe and scream as fire moved over them.

"What's the weather forecast?" Jay Paul said.

"Afternoon thunderstorms. Dry lightning this side of the big mountain. Our rain shadow."

Precipitation on the windward, usually the western, slope of a mountain mass almost always tended to be heavy. On the leeward slope, in what was called the rain shadow, the wrung-out air had little moisture left to fall. In California's Sierra Nevada, as an example, the western slopes with the heaviest snowpack in the

United States, were only a few score miles from Reno, Nevada, to the east, thirsty desert country. The bulk of Sierra Grande and its ancillary peaks drew almost all of the precipitation on their western slopes, leaving Sanrio a semi-arid area.

"You cheer me enormously," Jay Paul said. "Thanks."


JL was again in the Situation Room of the BIFC complex. On the Region 3 clipboard two more situation reports on BACKSLOPE had been posted. The fire was now an estimated 3500 acres in extent, and had reached into the Wilderness.

Fellow named Nero, JL thought bitterly, sat on his duff and played his fiddle while Rome burned. He, JL, also duff-sitting, listened to learned discussions on multiple use of forest lands—while this fire reached his lovely, unspoiled Wilderness. Too much. Entirely too damn much.

## 8

They had chosen to make their stand on top of a low ridge, and two crews, one SWFFF crew and Bessie Wingate's boys, were spread in a thin line taking down everything that would burn and clearing it back, leaving a swathe of bare dirt and three-inch stumps where the chain saws had gone through, as a fire line.

The sun was high, and hot, and the yellow issue Forest Service shirts and hard hats were not, as Bessie had put it, "any kind of goddam bikinis."

But sparks were flying, and the shirts and hard hats were protection, so you sweated until you stunk like a goat, and you cursed the fire and the terrain, and you chopped and shoveled and cut and scraped while the smoke that was everywhere now, thick and choking, made your breath come in short gasps to remind you that you were not at sea level but at seven thousand feet where oxygen was scarce.

The fire had roared up the narrow arroyo, reached a comparatively level area, spread out and slowed its headlong forward progress. The ubiquitous piñon and juniper were its fuel, with even green cholla and prickly-pear withering in the intense heat and bursting into flame with the hissing of steam sounding like a nest of snakes.

Behind the fire line, and above it, a thick grove of

the big trees, the beginning of the Forest's heart, waited helplessly. Birds had long since left and the small forest folk, the mice, the chipmunks, the squirrels and rabbits, each species in its own way, were fleeing in panic from the area of fire, deeper into the forest. The predators, too, the cats, the foxes, the martens and weasels, had taken flight; in their overriding fear of the flames ignoring the potential victims that were running beside them.

One of the SWFFF crew, Spanish-American, swarthy, wiry, with sharp features and angry eyes, waved his McCloud briefly at Bessie. "Hey, *guapa*," he said, and showed intensely white teeth in a broad grin at his joke. The word connotes cuteness, sexiness, and could not have been more inappropriately applied.

"Cut the shit," Bessie said without rancour.

"Okay. How about a beer? Ice-cold? How about that?"

"Now," Bessie said, "you're talking." She glanced down the slope at the spreading flames. "That mother's coming at us."

"Some like it hot, baby. It comes too close, I got me my shelter."

The shelter was simply a sheet of metallic, fire-retardant cloth, with hand and footholds on its underside. In a last-resort emergency, the fire-fighter swept a patch of ground bare, lay prone on it and drew the sheet taut over him, holding the edges of the cloth against the ground and hoping the flames would sweep harmlessly past.

"Me," Bessie said, "I don't aim to get into a fix where I have to use a shelter. And neither do my crew. Pete! Get the lead out! You're not leaning against the bar at the Antlers, goddamnit!"

The SWFFF crewman said, "Them Mescalero Apaches." Also SWFFF. "You know what one of them

100

said? He said that fighting forest fires was one thing the white man does that makes sense. How about that?"

"He's got a point," Bessie said. Her shovel had not been still a moment. With her strength, she uprooted whole plants and even small trees and heaved them back from the area they were clearing. She squinted downhill at the flames. "I don't like it," she said, "not even one goddamned little bit. Those big trees are too close. I can feel them against my back." She cocked her head toward the flames below them. "Hear that mother roaring at us. It thinks we're meat for the cooking."


Elsie Edwards had pulled on trousers and a shirt, fastening buttons and zipper with shaking fingers. The need to cover her nakedness was overwhelming, dominating all else.

Don was not dead as she had feared at first, but he was still unconscious. His breathing was steady enough, and as nearly as she could tell by fumbling at his wrist, his pulse was regular and reasonably strong.

She supposed that there was something she ought to be doing—for Don, for herself, or about the smoke that was heavier now and beginning to make her choke—but she couldn't seem to get her thoughts in order. What was the phrase—her act together?—and why should she think of that now?

She guessed, although she had no idea, really, that she was in a state of what they called shock, whatever that was. She was afraid she was going to be sick, and then as a lump in her belly began to grow like some horrible, malignant thing, she was afraid that she was not going to be able to vomit to rid herself of at least part of the dreadful feeling of shame and degradation that possessed her.

Rape had always been just a word one heard spoken

in awed tones, along with elaborate arguments constructed to prove that one either should, or should not, resist. Well, with a gun pointing at your head, and no doubt at all in your mind that the trigger would be pulled without hesitation if you did not obey commands, the question quickly became moot, and although Elsie was sure that she would never lose the sense of shame at her craven acquiescence, the fact of the matter was that she was still alive, and *physically* unharmed. The damage to her psyche was something else, but that, at the moment, was of lesser importance.

She knelt now beside Don, and her hands, like creatures under their own, not her, control, made ineffectual, stroking motions on Don's forehead. Maybe he would die; the blow to his head with the pistol barrel had made a dull, ugly thud and he had dropped to the ground without a sound as if his knees had suddenly become unhinged.

Dear God, what if he did die? Here in this unfamiliar wilderness? What if—?

Don's eyelids fluttered. His eyes opened briefly, unfocused, frightened; and then closed again. He made no sound, nor did he stir.

Elsie said, "Don! Don, darling! Please!" She waited, holding her breath.

His eyes opened again, wavered, steadied and began slowly to fill with recognition. He stirred, and his lips moved, uttering sounds Elsie had to bend low to recognize, understand. "What's burning?" he said. "Stove? Fireplace?"

"Nothing, darling. It's all right."

It was not all right. That realization was slow in coming, but it burst upon her with impact at last. The smoke was heavy now, too heavy, choking. And as she strained to listen she could hear crackling sounds as when — had it always been the day following Twelfth Night — her family used to burn the Christmas tree in the fireplace, carefully, as her father had always insisted, a single small branch at a time, the still-green needles crackling and hissing with the sounds she now heard.

She got to her feet and looked around. There — yes — she could see flames well above the ground, sweeping through the lower branches of a big ponderosa, leaving only twisted and blacked bare stems. The sight was terrifying.

"Don! Don!" Her voice was almost out of control.

"Help me up. Damn it, woman, give me a hand!" His voice was stronger now, and filled with urgency, and with the aid of her strong hand, he struggled to his feet and stood wavering, swaying without rhythm, muttering angrily to himself.

Elsie said, "The tent. Shall I take it down?"

"Never mind that." He was standing straight now, wavering no longer. "Give me your hand. Let's go."

"But our things!"

His head ached and throbbed, he had neither memory nor knowledge of what had happened, and his vision was still blurred, but his mind was clear enough to realize that there was danger present and unmistakable. Flight was their only course. "Never mind our things." He could even smile weakly in his crooked way. "We're what counts."

"You're still naked! We have no shoes!"

That, at least, made sense. "Grab what you can. Hurry, honey, hurry!"


A half-mile away, Felipe Vigil was still babbling happily. "Hey, man, that was some piece of ass, no? She was really but stacked! You got to hand it to anglo

103

chicks, some of them. They're like, you know, all solid and bouncy, like rubber, you know what I mean?"

"Greaseball," Frank Orwell said, "you'd better get your mind out of your pants." His voice was angry, rather than solemn. "We're goddam well going to need all the thinking both of us can do. Of all the stinking luck!"

"You clicking your teeth, man, but what you saying? What the fuck you talking about?"

"You smell smoke?"

"We been smelling smoke all the time. So?"

They had topped a low, almost bare rise. Orwell stopped and looked back. "See that?" He pointed to dark, angry smudges against the hazy sky.

Felipe looked. "So?"

Orwell turned and pointed in the direction they had been walking. "More smoke. See it? What we got, greaseball, is a goddam forest fire, and I've seen a couple and I don't never, *never* want to see another one close up."

Comprehension came slowly. Felipe looked both ways again. "So what we do now? You big anglo hotshot thinker, what we do?"

Orwell waved one hand toward Sierra Grande's lofty peak. "We haul our asses up that mountain just as fast as we can."

Mrs. Tyler Wayne frowned at the whitish flecks that drifted down around her.

"Ash, *señora*," Manuel said. "From the fire in the Forest."

"They should not allow it to come so close."

Tyler had known about such things, and from time to time had spoken his mind to the Secretary in Washington, who listened carefully. There had been that occasion, for example, when their "prescribed burning" had escaped the boundaries the Forest Service people had set, and Tyler had made a point of explaining to the Secretary that he certainly did not approve.

Mrs. Wayne had always found that nice Mr. Harmon—who either had no given names or chose to ignore them in favor of his initials, JL—most agreeably receptive and helpful, and she thought now that it would be quite in order if she went to see him about this falling ash. Mrs. Wayne and Tyler had visited Pompeii, and she had seen what falling ash could do if not controlled.

She smiled at the two gardeners. "I shall return," she said. "Don't you think you and Hilario might take a short rest, Manuel? The sun is quite warm." She walked back to the big house.

Adams, the Wayne chauffeur these last forty years, drove Mrs. Wayne to the Forest Service headquarters in the ageless shiny black limousine. Mrs. Wayne, in hat, short white gloves and a Neiman-Marcus summer frock went inside to call upon JL. She ended in George Jefferson's office. Jefferson got up promptly to greet her.

"My gardener," Mrs. Wayne said, "tells me that there is a fire in the Forest."

"Yes, ma'am."

"The young lady down the hall tells me that Mr. Harmon is in Idaho."

"Yes, ma'am."

"Mr. Harmon's card, which he was good enough to give me, says that he is—I believe the term is Fire Management Officer for the Forest."

"Yes, ma'am."

"Then," Mrs. Wayne said, "I fail to understand why he is not here, managing this fire. Ash is falling in my gardens."

Willard Spencer's first reaction to Aaron Swift's suggestion had been to ignore it. Spencer was not accustomed to running errands such as carrying checks to someone's office.

A second visit outside, however, and a new look at the strange copperish tinge of the sky had convinced him that the prudent decision would be to set pride aside, for this occasion only, of course. Accordingly, check in pocket, he presented himself at the Lewis Insurance Agency and demanded attention.

Bud Lewis himself appeared. "Here," Spencer said, and held out the check. He waited, but Bud Lewis made no move to take it. "Well?" Spencer said.

"Do you recall the due date on your invoice, Mr. Spencer?"

"Certainly not. I don't carry details like that in my head."

"Pity," Bud Lewis said. "The due date was May 18."

"So?"

"There is a grace period of thirty calendar days."

"I repeat, so?"

"The grace period ended Friday, June 17. Today is June 20. Your homeowner's policy has lapsed."

Spencer took a long, deep breath. He said with determined calm, "You joke, of course."

Nothing changed in Bud Lewis's face, nor did he speak.

"Then," Spencer said, "why was I not notified?"

"You were, Mr. Spencer. The invoice was mailed to you in April, well before the due date."

Again with determined calm in the face of stupidity, "Very well," Spencer said, and held out the check again. "Reinstate the policy."

Still nothing changed in Lewis's face. "There is a fire

in the Forest."

"I am aware of it."

"In view of that, Mr. Spencer, this is hardly the time to issue, or reinstate, a homeowner's policy."

There was silence. Spencer said, "Do you realize what you are doing? You are leaving my property unprotected."

"I am saving my underwriters a possible considerable loss," Lewis said. "That is my prime consideration."


Les Lawry said, "It's a goddam nuisance. We go to all the trouble to come into the middle of this Wilderness, and now they let a fire get started, so I suppose we'd better pack up and drive back out again."

Cindy Lou said, "A fire means a lot of people, doesn't it? Suppose they see us driving out?"

"What if they do?"

"That sign that said no motor vehicles allowed, what about that?"

"Doesn't mean a thing. Anybody asks, we say we didn't see it. Simple as that."

Tad said, "Pop." He hesitated. "If there really is a fire. A big one, I mean." He stopped.

"Don't worry about it, son. You stick with your old man, and we'll all be just fine. Just fine."

"What I meant," Tad said, "was, well, here's this stream. And if the fire gets bad, real bad, I mean, we could all get in the water, couldn't we? I've read about things like that."

"You just stick with your old man," Les said. "We'll be fine. You'll see. It's just a goddam nuisance. If the rangers had been on their toes it wouldn't have happened. We pay our tax dollars, and this is what we get."

Bart had mellowed, not much, but some; that was Stacy's early reaction. Maybe adversity, being up against something he could neither buy nor whip, had given him a touch of becoming humility, although the word seemed a strange one to use, however qualified, in connection with Bart Jones.

He appeared to have put on no weight, but the lines of his face had somehow softened and lost at least a bit of their harsh arrogance, although his eyes had not gained any warmth, and their expression retained what she had always thought of as the kind of fierceness one found in the eyes of a bird of prey — a peregrine falcon, perhaps.

Then what, really, did I ever see in him, she asked herself? And the answer came clear: toward him she had always felt the kind of kinship and admiration she had felt for the best roping horse she had ever owned, a gelding named Hank who was all business when a calf came out of the chute, but spent the rest of his time doing his level best to throw her and stomp her to death out of sheer cussedness.

"I must say," Bart said as he led her into the broad living room, handling his electric wheelchair with the same skillful ease he had once brought to driving a sports car when sober, "that you chose nice country for your retreat. That big mountain, now, a man could fall in love with that."

"No retreat," Stacy said.

"New life, then?"

"Something like that."

"Breeding quarter horses?"

"Saddle horses."

"That's too tame for you. You'll be wanting kids next. Wine, you said? You don't mind if I stick to martinis?"

As usual, her impulse was to come straight to the

point. "Why are you here?" she asked.

She had almost forgotten his lopsided grin, the expression of a boy caught with his hand in the cookie jar. "In a word," he said, "you."

"Come off it, Bart. Nobody ever meant that much to you."

"You underestimate yourself."

She had forgotten too how infuriating he could be sometimes. "All right," she said, "let's talk about something else."

"Like what?"

Remembering last night, "Bellevue Acres, for starters."

"Out of your line."

"Ken Delacorte's an old friend."

Bart sipped his martini. "Good football player. First-rate tight end."

"But no business man, is that what you're saying?"

"Bellevue Acres is a nickel-and-dime operation."

("By your standards," Ken had said, "it's not a very expensive shirt.") Remembering, Stacy said now, "And you're used to big deals, is that it?"

"There aren't too many things I can still do, and I need some fun out of life. You'll grant me that?"

"I don't know if I'll grant you much of anything," Stacy said. "I don't like giving blank checks."

## 9

In her logical, analytical way, Sophie Swift on this BACKSLOPE Monday occupied herself as if she were organizing a law case about to go to trial. One prepared for the worst, she had always believed, and then one could allow hope for the best.

Sitting in the June sunlight on the patio an 8x13 legal pad on her lap, she listed steps to be taken if the potential fire threat became an emergency.

First and foremost, the horses. The mare Impatient and her foal would go together in the horse trailer. The other two horses could be tethered behind the trailer and led slowly to safety.

Her favorite paintings would go in the rear of the station wagon, along with a few — but, unhappily, only a few — of the more precious books from the library.

The silverware, both flat and hollow-ware, all of which had been her grandmother's, she would put into pillow cases — favorite, and ingenious containers used by thieves, she understood — and carefully lower them to the deepest part of the swimming pool. There they would be safe.

Certain file drawers complete, containing her and Aaron's records over the years, also should best be loaded into the station wagon. One never knew when records, even those of yesteryear, might be demanded by, for example, the IRS, whose total insensitivity toward, and ignorance of, life's realities never ceased to amaze Sophie's practical mind.

Other small items of either intrinsic or sentimental value, small statuary, certain Indian rugs and baskets, a Zuñi fetish given to them as a housewarming gift, a pair of lamps bought to celebrate a successful lawsuit — items such as these she would also collect and put into the now overloaded station wagon, along with a few of her favorite cooking utensils.

Surveying the list, she smiled sheepishly when she discovered that she had made no provision for clothing, an oversight, she supposed, which was probably typical. No doubt Debbie, if she had thought to make any list of priorities, would have included clothing first. Sophie decided there was a message for her in that realization.

The wind had shifted, she noticed, and ash was no longer falling around her on the patio. She studied the big mountain and noted the clouds beginning to take shape, usual summer afternoon phenomenon. It was strange how easily she accepted the facts of Sanrio weather and comprehended the reasons and forces behind it.

In San Francisco where she had grown up, weather, as such, rarely played a role. It rained, of course, and fog did roll in through the Gate obscuring any view of Marin County, but there was not, or there had not seemed to be, the almost stately progression of the seasons that obtained here to which she was now so strongly accustomed.

She and Aaron had met at Stanford Law School, in their senior year had shared the editorship of the Law Review, had carried on a courtship which by most standards, Sophie conceded, would have been unexciting in the extreme, and had married the evening they had graduated. They had spent their honeymoon studying for Bar examinations.

Their marriage, Sophie supposed, had been more intellectual and companionable than fleshly, and she, in her unworldliness, had assumed that that was sufficient. Obviously, it was not, and she had had no idea that the pain of that discovery would be so intense.

It was axiomatic, of course, that attorneys, like physicians, were wise beyond measure when they dealt with the problems of others, or at least they pretended omniscience which to clients and patients frequently amounted to the same thing. But it was equally beyond cavil that in their own private lives they tended to stumble blindly, as if in a dark room, rarely being able to bring themselves to ask others for enlightenment, or even to admit that advice might be useful. During these past few months, Sophie had come to understand the meaning of the phrase, "learning the hard way."

With a final, appraising look at Sierra Grande's peak, she got up and carried her legal pad inside. A cup of tea while she waited for further developments, she thought, would help to pass the time. There was simply no point in putting into operation emergency plans which might never be necessary. In this decision, she realized, she was in a sense trying to propitiate the gods; pure futility, she was sure, but, so be it.

She was leaning against the kitchen sink, sipping her tea, when Aaron walked in, wearing a strained, unaccustomed, sheepish grin. "Just thought I'd check to see that everything was okay," he said.

Sophie turned so that her back was to him and set her teacup carefully on the sink shelf. She wanted suddenly to laugh aloud, to squeal, to sing, to dance, to do all manner of silly, girlish things she had seen female television contestants do when a winner was announced. Instead, turning again and smiling faintly, she said, "That was good of you, Aaron. But I think everything is under control, thank you. Would you like a cup of tea?"

There are few sights on earth as terrifyingly bowel-watering as a wildfire on the loose when faced close-up from ground level, which is the view fire-fighters customarily have. The monster has a voice, but it is not a constant as is the roaring voice of even a huge furnace. Rather, because temperatures within a wild-fire vary with the burning characteristics of the fuel it feeds on and with changing wind currents affecting its rate of oxidation, an uncontained fire can bellow or shriek, can explode with the sounds of falling bombs, can whistle or hiss with the piercing cacophony of sirens gone mad, or roar and rumble in a fashion to shake the earth and deaden eardrums.

Its appearance too is not the constant of even a fireplace fire, but, rather, is a continually altering palette of colors within the red range, occasionally laced, even interrupted, by roiling billows of black smoke, and its height and mass are as changing and unpredictable as storm-driven waves crashing against rocks and cliffs.

But unlike the sea, a familiar element in its proper context, wildfire is an intruder, totally out of place, insubstantial in that it is occasionally possible to glimpse *through* flames, but possessing a solid menacing reality to which all animal life race-memory reacts in sheer terror.

Jay Paul, at his command post within the Forest, was removed from the fire perimeter, and with past experiences on actual fire lines still very vivid in memory, guiltily happy to be where he was.

On the other hand, as Fire Boss, there was no

avoiding the responsibilities that came with the job, and by noon of this first day, he was close to despair. It seemed to him that everything that could go wrong, had.

To the north of the fire's center, wind-driven flames had capriciously attacked Sierra Grande's west flank, overpowered the crews attempting to contain it, and in sparsely wooded country were now racing through low brush and piñon-and-juniper growth toward the east-west line of Highway 14 which had once seemed too distant to worry about, but now looked like a fire line of last resort.

To the south toward the estates adjoining the Forest, the flames coming downslope were advancing slowly, but with apparent steadiness. And to the east of the spot where the fire had started, the monster had entered a part of the Wilderness and was heading toward the area known as Sheep Ridge. A good share of the problem, of course, was the presence of that great damned mountain Sierra Grande.

Around its mass, winds twisted and swirled in no immediately discernible pattern, and as that huge, admittedly colorful female crew chief Bessie Wingate had said at one point, "You fight fire in these here mountains, and you'd damn well better have eyes in your ass as well as in your face, because you never know what may come at you, or from what direction."

Through one of the broken lines, fire reached a stand of the big trees, the ponderosas, but that stand was fairly well isolated and it appeared that the fire could be kept from spreading farther. Futile hope.

Swirling winds at ground level picked up burning brush and fallen debris, flung it around as in a miniature whirlwind, and in the process completely jumped open surrounding ground and ignited lower branches of trees in the main stand of the Forest. Pine needles, as everyone who has burned a Christmas tree knows, flare like tiny torches, and their pitch-fed flames climbed higher and higher, creating their own small up-drafts of heated air until, "There she goes!" the crew chief said. "There's just no stopping the son of a bitch yet!"

"And so," the Line Boss reported by radio to Jay Paul, "we're going to need the kind of luck we don't seem to be having to keep it from spreading."

In another area, kids from the housing development, Bellevue Acres, irresistibly drawn to fire and excitement, seized a fallen, still burning branch, and ran with it as with a captured flag—and in the process managed to ignite a brand new area before they dropped the branch and ran home in panic.

The pilot of the chopper that had taken in one of the helitack crews reported catching glimpses of maybe half a dozen persons in the Wilderness. What made his report suspect was that he also claimed to have seen a jeep where no motorized vehicles were allowed, and it was well known that the last group to ignore that ban, two families of hunters from Texas, had been caught by JL who had taken them before the local Federal Magistrate Aaron Swift, who fined them and ordered that their two jeeps be towed out of the Wilderness by mule team, which had cost a pretty penny. There had been no known violations since.

On the other hand, on the chance that the sighting report was accurate and there *were* people in the Wilderness, in danger, it was up to Jay Paul to see that they were found and rescued. More worry.

Now came the word that a new area, over near a small lake that lay within the Wilderness beneath a three-hundred-foot cliff Jay Paul remembered seeing from the air, had somehow ignited and was burning furiously. "Just how the hell did that get started?" Jay

Paul demanded of no one in particular.

"Does it matter?" Phil Sommers said. "It's burning, and that's all that's important at the moment."

"Hell, yes, it matters. Is somebody torching trees? Have we got an arsonist on the loose? If so, we sure as hell want to know it and get the bastard caught and locked up."

"Andy McIlvain's still waiting," Phil Sommers said. "You want him to go in with a few of his people, take care of that new area and see what he can find out?"

"I'm saving the smoke-jumpers. All of them."

For what? Phil Sommers thought, but did not say aloud. Christmas?

On the phone from Albuquerque the Regional Supervisor, George Jefferson's boss, said, "Looks like you've got a bad one, George."

"This time of year. No rain. You know how it goes." And Jefferson thought he might get in a little dig as well. "And no prescribed burning."

"There's nothing I can do about that, George. Washington says no prescribed burning, that's how it is. By the time the governor of Idaho got through with the Department a few years back when prescribed burning up there got out of hand—remember?"

"Just thought I'd mention it."

"I see you've got your Forest team on it. What about JL's Regional team? I'm not trying to interfere, just asking. Think it'll go that far?"

"Could. The weather's against us. And I'm beginning to get civilian complaints."

"So am I. All the way from our senior Senator's office in Washington. That's expensive real estate, George. Expensive people own it. Fellow named Spencer, Willard P., know him?"

116

"As much as I want to." In a reassuring voice Jefferson added, "We'll get it whipped."

"I'm sure you will."

For that, Jefferson thought as he hung up, read: See that you damn well do. He called for his girl in the outer office. She appeared at once. "Get off a message to BIFC," Jefferson said. "We want JL back here. Yesterday."

In places the fire advanced slowly; in other places, wind-driven, it rushed forward in quantum leaps from a piñon here to a juniper there to a scrub oak farther up the mountainside already brought almost to the point of combustion by the rising currents of heated air.

In the slow advances there was deliberation that at times seemed almost contemplative, as with some great, devouring beast deciding which morsel to take next as it moved forward in its inexorable pace.

In the leaping advances there was a frenetic quality, a sense of hysteria, disorganization and a helter-skelter rush in which areas of brush, even individual trees were spared as if by a madman's logic.

Bessie Wingate swore at the flames and at her crew. She cajoled. With her, fighting a wildland fire was a personal vendetta, no quarter asked, or given. "Had me a house once," she had been heard to say in the Antlers one night. "Wasn't much, but I'd built it, me and Ted, and it was mine." She never explained who Ted was, and no one had the temerity to ask.

"Goddam fire come busting over the ridge, got into wild honeysuckle that had taken over. No stopping the mother. There went the house. And Ted. Damn fool, let himself get burned to death. What the hell, long time ago. Let's have another beer."

Now, moving into a new area of the fire line, Bessie was all business and attention. "Gus, you and Pete take that chain saw over yonder and take down that stand of piñon." Always at least two men on a job, never one alone. "The rest of you fan out and get hacking and scraping. I want this ground slicker than a baby's ass, nothing left for that mother down there to feed on. You hear me?"

Even above the crackling roar of the flames coming up the hill, her voice was clear and loud, probably audible in the next county. No one pointed this out.

To the neighbouring SWFFF hispanic, "You're doing a good job with that McCloud." The tool was a modified, highly efficient hoe which in the hands of a good man could scrape and cut and leave the ground as Bessie wanted it — clean and bare. "What's your name?"

"Eloy Jaramillo."

"Tell you what, Eloy. After this is all over, I'll buy you a beer at the Antlers. You know where that is?" Bessie's shovel had not paused. Her voice turned thoughtful. "You keep on working your ass off like that, maybe two beers. How about that?"

*"Muchas gracias."*

"That's okay," Bessie said. "A job of work like this separates out the men from the boys."


Stacy drove home from lunch in a thoughtful mood. She wished Bart had stayed back in Texas — out of sight, out of mind — but no matter what the old song said, wishing didn't change a thing. He was here, and intending to stay, and he was going to be a constant, irritating reminder of a life she had turned her back on.

It was not that she did things so much differently here. There were still parties, and gossip, and some folks who did things and others who just talked about them. Stacy supposed that wherever there was money in quantity, that was the kind of behavior you could expect.

But what was different was the attitudes of people toward each other. There was not the competitive spirit here that she had been used to, the desire to win at all cost no matter who got hurt in the process. She had that in herself, she was aware, and in her early years she had given it full rein and gloried in the results. Now she took a kinder, more sympathetic view of her friends and neighbors, and found the experience both pleasant and relaxing. It was a view Bart would never embrace, and that was where the problem was going to be.

There was no longer any doubt that there was a big fire in the Forest. And Stacy, looking at the rising smoke at the base of the big mountain, doubted if the calm assurance on the radio that all was under control could still be justified. She hoped that JL would be available and would give her the proper poop.

A pleasant female voice at Forest Service headquarters explained the situation, and Stacy hung up disappointed. Going off to Idaho at a time like this was not consistent with the image Stacy had formed of the man. *His* Forest, he had said, and sounded as if he meant it. Then why in hell wasn't he here taking care of it? Stacy's views on responsibility were unyielding.

There had been, for example, the night she had spent helping the vet, still wearing, and ruining, the long evening dress in which she was supposed to be gallivanting around town, while Dandy Sue, one of her mares, labored to give birth to the foal which grew up to be Sam, her favorite cutting horse.

There had been plaintive telephone calls that night, ending finally when Stacy said with careful clarity,

"You're a nice guy and I like you fine. But between you and my mare in labor, there isn't even a choice. You're way out of the running. So stop bothering me, god-damnit. Is that clear?"

Now she called Ken Delacorte at his office, and for a wonder he was in. "I'm beginning not to think much of your JL Harmon, hotshot fire-fighter," she said, and explained why.

Ken, still considering the possibilities of what he had uncovered in the Bellevue Acres matter, said, "Then I guess that makes us even, Stacy baby. I'm beginning to work up a considerable dislike for your Bartlemy Jones, fancy wheelchair and all."

It was precisely the right response, and Stacy found herself smiling. "Then," she said, "maybe we'd better get together and talk about it. What do you know about this fire that's going on?"

"I'll find out the latest and bring a report," Ken said.

# 10

The team that later sifted carefully through the situation reports and listened to direct testimony, decided that at this point, late afternoon of that first day, BACKSLOPE could have been contained by quick, decisive action.

The estimated area of the fire was now something over 10,000 acres, not yet a headline conflagration, but one which, because of its location, the difficulty of the terrain, the proximity of homes and the erratic local weather conditions could, and did, too quickly become a nightmare horror.

Granted, the afternoon thunderstorm arrived as predicted, with strong, gusting winds and dry lightning, in places driving fire-fighters back from yet more fire lines. But the thunderstorm period lasted only ninety minutes, and afterward in the deepening evening, winds dropped in velocity, and even in places gradually began to reverse themselves — upslope wind slowing, and as the air cooled becoming a downslope flow because of temperature gradient.

Jay Paul had his troops deployed, his communications in place and his air attack organized and operating. But Andy McIlvain's twenty-five smoke-jumpers, cutting-edge troops, remained on the ground at the airport; two hotshot crews, Category I fire-fighters, were in the wrong places, doing routine line work; only one bulldozer had been brought into action and although ground tankers were available within striking distance, none had been summoned because of Jay Paul's exaggerated respect for the rugged terrain.

As darkness gathered, the air tanker slurry drops slowed and then stopped altogether; the wind and temperature conditions that had nurtured the fire's beginnings the night before resumed their encouraging effects; fresh fuel on the ground—the result of the stricture against prescribed burning—came into play and the tide of battle shifted slowly but inexorably in favor of the attacker.

Nighttime fire in a forest is a fearsome spectacle. Flames leap and cavort, casting huge threatening shadows. The odors bring thoughts of hellfire and brimstone. Live wood branches crack like brittle bones and crash to the ground as widow-makers, or seem to shrink into minor, naked, blackened replicas of their former selves, abject and pitiful reminders of the holocaust that has passed. Flames in green forests roar, threaten and seem to shake the earth. Whole trees, weakened, topple and fall, crushing lesser growth, spreading the flames, erupting sparks as from explosions.

Against all this, once the fire has gained a beachhead in the big trees, man's efforts seem puny indeed, the ultimate in futility. It is also a test of fortitude and endurance, of determination that will not concede defeat, of coolness under attack and ability to endure. Nighttime wildland fire-fighting stretches you to the limit.

"You'll go where I goddamn well tell you to go and no place else," Bessie told her crew. "In the morning, because I don't think we're going to sleep this night, when I count noses, I don't want some jughead turning up missing. You hear me, you silly bastards?" The epithet was affectionate.

Eloy Jaramillo, three hundred yards away with the rest of his SWFFF crew, winked at the man on the line next to him. "That one," he said in Spanglish, "she go into the ring with the bull, she pick him up and throw him to hell over the barrera. He never know what hit him."

"So there it is," Ken Delacorte said. "Not good, but not out of hand. Yet. JL is in Idaho, at BIFC."

"So I was told. The question is, why?"

"Because Jefferson, his boss, the Forest Supervisor, sent him there and turned the fire over to Jay Paul and the Forest team. The same reason I sat on the bench sometimes when I ought to have been playing; because the coach told me to. You don't know about bosses, Stacy baby. Ordinary folks do."

"I'll take that," Stacy said, "but I'm damned if I know why." Maybe she did know, at that, she thought, remembering her father saying, "I'm not asking you, I'm telling you. You're going to learn to behave like a goddam lady if it kills you." She felt a little better about JL.

"Now your Bartlemy Jones dude," Ken said. "He's something else. Mean, is he?"

Stacy thought about it. "I guess he used to be, and probably still is."

"Way I figured." Ken explained what he had found out.

"And you stand to lose that shirt of yours?" Stacy said.

"Not necessarily. But a lot of other people stand to get hurt bad."

"Who are they?"

"Nobodys, with lots of kids and bikes and roller skates and when they're lucky a six-pack of beer on payday."

Stacy studied him curiously. "And you care about them?"

"Oh, hell," Ken said, exasperated with himself and with the position he had allowed himself to be backed into. "It's shooting fish in a rain barrel for your wheelchair dude. All he has to do is wave his money, climb into the driver's seat and start moving the levers that put the pressure on. For a time the profits roll in. When they taper off and begin to stop, he unloads at fire sale rates."

"And what happens to your nobodys?"

"They go right on struggling, trying to raise their kids and pay their bills and still have enough left over for that six-pack." He added, "And maybe they lose their houses."

"I thought you were the live-and-let-live advocate, but you care about them?"

"That doesn't make me Joan of Arc."

Stacy smiled. "But it does make you a nicer guy than I knew you were."

"I just have low tastes, is all."

Stacy's smile spread. "Maybe that's why you and I have always gotten along." She glanced out the window at the glow within the Forest. "What do you suggest we do to pass the time while the world burns?"


The moon, almost full, hung low over the eastern plains. To Frank Orwell, leading the way in switchbacks up Sierra Grande's flank, the moon resembled a gigantic eye, fixed on them, spotlighting their progress, Here, above timberline, there was no place to hide from its scrutiny, and he felt naked and exposed.

Felipe Vigil, panting along behind in the thin, cooling air, said, "*Basta*, goddam it! Enough! What we trying to do, set some kind of goddam record?"

Goddam greaseball, Orwell thought, but he did stop. He was breathing deeply, but not hard. "With that fire," he said, "this mountain's going to be crawling with people. You got that, greaseball? They—"

"You call me greaseball one more time," Felipe said, "and I cut your liver out and make you eat it. I've had enough of your anglo shit. So the mountain's going to be crawling with people, what are we, *brujos*? spirits?"

"We," Orwell said with heavy scorn, "are escaped convicts. You forget that? We—"

"And we wear signs that say so? Or these *gente*, people, men here to fire-fight, they carry pictures of us? You crazy, man! All they care about is fire. They don't give a shit about us."

Orwell thought about it. The goddam greaseball had a point, he told himself in surprise, and almost said so aloud, but stopped before the forbidden word popped out. He had seen Vigil in action, knife in hand, and he had no wish to see that particular spectacle again. Instead of speaking, he merely nodded agreement.

"So what do we do now?" Vigil said.

"We'll work around the mountain, spend the night up here and then early in the morning go down and see how things look on that side of the Forest."

"Going to be cold."

"Okay, it's going to be cold." Orwell wondered if there would be resistance, and what he could do about it if it came.

125

Instead, "Okay," Vigil said. "I just keep thinking about that chick. She here, she'd make me warm."

Don and Elsie too had stopped climbing and running, Don at the limit of his endurance. His headache remained, throbbing unbelievably with each heartbeat, blurring his vision, but his thinking remained clear enough.

"I think we're above it now," he said, panting, sitting exhausted on the ground, his head bowed. "Isn't that the sounds of fire down there below us?"

The crackling of flames and the crashing of falling branches and whole trees reached them clearly. And the rising smoke was heavy, choking.

"Are we safe here?" Elsie said. She was two selves, she thought, and felt that hysteria was near. One of her recognized the danger and worried about Don's condition. The other still could neither believe nor thoroughly comprehend what had happened to her; it was as if a curtain had been drawn in her mind, or a bad dream almost dissipated by awakening.

But the experience hadn't really been walled off, or blown away. It remained, vicious and unreal—

"I don't know what happened," Don said. His head was still bowed, and his voice was weak, but comprehensible. "I can't remember anything except your saying that you'd never been happier." He looked at Elsie then.

Suddenly, she was crying without sound, no sobs, no convulsive gasps of breath, merely her face screwed up and tears running down the side of her nose from eyes that were wide open, pupils distended, that seemed to stare, unseeing, into the distance, or into the past.

"Elsie!" Don said. "Baby!" He reached for her weakly

and managed to get his arm around her shoulders, but lacked the strength to hold her close.

"I'm all right," Elsie said. "All right. Honest. All right." The words kept repeating themselves, a litany lacking responses. The tears would not stop.

Beneath them on the mountain slope, the crackling sounds of flames and destruction heightened the sense of quiet drama that was building between them.

Don closed his eyes momentarily, took a deep breath and opened his eyes again, willing them to focus on the girl's face. "What happened?" he said. His voice was stronger now, and filled with urgency. "What happened? You've got to tell me."

Elsie shook her head. She fought the tears under control and wiped her cheeks and eyes with the backs of her hands. She shook her head again in stubborn silence.

"Baby," Don said, his voice patient now, "you have to tell me. We promised to share, remember? What happened to you happened to me too, but I can't remember what it was. Something, somebody—" He shook his throbbing head in exasperation. "It won't come to me. I—blacked out? I—?"

"You were hit on the head," Elsie said. "Two men with guns." She too closed her eyes and opened them. It was somehow easier now. "Yes." The words came slowly. "You have a right to know what happened." She told him.

If Mom hadn't told Pop to slow down, as in four-wheel drive they made their bumping, jostling way through the forest, Tad thought, Pop wouldn't have done just the opposite, as always, driven faster, and they wouldn't now be stuck. But good.

"Of all the goddam luck," Les Lawry said, and swung his legs out to stand up and have a look.

Cindy Lou sat unmoving, almost rigid. "I'm scared, Les." Her voice was shaking.

"What the hell for?"

"The smoke is heavier. There's fire, and it's close, too close! I can almost feel it! We never should have come here!"

"Oh, for Christ's sake! Tad, come here. Let's see what we can do."

With one wheel well off the ground and the jeep's frame resting solidly on a big, half-buried rock, there wasn't anything they could do but call a tow truck, Tad decided, but did not say aloud, which would only have made it worse.

"Think we can lift it off?" Les said.

Tad knew they could not, but all he said, was, "Maybe. We can try."

It only took two futile tries, and it was Les who called a halt. "No dice," he said. He was red in the face and puffing from the exertion.

"Maybe if Mom got out," Tad said.

"I said, 'no dice'. These damn jeeps are heavy. That's why they stand up. In the Army—"

"Les!" Cindy Lou's voice was rising. "Over there! Look! I can see the fire!"

So could they all. In the gathering dusk, first the brightening glow, and then the flames themselves were suddenly visible as the fire, like a malevolent attacking force bent on destroying them alone, swept through the trees, angry orange-red in color, its voice a crackling roar, its power and force throwing out fiery jets which consumed brush and undergrowth like a blowtorch.

The air was filled with its menace, and as they watched, a mature ponderosa, probably wind-weakened by one of the thunderstorms, swayed, hesitated and with a harsh, tearing sound began its slow fall to crash heavily on the forest floor. Sparks flew in every direction and new flames burst into being.

"Jesus H. Christ!" Les said. "Let's get the hell out of here! Come on!"

Cindy Lou said, "Our things!"

"Screw the things. Damn it, Cindy Lou, get your ass out of that jeep and come on! Tad, you lead!"

"Which direction?"

"How the hell do I know? Just away!"


JL caught a commercial flight out of Boise, and landed eventually in Albuquerque where a Forest Service aircraft was waiting.

"Short trip," the pilot said. "Learn anything in BIFC?"

"Too damn long a trip," JL said, "and I learned that if you keep shifting cheeks while you sit, it helps. What's about BACKSLOPE?"

"Jay Paul's got more than he can handle."

Outside as they flew there was only moonlight and the blinking wingtip lights of the aircraft. The dim glow from the control panel showed little of the pilot's face as JL studied it. "That's rough country to fight a fire in," he said. "Maybe it's not Jay's fault."

"Could be," the pilot said. He had no intention of getting crossways with JL. "Me, I just fly airplanes. You want to go straight to the airport?"

"Fly over the fire area. Low. I want a good look."

"Then tighten your seat belt. This thing will buck a little."

They flew in silence for a little time, the moonlight casting shadows on the ground, occasionally the lights

129

of an isolated house showing or the headlights of a car or truck speeding along the highways. This was lonely, empty ranch country, flat and uninteresting, not to be compared to what JL thought of as *his* Forest. He found himself anxious for his first glimpse of the mountains.

"There she is," the pilot said suddenly, "and we're still well more than fifty miles away." His pointing finger picked out a spot on the dark horizon lighter than its surroundings, and JL squinted to bring it into focus.

After a few moments he could make out the red glow, at this distance as harmless-seeming as the comfortable glow in a fireplace on a winter evening. But on the ground at the scene, it would be an entirely different story, or Jefferson would not have called him back.

On the ground, the area would be filled with the roaring, crackling sounds of conflagration, with the crashing fall of huge trees and the hollow, rushing winds of sudden air currents generated by the intense heat.

Ashes and burning debris would fill the air, and falling limbs—widow-makers—would be a constant threat. Brush, undergrowth and loose tinder would flare suddenly underfoot, while strange, threatening shadows would leap and cavort against shifting curtains of thick smoke.

Around the flaming area men and machines—bulldozers, backhoes—would be fighting to create a perimeter of containment, a fire break across which fire would not travel, and in some places they would succeed, but possibly only temporarily, and then be forced to fall back and begin their work all over again.

A fight with fire was war to the end, no quarter asked, or given, no respite allowed. In ancient times,

JL had read somewhere, opposing armies sometimes declared a temporary truce that each side might carry its wounded from the field and decently bury its dead. Not so with fire. Fire was one continuing battle, with the casualties, the blackened remains of houses too, left as the ugly testimony of what had been.

"Offhand," the pilot said, "I'd say you've got your work cut out for you."

JL's eyes remained on the increasing glow of the fire. "We'll whip it," he said. Because we have to, he thought; there is no other way.

# PART II

## 11

Late as it was, George Jefferson was waiting in his office at headquarters when JL arrived from the airport.

"You've had a look?" Jefferson said.

"We flew over the entire area."

"How's your ankle?"

"It's fine, George," JL said, "just fine. When I'm sitting on my ass it doesn't bother me a bit."

"Did you make smart-ass remarks like that at BIFC?"

"I just sat and listened. To damn little." *Damn it, George,* he wanted to say, *we've got a fire on our hands. Let's cut the crap.* Instead, he sat silent, forcing himself to be patient. George had a temper too.

Jefferson closed his eyes for a few moments. When he opened them again, "It's been a long day," he said. "Albuquerque called, Regional Office, then Willard P. Spencer called. Mrs. Tyler Wayne came in—" he looked curiously at JL. "She a friend of yours?"

JL kept himself under tight control. "I like her. When she has questions, I answer them. She's—out of touch, but—"

"If she wanted to pick up the phone and complain to three, four people, old Senatorial cronies of Tyler's," Jefferson said, "inside the hour the Secretary in Wash-

135

ington would be down on the Regional Office in Albuquerque, and on me like a ghost on a frame house. That's how out of touch she is. Ashes were falling on her roses, and that is definitely not allowed."

JL blinked. He nodded as patiently as he could. "I'll bear it in mind."

"You do that. Now how does it look?"

"Bad. And it's going to get worse."

Jefferson leaned back in his chair and gestured toward the map of the Forest on the wall. "Show me."

At last. JL took care not to limp as he moved to the map. With his forefinger he traced an irregular outline not too dissimilar from his original sketch in elliptical shape, its major axis running east-west, with a horn-shaped projection in the northwest where the flames had worked their way around Sierra Grande's flank and were headed for the highway. "This is roughly the area of the open fire—"

"How many acres? At a guess?"

JL shrugged. "Twenty thousand?" What real difference? The fact was that the fight had just begun.

Jefferson's eyes closed briefly. "Too damn many." He nodded. "Go on."

"I haven't seen infra-red photos," JL said, "but I'd guess that here and there—" Between the south boundary of the Wilderness and the line of large estates. "—where there's ground clutter so thick you can't walk through it, there are probably other areas already smoldering and ready to combust. We'll see what we can do about those."

He moved his finger to the big mountain's eastern flank above the Sheep Ridge area. "Morning sun, and the ground beginning to heat up creating air currents, the upslope wind will enlarge this area. Lots of timber up there."

"Can we stop it?"

"We'll try." He moved his finger again to the area just to the west of Sheep Ridge where the ground lost its steep slope in an alluvial plain. "But here's the big problem. Too close to houses, that development—"

"Bellevue Acres?"

"Right." JL paused. "All those houses, all those kids. And then, if we aren't damn careful, the town itself." He left it there.

Jefferson's eyes closed briefly again. He opened them and nodded. "And to the west and north?"

"The highway." JL's forefinger moved up the map to trace an east-west straight black line that swung suddenly into the southwest. "If we can contain it there—" He shook his head. "Depends on the wind." His forefinger moved again, back down the map to the line of the County road. "Here—" he began.

"There," Jefferson said, "you've got to be damn careful. The Museum's going to start a dig next month, so don't you send in backhoes or bulldozers and screw up the site or we'll have archeological buffs from all over the west screaming at us."

Always the strictures, JL thought, and railing against them did no good at all. To be scrupulously fair, he would have to admit that setting strictures was an essential part of George Jefferson's job, and you could not fault him for that. George, as Sanrio Forest Supervisor, was responsible for *all* aspects of Forest care and maintenance, not merely and solely fire suppression, however important that might be at the moment. George had to deal with the public, who, in the final analysis, owned the Forest. *The rest of us just work here*, he told himself, and said merely, "We'll be careful."

"And Vista Hill," Jefferson said, "and all those other big damned places abutting the Forest—there's that movie sex symbol, they call her, what's her name?"

Madge would have known. JL did not.

"The one with the big knockers," Jefferson said, "although I guess that's standard equipment. Anyway, the seven-figure spreads."

"They'll get the de luxe treatment." They wouldn't, and both men knew it. The fire-suppression effort JL would direct would try to protect *all* property, and in the process would lose some — by now that was inevitable — but whatever favoritism might be shown would be based on general, not specific, good.

That JL had been brought back to Sanrio in this precipitate fashion solely for the purpose of taking over the handling of BACKSLOPE went without saying. Nor did either man even by so much as a hint indicate that sending JL to BIFC in the first place had been a mistake.

Between them lay a wall of resentment contributed to by both sides and strengthened now to the point of impenetrability. Jefferson resented the fact that JL, who in the normal course of things would have been unchallenged first choice, had absolutely no interest in succeeding to Jefferson's job, and in Jefferson's view insisted on doing little things, such as that unauthorized parachute jump with Andy McIlvain, to show his independence.

JL, the fire-suppression specialist, resented strictures placed on his sometimes admittedly free-wheeling tactics. Jefferson, he would be the first to admit, was a good Forest Supervisor, and, as bosses went, a good boss. But the fact of the matter was that JL wanted no one looking over his shoulder second-guessing him or giving him orders. Stand-off.

"All right," Jefferson said, "it's all yours. Have the dispatcher call in what you need."

"Has Jay Paul been told?"

"That," Jefferson said, "is where your job begins."

As JL walked outside to his pick-up, he felt for the first time in twenty-four hours unshackled, at last turned loose on the job he knew and liked best. He could glance up into the sky and see the reflected glow of the fire in *his* Forest, the enemy. Preliminaries over, he thought, now the main event begins.

Jay Paul was sitting at a folding table staring glumly at a map. Electric lights had been strung from the portable generator here at the command post in the Forest, and portable toilets had been set up well away from the long mess tables. Radio antennae had been mounted high in nearby trees. From a catering truck not far away cooking smells warm and strong blended with the smell of smoke, faint, but unmistakable. In the deep shadows one crew, twenty men, were sacked out on the ground, blanket-wrapped against the chill of this high country June night.

Jay Paul looked up, saw JL, automatically began to smile in relief, and then, as full realization came, suddenly looked less than happy. "They called you back from BIFC?"

"I got tired of sitting."

"You're taking over." It was a statement, no question, and yet answer was required.

JL pulled up a chair and sat. This was always the hard part. "Look," he said, "for damn near twenty-four hours you've been working your ass off—"

"And getting nowhere."

"Well, maybe we can change that. Let's see your last situation reports. Then you go off and have yourself a cup of coffee. You might have somebody bring me one too." He settled himself deeper into his chair.

Taking over like this was never easy either for those doing the taking, or for those being superseded, and

139

sometimes could be downright destructive to morale. But there was no help for it, although there were several choices that could be made which just might alleviate immediate strain.

He, JL, had, at least for the present, a free hand. Whatever he needed he could tell the dispatcher to call for and it would be sent on its hurried way.

He had at call the members of his own Class 1 Regional fire team, forty-eight chosen supervisory personnel from across Arizona and New Mexico, any or all of whom were constantly prepared to drop what they were doing and come flying when summoned. All were authorized for out-of-Region assignments as well as assignments within the two-state area.

He had at call the vast resources of not only the Forest Service, but also the Park Service, the Bureau of Land Management, the Bureau of Indian Affairs and the Fish and Wildlife people. (It had always amused JL that no matter how much, in the uppermost echelons, the Departments of Agriculture and Interior might continue to carry on their ancient feud, struggling for power and domination, down in the working levels when there was need, aid was promptly given Department-to-Department without stint and without protest on a let's-deal-with-the-emergency-first-and-discuss-the-cost-later basis. BIFC, Boise Interagency Fire Center, itself was proof of this cooperation. JL sometimes wondered if the Secretaries or the supporting Congressional Committees had ever been there, or had absorbed the lessons to be learned.)

He could at need call on whatever resources the City of Sanrio or the County of Sanrio might boast, including police and sheriff's department law enforcement officers.

As long as he was dealing with National Forest, Federal land, he had the local Federal Magistrate,

140

Aaron Swift, to issue whatever legal authority might be required. And if fire, recognizing no boundaries, chose to leave the Forest and invade County or City property, JL could expect complete cooperation from local judges as well, to match that which Aaron Swift could be counted on to provide.

The fact of the matter was that with few exceptions, and these largely among newcomers, the people of the area, living in close proximity to the vast Forest, their physical and safety interests identical, were prepared in an emergency such as a fire to accept trained Forest Service leadership, and that, in the final analysis, meant JL.

Now, reading Jay Paul's last situation reports which showed clearly a deteriorating position, seeing and digesting errors both of omission and commission, JL balanced in his mind the benefits and the disadvantages of various courses of action he might take.

He could, for example, have the dispatcher summon his entire Regional Team to take over each supervisory function, or he could act selectively, replacing only those already in charge whom he considered incapable of doing the job on the kind of fire he was sure this was going to end up being.

He could call immediately for more line troops, or he could see to redirecting the forces already on the scene, thereby avoiding the confusion that sometimes occurred when too many new people arrived at a fire all at once.

He could either endorse or overrule plans Jay Paul had set in motion, such as the air slurry drops which so far had failed to accomplish what Jay had hoped they might. And so on.

As he read and considered his options, he glanced from time to time at his watch. Briefings for supervisory personnel on major fires were held at 04:30 and at

16:30, and the pre-dawn briefing time was approaching fast.

Once, young in the fire-suppression business, he had found it incongruous that someone like a Fire Boss or a Plans Chief would be sitting quietly apparently doing nothing while the world was going up in flames and troops on the fire lines were busting their asses to hold what territory they had as if their lives depended on it.

He had long since learned that it was because fire suppression was now an organized operation, directed by trained men who did sit and study and think—Fire Bosses, Plans Chiefs, Safety Officers, Fire Behavior Officers, meteorologists—that tragedies such as the Griffith Park, Los Angeles, fire accident that killed 25 men and injured 128 in 1933 in a relatively minor brush fire, no longer occurred.

Forest Service records showed that between 1926 and 1976, 145 men died on 41 fires from fire-related injuries. In recent years there had been *no* heavy losses.

Only trained personnel were allowed on a fire line, each man, or woman, carrying a "red card" which showed degree of fire-fighting proficiency and "step test rating" for endurance. No longer did the wildland fire-fighting agencies send trucks into towns and cities at need to take men from the streets, usually Skid Rows, as they once had to fight forest fires.

And no longer did untrained men assume leadership because there was no one else, and do the best they could with whatever they happened to have at hand or could get quickly, improvising, struggling, sometimes daring too greatly and putting lives at risk.

A major fire was conducted now like a major military operation, and the Fire Boss, like the commanding General, performed best when he had the time and the opportunity to study and think.

It was close to briefing time when Jay Paul reappeared. His face was set, and sullen. "Orders, boss?"

JL deliberately gathered together the papers he had been reading and got out of the chair before he answered. "Yes," he said. His voice was pleasant, but he was not smiling as he looked at Jay. "The first one is to get that chip off your shoulder. You're not going to do me any good in that frame of mind." He waited a moment and watched a subtle change in Jay's face. "Now," JL said, "let's go find out just where we stand."

The twice-daily briefings were held on a strict schedule and followed a predetermined routine. The Fireline Handbook issued by the National Wildfire Coordinating Group in Washington said that they were to take no more than thirty minutes.

To JL, never one to go wholly by the book, they were basically valuable in ensuring that all supervisory personnel knew what was going on throughout the entire fire-suppression effort. In this instance, through his knowledge of the terrain, his study of Jay Paul's reports and the weather forecasts, he felt that he was already up to date. What he was interested in were the supervisory people themselves and their attitudes. Taking over in the midst of an operation was always a tricky business.

First came the Roll Call. JL, with Jay Paul slightly behind him, sat off to one side and watched as each hand was raised, and identified the face that went with it.

These were all people from the Sanrio Forest, men he knew, whose individual capabilities he had long since catalogued in his mind, marking this one for eventual command, that one as best suited for middle-echelon, specialized but routine responsibilities.

Watching carefully as name after name was called

and answered, he decided that he was satisfied with the selection of those who attended the briefing; there were neither too many, some of whom might be unnecessary, nor few enough to leave out anyone for whom the session might be important.

Next, from Phil Sommers, Plans Chief, a brief background of BACKSLOPE's beginnings, and fire-suppression accomplishments to date.

Somewhere behind JL a voice, low-pitched but audible, said, "Very damn little, with good movement backward."

JL, stifling the temptation to look around, faced resolutely forward. At his shoulder, Jay Paul muttered to himself.

The Safety Officer reported next. "The usual hazards, but we got through the night with only one incident." His voice remained grave. "One man fell into a bed of prickly-pear. He's been plucked clean now." The spines of the local variety of prickly-pear cactus grew as long as an inch. There was a general murmur of sympathetic laughter, quickly gone.

At least, JL thought, Jay Paul's obvious feeling of strain had not yet reached through the supervisory ranks, and the men could still find rough humor in a situation. It was a good sign.

The Fire Behavior Officer whose job was to predict the fire's probable course came next, followed by the meteorologist. JL tuned out both reports as covering ground he was already familiar with.

The Line Boss, second in tactical command, followed, and JL attended him carefully. A bright boy, in JL's opinion marked to go far. His name was Ben Hastings, college-educated, a forestry major specializing in plant biology, trim, neat, handing out assignments that were as neat as himself. He read off a list of Division Bosses he would meet with after the briefing for special discussions.

The voice behind JL, the same one that had spoken protestingly before, said, "And what about us? We're lepers?" This time the voice was not low-pitched.

JL, without turning his head, said, "I'll talk with you later, Andy. Simmer down and sit still." Then he stood up.

He spoke to them all, deliberately keeping his voice quiet, calm, almost uninflected. Regardless of whatever inner doubts and worries he might have, he had long ago decided, it was mandatory that he present an attitude of confidence, even of serenity to those under his command. No matter that the habit had earned him the reputation of having ice water instead of blood in his veins: the results justified the subterfuge, and that was all that mattered.

"Dry weather for too long," he said, "so everything, including what we weren't allowed to get rid of by prescribed burning, was just plain ready to go at the first spark. We were all waiting for it. Now we've got it, and no rain in sight."

He looked around. "You've held it for twenty-four hours," he said. Not true; they had lost their fire lines in a dozen places, but his voice held no blame, no hint of criticism. "Now we've seen how it's developing, we'll see what we can do to make sure that it doesn't get out of hand."

His voice altered abruptly. "They brought me back from BIFC," he said, "because I wasn't learning anything. It wasn't that I knew it all, it was just that I wasn't listening, I was back here instead of there, so they said, 'What the hell, might as well send him home, he's no good to us here.'"

There were smiles, and a general sense of relaxation. No big changes yet, their expression said. JL's voice changed again, to a brisker tone. "All right, let's get at it." He pointed at Andy McIlvain, Jay Paul, Phil Sommers and Ben Hastings. "I want you four, Andy first. Alone. Ben, when you've finished with your Division Bosses."

JL could have written Andy McIlvain's resumé from memory. A degree from Cal Tech in aeronautical engineering, only an unfinished dissertation standing in the way of his PhD; 41 years old; unmarried and uninterested, not in women, but in the permanence of matrimony; a commercial pilot's license; winter season ski instructor; thirteen years as a smoke-jumper, the last eight as crew foreman; Department commendation for the new parachute design; hang-glider designer and enthusiast. Impatient.

"What's your beef?" JL said.

"You've got a fire, damn it. I've got a crew of fire-fighters, smoke-jumpers, good ones—"

"The best," JL nodded.

"And we've been sitting on our asses, pitching cards into a helmet, pitching pennies, waiting—goddamnit, I told Phil Sommers we could go into that terrain! Duck soup! With the new chute, even you could make it!"

"Thanks."

"But Jay Paul says he won't risk us—for Christ's sake, what are we here for? You've lost a whole section because he wouldn't let us go in at the start, that's six hundred and forty goddam acres! Now—"

"All right," JL said. "You've made your point. Now I'm here, and we'll use you. That's a promise. You're loaded up?"

"Eleven fire boxes lashed down, eleven men ready to suit up. If we need more in one spot—"

"Back to the airport," JL said. "I'll call you."

"Look—" Andy began.

"Move it! You've got your orders."

Andy hesitated and then slowly began to grin. "Yes, sir, Fire Boss, sir! On my way!"

JL merely nodded, and looked up, no longer interested in Andy McIlvain. His face was placid, untroubled. He beckoned to Jay Paul and Phil Sommers. "Come on over and sit down. Let's talk about a couple of things."

Jay Paul approached the table with his jaw set. "I refused to risk them," he said. "I won't lose men—"

"Sit down," JL said. "We'll get to Andy's jumpers in good time. They'll be there when we need them." He paused for emphasis. "And we will," he added.

## 12

In full daylight on this second day, the scene was wholly different from what it had been twenty-four hours earlier. Sierra Grande's towering peak was still plain against the limitless sky as winds above the ten-thousand-foot level swept it clean, but lower, the pall of smoke hung like smog, deepening in color closer to the treetops, dirty, grayish-brown, ugly and threatening.

From the city, no flames were visible, and even from the big houses abutting the Forest, like Vista Hill, Stacy's place, El Rancho Costa Mucho, Sophie Swift's property and Willard P. Spencer's now uninsured estate, stands of ponderosa pines, in places thick, in other places precariously thin, screened the actual conflagration from view.

But fire was there, ever expanding, and it made its presence, felt in the smoke it generated, thick, in places choking, seeping through closed windows and doors, leaving its distinctive smudgy prints on whitewashed walls and garden trellises; in occasional violent sounds as a giant tree relaxed its hold on the earth, and on life, and came crashing down through lesser growth; in the occasional sight of an animal fleeing in terror, a deer, a mother bear herding her cubs; two, or three, or half a dozen of the wild donkeys who bred in the Forest vastness and thrived on its protected lands.

Overhead there was an almost constant din as chartered twin-engine air tankers swept past at near treetop height and at direction from the ground opened their tanks to discharge in ragged, red clouds their loads of slurry on targeted areas. Their exploits, and in particular those of the small, single-engine Forest Service lead planes which established the flight paths for the tankers, had inspired a book entitled *Fly the Biggest Piece Back*, indicating something of the hazards of the operation.

Out of sight of the city or the big houses on the Forest's fringe, where terrain permitted, bulldozers carved fire breaks to halt the flaming advance, and ground tankers pumped water by the ton. But in rougher, steeper country, sweating, cursing line crews dug and chopped and scraped the ground clean by hand, carving their fire breaks and hoping they would hold, that no errant wind gust, perhaps caused by air currents heated and thus powered by the flames themselves, might catch a burning branch and carry it, airborne, across the cleared area into a fresh, virgin stand of trees.

Bessie Wingate, indefatigable, using her #2 round-point now as the shovel it was, now as a cutting tool, now as a lever until its hickory shaft threatened to break, nevertheless kept her eye on her nineteen crew members as a mother hen on her chicks, shouting frequent encouragement as well. "I think we're whipping this mother!" Her voice carried clearly. "Son of a bitch gets up here, it's going to have to burn dirt because that's all we're leaving her! Take it down clean! Slicker than a baby's ass! Way to go!" And to Eloy Jaramillo, twenty yards away, "What you got in your hip pocket, Eloy? That bottle? Whisky?"

Eloy looked up from his work with the McCloud and showed his fine white teeth. "*Salsa*. For the goddam C-rations."

"Hey!" Bessie said. "You got something there. They sure as hell taste like shit. All right, let's keep it moving!"

Andy McIlvain was in the spotter's seat abaft the open fuselage door on the port side of the Twin Otter, headset and attached mike in place, and his head well out of the open window as he scanned the forest beneath them. On the wooden bench that lined the starboard side of the bare fuselage, eleven smoke-jumpers sat, suited up and wearing their two para-chutes each, carrying their helmets with the steel mesh faceplates that swung and latched into place when they were ready to jump. The cabin was not soundproofed, and the constant rush of wind from the open fuselage door made conversation difficult if not impossible.

One thing, Andy was thinking with part of his mind, when old JL got into the act, things began to happen, none of this pussyfooting and horseshitting around that typified lesser fire bosses like Jay Paul who was so afraid of making a mistake that he damn near did nothing.

"We can handle these two quadrants," JL had said on the phone, both men miles apart looking at maps for reference as they talked, "but up in that northwest corner—got it?—where those contour lines get damn close together, I can't get trucks or choppers in, and—"

"We can go in," Andy said.

"Yes, I think you can." He knew the terrain and he knew the new chutes' capabilities. He did not hesitate. "I just want that line held so it can't fishhook around

150

and cause us trouble from the wrong side. Got it?"

"Duck soup."

"Okay." There was the hint of a smile in JL's voice. "Get on it. And save part of your crew in case we need you somewhere else as well."

"Charge!" Andy said, and hung up.

Now, studying the terrain beneath them, seeing the actual flames they were going to have to control, estimating height and distance, and searching for a possible drop site — "Got it!" he said loud into the fixed mike to the pilot. "Ten o'clock, that opening in the trees, see it? Come around and fly upslope, drop down maybe a couple of hundred feet. Your first pass right over the target, as usual."

He beckoned Jake, his number-two man, who would be in charge of this crew, and pointed downward.

Jake nodded, rose from the bench and crossed the cabin to hunker down in the open doorway, leaning out and holding himself inside the cabin against the plane's banking turn by the door jambs. He followed Andy's pointing finger and picked out the small opening in the trees. He nodded.

Andy pointed back at the visible flames, the rising smoke, and made a crossing gesture with his hand, indicating a line to be drawn.

Jake smiled faintly and nodded again. "Will do," his lips formed.

Andy reached beneath his seat and took up three weighted rolls of crepe paper, red, orange and yellow, and with his head well out of the window watched the ground as they approached the potential drop site. When they were directly overhead, he tossed out the paper streamers and simultaneously pushed the stop-watch button on his wrist watch. Together, he and Jake watched the streamers fall, clearly visible against the greenery below.

They landed a hundred yards beyond, and off to one side of the small opening, and Andy pressed the stop button on his watch. He glanced at it. Into the mike he said, "One minute and fourteen seconds. Take her down another two hundred and fifty feet for this pass, and alter course a hair to port." Their optimum drop altitude was 1200 feet, one minute of drop time. "Got it?"

"Roger." The plane banked steeply and came around in a sharp turn.

This time, Andy tossed out the three streamers when they were one hundred yards short of the clearing, and again timed their fall. All three streamers landed in the opening, and the time was one minute and two seconds. "Bingo," Andy said into the mike and as the plane began its sharp banking turn, he gestured to Jake to get ready.

Jake snapped the hook of his primary parachute's static line to the vertical cable anchored to the aircraft's structure and squatted on one leg in the open doorway, his other leg hanging outside, free. He locked the mesh faceplate of his helmet into place, and reached overhead to grasp the bar above the doorway. Without command, Benjie, Jake's jump mate came off the wooden bench, snapped his static line to the cable too and bent over Jake's shoulder in a ready attitude.

Andy verified that both static lines were secured to the vertical cable, and that both lines stretching across the fuselage floor were clear of any obstructions and could play out freely. His head out the window, he watched as they approached the drop site.

Precisely over the spot where he had dropped the last three crepe streamers, and without looking back from the window, Andy tapped Jake on the shoulder and Jake launched himself through the open doorway. Benjie followed immediately.

Andy watched as the two static lines stretched taut from vertical cable to doorway, snapped the rubber bands that held them in serpentine coils on top of the chute packs, paid out as the men dropped, and, reaching their full extension, pulled free the chute covering, allowing the chutes to deploy.

He then hauled in the two lines and the parachute casings attached to them, unsnapped the hooks from the vertical cable and tossed them behind the seat.

Two more jumpers took their places at the open doorway as the aircraft began its next fly-around.

When all eleven men were on the ground, Andy would start pushing out the packed cardboard fire boxes, each with its own chute, two at a time as they circled the drop area. The last item to go out would be a cardboard box without parachute, containing a single pair of climbing irons—just in case someone or something was caught high in a tree.

Of this final box, Andy had told one of his new crew members, "You get the hell out of the way of this sucker, because after freefalling twelve hundred feet, it's not about to slow up for anything until it hits the ground, and then your problem may be to dig it out of the hole it makes."

Now, still watching the ground, he saw Jake and Benjie land in the tiny opening among the trees, roll easily, come to their knees and, tugging on the shrouds, collapse their parachutes. Both men looked skyward, and waved. Andy merely nodded. "Luck," he said beneath his breath, and turned his attention to the next jump pair.

Into his microphone, speaking via the aircraft's radio and the tower to JL deep in the Forest, Andy said, "Eleven men with gear on the ground taking positions.

153

Jake will be in touch. We're coming in."

"Roger," JL said. "Stand by."

"That," Andy said, "seems to be the bestest thing I is at. Over and out."


Again Aaron Swift had not slept well, and those guilt feelings continued to run vaguely through his mind. The previous afternoon at the ranch he had drunk the cup of tea Sophie had made for him and listened to her list of planned preparations, all logical, sensible and somehow inexplicably pitiful as well.

"Records?" he had said. "I mean, figures on paper — they're important to save?"

"Yes." Sophie had seemed uncharacteristically uncomfortable, even embarrassed.

"Tell me why, Soph."

Her embarrassment deepened, but it was not in her to avoid a direct question. "Along with grandmother's silver," she said slowly, "and the paintings I intend to save and the few knick-knacks, the records are—" She spread her hands helplessly as the words ran down.

He knew her well, Aaron realized suddenly, indeed far better than he had until this moment understood. What she was saying, even without the words, was that the things she listed, the records among them, were her mementos of life, the total remaining reality of her existence, hence incalculably precious to her.

"Maybe you're right," Aaron said gently. "Records can't be replaced. As lawyers we both know that."

After finishing his tea, and hearing once more Sophie's assurances that there was really nothing he could do, Aaron had gone back to his office. There was a call from Debby at the Club, and as he went about returning it, he could picture her, young and lithe and shapely in one of her scant bikinis, stretched out beside the pool probably with a diet cola at hand, no doubt having found friends to talk to about the matter of clothes, recipes, entertainment, bestselling books and travel possibilities that loomed large in her life.

"A," Debby's breathless voice said on the phone, "would you feel like having dinner here tonight? Mary Sue tells me that the new piano player is super, and you know how you love the Club's roast beef. It isn't sensible for me to cook a standing rib roast at home just for two."

"Why not?" Aaron said. "I'll bring along my fiddle and we can watch Rome from there."

"You say the funniest things sometimes," Debby said. "I never know when you're teasing."

That night, lying awake in the pre-dawn blackness, Aaron was not at all sure that *he* knew, either, when he meant what he said and when he was merely throwing up a smokescreen of persiflage—which was ridiculous, of course, but there it was. Like the neurotic, he thought, who knows that two and two make four, but it worries him.

At his office that second day of BACKSLOPE, he had heard, as usual, pretty much all that was going on in Sanrio.

JL was back in town and in charge of the fire, which was all to the good. But it seemed to Aaron that during the night the fire had spread, and that was all to the bad.

Through his corner office windows he could see smoke deep in the Forest rising against the backdrop of the great mountain, where yesterday that quadrant had been clear, and he was tempted to call George Jefferson for a full status report, but he was by nature a patient man, and for the present at least, he decided, he would resolutely assume that matters were still well in hand.

155

He had great respect for both Jefferson and JL, who were professionals, devoted to their work, but he also had a countryman's understanding of just how thin the line was between a wildfire being brought under control, and one which, for any of a variety of reasons mostly climatic, could at any time burst its containment and ravage the countryside, destroying not only vegetation and valuable stands of lumber, but also houses, and threatening lives as well as property. A wildland fire on the loose was one of nature's most awesome forces, as terrifying and as pitiless as a tornado or a hurricane, and as devastating.

Aaron had seen mile after mile of blackened forests, burned-out houses, entire small towns destroyed, their populations driven from their homes with what they could carry to find shelter where they could and hope that some kind of help with food, water and medical supplies would eventually arrive on the scene.

But allowing his mind to dwell on possibilities like that was fruitless, worse, it was deeply depressing, so he concentrated on other, lighter matters.

Willard Spencer's insurance had been allowed to lapse, which would have been serious if it hadn't been so unnecessarily stupid. Aaron could work himself up to neither sympathy nor a sense of responsibility.

And Ada Loving, the film star about whom Debby had spoken in such ringing superlatives arrived at Aaron's office unannounced at mid-morning, and that completed the process of dismissing the fire in the Forest from his thoughts. Reports of her impressive body, Aaron decided, had not been exaggerated.

Ada Loving had purchased a home in Sanrio — or it had been purchased for her; details were unclear. In an interview with the local newspaper, she had said that she was enchanted by the climate and the scenery and the friendliness of the folks who lived in Sanrio, and she had confidently predicted that the area would burgeon and prosper mightily as soon as its charms became more widely known, something she was going to help happen.

Movie-goers, particularly young movie-goers in droves had found the great deal that they had seen of Ada Loving enchanting; in person, up close, she was irresistible.

"My business manager of course handled all details of buying the property," she told Aaron, "but he told me that in any kind of emergency, you were the person to depend on."

There was more than native shrewdness behind the carefully contrived facade, Aaron decided; Ada Loving was quite obviously of the opinion that sexy actresses were not supposed to be intelligent, and behaved accordingly; but glimpses of her real self showed through. "Flattering of him," Aaron said. "Do you have an emergency?"

"I don't know. Does this fire count? In Malibu it would."

"Happily," Aaron said, "this is not Malibu yet. And so far, the fire is merely a fire, no threat to life or property."

"But it could be?"

"With bad luck, very bad luck, it could be."

"You kid me not. Thank you for that." The celebrated blue eyes were steady, intelligently appraising, all coquetry set aside. "Who is in charge? And how do I meet him?"

"To make sure that a little extra care is taken to protect your property?"

Nothing changed in Ada Loving's eyes or her friendly smile. "Why not?"

"Matter of viewpoint." Aaron wore his courtroom manner. "The Forest Supervisor is named George

Jefferson."

"The boss man?"

"The top of the local totem pole," Aaron said gravely. Let George fob her off himself.

As Ada Loving left his office, Aaron decided that the view from the rear precisely balanced the view from the front, a miracle of anatomical engineering.


JL glanced at the note Jay Paul handed him, and then glanced again and this time read it carefully. "A burned-out jeep? In the Wilderness?"

"Texas plates," Jay Paul said. "We had a reported sighting yesterday from a chopper. This confirms it. One of Andy McIlvain's smoke-jumpers found it."

"No people?"

Jay Paul shook his head.

"Get a chopper in. See if it can spot them." JL's voice was doubtful. "If they know they're not supposed to have driven in, they may not want to be seen. If they have a choice, that is. One thing about a fire: it smokes out lots of things, including people."


Elsie Edwards came cautiously back into the uppermost fringe of the big trees where Don sat on the ground, legs outstretched, his head resting, eyes closed, against one of the massive trunks. There was a purple bruise above and behind his right ear where the pistol barrel had struck, but the continuing throbbing ache included his entire head and part of his neck.

The fact that he was conscious indicated that it was probably no more than a mild concussion, he had decided, and Elsie had verified that neither of his pupils was abnormally contracted or expanded so he thought he could consider that further indication that he was not seriously damaged. But, oh God, his head ached!

He opened his eyes as Elsie approached, and what he saw in her face took his attention for the moment at least away from his own condition.

"What is it? I mean, you look as if you'd seen—"

"I have. I—did!" Elsie was holding herself under as tight control as she could manage. "They're—there! Above us! In the open!"

It took a moment to sort out the words and their meaning. "The two men? With guns?"

Elsie had crossed her arms over her breasts. She caught her lower lip in her teeth, and nodded, a jerky, mechanical motion, filled with emphasis.

"Did they see you?"

Her head moved sideways with the same stiff effort.

"Then we're all right here," Don said, "unless the fire comes up the slope."

"It—does, doesn't it? Doesn't it? Move upward, I mean?"

"Sometimes. Maybe. We'll just have to wait and see." Between Scylla and Charybdis, he thought, and he helpless as a mouse.


"Will you look at that damned jeep?" Les Lawry said. "It looks like it took a direct bomb hit." Around them the ground still smoked and smoldered where fire had passed through. They picked their way with care.

"Our things!" Cindy Lou said.

"We're alive, aren't we? Instead of being barbecued like we would have been if we'd stayed here?"

"But we shouldn't have been here in the first place!"

"This is the hell of a time to bring that up, damn it. We—"

Tad said, "I hear a helicopter."

"Okay," Les said. "Take cover. Over there, in those rocks."

"But, Les, they could help us! Take us out!"

"You want me in the slammer? Of all the goddam rotten luck! Come on!"

## 13

Reports, maps and even infra-red photographs were all very well, but, in JL's opinion, there was no substitute for seeing the situation yourself. Sitting now in the Forest Service helicopter, soft pencil in hand and map-folded-on-clipboard on his lap, he studied the fiery battlefield below with an appraising eye. The situation, he decided, was less than good.

By quantum leaps in terrain too steep for bulldozers, one front of the fire was advancing up the Sierra Grande's slopes, in its savagery obliterating all low growth and leaving the big pines as naked and blackened skeletons, some still standing, others collapsed on the smoldering ground.

The flames were not constant, as in a furnace, but, rather, acting almost as if driven by gigantic blowtorches, they suddenly flared up here, and as quickly receded there once fuel immediately at hand was consumed. But the advance continued.

Smoke rose in great billowing clouds, and although above the racket of the chopper's engine and blades no sounds from the ground could be heard, the mind readily absorbed the turmoil that was a part of the destruction.

Further on, in the area of ground clutter too densely packed to walk through—the result of uncontrolled second growth following a long-ago fire—ominous smoke tendrils were rising, testimony to the hidden build-up of ground level temperatures which, unopposed, could rise steadily until the entire area suddenly took flame, immediately extending the fire's perimeter to include a thousand more acres.

Even ground crews were useless here because of the impenetrability of the tangled growth. In a situation like this, you took your gamble on what appeared to be the lesser of two bad choices.

JL plucked the hand microphone from its control panel bracket, and called Ben Hastings, the Line Boss, deliberately short-circuiting Jay Paul.

He gave the coordinates from the map on his lap. "That area we wanted to clear out with prescribed burning," he said, "got it?"

"Roger."

"It's smoking now. Before it reaches flash point, I want it opened up so ground crews can get at it." He wondered if he was going to have to explain how it was to be done. To Jay Paul, he thought, he might have.

"Roger," Ben Hastings said again. "Spaced explosives—will do." His voice held approval.

"We'll spread fire by doing it," JL said, pleased by the immediate understanding, "but it'll be fire we can get to instead of the incendiary bomb we can't touch now."

"Understood," Ben Hastings said. "I'll take care of it, JL."

"Any word from the people with that jeep in the Wilderness?"

"Negative. The chopper is still sweeping the area. My guess is they're keeping under cover."

"Then they're making the wrong choice," JL said. "Over and out."

He made a swinging gesture to the pilot, who nodded and took the helicopter off in a new direction. Flying low over flaming areas the machine bucked and sometimes pitched sickeningly in rising air currents. Neither man paid heed.

"As a fire," the pilot said, "this one's a ring-tailed bitch. Or will be, when she gets her full growth."

JL nodded. He wore his faint, enigmatic smile. "You look to be right."

They came over the tiny opening in the trees where Andy's smoke-jumpers had gone in. The pilot stared at it in awe. "Jesus, they went in there? By parachute?"

"Good men," JL said. He pointed. "There they are."

"They're damn magicians," the pilot said.

The jumpers were spread out in a thin, spaced line, with two crosscut saws at work and hand tools for the clean-up, cutting a wide, clean fire break. JL nodded approvingly. With any luck, it would keep the fire in that mountainous sector from curling around as he had feared it might.

One of the men on the ground looked up and waved, thumb and forefinger held in a circle. JL waved the clipboard in reply. "Damn good men," he said, and waved the pilot off to a new sector of the perimeter.

Here the boxlike houses of Bellevue Acres, beginning only a few hundred yards from the nearest fire line, marched off in closed, orderly if less than immaculate ranks. Bicycles, stateboards, dogs and kids decorated the scene. But smoke from the nearest flames, JL noted, was blowing away from the development. No present threat there.

Farther on, vast by contrast, were the rolling green lawns and tended flower beds of Vista Hill, Mrs. Wayne's property, the main house, Territorial in style, of solid brown-stuccoed adobe, with tile roof and neat white trim, dominating the landscape as Sierra Grande dominated the skyline. It, too, was at present un-threatened.

They flew on, and JL, pointing down, said mildly, "Our one real bright spot — that highway. Natural fire break."

The highway was two full lanes wide, with a verge mowed by sickle-bar supporting only low grass and cactus insufficient to feed fire of any strength. On either side, the big ponderosa pines grew in healthy profusion.

"One front," JL said, "where we won't have to worry about containing the fire." Be thankful for small blessings, he told himself, and resumed study of the map he had been marking as they flew.

In response to George Jefferson's question last night, he had guessed that the fire had overrun maybe twenty thousand acres, something over thirty square miles. Looking down from the map now on the blackened, smoking and in places still flaming devastation that had been lovely Forest, he decided that the area had increased overnight by perhaps twenty-five percent, maybe even a little more. All boundaries had been pushed back, and only the one barrier of the highway looked secure.

Containment, there was the key; surround the monster, force it to exhaust its fuel and burn itself out. It sounded simple enough, but JL had often thought that the process of containment, particularly in mountainous terrain and swirling wind currents such as they had to deal with here, was a great deal like trying to pin down a blob of mercury on a flat surface. You applied pressure, and immediately what you were trying to contain separated into parts that skittered off in new directions. The analogy was not exact, but it did illustrate some of the difficulties.

In relatively flat terrain it was frequently possible to

pick your perimeter fire line, with bulldozers and hand tools develop a fire break, or, if conditions were right, denude a fire break by setting a backfire. Then when the monster approached, it would reach the line where fuel was no longer available, and that would be that.

But here, in this mixture of low growth, medium sized piñon and juniper and big trees—aspens, pines, cottonwoods, and the like—growing in country that stood on end, in places far too steep for men to work, let alone machines, and convection currents of air plus normal winds swirling in all directions, a neat, text-book fire break line was simply not possible to achieve.

Here, you fought the beast hand-to-hand, constantly aware that it might at any time outflank you, or leapfrog your position, that it might enter a narrow arroyo, a draw, and, driven upward by its own heat, increase in speed and temperature that sometimes even seemed to turn the air itself into invisible flame that could ignite trees and brush dozens of yards beyond the line where you thought the fire was contained.

The pilot said suddenly, proving that he too had been thinking along the same lines, "You ever feel you've got a fire you can't whip?"

"No," JL said, and mentally crossed his fingers at the lie. "You whip them all eventually."

"Tonight," the pilot said, "I'm going to pray for rain."

JL nodded. "We'll take whatever help we can get."


Stacy went out to her corrals surrounding the big barn, and Pancho, Juanita's son, immediately appeared to follow on her rounds.

Pancho was fifteen, small and wiry, with strong, gentle, horse-sensitive hands. Stacy had walked in one day to find him straddling a bale of hay in the barn, practising changing a stick that represented a racing whip from hand to hand. He was embarrassed that she caught him thus.

"The only way," Stacy said approvingly. "You want to be a jock, you practise it all, all the time." Wherever that determination to excel turned up, it was something to be admired, and encouraged, not ridiculed. Her father again: "You can run out front, honey," he had said, "or you can run back with the crowd. Up to you. But there's something to bear in mind: not everybody has that choice; most, no matter how hard they try, are always going to stay with the crowd, so when you find one who looks like maybe he *can* be a front-runner, give him all the help you can."

The postage-stamp racing saddle Stacy had sent away for after her discovery of Pancho's ambition rested on its own rack in the tack room now, bright and polished with saddle soap until it glistened in the lights. Pancho had tried it on Sam once, and been pitched over the corral fence and almost into the next county for his effrontery.

"Sam," Stacy had pointed out, "is a cutting horse, and he knows it. And cutting horses don't mess with racing saddles."

"*Sí señorita.*" It was obvious that Pancho would remember.

Now, "The smoke's not bad yet," Stacy said, "and if it doesn't get any worse, we won't have anything to worry about. I want you to stay out here, Pancho, and if the horses start getting spooked, let me know immediately." She studied the boy. "Big responsibility. Can you handle it?"

"*Sí señorita, con gusto* — with pleasure."

Stacy nodded, and reached through the corral fence to snap her fingers in summons to Sam who walked over, ears forward and blowing softly with pleasure, presented a velvety nose to be stroked.

"You help keep track of things too, Sam," Stacy said. "If there's any problem, we'll get you all out in plenty of time."

As she walked back toward the big house she reflected that they were all treating what was happening in the Forest as something distant, remote, to be spoken of almost as if it were not real. She wondered if civilian populations looked on war in the same way—until it actually descended upon them and shattered their lives. The this-may-be-happening-but-it-won't-touch-me syndrome was probably universal, she supposed, and those who refused to accept it were considered alarmists—it was no doubt as simple as that.

She realized that she had been aware for some time of the staccato sounds of a helicopter, and she looked up now as the sounds suddenly increased in shattering volume and the craft swept overhead in its awkward, seemingly crablike way. Automatically, she waved, and saw an answering wave, and a face looking down—either JL or her own imagination, she thought, and hoped it was the former. Funny, but if he had come back and taken charge, she could feel a definite strengthening of her sense of security.

She realized that she knew very little about him, and most of that from Ken Delacorte, but even in her few encounters with JL she had developed a feeling, good vibes, as some of her friends might say, the kind of thing you tended to heed, just as you heeded the opposite—bad vibes—when they came to you from man or beast.

"We're animals, honey," her father had said over and over again, "and don't let anybody tell you different. And we react to folks just like a horse does, or a dog. I don't mean we wag our tail or whinny and nicker, but it's the same thing. Some men I like first time I lay eyes on them. Others I wouldn't trust as far as I could throw them. I don't know what it is, but it sure as hell is there—just a feeling, but you'd damn well better pay attention to it."

She heard the explosions then, muffled, spaced, sounds as of large doors being shut on distant, empty closets. She looked toward the Forest, saw the spaced columns of smoke rising and felt her first real intimations of unease.

The sounds of the explosions reached George Jefferson's office too, and Ada Loving in one of the visitors' chairs, shapely legs crossed and magnificent bosom very much in evidence, said, "Does that have significance, Mr. Jefferson?"

George Jefferson was uneasy in this female's presence, and he had a good idea that she was well aware of it. His conversation tended to be edgy. "We don't usually set off explosions just for fun, ma'am," he said, "so I imagine there's a reason for it. I'll find out in the evening situation report."

"In the San Francisco fire that followed the 1906 earthquake," Ada Loving said, "I have read that they dynamited whole blocks of buildings."

"Here, ma'am, we tend to rely on fire breaks our crews cut, by bulldozer or by hand."

"And if houses get in the way?"

"Our first duty is to protect life and property."

"But you would rather that we didn't build, or live, quite so close to the Forest?"

"That, ma'am," Jefferson said, his patience at an end, "is a sure as hell fact." He rose from his chair. "Now, if you'll excuse me."

Ada Loving rose too, smiling. "I'm sure you will do what you can, Mr. Jefferson," she said. "I am confident that our properties are in good hands."

The spaced explosions—explosives lowered by helicopter and detonated by remote control—had blown a rough but open path through the tangle of brush and ground clutter. And they had, as JL anticipated, spread tendrils of fire and smoldering fuel in all directions. The two hotshot crews that attacked the area, one from either side, had their hands full.

Gordy Walker, crew chief of the Los Ojos hotshot crew (Category 1), invariably approached a new assignment with extreme caution, thereby causing suppressed snickers among the crew who knew that within a matter of minutes old Gordy would get into the spirit of the thing and start charging whatever their objective was with a fury that had to be seen to be appreciated. It was suggested that Gordy's mother must have been frightened by a burning bush, and that she had managed to pass along to her child a hatred of anything that caught fire.

Now, muttering to himself between commands, he spread his crew around in pairs to douse whatever was already on fire, and to widen and clean out the pathway-break the explosives had left. "But take it slow and easy, goddamnit," he told them. "There's still smoke coming out of some of that brush and it could go up in your face without warning." To an experienced crew like his, totally unnecessary cautionary advice.

Terry Young, the crew's free spirit, said, "Yes, *sir*! Will do, sir! Easy does it, sir!"

"And screw you too," Gordy said without rancor and plunged in with his favorite tool, a brush hook, its sickle-shaped, axe-handle mounted blade honed to a fine edge.

Ben Hastings, Line Boss, on the phone to the heliport and the chopper pilot who had lowered and detonated the explosives, said, "How many charges did you put in?"

"Ten, like you said."

"Right. And did you count the explosions?"

"They all went off."

"Damn it, did you count them? Because I only heard nine."

"Well, hell," the pilot said, "they must have all detonated. I mean—"

"Never mind." Ben's voice was sharp. "Stay on the line." He turned to the communications man. "Get on the walkie-talkies and get those two crews out of there. Fast! I want acknowledgement when they're clear."


Gordy paused in mid-swing of his brush hook, took his walkie-talkie from his belt to acknowledge the sudden beeping. He listened. "Oh, for Christ's sake," he said in disgust, raising his voice, "Out! All of you, goddamnit, out! There's a live explosive in here somewhere!" Into the walkie-talkie again, "Why the hell can't they get it right the first time? We've got fire to fight here."


Ben Hastings said to the chopper pilot, "Get in the air, fly over the area and give it another signal. If it detonates, fine. If it doesn't—"

"They all *had* to detonate!" the chopper pilot said. "I mean, why would nine go off and not the tenth? It doesn't—"

"Just haul your ass out to your chopper and get into the air," Ben said. "We've got fire spreading, and crews

170

can't move in until we're sure. Got that?"

They heard the chopper approaching, and watched it come in at treetop height. It hovered over the blasted pathway through the brush and clutter now burning briskly. "Come on!" Gordy said under his breath. "Goddamnit, come on!"

One of the crew said, "What's going on?"

"He's trying to detonate the charge by radio signal, dummy," Terry Young said.

They waited, watching, until the chopper flipped up on its side and slid back the way it had come in its crabwise way. In the blasted pathway there was only the sound of crackling flames.

"Shit!" Gordy said, and took up his walkie-talkie. He identified himself. "I'll go in," he said. "I'll find the mother."

"Negative." This was Ben Hastings's voice.

"Damn it," Gordy said, "we're going to have fire we can't handle if we just stand around here with our finger up our ass. It's already spreading."

"I'm aware of that," Ben said. "But you—"

"Then you just stay the hell aware of it," Gordy said. "And when I come back out, we can go to work. Over and out." He handed the walkie-talkie to Terry. "You hang on to this, bigmouth." He turned and headed down the jagged pathway at a trot.

"And so," Ben reported to JL, "the feisty little bastard went in, found the charge, and heaved it as far as he could into an area that was already burning. After a while, it detonated harmlessly, and that was that." He shook his head. "What do you do with people like that?"

"Try to protect them," JL said, "and then say a little prayer of thanks when they refuse protection. Or bury them. One."

# 14

His name, as they discovered later, was Jerry Michaels, and you would have thought he had been driving tractor-and-semi-trailer rigs, eighteen-wheelers, long enough to know better, but there is never a way to predict how a man will react in panic.

Ever since Albuquerque the CB had been crackling, not with Smokey reports or road and weather conditions, but with talk of BACKSLOPE, although none of the truckers had yet heard the actual name.

"I saw that damn fire on my north yesterday," one trucker reported, "and it's the hell of a lot bigger now. You can see the smoke for fifty, seventy-five miles."

"Fire that big," another voice said, "uses up all the oxygen. Gasoline engines get too near, I hear tell they stall out."

"How about diesel?"

"Diesel's different."

"The hell. Diesel needs oxygen too."

"Diesels don't have carburetors."

"Neither do these fuel-injection jobs, but they still need oxygen."

That argument was inconclusive, and good for fifteen-twenty miles. Jerry Michaels stayed out of it. He wasn't going anywhere near that fire if he could help it. But just listening passed the time.

It was a four-wheel-drive pick-up, a 4x4, breaking in that caught his attention. "They've closed Route 123. The fire's the reason."

The radios were silent briefly. Then someone said, "Let's have a 10-9 on that, good buddy."

"10-4. They've closed Route one-two-three from Bart's Corners where it leaves Route 7."

"Is Route 7 still open?"

"Last I knew."

"10-4. Appreciate that information."

Another voice asked, "How about Route one-four?"

"It's open. For now."

Route 14, one-four, was Jerry Michaels's road, full width, two-lane, a few curves, but nothing serious. Once, back in mid-winter, it was closed for a spell, but it shouldn't be closed now. Good thing, too, because turning around a full-length tanker rig like Jerry's on a two-lane road unless you had an open space to back into was not the easiest thing in the world.

Some ratchet-jaw, probably over on the Interstate, said apparently to nobody in particular, "All that smoke reminds me of a fire I seen north of LA one time. Flames till Hell wouldn't have it . . ." The voice droned on in the steady, determined tempo of the non-stop talker. Jerry, with the ease of long practice, tuned it out of his consciousness, but left the CB on.

He was in no great hurry, and he held the eighteen-wheeler at a steady pace just under the sixty mph the cops in these parts would generally allow. The big mountain, Sierra Grande, was on his left now, showing even up near its peak streaks of smoke the upper wind currents hadn't quite been able to dissipate.

In this country, as anybody who had lived here for any time at all knew full well, you treated fire with respect; as you treated water, or, rather, the customary lack of it. Fellow who seemed to know, one of those university-types who turned up in strange places usually driving 4x4's, had told Jerry once that way back in 1540 a dude called Coronado had come through here with some soldiers and gone as far east as Kansas.

Jerry had pondered long and hard and failed to understand how anybody in his right mind could have had the guts to go all that way without knowing when, or even if, they were ever going to find water just to keep alive in this big, damn country.

It was a land that penalized mistakes, something always and always to remember. Given the chance, the sun that now felt pleasantly warm through his windshield could and would desiccate you. In any of the small arroyos he was driving past, bone-dry for months on end, years, a flash flood could come romping down out of the mountains without warning and pick up even a rig as big as his and throw it right off the road. There were freak winds and dust storms and in winter blizzards that swept in piling drifts higher than a man could reach in temperatures you would not believe. And now there was fire, and who knew where that would end?

Automatically his eyes swept his control gauges — oil pressure, engine temperature, fuel level, ammeter, and finally speedometer. All okay. He glanced left and right at his outside mirrors and saw only the steady sides of the semi-trailer tank following obediently with its load of six thousand gallons of gasoline.

The CB speaker came alive again: "They're blowing charges in there, deep in the Forest. Rather them than me. Damn explosives can be tricky."

"Break one-nine." A new voice.

"Come on, breaker."

"Route one-four is still open both ways, but where it cuts close to the big mountain, it looks like they're fixing to set up a roadblock."

"10-4. Appreciate that information."

Instantly, Jerry Michaels was all attention. He took down his hand microphone. "This here is Singlejack. Come back, breaker. You say where Route one-four gets close to the big mountain? Where that Forest road comes in? Over."

"10-4. That's the place. I seen flames through the trees, and they got a Forest Service truck with road-block signs they hadn't yet put up, time I rolled past."

Jesus H. Jumping Christ, Jerry thought; fire close enough to the road to be seen through the trees, and him with thirty-six thousand pounds, eighteen goddam tons of gasoline in his tanks.

Automatically, he slowed and began looking for a likely place to turn around. No dice. It could be done, but it would take time and patient maneuvering, and, besides, the goddam shoulder looked soft, maybe too soft for his rig's weight. And all he needed was to get the rig stuck if fire was that close. Goddam.

So there was nothing else to it, and that was for damn sure. If there was one thing you learned pushing a big rig along highways all these years, it was that there were times to hit the brakes, and other times when nothing but the hammer down all the way would get you out of a tight spot. He floored the accelerator, the big diesel roared in response and the whole rig began to gather speed.

The hell with a roadblock. He was pushing not much shy of thirty tons of rig and load, and if anything tried to stop him it was going to be too goddam bad. Let the cops come after him; they could settle all that later. Right now what he was going to make damn sure of was that he wasn't hung up, just a sitting duck while those flames in the trees came closer, and closer.

The tires began to sing on the pavement, and Jerry could feel the gasoline load sloshing a bit in the less-

176

than-full tanks. Never mind that. The road was good and the curves ahead not too bad, and at this speed in no more than three-four minutes he'd be past that point where apparently they were about to set up the roadblock—if they hadn't done it already—and from there on it would be strictly downhill, running away from, instead of straight toward, the point of greatest danger.

There was a righthand curve ahead, and he swung a little wide across the double center line to flatten his arc. Plenty of road, no sweat, even at the speed he was now traveling. He bent over the wheel, studying the roadway, estimating distance, swinging force, speed—

And here, coming in the opposite direction around the curve came a Forest Service truck speeding along to set up warning signs for oncoming traffic.

Instantly Jerry tightened his turning radius a little, and a little more to give the truck enough room. He was running a bit faster than he had thought, and the resistance of the front wheels to sharper turning surprised him.

The oncoming truck had already swung clear over to the edge of the pavement to avoid collision, and the driver's face through the windshield was a picture of shock, surprise, anger and fear, mouth open, no doubt shouting inaudible words in these brief moments.

By sheer strength, Jerry hauled the big tanker rig into a tighter turn, managed to re-cross the double center line and suddenly felt the inside wheels of the tanker-trailer begin to lift. Loaded tankers tend to be top-heavy, and this one, obeying the tilting movement of the gasoline load, was no exception.

The tanker-trailer went over first, by its weight carrying the tractor with it almost without resistance. At high speed the entire rig smashed on its side on the pavement and by its momentum continued, sliding, throwing a shower of sparks.

Gasoline poured from the ruptured tanks. Ignited by the flying sparks, it burst into streams of flame that ran across the highway and across the mowed verge.

But it was the gasoline vapor within the partially emptied tanks that did the damage. Suddenly mixed with air to form the same combination that explodes in automobile cylinders, its power potential far greater than that of dynamite, showered by the sparks that still flew from the friction of sliding metal against pavement, the entire load went up in one gigantic blast that tore a crater in the pavement and flung pieces of burning metal in all directions. A towering column of black smoke rose swiftly to mark the spot.

Ben Hastings, Line Boss, took a deep breath and approached the table where JL studied the afternoon situation reports. "Yes, Ben?" JL said.

"We've lost our north fire line," Ben said.

JL leaned back in his chair. He forced his face to remain calm, placid in the face of this news. The one sector he had considered secure, he thought, was now just one more danger point with no further natural barriers like the highway to contain the monster. "It jumped the road?" Had to be; no other ready explanation. Maybe errant wind currents—

Ben was shaking his head. "Not exactly. A trucker apparently panicked and spread a tanker loaded with gasoline across the highway. It blew up, of course."

JL blinked, but that was all. A freak accident, happen one time in a million, maybe. No matter. It was done. "And the trucker?"

"They may find pieces of him, and they may not."

JL blinked again. Then slowly he nodded. "All right, Ben. Get dug in on a new line as best you can."

Dismissal.

Ben opened his mouth and then closed it again. In silence he turned away. The man was not human, he thought; totally without feelings. Unbelievable.

JL went back to staring at the situation report in front of him, and found that he could not concentrate. He wondered who the trucker was, and how and why he had panicked. Our job, he thought, is the protection of life and property, so we are in a sense responsible. Not really, of course; not in a legal sense. But because of the fire, a man was dead, just like that. How many more would there be? We're at war, he told himself, and in a war there are casualties. It was scant comfort.

There was a new sense of urgency at the 16:30 briefing that afternoon. Phil Sommers, Plans Chief, spoke somberly of the fire's progress during the past twelve hours, and neither the meteorologist nor the Fire Behavior Officer could add any word of cheer.

"And it's not going to get any easier," JL said, addressing the group. "No rain in the forecasts, probable wind, the usual afternoon thunderstorms with dry lighting." His manner, he knew, appeared almost unconcerned. But would it have helped to present a face of gloom? "All right, let's get on with it." As he turned away he beckoned Ben Hastings and Jay Paul.

The two men followed him in silence back to the table he had commandeered as desk. "Ben and I are going to take a little jeep ride," JL told Jay. "You take over here. We'll be in touch on the radio."

Ben drove; JL, map and clipboard on his lap, hung on with his free hand. "More than twenty thousand acres so far," JL said, his voice still under tight control. "And it'll get worse before it gets better." How much worse, was anybody's guess. "Depends in part on the winds." Despite himself, a little of his worry sounded in his tone.

Ben glanced at him curiously. The man did have feelings, after all?

"Our normal weather pattern is southwest-northeast," JL said. Ben knew that already, of course, but JL wanted his thoughts strictly in order. "But sometimes it reverses, and strong wind out of the east—"He shook his head.

"A lot of Forest there," Ben said, nodding. "It could burn all the way across Arizona if it really got out of hand. God knows how many acres, miles. Do we want more line troops?"

"Think it would help?" The teacher making a pupil think for himself.

Ben's answer came slowly. "Not really. Not now."

"Neither do I." There was approbation in JL's voice. "Turn here. Uphill. Let's have a good look at this sector."

Bessie Wingate, leading her crew down the trail, stopped at JL's signal, and walked over to the jeep.

"How's it look?" JL said.

Bessie was dirty and tired and unwilling to make small talk. "You really want to know, or you just asking?"

JL smiled faintly, and waited.

"Stinks," Bessie said then, slightly mollified. "The son of a bitch has pushed us halfway up the mountain, whipping us every foot of the way. I told Jim McColl— his crew relieved us—that as far as I can see, we've lost this whole sector and we might as well admit it and cut our losses." Beneath her yellow hard hat and through the smoke smudges on her face, her belligerence was plain. "And what do you goddam well think of that?"

JL merely nodded, expressionless. "I think you're right."

Ben Hastings, watching in silence, opened his eyes a little wider in surprise.

"Another one hundred, two hundred yards, maybe a little more," Bessie said, "and the bastard'll run out of fuel anyway. Timberline. We're wasting manpower fighting for that last shitty little bit."

JL said, "You agree, don't you, Ben?"

Ben didn't agree, and yet when you looked carefully, you saw that there was some logic to the concept. He nodded.

JL said to Bessie, "Send one of your men back up to tell McColl to let that sector go, and pull his crew over to protect against the fire fishhooking into fresh timber when the downslope breeze begins near sundown."

"I," Bessie said, "will be thoroughly goddamned." She gestured broadly with her shovel. "Who ever heard of anybody listening to the poor bastards on the fire line?"

"And you," JL said, "catch somse food and some rest."

"Shit," Bessie said, "we could go on all night, if we had to."

JL smiled. "We'll need you tomorrow. Let's head back down, Ben."

Ben drove in silence for a time, his face thoughtful. "Sacrificing a little timber for morale, is that it?"

"A good trade-off," JL said. "And her idea does have merit." He pointed off to the right. "Let's see what the situation is over here."

Bellevue Acres, with smoke heavy in places and in others temporarily cleared by convection currents.

"About six hundred people, all told," Ben said. "One hundred and thirty houses." He was silent, looking around at the cluttered driveways and scruffy lawns. "Put it all together, and it wouldn't be worth much more than one of the big places farther on."

"In money, or in people?"

Ben glanced sharply at JL's face, and said nothing. You rarely knew what the man was really thinking, Ben thought, so your best bet was to tread warily.

"If the breeze holds as it is," JL said, "we have no worries here." He gestures with the clipboard. "Vista Hill. I want to reassure Mrs. Wayne."

The two gardeners were still at work. They watched the jeep curiously, saw JL and waved. JL waved back. "Right up to the big house," he said.

Back in the Forest, Ben was thinking as he drove, there were hundreds of men—and a few women, like Bessie, exceptions—in a battle against the destoyer, fire. The battle fatigue he had seen on the faces of Bessie's crew would be lined into almost every face. The deep anger he had seen in Bessie herself would be gnawing at every man's innards because fire becomes a personal enemy, evil incarnate, unfeeling, uncaring, dedicated to sheer destruction, unforgiving, and un- forgiveable, capable of arousing man's deepest emo- tions: blind panic, and hatred.

And here they were, he and JL, the top command in this war, driving up to a big house to speak with an old lady. Unreal.

"It's her Forest too," JL said as if he had been reading Ben's thoughts. "Along with all those people in Belle- vue Acres and the rest who live around here, and elsewhere, the Forest belongs to her. We just work there and try to take care of it for them."

# 15

Mrs. Wayne said, "How thoughtful of you to stop by, Mr. Harmon, just to reassure me, I know. Tea? Sherry?"

"Thank you, no, ma'am. I'm afraid we're a little pressed for time."

To Ben Hastings, the sense of unreality was deepening by the moment. JL, whom he had always considered hard-headed and pragmatic — despite rumors he had heard of a hobby of painting landscapes in oils — seemed to have flipped.

"I quite understand," Mrs. Wayne said. "And I do want to say how much safer I feel now that you are back from — was it Idaho? — and taking charge." Her manner was thoughtful. "Tell me, Mr. Harmon, is this fire the result of what I believe you call prescribed burning? I recall that my husband once had occasion to take that up with the Secretary."

"No, ma'am," JL said. "Prescribed burning had nothing to do with this fire." He was his calm, pleasant, usual self, and yet Ben could sense now a feeling almost of urgency that had not been noticeable before. "As a matter of fact, ma'am," JL said in that same polite way, "if we had been allowed prescribed burning, this fire might well not have become what it has."

Mrs. Wayne thought about it. "I'm afraid I don't understand. Could you make it all a little clearer for me?"

JL did, explaining about the fuel that accumulated on the ground in the Forest, and about the uncontrolled second growth they had had to open with explosives, all of it contributing to the threat of a large conflagration if and when, as had happened, dry lightning struck or someone was careless with a campfire.

Ben listened in wonder, seeing at last the purpose of this visit.

Mrs. Wayne remained thoughtful, and when JL was done, "I see," she said. "I was not aware of all the ramifications, Mr. Harmon, and I thank you for informing me."

JL stood up. Ben rose with him. "We just wanted to make sure that everything was all right here, ma'am," JL said in his guileless way.

"And I do appreciate it," Mrs. Wayne said, and walked with them to the door.

Back in the jeep, going down the long drive, "You were making a pitch," Ben said, feeling the sense of unreality no longer. "Will it do any good?"

"If George Jefferson's right," JL said, "she can pick up the phone and call a couple or three Senators, and the Secretary will damn well listen."

"And maybe, just maybe," Ben said, "we'll be allowed to care for this Forest the way it ought to be cared for."

"Worth a try," JL said. And he added, "Who's this?"

It was a large station wagon pulling alongside, the driver obviously wanting conversation. "Humor him," JL said. Ben pulled over and stopped, and they waited while the driver climbed importantly from the station wagon and came back to them.

"I am Willard P. Spencer," the man said. He gestured. "You are approaching my property."

JL wore his faint, enigmatic smile. He nodded silently.

"I wish to have a crew of your men," Spencer said, "patrolling the perimeter of my land to see to it that this inexcusable fire does not damage my property. I have been in touch with your Regional Office in Albuquerque, and they assure me that everything possible will be done to protect my holdings, and those of others."

"It most certainly will, Mr. Spencer," JL said. "You have my word on it."

Ben sat quiet, expressionless.

"And now if you will excuse us," JL added, "we'll get on with seeing that it's done." He smiled again and nodded as they drove away.

They rode for a little time in silence. "Jesus," Ben said, "is he real?"

"Not only real," JL said, "but in his own way representative too. There are lots more like him."

"How do you stand it?"

"Sometimes I wonder."

They rounded a curve. JL pointed ahead. "Stop here," he said, and wondered at the sense of urgency, almost a sudden physical need that he felt.

Stacy, in her customary jeans and boots and a shirt with sleeves rolled up on her slim, strong arms was standing beside the Cummings mailbox, a bundle of mail in her hands. "I heard you were back," she said, and added without embarrassment, "I felt better knowing that you were in charge."

JL tried and failed to think of a reply. He was conscious that Ben was watching him curiously.

Stacy nodded her head toward the Forest and Sierra Grande, its sharp outlines softened by smoke. "Am I shying at shadows, or is it worse?"

With this woman, JL thought suddenly, he would never be able to say other than the truth. "I'm afraid it's worse." He felt impelled to add, "but still not to worry."

"My horses."

"I've thought of that." He spread his hands.

"We'll cope." Stacy's eyes studied his face with a strange intensity and it was as if Ben were not even there. "And after it's all done," Stacy said, "you can come over one night, and tell me about it."

"I'd like that."

Stacy said then almost as if suddenly embarrassed and searching for a change of subject, "Clouds over there. Rain?"

JL followed her pointing finger, and shook his head. "Unhappily, no. The best we'll get is probably virga and that won't help a bit." He saw Stacy's faint frown of puzzlement, and explained his term. "Virga is precipitation that doesn't reach the ground. It evaporates first. What you see over there that looks like a ragged curtain. In this thirsty country you see a lot of it."

"So," Stacy said, "all you can do is hope."

JL's faint smile appeared. "That's about the size of it. We have a lot of practice at hoping. Ben, let's get back to work."

Stacy made a vague gesture with the hand that held the mail. "Luck," she said, and watched them drive off. She was not at all sure why, but she admitted to herself that she was becoming more and more impressed by, and even interested in, JL Harmon.


In the jeep the radio came alive with Jay Paul's voice from the command post saying, "Come in, JL. JL, come in. Over." There were undertones of excitement verging on hysteria behind the words.

186

JL picked up the microphone and spoke out his name. "Over," he added.

"We've got a new break-out," Jay Paul said. "Beyond Route one-four. Isolated. It's either spontaneous or incendiary. And Los Ojos reports two convicts missing." The words were coming faster and faster. "Maybe they're responsible. Maybe they—"

"Slow down," JL said, breaking in. "You're racing your motor. Have the convicts been spotted? Over."

"Negative."

"Then they could be anywhere, doing anything. Have you sent an attack crew in to the new area?"

"Not yet. I wanted to—"

"Then send one in. Now. And forget the convicts under the bed." Despite himself, JL realized that his impatience and annoyance were showing. He glanced sideways at Ben Hastings, whose face was carefully turned forward, his eyes on the road. "Over and out," JL said into the mike, hung the instrument on its dashboard hook and leaned back in his seat. "You heard," he said. "Do you think we have an arsonist at work?" His voice was quiet again.

"No."

"Why not?"

"It just isn't likely here."

Privately, JL agreed, but still he pursued it. "Explain that."

"I don't have too much faith in statistics," Ben Hastings said, his eyes still on the road, "but sometimes they do give a basis for judgment."

"And?"

JL knew the facts just as well as he did, Ben was thinking, but JL didn't ask questions without reasons, so he deserved an answer. "No more than 5% of our wildland fires here in the west are incendiary," Ben said. "Those are our compiled stats, and there's no reason to doubt them." His voice altered suddenly. "Oh," he said. "I see what you mean. Jay comes here straight from the southern piney woods, and there they have up to 55% incendiary fires."

"And habit dies hard," JL said, nodding. A bright boy, Ben, he thought. "Something to remember."

Ben shook his head slowly. The sky was darkened by smoke, the taste of conflagration was in the air they breathed, awareness of the growing magnitude of BACKSLOPE was all around them—and JL could go from detail to detail, from Bessie Wingate to Mrs. Wayne to Willard P. Spencer to Stacy Cummings to Jay Paul without even shifting gears, and yet still keep the big picture in mind. "You don't miss much, do you?" Ben said. There was admiration behind the words.

JL's face was expressionless. "Only in some directions," he said. "In others, I can't even see the main point until my nose gets rubbed in."

It was at times like this, commanding a large operation, keeping all the details in hand and in proper relationship, well aware of his competence—it was then that his shortcomings in other facets of life came so strongly to mind.

He was not a learned man, and from time to time he supposed that a lack of advanced education had hampered his development, although he was not really sure that this was so because what in his opinion he lacked came not from books or study, but from one's own self. It was as simple as that.

In JL's estimation, the world was divided into two kinds of people—specialists, and whole men and women. Specialists could be useful, even necessary; but the whole man, the one who could find a handle on any situation and somehow cope with it—this was the man you could look up to, and follow. And in JL's estimation, this was where he himself fell short.

His basic problem, he had long thought, was that his competence lay more with *things* than with *people*. This had been Madge's contention, and she had rarely missed an opportunity to bring it up.

"Trees, bushes, rocks, mountains, even those damn clouds you try to paint—they all mean more to you than real people," Madge would say. "You don't like cities because they're *people* places. You'd much rather sit and stare at a running creek that doesn't even have fish in it." Madge was a country girl, and her love of cities was that of the deeply involved convert—uncritical, ecstatic and unswerving in its devotion.

"You may be right," became for JL the easiest and least contentious reply. And, he had told himself on a number of occasions, maybe at that she *was* right.

Oh, he was easy enough with people—men, that was, not with women—and his range of acquaintance was almost limitless. He had maybe three, four that he thought of as friends—Andy McIlvain, Ken Delacorte, for example—but if and when Madge pushed him hard, he really couldn't say that he had any intimates.

"Except you," he would sometimes point out.

"That isn't the same at all."

"We get pretty intimate sometimes."

"That's not a nice way to talk."

"Why not?"

"If you don't understand, I can't explain it. Anyway, I'm talking about men."

"You don't seem to have any close women friends."

"You've never given me the chance. We've never lived in a real town, a city where I could meet interesting people." Like those in the movie and TV magazines was what she meant, but Madge had never said this aloud.

Sometimes JL tried to justify what amounted to his

singleness of purpose by pretending to believe that he was merely doing his job and doing it well. But that argument, examined, fell flat because there were others, Andy McIlvain for example, who were just as devoted to their work, but who also managed to live separate, wholly different lives when they were off-duty. JL had his oil painting, and that was about it, and even there, as Madge had pointed out, his choice of subjects was strictly limited.

Ben said suddenly, "Why don't I drop you off at your house? Jay and I can take the night shift and you can catch some sleep. You've been on your feet for how long? Anything urgent comes up, we can always phone you."

JL thought about it. "How do you and Jay get along?"

"Well enough."

"Who's your relief man?"

"Jerry Weinstock."

JL knew him. A good man, and that, in itself, was another high mark in Ben's favor — that he would obviously not tolerate less. "Turn your line boss duties over to him," JL said, "and you hold Jay's hand. I don't want to replace him unless I have to." It was a ticklish situation he was creating, he knew, because Jay was technically Ben's superior. On the other hand, in merely this one day, he, JL, had learned who was the better man. He glanced at Ben's face which showed nothing. "Think you can do it that way?"

"If you say so."

"Any argument between you and Jay on something you think can't wait," JL said, "I want you to call me pronto."

"Will do."

They drove for a time in silence. Almost exactly at the summer solstice as they were, twilight lingered in the smoke-hazed sky.

"It's going to be a long night," JL said, "and you're going to lose more ground. Expect that. Nighttime cooling will produce downslope winds. You know that, but it doesn't hurt to emphasize it. In places, you're going to lose your fire line. You know that too, but somehow at night, when you're the man in charge, every piece of ground you lose seems that much more important, even disastrous. It isn't."

Ben listened as he drove, and thought that this was a side of JL he had never seen before, a kindlier, more sympathetic side, explaining and warning rather than simply ordering. He wondered why the change, but did not see fit to ask.

"Funny thing about nighttime," JL said. "Fire always seems bigger, and hotter, and spreading faster. I've seen whole crews go through hell just sweating and swearing in daytime, and then suddenly see things that aren't there and panic at night. Even when you don't see things, or hear them, you may begin to wonder if you are going to hack it, or if the fire's going to run away from you in the end and not stop until it runs clear out of fuel." Again he glanced at Ben's face. "You know what I mean?"

"I think so."

"The thing you have to remember," JL said, "is that fighting a fire isn't really like fighting a war. People say it is, but they're wrong. In a war, you can always surrender, throw down your weapons, throw in the towel — and the fighting stops. But a fire won't accept surrender and there is no way to make it stop. You whip it, or it whips you and all the people and all the property you're trying to protect. There's the difference, and it's a big one."

He felt a little silly expounding platitudes like this, but as nearly as he could, he wanted Ben to get into his, JL's, mind, to think as he thought, and to react as he would react. Impossible, of course, but all he could do was try.

Sleep did not come for JL, which was unusual, because he had trained himself to sleep just about anywhere anytime. Worst of all, the thoughts that plagued him into wakefulness were futile.

He could not shake the memory of Stacy Cummings saying that she felt better because he was in charge, nor the warm certainty in her voice when she said that after it was all done, they would talk. He tried not to read meaning into her words, and instead found all manner of ridiculous possibilities running around in his mind.

He also tried not to think that if George Jefferson had allowed him to stay here and handle the fire from the start instead of bundling him off to Boise, the crews on the line would now be simply cold-trailing, patrolling the perimeter, to make sure that nothing started up again out of the near-dead ashes, instead of fighting step by step in the sharp, acrid, choking smoke, facing the terrifying nighttime flames in what in too many places was merely a rearguard, not even a holding, action.

He got out of bed at last and padded into his studio as into a refuge, not turning on the lights but merely standing staring through the large window at Sierra Grande's dim bulk reaching high into the moonlight and at the flames clearly visible on its lower slopes and in places much higher, while the futile thoughts and ridiculous possibilities went on and on.

He did turn the lights on briefly, looked once more at the unfinished canvas on the easel and was tempted to take it off and put it in a corner, face to the wall, a part of his life for the present set aside.

Instead, he turned the lights off, went out of the studio, and in the bathroom sloshed cold water on his face before putting his boots back on and going to the telephone to call Ben for transportation. Morning would come eventually, and in even hazy daylight things would appear a little, if not much, better.

On the mountain the evening downslope breeze coming off the snow probed the trees and set aspen leaves to whispering. It was cold.

"So now we stuck up here on this goddam mountain," Felipe Vigil said. "How long we stay here?"

Frank Orwell resented the implication that it was all his fault. "You saw the fuzz when we tried to go down." Not all that many police, but the shock of finding any had seemed to increase their numbers. "State fuzz, too," Orwell added, "Not just local yokels."

"So now they know we here."

"Not necessarily —" Orwell almost added, "you greaseball," but stopped the words just in time, and made himself calm down. "We stay out of sight, they may think we got off the mountain ahead of them and are halfway to Arizona by now." Probably wishful thinking, but Orwell had long ago discovered that any hope, however forlorn, was better than admission that there was absolutely no way to go.

"And cold enough to freeze the *cojones* of a stone *mono*." Vigil's outlook tended to vacillate between bright optimism and dark hopelessness. "We freeze tonight for goddamn sure."

"I thought the anglo chick was keeping you warm."

"You real funny anglo *hijo de puta*," Vigil said. "How about a fire?"

"No way. Those fire-fighting crews maybe couldn't care less whether or not we're up here, but they spot a fire and they'll bust their asses to get to it and put it out. Probably five, six in a chopper, and then what do we do?"

"You bigshot anglo brain, you tell me."

"Walk and try to stay warm. Think about the anglo chick." Orwell even smiled. "As a matter of fact, I could use some more of that myself."



Les Lawry was more exasperated than usual. "God-damnit, Cindy Lou, whyn't you watch where you're going? I look around and there you are either on your face or on your ass, and—"

"Mom's hurt, Pop," Tad said. He dropped the branch he had broken off to use as a walking staff, and knelt beside his mother, trying to remember his Boy Scout First Aid. "Here?" He touched her left ankle gently. "Can you wiggle it? Not much, just a little to see how bad it is."

"Oh, for Christ's sake!" Les said. "Can you walk, Cindy Lou? Tell me that. Can you walk?"

"I think we're going to need help, Pop," Tad said. "I don't think she'd better even try to walk."

"Well, goddamnit, she can't just sit here!"

"We could carry her. Scout's lift."

"What the hell is that? Besides, do you know where in Christ's name we are? You're the Boy Scout. How about trees and what is it—moss only on one side?"

"I'm sorry, Les," Cindy Lou said. "I didn't mean to twist it."

"Okay, okay," Les said. "Now let me think."

"If we hadn't come here in the first place—" Cindy Lou began.

"Not now, Mom," Tad said quickly. "Let Pop think."

Les looked at the boy. "You got any ideas?"

Tad had been thinking about their situation for a long time. He said now in a hesitant voice, "I think we're safe enough here."

"What makes you think that? Speak up, boy, how come out here in the middle of a forest fire we're all of a sudden safe?"

Tad looked around at the blackened desolation. "It's all burned over. There's nothing left to catch fire."

"He's right, Les," Cindy Lou said.

"You've got a bad ankle," Les said. "You stay out of this." He too looked around. "So, okay, maybe we're better off here than I thought." Grudging admission. "I didn't think about it much. So what do you think we do now?"

"Maybe we'd better stay here," Tad said, "until it gets light."

"Then what do we do?"

"We can lay out a signal for a helicopter to see."

"Oh, Les!" Cindy Lou said. "Then they can help us."

"Yeah." Les thought about it. "But they'll want to know about the jeep." His face brightened suddenly. "Got it! We'll say we were trying to get away from the fire, and that's why we drove into the Wilderness. To save our necks. How about that? True, isn't it?"

Tad looked at his mother. Cindy Lou looked at the ground. Neither spoke.

"Okay," Les said. "Now what I want to know, is how bad is that goddamned ankle? Can you walk on it if you have to? Tell me that, Cindy Lou."

"If I have to," Cindy Lou said, "I can try."

"Okay," Les said again, in command once more. "Now Tad, you see about getting a nice level place and sweep it clean of ashes. Use a branch. A tidy camp, that's what we want. And we'll just stay here until morning. That's the way I see it."

196

"I'm not being logical," Elsie Edwards said. "I know that. And I'm not being brave, either. I'm being just what I've always hated—stupidly helplessly female." Funny, the tears were no longer even close. But a tight, visceral feeling she was afraid would lead to vomiting was something she could not control, let alone ignore.

"You're doing fine," Don said. "Just fine." Words were so *damned inadequate*! "My fault." He tried to smile. It was a poor effort. "We should have chosen the Dorchester after all, even if we couldn't afford it. Or one of those gingerbread—"

"Stop it!" Elsie was silent a moment, fighting down the nausea. She said in a calmer voice, "How's your poor head?"

"Better. Really, honestly, better. I can focus now, just like ordinary people." Almost true. The terrible throbbing had subsided to a constant lesser level of ache, and his mind felt clearer. He tried to sound calm, competently objective. "We're very close to the timberline," he said. "Above it, we're safe from fire, but not from those—rapists." It was difficult to say the word aloud.

Elsie sat silent, for the moment unable to speak. It was over, she told herself, and she was alive, physically unharmed if psychically bruised beyond anything she might have imagined. If it were to threaten again, she thought, I believe I would kill—either them, or myself.

"The problem is," Don said as logically as he could, "the only place we can be completely safe is below the fire. And—" Again he attempted a lighter touch, accompanied by a wry smile. "—the trouble is that I don't see quite how we're going to get there from here."

Elsie took a deep breath, held it and let it out slowly. "You're trying," she said then. "I know that, honest." Her eyes searched Don's face. "But I don't want to be shielded or sheltered. Not any more. It's all changed now." Miraculously, all at once the nausea was gone, and in its place was steady anger, banked and glowing. "We can't go up and we can't go down. That's what you're saying, isn't it?"

Don said slowly, "Pretty much." The sudden change in her was almost palpable and somehow shocking.

"We can't go up," Elsie said, "because you're thinking of me. So am I. But I'm thinking of you too. They'll do again what they did to me—or they'll try. But they'll kill you. They're that kind of animals. One of them, the anglo, almost shot you before, when they had—finished with me. This time they'd do it."

Don closed his eyes briefly and tried to imagine how it had been. "I didn't know that," he said.

"We can't go down," Elsie said, "because of the fire. But at least it's—clean. The smoke even smells clean—if that's possible."

"The evening breeze blowd downhill now," Don said. "That's how it happens in these mountains. It may hold the fire, at least temporarily. And there's a moon." He was weighing conditions, considering their situation from as many angles as he could. "We can move further on around the mountain, just below timberline as we are here."

"How far? There's that lake you've told me about. And the cliff above it. We'll have to go up when we reach that."

Don nodded in silence.

Elsie nodded her head toward the fringe of trees and the open mountainside above them. "What will *they* be doing?"

"Probably the same thing."

"So we'll meet?"

"We'll try not to." Don shook his head angrily. "That's the best I can give you at the moment, baby."

198

Elsie nodded. "Then for now, it has to be good enough."

"I'm sorry."

A shake of the head this time. "No apologies," Elsie said, and gestures down at herself. "I'm the cause. If I weren't a woman they wouldn't be interested."

Don could smile at last and mean it. "Neither would I," he said.


Three times during the night Stacy awakened and in her nightgown padded through the house on bare feet and out to the patio to listen for any indications of restiveness or near-panic from the horsebarn. All she heard were the normal night sounds, an occasional stamping hoof, a long sigh, the rasping, grating noise of friction as one of the animals rubbed himself against unyielding wooden structure.

The taste of smoke in the air seemed stronger, she thought, but that could well have been no more than nighttime imagination. But the glow above the forest, like the glow above a city at night, only stronger — this was not imagination; and high on the mountain's slopes, open flames were visible, these as well entirely too real.

The moon was close to full, and even through the smoke haze it cast black shadows that seemed to her, as always at night, alive. With only a small, practised effort, she could turn the big cholla into a crouching bear, the carefully scattered lichen-covered rocks among the gravel into a herd of snuffling peccaries, the row of poplars into a giant's fence and the deep, internal corner of the patio into a secret cave entrance.

Growing up alone, she had created her own world, and kept it to herself, secure from prying, perhaps scoffing, grown-ups. She supposed most kids did that.

Perhaps it was because she had never had real intimates that the habit remained, still strong, still secret. It was not a refuge in the true sense, this secret world of hers, something to retreat into when things got too rough. By and large the rougher things became, the better she responded to them.

"They sure God got things a little mixed up when they put you together, honey," her father had said more than once, smiling a little in that admiring way he sometimes had when he dealt with her. "You've been taught to be a nice gentle filly, and every so often you turn up wildcat. What in the world did Bobby Joe (or Willie or Duane or Buford) do or say to lay your ears back and bring you out snarling and spitting?"

Smiling, the sudden temper flash already past, "The son of a bitch thinks he can take me for granted, and I just thought it was time to set him straight."

"That the way they talk in Boston?"

"They may. At least, now they know the words."

On this night, standing in the patio in her bare feet, surrounded by the interesting, but not threatening shadows—the bear, the peccaries and the rest—she faced the scene, the flowing sky and the open flames high on the mountain while she considered the implications and possible courses of action.

"Prepare for the worst and hope for the best is the way a lot of folks operate," her father had said. "But I've found that most times you can narrow it down quite a bit by taking the worst possible case and the best possible case and figuring that what's going to happen will most likely be somewhere in between."

The worst possible case, of course, would be a violent wind shift that would drive the flames in her direction, And Stacy had no illusions that against that threat JL and all his people would be able to put up more than a stubborn rearguard resistance until the wind shifted again. And what might remain of her house, the horsebarn, the other outbuildings and all the lovely property after the flames had finally been extinguished did not bear thinking about.

The best possible case would be sudden, continuing heavy rain, but JL himself had scratched that possibility and done it in a way that Stacy liked. He had not cursed the luck or in any way tried to fix the blame. Nor had he sounded like a perpetual pessimist who went through life glorying in the cynicism of expected defeat.

Instead, his attitude had said clearly, "Tough tit, but that's the way it is. It's a fair fight. Let's get on with it."

And so, assuming conditions somewhere between the two extremes, she set her plans, which meant first establishing priorities.

The horses were her primary concern. To an animal, they gave her obedience and loyalty; some, like Sam, also gave affection. They were her charge, her responsibility, and she would not let them down.

Juanita and her son Pancho also relied on her, of course, but in a sudden emergency they could fend for themselves simply by getting into Juanita's car and driving away. Stacy would issue orders to that effect, although she had an idea that young Pancho, whose devotion to the horses very nearly equalled her own, would refuse to budge until all animals were seen to safety.

And then, of course, actually no concern of hers but still impossible to ignore, there was Bart Jones in his wheelchair. Thinking of him as she stared up at the flames on the mountain, watching their leaping, flashing, terrible splendor, she was reminded of that old ethical question — whom do you rescue from the burning building, grandma or the baby?

Suppose it were to come to a choice between seeing

Bart or the horses to safety? Ridiculous, no? "Ridiculous, yes," she said aloud, and, annoyed with herself for seeking trouble, padded on her bare feet back through the sleeping house to bed.

Well before midnight, Ben Hastings decided that JL was right: at night even with an almost full moon showing hazily through the smoke-filled air, things looked different, somehow more threatening than they had in daylight. He had noticed the phenomenon before, but it was only now, feeling the full sense of the responsibilities JL had obliquely put upon him, that the nighttime difference took on real importance.

For example, from the chief of one of the farflung line crews, through his sector boss to *his* division boss to Jerry Weinstock, Ben's night replacement as line boss, to Jay Paul and Ben jointly came word that someone was setting off dynamite charges near the fire perimeter which was now into State, no longer Federal land, and what to do about that?

"Now I know we've got an arsonist out there," Jay Paul said, "and if he's using dynamite, God only knows what'll happen next, or where. We'd better call in State Police and tell them we've got a firebug loose. Maybe it's even those escaped convicts."

In broad daylight, Ben thought, he would have put Jay's attitude down to simple over-reaction. Now it seemed closer to hysteria. "Maybe I'd better take a run out there and see what's doing," he said. "Messages do get garbled." Unconsciously, he was modelling himself on JL, keeping his own reaction as mild, as apparently unconcerned, as possible.

"Hell's fire," Jay said, "how can there be any doubt? People don't just go around setting off dynamite charges." He shook his head angrily. "Okay. Go ahead.

But let me know soon as you can."

The crew chief on the perimeter was grimy and short-tempered. By the light of flames that leaped and cavorted through a patch of scrub oak and a sprinkling of juniper clinging to broken ground, Ben could make out streaks on the crew chief's face where sweat rivulets had dissolved channels through the accumulated dirt. His eyes seemed overlarge, as if carefully outlined in oriental kohl make-up. "Dumb son of a bitch," the crew chief said. "Stupid goddamn fool. I told the mother—"

"Let me have it from the top," Ben said, sounding like JL himself as he had spoken patiently to Bessie Wingate on the jeep trail. "Who was setting off charges?"

"Goddamn fucking Highway Department idiot. Orders, he says. They're widening the highway over yonder, so come quitting time they set off charges, and clear away the broken rock the next day after the dust settles. You know what the son of a bitch told me?"

Ben waited in silence, again as he had seen JL do.

"He said," the crew chief said, " 'So okay, you got a goddamn fire. That's your worry. I got a job to do, and you can take your goddamn fire and shove it. I'm through for the day and I'm going home.' "

"Okay," Ben said. "I'll take it from here. There won't be any more dynamite charges."

"They could just as easy as not set another goddamn fire, couldn't they? With things as dry as they are, what in hell are they doing blasting around forest land, anyway?"

"Good question," Ben said, and turned back to his jeep radio to pass the word to Jay Paul, whose reaction was explosive.

"Jesus H. Jumping Christ!" Jay said, the words coming over the air like so many exploding firecrackers. "Now we've got the goddamn civilian Highway

Department deliberately fouling us up! How do they expect us to bring a fire under control when everybody is working against us?"

"I'm coming in," Ben said, still that calm way. "Over and out."


In the darkness, Debby said, "You're worried, A. I've been watching. Is it the fire?"

"Imagination," Aaron said. "Yours."

"No." Debby's voice was definite. "Last night—I guess it's night before last now—you said that funny thing about bringing your fiddle and watching Rome from the Club. You were talking about that Emperor with the funny name, weren't you? The Roman one?"

Aaron was silent, vaguely shamed. He had no business teasing her with references she could only partly comprehend. She deserved far better than that. Kitten she might be, but she also had a sensitivity, wholly intuitive, which he could in no way match, or even comprehend. And so it behooved him to tread carefully lest he hurt her.

"And you haven't been sleeping tonight," Debby said. "I've been listening, and you haven't. I can always tell."

"I snore?" Mock solemnity. "You never told me."

"You don't snore, A. But when you sleep, you breathe quiet and evenlike, and tonight you haven't."

Aaron said gently, "That means you've been awake too. Why?"

"I don't like the smoke. And I'm worried about you."

What was that silly TV ad, Aaron thought, the one that said now was the time to brew some particular brand of coffee? There were times when the absurdity of the world seemed without end. And the absurdity of himself, a middle-aged man trying to cope with a young woman's unease and having no faintest idea how to go about it. He said, "At least you have reasons. I don't."

"Honest, A? There isn't anything bothering you? Anything I've done? Or maybe haven't done?"

"Sins neither of commission nor omission." He sounded, damn it, as if he were grading a term paper, not talking to a troubled wife. His normal world, the world of the brief and the courtroom had absolutely no place in bed. "I'm being difficult, honey," he said. "And I have no reason for that, either. Forgive me, please."

"It's all right, A. Honest." There was a silence. "Is there anything you'd like? I'm not very good at saying it. I guess I never learned to put these things into words. But if, you know, you'd like—"

"Slap and tickle is what the British say," Aaron said, trying to ease the embarrassment.

Debby giggled. "That's a funny way to put it. But, okay, I guess we know what we mean, don't we?" She giggled again. "I sound like a bride, don't I, and that's pretty funny too, isn't it?"

"You sound," Aaron said, "like a girl who grew up with old-fashioned values which are very rare these days. Along with them seems to go a touch of prudishness, too, and maybe that's unfortunate. But the balance is so heavily on the side of good, that there simply isn't any contest. I like you just the way you are, honey."

"That's nice, A." There was one more soft giggle. "But you haven't answered my question. About—slap and tickle, I mean. Would you like that?"

Aaron wondered if the TV writers of commercials would suggest brewing coffee at a time like this, too, and decided that he wouldn't put it past their sniggly little souls. "You know, honey," he remarked in a conversational tone, "that is far and away the best offer I've had all week, and I accept with pleasure."

"I never knew anybody who talked like you," Debby said. There was warmth in her voice. "I guess it comes from going to court so often." There was pride in her voice too. "Let me get out of my nightie."


JL was at the command post, a cup of steaming black coffee in front of him when the phone call came. The night dispatcher said, "Call for you. I didn't know whether to patch it through or not. A woman, name of Cummings—"

"Put her through." Were thoughts really telepathic?

Stacy said, "I apologize—"

"No."

"I don't scare easy, but my horses—" She left the sentence unfinished.

JL had already talked with Jay Paul and Ben and read the reports. "For the present, you're okay."

"That's good enough." There was relief in her voice, and then a sudden change of tone. "And how about you? I tried your house."

"I'm okay, too."

There was a short silence. "Keep it that way," Stacy said, and hung up.

JL put the phone down gently, wearing, and feeling, his first smile in days.

Ben studied him curiously. "Anything wrong?" Ben said.

JL shook his head, smiling still. He said nothing.

## 17

Billy Bob Barker, pharmacist, was the mayor of Sanrio. ("The Fastest Growing Little Town in the Southwest." Not wholly true, but who was to argue?)

Billy Bob opened his pharmacy promptly at 08:00 on this morning as he had done every weekday morning for the last twenty-seven years. His first visitor, not a customer, was Willard P. Spencer.

"I am far from satisfied with the progress that is being made in bringing this fire under control," Spencer said. "You are the mayor, and I, as a citizen, hereby register my dissatisfaction."

Billy Bob was by nature a peaceable man with a deep faith in the power of negotiation. "Why," he said, "old JL is the best there is, Mr. Spencer. George—that's the Sanrio Forest Supervisor—has all the faith in the world in him."

"That may be, but there are no results yet to justify that faith, and I for one think a change is in order. If I must, I will telephone Washington and register my complaints there." The threat was largely bluff, although Spencer did have Washington acquaintances in high places, old family friends.

"Well, now, there's no call to do that," Billy Bob said. "This here's a local fire, maybe a little bigger than most, but in its way the kind of thing we have to put up with every year. And JL has always coped real good.

He knows the Forest, none better, and—"

"Nevertheless," Spencer said, "when I can see flames from my patio, I am no longer complacent." Particularly since he no longer had insurance, but he left that unsaid.

"Well," Billy Bob said doubtfully, "I can talk to old George. He's Federal, of course, and me being mayor of the town doesn't cut too much ice, but I can give her a try."

"You do that," Spencer said, turned away and walked out, almost running into Ada Loving whose smile and fabled body in halter and shorts he admired, but failed to recognize. Spencer was not a movie-goer.

"Sunscreen," Ada Loving said, advancing on Billy Bob whose chin was just about on a level with those incredible breasts. "They have funny numbers, I understand," Ada Loving added, "or, rather, I don't understand, but my dermatologist says to use the highest number." She smiled again, showing perfectly even, expensively capped white teeth.

"Yes, ma'am," Billy Bob said, and scuttled to the sunscreen shelf.

Ada Loving bent over a glass case to study its contents, thereby consciously exposing her breasts almost to their nipples. "Isn't this fire terrible?" she said without looking up, and added with no change of either tone or emphasis, "You do have a lovely selection of perfumes."

Billy Bob, a clutch of sunscreen bottles in his hands, stared down the front of Ada Loving's scant halter and swallowed hard. "Terrible," he said. "Yes. And nice perfume, like you say." He stood frozen.

Ada Loving straightened, but not too much. Her smile was brilliant. "I'm a stranger in town, but you probably know that already."

"Yes, ma'am." Betty Sue, his fifteen-year-old daughter, Billy Bob was thinking, was going to squeal and almost faint when she heard that Ada Loving was actually in the pharmacy and standing *that* close.

"And when you don't know anybody," Ada Loving said, reading his thoughts as easily as if they had been displayed on a prompter, "you don't really have anyone to lean on." She moved her shoulders gently. The action did strange things to the halter and the flesh the halter partially contained. His Honor's eyes, she thought, were almost standing out on stalks. "And I'm terrified of fire," she concluded, "especially when it's coming closer." Over to you, buster.

Billy Bob licked his dry lips. "We don't none of us like fire very much," he said.

"I'd feel so much better, safer," Ada Loving said, "if a few of those brave men in the yellow shirts and hardhats could be just a little nearer to my house. You don't think that could be arranged, do you? I mean, you're the mayor, a very important man, and if you asked—?" She left the sentence unfinished.

Billy Bob was not unacquainted with approaches of just about every size and character, hinting or asking right out for favors that ran all the way from fixing speeding tickets to arranging variations in zoning regulations. None had been quite of this quality or appeal, true, but the basic similarities remained. He side-stepped with the ease of long practice. "Well, I'll tell you, ma'am," he said, "I can't promise anything. Not a thing."

"Of course not." Ada Loving knew her way around too.

"But," Billy Bob said, "I could talk to somebody, maybe, and see what might be arranged. Just might, you understand."

"Of course. And, believe me, I do appreciate your concern. I mean, not knowing me and all, to go to any trouble at all would be just dear of you, and I would appreciate it."

"I'll see what I can do." Billy Bob drew his eyes reluctantly from the fleshly feast and stared at the bottles in his hands. "Now about your sunscreen. I'd recommend this one, unless you have a different choice."

"That one will be just fine," Ada Loving said. "I trust your judgement completely."

As Ada Loving walked out, Billy Bob watched her shapely bottom undulating gracefully, and reflected, as Aaron Swift had, that it was remarkable indeed that the rear view of the woman was every bit as appealing as the view from the front.

When she had turned out of his sight, he went out to the sidewalk himself, partly to follow her progress down the block, but partly also to gaze up at the sky and the big mountain and to assess the smoke that rose from the Forest.

Willard P. Spencer was a horse's ass, Billy Bob had already decided, and probably all there was to Ada Loving was already on display, but, damn it, both of them were absolutely right in their concern: the fire did look worse this morning rather than better. It was just possible that JL had fought too many fires and was no longer the man he once had been. A call on old George Jefferson would not be wasted time and effort after all.

BACKSLOPE made the local TV7 news that morning, with spectacular air shots taken from the TV7 chopper and gee-whiz commentary from TV7's ace newsman, Charter Norris. "TV7 has attempted to contact JL Harmon, Forest Service Fire Management Officer, who was long ago and with reason dubbed 'the anonymous man'," Norris's solemn voice said, "but all efforts have failed. And the fire is no closer to being controlled now than it was at this time yesterday. Sanrio residents are beginning to wonder if the town itself is in danger."

George Jefferson, on the horn to JL at the command post, said, "Is it?"

JL, with the reports from the 04:30 briefing in the forefront of his mind, said, "is what what?"

"TV7 says people are beginning to wonder if the town is in danger."

"Carter Norris reporting?"

"He has a big following, JL. Folks believe him."

"They believed Chicken Little too. The town is not in danger unless—"He left it hanging.

"Unless." Jefferson said the word musingly, fully understanding its implications. He said, "Unexpected, violent wind shift?"

"That could make things difficult. Any kind of high winds could. Power lines down, starting small scattered fires. A trailer park torn up and gas lines ruptured. You know all that as well as I do, George. We were going to have a green belt around the town, remember? It would have acted as a firebreak as well as a park."

"Do you need more troops?"

"We may, but not yet."

"What's the weather forecast?"

"More of the same. No precipitation in sight, at least none that could help us."

"Injuries?"

"It's all in the status reports, George."

"I've read them. Between the lines too. Do you want to replace Jay Paul? If you do, go ahead. I made a mistake. I admit it."

"I'm keeping him on a tether. He may be all right yet."

There was a silence. Jefferson said at last, "I'm getting pressure, JL."

"I gathered."

"All the way from Santa Fe, *and* Washington."

"Santa Fe?"

"The Governor. Who wants to be Senator."

JL was silent.

Jefferson said, "Backfire? You've considered that?"

"Do you want to replace me, George? Ben Hastings is a good man."

"I won't even answer that. How's your ankle?"

"And I won't answer that, George. That all?"

JL hung up and leaned back in the camp chair to look up at Andy McIlvain. "You've got a beef?"

"I've got thirteen men, counting myself, unassigned."

"I need you on standby. If I didn't, you'd be out there on the ground somewhere."

"Damn it, pappy, you know what it's like sitting around. You remember that, don't you? Where do you think you may need us? Maybe we could go in now and—"

"I don't know where I'll need you."

Andy let his breath out in an explosive sigh. "Oh, Christ! You've got one of your visions, is that it?"

"Not really."

It was not visions that he had, JL thought, but rather occasional *feelings*, hunches, maybe, whatever they were, sometimes too strong to ignore. You could plan a campaign to suppress this or any other wildland fire, taking into account climatic conditions such as temperature, humidity and wind, the terrain and the kinds of fuel the fire would feed on, the availability of fire-fighting forces and equipment and even the capabilities and morale of the troops—and sometimes you would *know* right from the start that you could not cover all contingencies, that something, as with that exploding gasoline tanker truck, would be bound to pop up when you least expected it to alter the situation.

Suppressing a wildland fire, like fighting a battle, was not pure move-and-counter-move as in a bridge hand or a game of chess. It was, or it could be, more like roulette, sometimes defying the odds, regardless of what the book said.

"I don't know where I'll need you," he repeated, "or what I'll want you to do. But I want you in reserve, available." That feeling was overpowering.

Andy said, "George Jefferson would wet his pants if he knew how you sometimes run a fire, part by the book, part by the seat of your pants and part sheer hunch." He shook his head in slow wonderment. "Like up Valle Ciego way—what was that fire's name? Hellfire we called it, and it was, but how did you know it was going to run that ridge the way it did?"

"I didn't." JL smiled faintly, remembering. "But it was always a chance. So go on back to the field and toss more cards into a helmet or pitch more pennies. But be ready to suit up in a hurry."

Andy started toward his jeep, then stopped and came back. "That Ada Loving, the sexpot in the movies. You know she's in town?"

JL nodded silently.

"She was on TV this morning," Andy said. "Jesus, what a body!"

"Maybe you'll have a chance to rescue her," JL said, "throw her over your shoulder like they do in movies. Now beat it."

The 04:30 briefing had gone about as JL had anticipated it would, which was to say with a strong undertone, not of pessimism, but of near-anger at continual frustration as weather and circumstances such as the exploding gasoline truck seemed to conspire against all their efforts; and a deep determination that, as Ben Hastings, not normally a profane man, put it, "we'll whip the son of a bitch yet, regardless."

In their pre-briefing conference, Ben had told JL, "We lost ground all around, as you said we might." He shook his head. "The nighttime winds seemed to blow in circles, and a couple of areas we thought were secure, got hit, and wiped out, before we even knew it had happened. Here, for example." He put his finger on the large-scale topographical map.

JL glanced at it and said without hesitation, "Lodgepole pine." He nodded. "It goes in a hurry."

"If it had been ponderosa," Ben said, "we might have had a chance to get organized in time. Sorry about that."

JL shook his head. "It happened, just the way it happens all the time. We try, but we can't be everywhere in force at once." I'm sounding like a coach giving a pep talk, he thought, and glanced at young Ben's face for impatience at the platitudes, but found none. "How did you handle that Highway Department hassle?" he said.

"I called Santa Fe and got the Cabinet Secretary out of bed. He didn't like it, and I imagine the Highway Department chief isn't going to like it, either, but there won't be any more blasting." Ben hesitated. "Maybe I stepped out of line—"

"I'll back you," JL said, "and so will George Jefferson, and Regional Headquarters in Albuquerque. When you're dealing with just plain damn fools, there's no sense trying to pussyfoot." He nodded again. "Good job all around. After the briefing, get some sleep."

Now, the briefing over, Ben and Andy McIlvain gone and daylight scarcely begun, here came Stacy Cummings, riding that big sorrel gelding named Sam as if she and the horse were one. She stepped down from the saddle with a movement as natural as stepping out of an elevator, and, leaving the reins dangling and the big horse thus securely tethered, came over to the folding table. She was unsmiling.

"Don't get up. I'll sit for a moment." She pulled up a camp chair and sank into it, obviously ill at ease.

She said without preamble, "I shouldn't have called you, bothered you. I'm sorry. Things—look different at night." She hesitated. "Some things."

"I was glad you called." Simple truth. The warm smile in his mind remained.

There was silence between them. Stacy broke it. "I heard that pompous ass on TV," she said. "I wouldn't talk to him either."

"But you, like everyone else, want to know how it's going." JL nodded. "I don't blame you. Well, here's the picture." It occurred to him briefly to wonder why it was that he should find it so easy to be open with Stacy when his usual habit was to keep his thoughts and worries to himself. No matter. It was just—different, somehow.

Stacy waited in silence.

"We've taken a licking so far," JL said. "It was bad yesterday, and we lost more ground during the night."

"And you don't like to lose," Stacy said, understanding plain. "Neither do I." She hesitated. "In some ways, we're alike, you and I. Maybe that's why we struck sparks at the start." Her quick gesture dismissed their similarities. "Any help coming from the weather?"

"None. If anything—"

"Wind change?" Stacy caught the look of surprise that crossed his face, and was quickly gone. "I've been thinking too," Stacy said, "best possible case and worst possible case—you know about those?"

JL picked up a pencil, stared at it and set it down again. He faced Stacy. "I won't tell you you think like a man," he said. "I don't think you'd like that. But you do

215

look at things, don't you? Yes, we may have sudden, strong wind change."

"How bad is that?"

"Depends what we can do between now and then. If we can contain the fire in that quadrant, get it tightened down, under control, then wind may not hurt us much. We'll be able to cope with small break-outs."

Stacy said slowly, "Go on. What's the bad part?"

"But if we're just holding our own," JL said, "no more than that, wind change can hurt us bad. If the fire crowns in that part of the Forest—"

"You're talking about my side, aren't you?" Stacy said. "Mine and Bart Jones's, Willard Spencer's, Sophie Aaron's, Bellevue Acres, Vista Hill—and the town beyond?"

"I'm afraid I am." She did not need a diagram, JL thought; she saw things quickly, and whole.

"You're moving men and equipment into that side," Stacy said, as if she had read his mind. "I rode through and saw." She stood up then. "Thank you. I admire honesty."

"I'll see that you have warning," JL said. "If it's necessary."

"Thank you for that, too." Stacy turned away, walked to Sam, gathered up the reins and, stepping into the stirrup, swung lightly into the saddle. She faced JL again. "That date we have—" She smiled briefly. "—to talk things over when all this is done." She hesitated. "As far as I'm concerned, it's still on."

"I'm looking forward to it," JL said, and this time the smile came out into the open.

## 18

It is not a matter of record who arranged the first meeting between Bart Jones of El Rancho Costa Mucho and Willard P. Spencer, but it is known that the meeting took place over lunch in the dining room of the Inn of the Mountain which sits on high ground— 320 wooded acres of it—overlooking the Sanrio Valley, the town, the Forest and in the middle background, dominating the landscape, Sierra Grande itself, on this day smoke-shrouded and secretive against the clear, brilliant sky.

Bart was waiting at the table in his wheelchair when Spencer arrived, late, as usual. " '*L 'exactitude est la politesse des rois*,' " Bart said as they shook hands. And he added in response to Spencer's frown of non-comprehension, " 'Punctuality is the politeness of kings.' The aphorism is supposed to be Louis XVIII's, and if it is, it's the only sensible quote I've ever heard from him." He was smiling, but the smile did not reach his eyes. They retained that fierce expression Stacy had long noted, and to herself compared to that of a peregrine falcon.

Spencer sat down. He unfolded his napkin, uncomfortably aware that he had been challenged. "I was detained," he said, which was not true; he had merely been his usual slothful self. "Besides, it is without importance."

"I doubt the first part, and reject the second," Bart said. He watched Spencer's eyes widen in surprise, and then assume an expression of stiff distaste in the presence of such bluntness. Bart said, "If and when you get to know me better, friend, you'll find that I don't put up with horseshit. Not from you, not from anybody." In the stunned silence he waited, but there was no reply. He said then, "Now that we have that straight, what would you like to drink?" He indicated his half-empty glass. "They make a good martini, if that's how your taste runs."

Until the waiter arrived with two martinis, one, as suggested, for Spencer, and a second for Bart, they talked merely of the spectacular view. "No city smog," Bart said, "no industrial smoke, just God's clean air, when there isn't a fire to spoil it."

Spencer spoke his first words in some time. "The bucolic ideal," he said, his voice heavy with irony.

"Absolutely right, friend." Bart's voice held no mockery. "If you could cut it up and box it for export, you'd make Apple computers look like penny ante pikers."

When the waiter was gone, "My ranch is for sale," Spencer said, still with heavy irony, "if you'd like to start with it."

"I know." Bart's face showed nothing. "*If* there's anything left to sell, that is, when they finally bring that fire under control. A total loss with no insurance can be rough." Again he watched the shock of surprise in Spencer's face. I'd purely love to play poker with you, Bart thought. Aloud he said, "I'm new here, true, but I get around some. And I ask questions, and I listen to the answers. You're not in a very good spot, are you?"

Spencer took a deep breath. "I resent —"

"Folks poking into your private affairs? But nobody's

really private, friend. You may think you are, but it ain't so. Your banker and your broker and your insurance man, not to mention the IRS and the credit ratings people who okayed all your credit cards, along with your doctor and your lawyer and probably your State revenue folks—you may think you're walking around wearing clothes, but, believe me, friend, you're naked as a jay bird if anybody wants to trouble to look. Everything you are and everything you have is in a computer somewhere, and all it takes is punching the right numbers to bring it up on the screen. We're all in the same fix, everybody who is anything or has anything worth cataloguing."

Spencer sipped his martini and with difficulty regained his composure. "Unpleasant thought," he said.

"All those grubby little peasants in a position to know your secrets?" Bart nodded. "Yup. Unpleasant as hell, but real, too."

Spencer said, "I am sure I wasn't invited here merely to hear these distasteful facts."

"Right," Bart relaxed in his wheelchair and studied Spencer carefully. Almost exactly what he had expected, he thought; nothing much there but the name and the connections, but they would be sufficient. "Ever been in real estate?" he said.

"If you mean as a commercial venture, certainly not."

Bart nodded. "Engaging in sordid trade has never been your bag. I appreciate that." His voice merely stated a fact, without judgement. "But you have taken a flyer or two in the markets. I know about that too. And the commodity market can be what you might call volatile. Friend of mine dropped a bundle just by going to the john at the wrong time. His broker closed him out when pork bellies took a sudden dip." His eyes were steady on Spencer's face. "You dropped a bundle, too,

219

a big enough bundle to make quite a thud when it hit. All kinds of echoes and repercussions. Not quite in the same class with the Hunts and their silver caper, but big enough."

"Is there a purpose behind all this?" Spencer's tone was filled with indignation.

"Yup. Sure is. You know Bellevue Acres?"

"That wretched development near my property? All the children and the dogs and the television antennaes like a metal forest above the clotheslines eternally filled with washing?"

"That's the place."

"May I ask," Spencer said, "just what in the world that may have to do with me?"

Bart finished his second martini. Beyond a faint sense of exhilaration that so far everything had gone exactly as anticipated, he felt no effect from the drinks. "Maybe we better have another," he said, "and then I'll tell you."


Sophie Swift was already in her office when Aaron came in that morning. She wore an off-white tailored blouse, a light skirt and low-heeled pumps. Her grandmother's fine pearls peeked from the throat of the blouse and showed off well against Sophie's tanned skin. The effect was tailored, businesslike and cool, fetchingly like a *New Yorker* ad for one of the better stores.

Aaron, pausing in the doorway, said, "You didn't have to leave the ranch, Soph. You seemed more comfortable there."

"I can't spend my life worrying about what may never happen." She touched papers before her on the desk. "What is all this about Bellevue Acres, Aaron? Ken Delacorte, the bank, now this new man Bartlemy

Jones?"

Aaron came in and closed the door behind him. He sat down in one of the leather visitors' chairs. "I suspect shenanigans. Technically, none of our affair. Ken is not helpless."

"But?"

Aaron sighed. "It's beginning to look as if Bart Jones is indeed, in Ken's homey phrase, a 'sharpie in a wheelchair'. They know him well in Houston and Dallas and as far west as Denver—"

"You've made inquiries. Why?"

Aaron sighed again, this time to mask embarrassment. "Bellevue Acres is not very much, you'll agree, Soph. It is no ornament to Sanrio. On the other hand, it was conceived honestly, by Ken, for an honest purpose, to provide low-cost, decent housing, and, in the process, to make an honest profit. It is no rip-off. The walls of the houses don't crack, and the roofs don't leak, and water and sewerage are both as they should be. Most important, there's been no gouging on floating mortgage rates." He stopped. "What's funny, Soph?"

Sophie shook her head gently. "Not funny-funny. Admirable-funny. Every so often that part of you peeks out from the place where you hide it. You're about to do battle on the side of justice. I recognize the signs."

"The trouble is, Soph, there's nothing to fight. Mr. Justice Bentley of the Court of Appeals up in Denver told me once that trying to deal with a case that was before him was like trying to goose a ghost—all you got was a handful of sheet. That's where I am with Delacorte, Bellevue Acres, Bart Jones et al."

"The frontier humor peeks out from time to time too," Sophie said. She was smiling.

Aaron got up. "To work. Good to see you back, Soph. The office seems empty when you're not here."

He looked at her as if he had never seen her before. "New outfit? Becoming." He missed the look of wistful pleasure in her face.

In his own office, Aaron took off his jacket, hung it neatly on the coatrack, took his reading glasses from the breast pocket and laid them on his desk. Normally, he would now have sat down in his high-backed swivel chair and started the day.

Instead, he walked to the broad windows and stood for a little time staring at the big mountain, the rising smoke, the haze that shimmered in the foreground distorting the outlines of buildings no more than a few blocks away. Bad, he thought, and getting worse. JL and his people had better get a handle on this thing soon or all kinds of hell could result.

But he was uncomfortably aware that his thoughts were not really on the fire or its potentialities, but, rather, on Debby and last night; and this, he supposed, was some kind of commentary on human pettiness, that in the face of potential widespread catastrophe he should find himself concentrating instead on his own small life.

Debby was a young, stunningly desirable female, all taut curves, unexpected firmness and astonishingly lithe strength. But these attributes she had always possessed. Last night she had been qualitatively different.

Last night there had been an urgency in Debby that far transcended desire, almost an hysterical note in her frenzy arising from Aaron knew not what source. And the words she had spoken afterward had been strange and puzzling too.

"I love you, A. And I depend on you too. That sounds funny, doesn't it, but it's so."

Aaron could not for the life of him remember what he might have said to that.

"You see people all day," Debby said. "They depend on you too, and you tell them what to do. Isn't that so? Now will you tell me?"

"About what?"

"That's just it, I don't know."

"Unknown malady?"

"Please, A, be serious with me."

"Sorry." He realized that he meant it.

"It isn't the fire," Debby said, "or anything like that, at least I don't think it is. It's you, really."

"What about me?"

"You been—funny. Not, you know, funny ha-ha, but funny-different."

"How? In what way?"

"I don't know. I'm not a big brain, A. You know that already. I—feel things even when I don't understand them."

True enough; her almost extra-sensory perception was sometimes startling. "I know," he said. Smiling in the darkness, he added, "In other times, you might have been burned as a witch."

Debby giggled. "You say the funniest things. I don't always understand them, A, but I can tell when you're laughing at me, or with me, and I like it when we're laughing together. Like now." She snuggled warmly against him. "Thank you for talking to me."

"I didn't say anything."

"Yes, you did. You said a lot. Goodnight, A."

In no time at all, Aaron remembered now, she was asleep, curled as always in her kitten position, her breathing deep, even, untroubled. It was almost dawn before Aaron himself found sleep.

The telephone on his desk buzzed now, and he crossed the office to pick it up. The Mayor on line one, the switchboard girl said, and Aaron scowled at the far wall. "Very well." He punched the selector button.

"Billy Bob, what brings you out of your mortar and pestle?"

"TV7 says—"

"I saw Carter Norris's show."

"Well, what do you think, A? Even if it isn't all true, it's bad publicity. Keeps tourists away."

"We could bill it as the biggest fire on earth. That would pack them in."

"Damn it, be serious, A. What're we going to do about this?"

"I'd say that's very much up to JL. I don't know a McCloud from a brush hook, and don't care to."

"You think JL's still up to a big fire?"

Aaron was frowning now. "That means what?"

"Well, hell, a job like that, seems to me a man goes over the hill pretty fast. Or can. Damn it, he headed for Idaho soon as the fire was reported. Why'd he do that?"

"My advice to you, Billy Bob, is to stick to your pharmaceuticals and leave fire-fighting to George Jefferson and JL. You—"

"I got a responsibility to Sanrio, A. They elected me."

"So they did. Several times. And you can best discharge your responsibility by telling everybody you see that everything is okay, fine, copacetic, instead of spreading doubts—"

"Suppose it isn't? What if we get a wind change? What then?"

The thought had been in the back of Aaron's mind ever since BACKSLOPE began to show signs of becoming a full-fledged stemwinder of a forest fire.

Western mountain bred, he knew what wind-driven flames could do in brush and stands of timber; how a fire that crowned could create its own wind currents blowing at near-gale force, flinging burning material

224

high into the air and carrying it distances that could not be believed to start fresh conflagrations far from the main fire body.

A fire that crowned was a fire out of control, beyond man's puny powers to manage or even contain. And forests were not the only prey. It was the fire storm, rather than the earthquake which began it all, that destroyed a good share of San Francisco in 1906; it was the fire storm raging out of control that destroyed Hamburg's center long after the Allied bombers had returned to their bases. Fire out of control could consume Sanrio as surely as fire in the grate consumes a log.

"Well, that," Aaron said to Billy Bob in his easy courtroom manner, "is what used to be called before inflation the $64 question." His relaxed tone belied the evasion it contained. "Do you have any weather information that suggests a wind change, Billy Bob?" he said.

"Well, no. But—"

"Nor do I. And, you know, I can't really remember the last time wind came romping around Sierra Grande and headed in our direction. Can you?"

"No, I can't, but, damn it, A, it *could* happen now, couldn't it? Answer me that?"

"And it could rain too, Billy Bob, even though there isn't a cloud in the sky at the moment. Think of that too."

There was a short silence. "Well, hell," Billy Bob said, "maybe I'm just spooked. That Ada Loving woman was in this morning, and—"

"When I look at her," Aaron said, "wind changes and forest fires are the last things in my mind. Fires of a different kind, maybe, but you don't start those with a match."

Aaron hung up on that note, and sat for a few

moments remembering how Ada Loving's presence had filled this office. A line from Shakespeare ran through his mind— ". . . such stuff/As dreams are made on." He smiled at that, thinking again of Debby and remembering another quote, this one from Kipling: "I've a neater, sweeter maiden in a cleaner, greener land."

# 19

Ken Delacorte had seen the TV7 news too, and while he shaved he thought about it. After breakfast he drove as close to JL's command post as he was allowed and walked the last mile or so. The exercise felt good.

"You're busy," he told JL, "or if you aren't, you damn well ought to be." Between these two there was ease. "So," Ken said, "I won't take but a moment. I've got a question."

"Shoot."

"You want me to bust Carter Norris in the beak? He's been asking for it a long time, and it would be a pleasure."

JL produced his faint smile and shook his head. "Let him live. Assaulting the press is a mug's game."

Ken shrugged. "It's your fire. How's it going?"

"Well enough."

Ken nodded solemnly. "I had a coach once. Halftime he gave us a pep talk. 'They've stopped our running game and they've stopped our passing game, and they're scoring at will. Now let's go out and finish them off.'"

He walked back to his car, started for town and then changed his mind and drove instead to Stacy's place. She was in the large corral, mounted on a bay gelding, guiding him without seeming effort through a maze of plastic pylos. Pancho was perched on the top rail of the corral fence watching.

"Business as usual?" Ken said.

Stacy rode over and brought the gelding to a halt.

He stood as in a show ring, motionless, poised. "They need their workouts," Stacy said. "I could do with less smoke, but so far the horses don't seem to worry. And JL promised warning." She swung down from the saddle, and Pancho, agile as a squirrel, came down from the fence to take the reins. "You came to talk?" Stacy said. "Let's go inside."

They sat in Stacy's library-office on the large leather sofa, a cushion's width of distance between them. "Bart Jones?" Stacy said.

Ken shook his head. "He's there, and I trust him about the way I trust a Gila monster, but this fire is more important. JL's worried, and I can't recall the last time I saw that. That may be your warning."

"He sent you?"

"Strictly my idea."

Stacy studied his face. "Something stirred you up. Tell me."

"Simple," Ken said. "You. I don't want anything to happen to you."

"I can take care of myself."

"Sure you can. Nobody better."

Stacy made a small, quick gesture of impatience. "You're talking in circles, Ken. We've known one another a long time, and you usually make more sense than this."

"And you usually see things a little clearer. I'm the guy next door, only I'm not. I used to be, but I gave that up a long time ago."

Stacy turned silent, thoughtful. She said at last, "You never said anything about it. You never gave any kind of indication."

"I haven't done so badly," Ken said in apparent digression. "Give me that. If Bellevue Acres goes on as it has, I'm fairly well fixed. For now, anyway. But what I'm worth, even on paper, wouldn't keep you in hairpins for a week."

"So I'm supposed to treat you like a lackey? Come off it. The man-woman bit wasn't set up with money in mind. You want to go to bed with me? I can't think of a nicer guy for a roll in the hay."

Ken shook his head sadly. "As long as I've known you, you've done this," he said.

"What?"

"Fallen right back on stableyard talk when you don't know what to say. You aren't soft. You're tough, resilient. It's just that you don't want anybody to get close to you and find out that you aren't—brutal."

Again there was silence. "You know me about as well as anybody, I guess," Stacy said.

"Maybe too well. Okay, I won't push it. Are you still carrying the yearns for Bart Jones?"

"No." The word was emphatic.

"He's in your mind a lot."

"I'm trying to find a way to bury him at the crossroads with a stake through his heart."

"Exorcise him like a demon?" Ken watched her faint nod. "I wish you luck. How about JL?"

"That," Stacy said with even greater emphasis, "is ridiculous. And what is this, anyway, some kind of catechism?"

"I'm taking a look at the opposition."

"Damn it, Ken—" She stopped, and smiled sheepishly. "I can't get mad at you. Not really."

"I'm still the guy next door?"

"My offer holds. If you're interested."

"At the moment," Ken said, "I'm not." He smiled suddenly. "Do you give rain checks?"

Ben Hastings was back at the command post before noon after only a few hours sleep. "Nothing else to do," he told JL, "so I thought I'd come down to see what's

229

new." A blatant lie, and both men recognized, but ignored it.

JL had the latest aerial infra-red photographs of the fire area on the table in front of him. "Pull up a chair and have a look," he said. "Here, here, here and here—" His pointing pencil moved quickly. "—we have open flames, these black areas. We're moving men to block their spread, and where we can, where they can work, we've shifted in 'dozers to help cut breaks."

"Slurry drops?" Ben said.

"Slurry drops are fine, but you can't hold a whole long fire front with them alone." Again, JL thought, he was, inescapably, the pedant, the teacher. Why? He could sort the reasons out later. Right now he wanted Ben Hastings to learn and learn. "Saturation bombing was going to win World War II," he said, "only it didn't work out that way. They needed the men on the ground to take, and hold territory. In a sense, we're in the same position. There is no substitute for the crews with the shovels and brush hooks and chain saws and Pulaskis taking the fight right to the fire." He added, "The poor bastards."

Ben, remembering that encounter on the trail yesterday, said, "Bessie Wingate." He was smiling.

"She's back in there," JL said, "and so is Gordy Walker, the hotshot crew chief who went in after the unexploded charge. They're all out there, working their asses off while I sit here trying to figure out a new attack." He stared glumly at the infra-red photographs.

Ben said, as George Jefferson had said before him, "Backfire?"

JL nodded. "It may come to that, particularly if the wind shifts, but I hope it doesn't. Backfires can get out of hand too, but just in case I've called in a chopper fitted with helitorch equipment, jelled gasoline to set a backfire along a prescribed line. If we decide to use it, you'll ride a following chopper and call the shots."

Ben put his finger on the infra-red photo. "Houses here, and that nearby gray area looks hot. That's chamisa in there with some russian thistle. It'll go up fast."

JL nodded and leaned wearily back in his chair. "You get on it," he said. "I've got some thinking to do." His voice altered suddenly as a new thought appeared. "We may find that helitorch useful yet."


Mrs. Tyler Wayne left Hilario and Manuel working carefully in what she thought of as her English garden—primroses, foxgloves, canterbury bells, shasta daisies, lobelia in the borders, salpiglossis impatiens—and went back up to the big house to rest.

Even without modern air-conditioning, which Mrs. Wayne disliked, it was cool inside. The broad porch overhang shielded the house from the high sun in the summer, and allowed the low rays of winter to enter freely; and the thick whitewashed adobe walls retained that solar heat in the winter and in summer, lacking thermal build-up, refused to change in temperature from their steady, even pleasant level day or night. In addition, Vista Hill placed as it was on high ground could be counted on to enjoy a cooling breeze even when the air was still down in the town itself.

A maid brought Mrs. Wayne a cooling glass of iced tea which she sat sipping quietly. Sierra Grande, its remaining snow patch coming into view and then disappearing as smoke clouds swirled, dominated the middle foreground. Mrs. Wayne had always thought of the great mountain as guardian of the valley, and as such it held both her affection and her respect.

Once in her younger days she and Tyler had climbed the mountain and eaten a picnic lunch just beneath its peak while they gazed in awe at the thousands of square miles of broad land laid out in a circle around them, the horizons impossibly distant and yet seemingly close enough to touch.

There they were staring at the southern foot of the Rockies, the Sangre de Cristo mountains, snow-covered still; there into Oklahoma; there Texas, and below it Mexico; there Arizona and to the north Colorado. That day, which Mrs. Wayne had never forgotten, Sierra Grande had seemed the center of the world.

On their way down, she remembered, they had seen tiny picas guarding their gathered hay amongst the rocks; and a family of curious mountain goats, the kids romping on narrow rock ledges with only a thousand feet of empty air beneath them, as if they played on a living room floor, while the adults watched in seeming pride, entirely unafraid of the humans clambering carefully down the faint trail. Another world; and it was no wonder, Mrs. Wayne had always thought, that the Indians—in this locale, Apaches—considered the mountains sacred.

In the near foreground she could clearly see Bellevue Acres with its bustle and its clutter. She had considered attending the City Council meeting at which the variance allowing higher density of homes in the development had been discussed, and had decided against it.

Tyler, she had thought many times since, would have gone, argued forcibly against change and likely carried the evening. Perhaps she had let him down by not following suit. No matter, it was done now, and if she found the view of scruffy lawns, scraggly gardens, washing hung out to dry and dogs running free too distasteful, she could always look in another direction.

The fact of the matter, of course, something which she admitted only to herself and only at rare intervals, was that she was tired, perpetually, peacefully, unresentfully bone-tired. And the fatigue had nothing to do with health; it was purely and simply an attitude of mind that had been growing for years, perhaps beginning when Tyler died.

Colors were no longer as bright as they once had been, nor as exciting; conversation, particularly with strangers, was frequently an effort where once it had been a challenge and a joy; travel no longer interested her. And this fire now—

She looked up as the maid approached carrying a telephone extension which she plugged in. As she handed the phone to Mrs. Wayne, "A Senator Bronson calling from Washington," she said, and walked quickly away.

Mrs. Wayne was smiling as she raised the phone. "Hello, Will," she said.

"Myra. How good to hear your voice. It's been a long time, too long."

"I'm not one of your constituents, Will." The smile was in her voice now. "You don't need to butter me up, even though I love it. You have something in mind."

There was hesitation. "You have a fire in the Sanrio Forest," the senator said.

Mrs. Wayne looked out past Bellevue Acres to the wooded and smoking lower slopes of Sierra Grande. "We do indeed."

"Is it being properly handled? I have had reports, complaints—"

"I choose to believe so, Will. I know the young man in charge, and I consider him eminently qualified."

"Bureaucrats become entrenched, Myra. You know that as well as anyone. Tyler knew it too. They become careless, sloppy, set in their ways—"

"Like politicians, Will. Only some politicians, of course."

The senator's tone changed. "Are you all right, Myra? Safe?"

"Safe on my hill, yes. Perhaps secure is the better word." Mrs. Wayne wondered where that concept had come from so suddenly.

All at once her eye was caught by two boys down in Bellevue Acres, both on bicycles, both accompanied by dogs. They rode shouting across one of the scruffy lawns; the sounds of their voices reached clearly through the open windows of the large room. Mrs. Wayne wrinkled her nose in distaste.

"There have been an unusual number of large fires this summer," the senator said. "I detect a certain laxness in the entire Department—"

"At the next election, throw the rascals out, Will. Isn't that the customary aim?"

A young woman, obviously pregnant, came out of the house with the scruffy lawn the boys had ridden across and screamed after them. Her voice, too, reached clearly to the Vista Hill house.

"I'm worried about you, Myra," the senator's voice said. "The reports I have of this fire—"

"No doubt exaggerated, Will." Or maybe not, Mrs. Wayne thought, watching a sudden flare of flames rising above the Forest tree level and as quickly disappearing.

"Nevertheless," the senator said, "I am going to call the Secretary and ask for an accounting on your behalf."

Mrs. Wayne was thinking of JL and what he had told her. "You might also tell him, Will, that if it were not for his ban on what I believe is called 'prescribed burning', I understand that this fire might not have reached its present proportions."

Was there hesitation? "I will mention that," the senator said.

234

You do that, Mrs. Wayne thought as she hung up.
And maybe it will help. Looking out at the smoke, she
felt a little better.


Bessie Wingate said to no one in particular, "If you
ask me, this mother is goddam well determined to burn
the mountain clean, right up to timberline." Her tone
changed, but did not increase in volume; there was no
need, it was already audible throughout the entire
area. "You, Pete, and Stinky, haul ass over yonder
with that saw and take down that lone pine. It can be a
goddam stepping stone if wind carried a burning
branch to it."

She loved the forest, and she hated the wanton
destruction that was spreading within it. To her, there
was something basically wrong — although she knew
there was no alternative — that they themselves had to
destroy living things, like that healthy lone pine, in
order to save. In a saner world there would be no need
to sacrifice even the few in order to protect the many.

At each fire — and by now there had been so many in
her experience that it was impossible to keep them
separated — her personal reactions, like the lines on a
temperature chart in a known illness, followed almost
the same course.

First was simple recognition that a job of work was
there to be done, so let's get on with it. In straightforward physical work there was satisfaction and a sense
of accomplishment; only an occasional glance over
your shoulder could show how much you had done,
and how well.

But some fires fought back stubbornly, refusing to
succumb to initial attack, mounting flanking movements of their own in retaliation, sometimes almost
seeming to summon up unexpected wind demons at

the wrong time to thwart what ought to have been sufficient efforts at suppression. That was when determination moved in and took over, and the contest became *mano a mano* — one on one, as the sportswriters had it these days — a personal thing in which emotion took hold and began to grow.

Bessie was not acquainted with the ancient formal agreement of no quarter asked or given, but she was quite accustomed to the results, she and her crew against the fire, catch-as-catch-can, rough-and-tumble, no-holds-barred, we're-going-to-whip-you-you-son-of-a-bitch-if-it-kills-us. It was then that the adrenalin started to flow freely, as now.

Through the trees above which they were cutting their fire break, a perpetual glow marked the approaching flames, with an occasional bright burst of fire as a pitch-filled piñon went up like a torch. The sounds of the fire were constant, a roaring, crackling furnace sound, punctuated by the crash of a huge tree collapsing or, on fire its full length, sprawling headlong down through lesser growth, causing an instant upsurge of sparks and open flames.

The heat of the fire reached them too and carried with it the heavy smoke fumes which were sometimes, as Bessie knew, all too lethal. Carbon monoxide concentration in wildland fires, especially in canyons, could rise to more than 800 ppm (parts per million), more than enough to cause death from no more than brief exposure, or lasting deleterious effects even if death did not occur.

When, taking a brief glance downhill toward the fire front, she saw two running figures dodging among the trees on a course parallel to, rather than away from, the flames, her first thought was that some fire-fighters had lost their marbles and, in panic, their sense of direction as well, and she raised her voice again in a great shout.

"Come out of there, you goddam fools! You're too close to the front! Head uphill! Uphill, you silly bastards!"

The running figures disappeared, and Bessie, leaning briefly on her shovel to wipe the sweat from her forehead with one dirty yellow shirt sleeve, said audibly, "I'll be a son of a bitch, am I losing my goddam mind? Did you see anything, Charlie?"

"What? And where?"

"Okay," Bessie said, "so you didn't. I guess maybe I didn't, either. Who in hell would be wandering around down there with a fire front coming uphill at them like a mad bull in a field? Sweat in my eyes, likely, no more than that."

Elsie and Don Edwards had heard the sound of Bessie's voice, but the roar of the fire had drowned out the words. They ran on, as close to the approaching fire line as they dared.

At this elevation, somewhere around 9000 feet, the thin air seemed to contain far less oxygen than smoke, and their breath came in great gasps. To Don, whose head had become again one huge aching throb, a bass drum sounding each rapid heartbeat, running at all was sheer torture. But he had caught the sense of near-hysteria from Elsie, and for the present at least his legs obeyed his mind's weakening commands.

For Elsie, the feeling was that of being on a treadmill in a nightmare situation the cause of which she found hard to remember. I'm going mad, she thought at one point, because I don't understand what is happening, or why. One moment they were alone in their own tiny place in the forest. The next, the world was turned upside down and what had been secure and happy was suddenly destroyed. But, for what reasons? And where had sanity gone?

She was aware that Don beside her was stumbling now, close to the limit of his endurance. She was suddenly aware too that the faintly cooling breeze of her cheeks had shifted sides and was coming now from above them on the mountain, and that the actual flames below them were farther away than they had been.

Elsie slowed, caught Don's arm and drew him down to a stumbling walk beside her. "I think," she said, finding the words not only hard to form through gasping breath, but also difficult to say because they seemed to offer hope, "that we're — safe. For now. Sit down. Rest." And when he had sunk to the ground like a doll unhinged, she knelt beside him and touched his cheek with great gentleness. "Poor baby," she said, "All my fault." When Don's head waggled feebly, Elsie patted his cheek again. "Yes, it is. Now be quiet. Rest. I'll — have a look."

Don sat where he was, his arms resting on his bent knees and his head bowed over them. He no longer had any idea where they were, or any clear picture of what had happened during the past few daylight hours. He seemed to remember that at one point Elsie had whispered urgently, "There they are again! They're still here!" But his head throbbed so violently now that he could not be sure what was real and what mere fantasy, so for the moment he gave up any attempt to sort it all out.

What had apparently happened to Elsie back there in front of their blue nylon tent was wholly unbelievable, and yet — this he knew with deep, inescapable certainty — was also completely true, and there was nothing at all that he could do about it.

He should not have brought Elsie here to the forest. It had seemed such a great idea. No people, nothing to bother them, just cool green cleanliness and splendor as if they two were alone in time, discovering the world from a new viewpoint, together. Instead, this scenario of horror, a bad film directed by a madman, a bad dream from which there was no awakening.

Sitting unmoving, eyes closed, he tried to remember at least the contours of the mountain he had studied so carefully on the topographical map. The way they must have come, with the body of the fire on their left and below them, they were traveling clockwise around the mountain's mass. So far, so good.

They had not yet come to the cliff he remembered from the map. It had appeared to be a cirque above a lake, the edge of the cliff not far below timberline. Sometime after this nightmare began, he seemed to remember that he had had an idea about that cliff, and he groped for it now.

Was it possible — the ratiocination came very slowly — that the fire might have been thwarted in its spread by that cliff area? The contour lines on the map had been piled one almost upon the next, he was quite sure, in such density, that no vegetation could possibly have grown on what was apparently an almost vertical stone face. The fire, then, would not have found fuel for the few hundreds of yards of the cliff's width, and if that was so, it seemed possible that beyond that area he and Elsie might be able to descend to safety.

Elsie was suddenly back. She was breathless again, but her expression had lost some of its tenseness, and the wild, unnatural glare had disappeared from her eyes. "Nothing," she said, and in the single word there was triumph. "When you're ready, we can go on." She dropped to her knees beside him. "Oh, God, darling, I think —"

"Well, well, well, well," Frank Orwell's voice, "will you look who we've got here?"

"*Guapa*," Felipe said, "*guapissima*, but this time with clothes on,"

Each man stepping out of the shadows held a knife. Orwell gestured menacingly with his. "If you're thinking of getting up," he said to Elsie, "just do it slow and easy. And you, buster, just stay right where you are."

Elsie put her hand on Don's shoulder. "Don't," she said. "Whatever you're thinking, don't You—can't. Don't you see, it wouldn't do any good at all?"

"You think good," Felipe said, "real good."

Elsie took a deep breath. "What do you want?" Surprisingly, her voice was steady.

"Why, honey, we liked the sample." This was Orwell. "We been talking about how good it was. You'd be real pleased if you knew."

Elsie was silent, motionless, her hand still on Don's shoulder. She looked from man to man, studying the faces, the eyes. There was, she thought, no pity, none. Her mind felt strangely cold, analytical. She waited.

"Stand up," Orwell said.

Don said, "No. No, damn it! What kind of animals are you?"

"Hush," Elsie said, "please hush, darling." She rose from her knees and straightened herself.

"Now move three, four steps away," Orwell said, and watched Elsie obey.

"Run!" Don said.

"Better not." Orwell again. He had moved quickly and he dropped to one knee and pressed the point of his knife against the side of Don's neck. "That is, unless you want to see his throat cut. That's how you slaughter a pig, did you know that, honey? It's easy. Messy, but easy."

Elsie closed her eyes briefly. She opened them again. "Please, darling. Don't do anything. No matter what. Please. He'll do it."

"She catches on good," Orwell said. He made a small gesture with his free hand. "Okay," he said to Felipe, "she's all yours. I had first shot last time. Your turn."

Felipe held his knife with practised relaxed ease. He gestured with its glittering blade. "You hear the man, *guapa*? Is good. But you bare-ass last time. That was better. The shirt—take her off."

Don said, "Don't—" He stopped as the knife point broke the skin and a thin trickle of blood rolled down his neck.

"Please, darling! Please!" Elsie's voice came out almost in a scream as she quickly pulled the shirt out of her trousers. She unbuttoned it with slow reluctance, held it closed for a moment and then opened it wide exposing her full breasts, and let it fall to the ground.

"You ever see *tetas* like these?" Felipe said admiringly. "Real fine, no? Okay, now the pants."

Elsie said, "Just leave him alone. Please. I'll do what you say. Anything."

"You bet your sweet life you will," Orwell said. "Now get those pants off, goddam it, or—"

The sound was a blend of roar and scream, high-pitched, hoarse, filled with fury and entirely terrifying. Bessie Wingate, enormous and overpoweringly visible in yellow hard hat, grimy yellow shirt and forest twill trousers, her omnipresent shovel clutched in one hand, burst out of the forest shadows on a dead run. "You son a bitches!" Her voice echoed and reverberated through the trees. "You goddam son a bitches!" She headed toward Felipe.

Felipe was agile, and practised. He sprang back from Elsie, and the knife in his hand seemed alive as it flashed in the air. *"Que vaya!* fat one, beat it before I cut your gizzard out!" It was a snarl. He advanced a single menacing step, another.

Bessie did not hesitate. She swung her shovel with

the full strength of both brawny arms in a flat arc, edge forward. It nearly severed the arm Felipe flung up to protect himself, and continuing almost unchecked slammed into Felipe's side with an ugly, tearing sound as of a cleaver hacking into a joint.

The knife fell unnoticed to the ground as Felipe staggered no more than two paces backward and collapsed in a bloody, moaning heap.

Bessie faced Orwell who had risen to his feet. "Now you, you bastard!" She advanced, the shovel held at the ready.

Orwell turned and ran.


"Son a bitch come at her with a knife," Stinky told the State police lieutenant. "Me, I'd sooner go up against a bear with nothing more than a goddam willow switch."

"There were eighteen other witnesses just like this one, aside from the bride and groom," JL said. "Bessie was leading her crew under orders to a new sector where we hope to push the fire back. They saw and heard it all—the attempted rape, the threat on the husband's life, and the knife attack."

"Seems cut and dried," the lieutenant said. "Clear self-defense." He was silent a moment, shaking his head slowly. "Jesus," he said, "what kind of a woman is this, anyway? A runaway truck couldn't have done more damage."

"She's been on the fire line almost four days now," JL said, "and when you've been at it that long, you work up a pretty fair head of steam. You don't fool around anymore."

## 20

By early afternoon, the party around Ada Loving's swimming pool was in full swing. Ada herself, tanned to the smooth flawlessness of a slick paper Coppertone ad, wore a white bikini which Joey Simpson, screenwriter, described as, "A G-string and pasties. In dear, lost, innocent days, as a costume it would have wowed them on a Minsky runway."

There were times, as now, when Ada temporarily put aside her usual wide-eyed attitude of vapid stupidity. "As at the Old Howard," she said, smiling sweetly, "when you were a Harvard undergraduate, no doubt."

Joey made a small bow. "Confronted with your other attributes," he said, "one tends to forget that there might also be a brain behind that lovely face. But you will forgive me if I ogle?"

"It's good box-office, darling."

There were twenty guests at the party, all but one of them imports from the Hollywood area. The lone exception was a man named Leon Sturgis, who wore carefully faded jeans, ostrich-skin cowboy boots and a short-sleeved Sulka shirt which showed off to advantage the heavy mat of black hair on his chest, and the gold chain around his neck. "Tax shelter with cash-flow is the name of the game," he told a group around the portable bar, "and if you have it, *and* enjoy yourself in a place like Sanrio at the same time, why that's a license to steal."

"Smog for smoke," one of the imports said. "I'm not sure you gain much. They both make you sneeze."

"The smoke is temporary," Sturgis said. "There is the difference."

Ada, despite her costume or lack of it, was not insensitive to the anomaly of poolside-party-as-usual-while-countryside-burns. It smacked of house parties on country estates while the plague raged in town. On the other hand, charter flights and laid-on limousines to carry guests from the airport were not arranged on a moment's notice, and last-minute cancellations were bad PR, so the decision had been made to carry on as planned, regardless. Profits from the sale of yet-to-be constructed $250,000-and-up condos and town houses were not to be taken lightly.

Ada had often wondered who really controlled the pursestrings and made the decisions, not that it mattered as long as she was paid as agreed, and on time. The public had not wearied of seeing as much of Ada as R-ratings allowed, but scripts giving her the chance to display her charms had been few and far between lately.

Sturgis, drink in hand, wandered over from the bar. "They've sent us a pretty dead group," he told Ada in a quiet voice. "What can we do to stir them up? A drive through the Forest?"

"You've heard that there is a fire going on?" Ada's voice too was quiet, and her smile did not fade.

"Sure. We'll show it to them firsthand. Excitement. Life in the raw."

"Include me out," Ada said. "Folks here are taking it seriously. So am I."

And here came Ken Delacorte, looking around curiously at the strangers, nodding in a friendly way to

Ada and giving Sturgis a cold stare.

He had met Ada a few times during his short time in Hollywood, and since her move to Sanrio he had squired her around on occasion, often enough to suspect that beneath the stunning exterior there was someone worth knowing.

He had never met Sturgis, but from his days in big-time college football on through the pros and briefly in Hollywood, he had known dozens like him, always on the fringes and on the make; human jackals, in his opinion. He acknowledged Ada's introduction with a faint nod.

Sturgis made his position clear at once. "You're in real estate too," he said, and nodded. He indicated with a nod of his head those around the pool. "But these are our pigeons."

"Pluck them clean for all I care," Ken said. "But I think you—" He spoke now directly to Ada. "—would do well to think about where you might go if things get completely out of hand."

"Paul Revere," Sturgis said, "warning that the British are coming?"

"Are things going to get out of hand?" Ada said.

"They could. We all hope they won't, but that's big fire."

"The Forest Service clowns," Sturgis said, "are screwing up as usual?"

"You know," Ken said, "some day somebody is going to pick you up, Sturgis, and set you down so hard you'll find your ass up between your shoulder blades. I might even do it myself. Now go play with your Hollywood pigeons."

Ada watched Sturgis walk off, still wearing his easy smile. She said, "You're not usually that belligerent, Ken."

"You're much woman, honey. You know it and I

know it. But—"

"We might make a good pair."

Ken nodded. "We might. And believe me, sometimes I'm real tempted."

"But then you think of Stacy Cummings and all that oil loot—"

"That's a cheap shot, honey."

Ada was silent for a few moments, thoughtful. Slowly she nodded. "I apologize." She turned on the famous Loving smile. "I don't very often, you know." She gestured toward the bar. "Would you like a drink? It is, after all, my house. On paper, anyway. Or," she said in a different voice, "are there others to warn? Are you self-appointed town crier?"

Ken looked across the pool area to Sturgis and the other guests. He looked again at Ada. "Don't let too much of them rub off on you," he said. "Wave the body around all you want. That isn't you, it's just something you happen to have been born with. But hang on to the real part. Keep it the way you'd like it, don't cheapen it. Do I sound like a shrink or a Bible-banger?"

"Strangely enough," Ada said, "you don't. I'll bear it in mind."


JL leaned back in his chair to listen to Bob Hastings's report. "Those houses are all right so far," Ben said, "and with luck we can keep them that way. But I've evacuated two of the families. Had to."

There was that in Ben's voice that caught JL's attention. "Trouble?" JL said.

"Argument. You can't really blame them. Fellow named Oliver, Ross Oliver. Know him?"

JL nodded. "He's been big on Sodom and Gomorrah for quite a while. He mentioned that?"

"He thinks all of Sanrio ought to be destroyed. But

he wants *his* house saved, and he's going to see to it."

Oliver had had a shotgun, and he had met Ben at his property line, a plump little man who looked as if he ought to wear a smile instead of his portentous frown. "I aim to protect my own." He spoke the words with deep conviction. "And I'll have help. All I need. The Lord is on my side."

"A little boost from us might make it easier."

"I'll manage, young fellow." He gestured with the shotgun.

Ben did not like the situation, but he stood his ground and tried to appear relaxed. "You have a wife, Mr. Oliver? Kids?"

Oliver nodded supsiciously, in silence.

"Don't you think," Ben said solemnly, "that it might be well if we saw them off to a safe place to let you and the Lord concentrate on the house?"

For as long as it might take to count to ten slowly Oliver considered the suggestion, his eyes never leaving Ben's face, and his finger never relaxing on the trigger of the shotgun. At last he nodded, and raised his voice in a shout. "Emma!"

Emma appeared instantly on the porch. She wore a long dress and an apron, and her hands were folded submissively as she waited.

"Bring the young ones," Oliver said. "Go with this young fellow. I'll stay here and attend to the house."

"Ross—"

"Do as I say, woman. I want no argument."

"So," Ben told JL, "I took them over to Bellevue Acres, and a young pregnant woman took them in and gave each kid a bottle of coke to make up for being in a strange place, while Oliver stayed behind and turned his garden hose on the roof to take care of any stray sparks." He shook his head. "Civilians," he said.

JL merely nodded. Ben had done well, he thought,

247

probably better than he himself would have managed. "Anything else?"

Ben extended his fist and opened it to display a stem and leaves of greenery. "One of the troops picked this up." He touched the map with his forefinger. "Found it over here, a big field of it. He wasn't sure what it was."

JL shook his head. "Neither am I."

"*Cannabis indica,*" Ben said, and showed his quick grin, as quickly gone. "I'm a plant biologist, remember? Marijuana, Mary Jane, pot—call it whatever."

"Growing wild?"

"Doubtful. It's a cash crop, big cash."

"And we missed it." Self-accusation.

"How many million acres in the Forest?"

"Doesn't matter," JL said. "We missed it."

"We could send in a crew."

JL shook his head. "One thing at a time. We'll deal with it later." He sat up straight and bent over the map again, the marijuana for the moment set aside. "Now here's what we're going to do. A limited backfire right here." He drew a line on the map running southwest to northeast above Sheep Ridge. "We'll use the helitorch. You fly behind it in another chopper and call the shots. No more than this area I've outlined, and I want a hotshot crew on the scene to keep it contained."

Ben studied the markings on the map and brought to mind the terrain, which was hilly, with thick brush, scattered piñons, junipers and one stand of cottonwoods as he remembered it, near the bed of an intermittent stream, now, with the summer's absence of rainfall, totally dry.

The logic of a backfire here was irrefutable, he thought; by preemptive burning, scorching to the ground the area JL had marked before the actual danger arrived, they could deny the fire further fuel when at last it burst from the deep Forest, and perhaps,

248

in that sector at least, stop it in its tracks.

On the other hand, there were always dangers connected with backfires, which could get out of hand. "If the wind shifts—" he began.

"The longer we wait, the more likely a wind shift becomes."

Ben nodded. "You're the boss."

"That's right," JL said, and showed his faint, enigmatic smile.

JL sat quiet at the improvised table long after Ben had gone. It grieved him that the Forest hush was now constantly disturbed by the clamor of men and equipment—jeeps, trucks, ground tankers, bulldozers, the distant snarl of chain saws, and the sudden painful sounds as living trees, the saws' victims, came crashing to the Forest floor. The fresh clean Forest odors, too, were submerged in the heavy smell of smoke, and in the nearby cooking smells from the caterers' kitchens so unlike the proper subtle scents of the occasional campfire and bacon or fresh-caught trout sizzling with coffee brewing in the pot.

In each major fire, too, situations arose which could not have been foreseen, and, worse, were almost never handled satisfactorily, thereby creating a residue of what he could only look upon as personal failure.

Early this morning, for example, one of the chopper pilots had spotted within the Wilderness ground signals—rocks set out in a geometric pattern—and when he hovered to investigate, he saw three persons, a man, a woman and a boy waving frantically and motioning for him to land in a nearby clear area, indicating that the woman was hurt.

But machinery of whatever kind is forbidden in Wilderness areas at all times, so the chopper pilot, instead of landing, radioed a report.

Eventually a saddle horse and two men were sent to

the scene, and it was not until sometime later that JL was told of the situation. By then the woman was already on the horse and the rescue party was on its way out, so there was no point in interfering. But the incident left a bad taste, and would, no doubt, be told and re-told as an example of Service insensitivity. We are, JL told himself as he had many times before, damned if we do, and damned if we don't.

Thoughts of that situation involving Bessie Wingate, the honeymoon couple and the two escaped convicts continued to bother him too, although by no conceivable standards could he or any of his people be considered even vaguely culpable.

But rape and violence had no place in the Forest, and by their mere presence they polluted the atmosphere far more unpleasantly than any amount of smoke or fire which were, after all, the results of natural causes.

One of the convicts was still on the loose, of course, and in the confused way that things worked was bound to turn up again under awkward circumstances, with his knife and the handgun several members of Bessie's crew had noticed, which, presumably, the man had not wanted to use lest he attract attention by firing it. He would not now be so cautious, and so he had to be considered dangerous.

The State Police knew the man was still around, but JL had warned them to stay out of the fire area in which experienced fire-fighters would be hard enough put to keep themselves out of trouble in the event of a sudden wind change.

And wind change was coming; that much was sure. All available meteorological data agreed on this one point. The high-pressure ridge that had sat over them these last few days was stirring itself and beginning to move eastward, and because, as in the old adage,

Nature abhors a vacuum, new air would move in to take its place and the pressure gradient would probably be shifted into a new, different and more dangerous quadrant.

Something else was changing too, and this change was in himself. Once, although he had never given this any particular thought, he had considered himself independent in thought and action, his own complete man, needing no one else.

Now, thinking of his talk with Stacy this morning, he realized what a relief it had been to share, not his troubles, but his estimate of the situation with someone as quick, as understanding and as sympathetic as she had been. Maybe there was something after all to the concept that at about his age, fortyish, reassessment of yourself did occur, values did change, and that independence he had clung to no longer seemed so important.

His handling of Ben Hastings was another example, because it had been and still was for all the world as if he, JL, were determined to train a successor in order that he might step aside with a clear conscience. Step aside to what? He had no answer. Like the field of marijuana, that, too, could wait.

He sat up straight to study the map again. The backfire he had sent Ben to set up and carry through was a gamble. That could not be denied. But *if* the wind direction held steady as it was for only a little time, the odds in favor of the gamble were high. When the fire perimeter reached the backfire area, as it almost certainly would, it would be stopped for lack of fuel, and with diligence and a little of the luck that was always necessary, that area at least could then be sealed off and considered relatively safe. If the wind change came sooner than expected, why, that was another story that did not bear thinking about.

It was how these things were done, little by little and bit by bitter bit, precariously establishing a bastion beyond which the flames could not spread, holding that area securely and at the same time throwing men and equipment into a new sector, there to fight for, conquer and hold fresh ground from which to launch new attacks. On a minor fire, simultaneous assaults on all fronts were possible. On BACKSLOPE, where fire, the enemy, was well established in force, piecemeal attack was the only way.

He remembered trying once to explain that to Madge. It had been a waste of time. And here came thoughts of Stacy again, because she would have understood, and listened with interest. He was tempted to call her now, but the phone on the table rang, and automatically he picked it up and spoke his name. George Jefferson said in an overly hearty voice, "How's it going, JL?"

Nothing changed in JL's face. "Ginger-peachy," he said. "Or, if you prefer, jolly good."

"Damn it, JL, I'm serious."

"I assumed." JL sighed. "For the record, we've had one double rape and another double attempted, a near-killing in self-defense, a comic-book rescue from the Wilderness, a field full of marijuana apparently planted, and a Bible-banging citizen defending his property with a shotgun presumably loaded. We also have an armed, escaped convict loose in the Forest, as well as a major fire on our hands. In other words, so what else is new?"

There was the sound of heavy breathing on the line. Jefferson said at last, "I appreciate your position, JL."

Big of you, JL thought, but did not say.

"But you'd better appreciate mine, too. I've had a call direct from the Secretary's office in Washington. Not from the Chief Forester, the Secretary. A Senator named Bronson is breathing on him and wants a status report on the Sanrio fire. And," Jefferson said quickly, "don't tell me it's alive and well. Save remarks like that for later."

JL thought, as he had before, that he would not be in Jefferson's shoes for all the tea in China. "Look at your map," he said, and began a concise report.

"We lost our north line at Highway one-four when that gasoline truck blew up. The fire is now across the highway and into lodgepole pine, and I estimate that we stand a good chance of losing the entire stand before we can stop it. . . . To the east, the the daytime updrafts have been pushing us back up the mountain, and the line may eventually reach timberline before it runs out of fuel. . . . To the west, we've established a line that is presently holding where Highway one-four swings south. Barring another freak like that gasoline tanker, we should be secure there. . . . To the south and southwest—there is where our major problems are."

"Threatening the town," Jefferson said, "and all those outlying houses." His accompanying nod of comprehension was almost visible.

"We're setting a backfire on Sheep Ridge," JL said, "and hoping we don't get a wind change before that's done. There's a front moving in—"

"Any rain predicted?"

"Not even enough to settle the dust."

Jefferson's voice came slowly, and with resignation. "How many acres so far?"

"Twenty-five thousand, more or less," JL said, "and still counting."

There was a short, pregnant silence. "Hang in there," Jefferson said, and hung up.

JL put the phone on its stand and sat quiet for a few moments. He had been thinking about Stacy, he told himself almost guiltily, and about Madge as well, but to a much lesser degree.

Part of this change he was noticing in himself, he realized suddenly, was the fading of his image of Madge; the picture of her in his mind, like a dream upon awakening, had lost much of its form and color. She now belonged in another world.

So be it.

## 21

Stacy stripped, bundled up underclothes, shirt, socks and jeans and tossed them into the dirty clothes hamper. Much as she loved horses, she thought as she headed naked for the shower, she detested women — or men too, for that matter — who always smelled as if they had just come from the stables. She remembered that it had not always been so.

"We have a house," her father had told her one evening long ago, "and we have a horsebarn. They aren't the same. When you come to the dinner table, by God, I won't have you stinking of sweat and horse manure. You go back to your room and get out of those clothes and scrub yourself clean. When you smell like a human again, you can have your dinner."

Stacy could not remember what she might have said to that, but whatever it was, it just bounced right back at her.

"You heard me, girl. I haven't raised a hand to you in a long time. Maybe you're overdue. You'd better not crowd your luck."

Times like this, she thought as she lathered herself, funny, unexpected times, even the sound of his voice came back to her so vividly it hurt. And once the memories began, they were difficult to shut off.

Another evening, she remembered now, much later,

but also dinner-time, the two of them alone at the big, polished table with lighted candles and silver candlesticks in the huge, etched hurricanes that had come from her mother's family, along with the heavy silver flatware, a wedding gift, with its single, engraved, ornate lettering on the gleaming metal. "Why haven't you ever married again?" young Stacy had said, and could not for the life of her even now understand what had worked her courage up to asking that question.

"I'm too ornery," her father had said, and showed his fond, crooked smile.

"I'm serious."

Her father studied her across the table. "Trying to find a clue to something in yourself, honey?"

"Maybe. I don't know."

"I'm luckier than most," her father said then. "I found one woman, the right one. Damn few do. Damn few like me, that is. I'm a loner, honey. I don't take easy to folks up close. I like folks, but I want a little distance between us. There's something of that in you too."

"I know."

"Not too much, I hope."

Stacy could smile sheepishly. "That's the part I don't know."

Her father took his time. "Horses aren't a substitute for people, honey," he said gently then, "and winning prize saddles, let alone prize money, isn't, like the man said, the be-all and the end-all. Maybe you're beginning to find that out?"

Stacy's smile was easier now. "We started out talking about you," she said.

Her father shook his head. "I think all along we've been talking about you. I've had my time. You're just beginning yours." His grin turned full and wide. "I read palms too," he said. "The future told any time. Now eat your dinner. You're the one talked me into

256

hiring the fancy lady chef who whomped up this meal."

Of course, Stacy thought now as she came back into her bedroom after her shower, there was a tenuous connection, as there usually was, between remembered incidents or conversations, and the present. In this instance, the connection was Sophie Swift.

On the telephone, at first Sophie had been almost her normal, businesslike, lawyer self. "I wonder if it would be convenient for you to meet me this afternoon, Stacy? Say five-thirty?"

So unusual as to be almost startling. "Why," Stacy said, "why, I think so."

"I realize that with this fire — your worry about your horses, I mean — I am importuning — I understand that, and I'm sorry — I don't usually impose."

Stacy had never heard Sophie this close to incoherence, or even anything less than precise. "Of course I'll meet you. Where?"

"I thought maybe the lounge of the Inn. It is quiet, I'm told. I mean—"

"We can talk," Stacy said. "Of course."

"Thank you," Sophie said. "Thank you very much."

Whatever it was, Stacy thought now, although she already had a pretty fair idea, jeans and boots were not the costume. Instead, panty hose, a dress, heels — Ken Delacorte would smile and ask if she had joined the cocktail circuit, but Stacy found herself thinking more about JL and how he would react, seeing her in other than man's clothes. He would approve, she guessed, and wondered at the depth of her hope that he would.

Sophie was waiting at a table for two in one corner of the lounge, sitting very straight and proper in the upholstered wingback chair, ankles crossed, wearing the same handsome clothes she had worn to the office

257

that day. Despite her tanned skin, her face seemed pallid, even drawn.

She could not remember when she felt like this, so—helpless and indecisive. Nor, until now, had she realized how *alone* she was in this wide world, and the shock of realization came with numbing force.

She had no close friends. She supposed that she had never really known what close friends were—never any giggling girlish confidences, never even at college the kind of earnest late-at-night ponderings of life, love, and the *meaning-of-it-all*.

There had been Aaron, period, with whom she could discuss whatever needed discussing, business, personal, whatever; equals, an intelligent male and an intelligent female bringing together, not opposing, but different points of view in harmony and understanding.

But now Aaron was beyond her reach, living in his own new world, and she was sinking deeper and deeper into the shadows of a lonely existence she had never known before.

And her invitation to Stacy was a cry for help to someone who had shared that brief moment of nonsense, oddly revealing, when Stacy had said that she talked to her horses, and they talked back. Incredible, but, oh, so real!

Looking up, making herself smile, "Thank you for coming," she said as Stacy approached.

"It's good to see you. Even as neighbors we don't—"

"And thank you for not asking if anything is wrong. Of course it is. You already understand that."

The waiter arrived. Stacy ordered a glass of white wine. The interruption was welcome. "Aaron?" she said.

"Of course."

"I'm not very good at these things, Soph." *I'm a loner,*

258

*honey*, her father had said. *There's something of that in you too.* "In fact, I'm not very good at all."

"You enjoy solitude. I don't. How do you do it?"

With mirrors, Stacy thought, and would not for the world have said. The question was unanswerable. She sat silent.

"Your horses," Sophie said.

"They're a help."

Sophie studied her curiously. "Do you need help? I never thought you did. I am surprised."

"Whole and perfect and impenetrable?" Stacy said. "Like a glass paperweight?"

Sophie's response was immediate. "I didn't quite mean that. Maybe what I said sounded—harsh. I'm sorry."

"It doesn't matter a bit, Soph. You and Aaron—"

"Lawyers," Sophie said, "are very good at telling clients what to do, how to run their lives. Now it's a case of: 'Physician, heal thyself.' And I don't know how to cope."

Through the large view windows across the lounge, the mountain rose grandly, shrouded now in smoke. Stacy stared at it. "When things get out of hand," she said, "they seem to do it all at once, don't they?" She looked again at Sophie. "I wish I had wise advice, Soph, I really do. But I don't."

"I like Debby." Sophie's voice was judicial, delivering considered judgement. "She is good for Aaron."

"You are generous."

A faint smile appeared and was quickly gone. "I am trying to be objective. The fact of the matter is that I like her, and—I never thought I would say this—I hate her too. Isn't that an ignoble confession?"

"I didn't even hear it," Stacy said.

It was as if she had not spoken. Sophie's thoughts would run their course unhindered, as if words too long forcibly contained had finally burst their confinement and were now free and demanding expression.

"A friend, a psychiatrist, told me once," Sophie said, "that recently widowed women were frequently forgetful, she had noticed, and often unable to make decisions. I have noticed these symptoms in myself, and they alarm me. I am not self-sufficient, as I once thought I was. Can you understand that? No, I doubt if you can. You have always been the epitome of self-sufficiency. Can you tell me the secret?"

Cold showers and pure thoughts, Stacy was tempted to say in flippant response, and stifled the impulse. Because maybe I am not as self-sufficient as I once was, she told herself, and again found JL in her thoughts. Strange. "Maybe there is none, Soph," she said.

Again, she might as well not have spoken; Sophie's words continued unabated.

"You take for granted what you have," Sophie said, "until one day you lose it. That is trite, but true. I have seen it with clients, to whom the prospect of losing liberty exists merely as an abstraction they cannot be persuaded is in any sense real — until the day the verdict is handed down, and the sentence, and they are led away. Then, all at once, realization takes place, and it is shattering."

It was embarrassing to have to listen to, Stacy thought, and yet in a strange and almost perverse way she was glad that it was she whom Sophie had chosen for her confidences. Her own reactions astonished her too because instead of amusement or even scorn, what she felt was pure compassion and a deep sense of empathy for another being in pain. It was, she told herself with strange, new anger, a feeling she had previously reserved almost entirely for horses rather than people.

"I think another glass of wine, Soph," Stacy said when, at last, the spate of words slowed. "And then why don't we have dinner here? I've heard that the food is good."

Sophie, calmer now, leaned back in her chair and produced a faint smile that, nonetheless, contained pain. "Thank you again," she said, "this time for not patting me on the head and telling me that everything is going to be all right. I must tell you that this is a chastening experience for me, and I hope I remember it the next time I am tempted to tell a client, wrongly, that he has nothing at all to worry about. I would very much like to have dinner here in your company."

The hotshot crew JL had ordered was in place on the scene of the backfire JL had planned, twenty highly experienced and expert fire-fighters, thoroughly briefed on the purpose of the operation. Gordy Walker, crew chief, as usual urged caution.

"I smell weather coming," he told them, "which may or may not mean a wind change, so be careful, goddammit, and stick right to JL's plan, you hear?"

"Aye, aye, Bwana," Terry Young the free spirit said, "your wish is our command."

"And up yours, too," Gordy said without rancor. "Okay, let's spread out. The chopper's already on its way."

Ben Hastings, the contours of the map on his lap already fixed in his mind, rode shotgun in the second chopper, a hundred and fifty yards behind the helicopter-helitorch from which had been lowered the flexible hose that would drop the flaming jelled gasoline. Ben wore a headset and mike attachment leaving both hands free.

He said into the mike now to the leading helicopter,

"You're right on course. Start your fire on the far side of that next low ridge, and hold it steady as you go. Do you read me? Over."

"Roger. Over."

"The backfire line we want is a little more than a quarter of a mile long," Ben added, "terminating well before the heavy tree growth begins. I'll give you ample warning."

"Roger. Like the Limeys say, a piece of cake. Over."

I hope so, Ben thought, and was unaware that he had said it aloud.

The pilot next to him said, "Shouldn't be any sweat, unless the wind changes suddenly. As it is now, the upslope currents will carry the fire away from anything that counts."

Ben nodded. "That's the general idea."

But deliberately dropping fire from the sky always seemed to be, and was, a risky business. Too many variables, like small errant wind currents, eddies, really, what the fixed-wing aircraft pilots, the glider pilots in particular, knew as clear air turbulence. And burning jelled gasoline could not be snuffed out like a match; it persisted until it had burned itself out no matter where it landed. Still, this was the sensible, efficient way to go about the job.

When they were able to look over the low ridge ahead, Ben saw on the ground, spaced along the line of the fire they were going to set, and well below it for safety's sake, the hotshot crew standing ready as ordered. That madman Gordy Walker, who had gone in after the malfunctioning explosive charge, Ben noticed, was in charge of the crew, which was something of a comfort because it meant that if anything were to go wrong, Gordy would see that his men busted a puckering string to cope. He felt unaccountably better when Gordy waved up at the choppers with his brush

262

hook, and with his free hand made a circle of forefinger and thumb.

And then the first string of flame dropped from the hose beneath the helitorch ahead, and Ben watched the hanging fire reach the ground almost exactly where planned. Instantly a clump of chamisa was ablaze. Its flames spread until they reached the outer branches of a healthy piñon which seemed momentarily to resist conflagration, and then all at once went up like a flaming torch, throwing sparks in every direction. As the line of flaming jelled gasoline moved on, Gordy's men moved closer to the fire to attack scattered flames that had been started downslope.

So far, so good, Ben thought, and resisted the impulse to cross his fingers. Into the mike he said, "Bang on target, and you're right on line. The wind currents aren't too bad? Over."

"Like I said, a piece of cake. I always wanted to be a firebug. Over."

They flew straight along the line JL had marked on his map, one behind the other, the line of fire beneath the helitorch shearing cleanly through brush and low trees as a cutting torch burns along a chalked line through metal plate.

JL's chosen front for the backfire was strategic, Ben was thinking. It was far enough downslope from the heavy stands of big trees that windblown sparks would not easily reach dangerously heavy fuel; and yet far enough above the large private holdings such as those of Ada Loving, Stacy Cummings, Sophie Swift and Willard Spencer, as well as Mrs. Wayne's Vista Hill and the Bellevue Acres development, that they too, would be well protected.

Beyond the end of the planned backfire line, the heavy big tree growth began again, and this finger of the Forest pointing downslope posed the greatest threat

263

to the town itself, and at the same time posed a flanking threat to the big houses and the development as well. But if the planned backfire accomplished what was intended, its burned-over area could be considered secure, and the full force of their counterattack could then be concentrated on the Forest finger.

This was a real granddaddy of a fire, Ben thought, by far the largest he had been up against, but old JL commanding the defense was no babe in arms, either. What you might call a fair fight.

The helitorch was approaching the end of the backfire line as marked on the map, and Ben spoke again in his mike. "On the rise of that next ridge," he said, "cut off your fire. We want to give the ground troops plenty of room to get around the end and keep it from spreading into those big trees. You've got plenty of fuel? Over."

"I'm loaded. The rise of the next ridge—will do. Over."

Ben let out his breath in a long, slow sigh. He had not realized how tense he had been, and now that the successful end was in sight, he could feel the fatigue in his muscles from the sustained strain. Watching the helitorch approach the cut-off point, he whispered, more to himself than to the man next to him, "Okay, cut it off, and we can go home." There was intense relief in the words.

But the string of fire continued unabated, and through Ben's headset the helitorch pilot's voice came clearly, "Shut off, you bastard! What the hell gives? Shut off!"

"You're too far!" Ben said into the mike in sudden alarm. "Too goddam far already!"

"I know it! The fucking valve's stuck! It should—"

"Then turn back! Stay away from those big trees! You read me?"

The pilot next to Ben said suddenly, "Jesus!" And there was that in his voice that turned Ben's head quickly to stare at him.

"What—?" Ben began, but the pilot was merely shaking his head and pointing straight ahead at the helitorch still dripping that string of burning jelled gasoline from its dangling hose.

The helicopter was right on the edge of the big trees now at an elevation of perhaps forty feet and trying to turn back, but in the process it was losing elevation at an alarming rate.

"Pick up, you son of a bitch!" This was the helitorch pilot's voice coming loud and clear in Ben's headset. "Up, up, up, goddamnit!" They were his last words.

Beside Ben his own chopper pilot said softly, "Too goddam late. He took his eye off it, the poor son of a bitch. There she goes!"

One moment there was the helitorch, the dangling hose, the string of flame clear against the greenery of the big trees. The next there was only a ball of fire rising incredibly, flames and currents churning within its maw; and almost simultaneously there came the thunder of the explosion and the blast of rushing air from it that rocked their own chopper. The helitorch-helicopter had disappeared.

Three of the big trees instantly burst into flame. More followed. On the ground Gordy Walker led his hotshot crew at a dead run toward the inferno, his walkie-talkie already up to his mouth.

Ben's pilot took their chopper up, and, banking, away from the immediate scene. "We can't do anything here," he said.

Speechless, Ben nodded in agreement, and closed his eyes.

The pilot's voice began in a monotonous tone, a steady, slow stream of words almost as if rehearsed.

"These goddam choppers don't like to fly," he said. "You learn that. They resist it. A fixed-wing aircraft wants to get off the ground and into the air, but these don't. And once you are airborne, you keep your eye on what you're doing, or you're dead. You learn that early, too. He just forgot it, and fussed instead with that gasoline fire shut-off." He turned his head to look at Ben. "You ever heard of the dead man's curve? No? Well, it's a graph of speed and altitude and what you are able to do when. He just didn't follow it, and where he was, there wasn't any second chance."

## 22

JL, leaning back in his folding chair, hands resting immobile on the map spread on his table, looked up to watch Ben and listen quietly. "There are times," he said when Ben was through, "when you can't win for losing. You've noticed that?" He nodded as if answering his own rhetorical question. "You've moved crews in? Ground tankers? You've established a line?" He nodded again.

"The rainmaker," Ben said, referring to the meteorologist, "still says wind change is coming. It doesn't look good."

"So what else is new?" JL studied Ben's worried face. "We're going to whip it," he said gently. "Count on that. We'll have more setbacks because when you get a fire this big that's the way it goes. But in the end we'll whip it."

The phone rang. JL picked it up and spoke his name. George Jefferson's voice said, "What is this about a helitorch exploding? How? And where?"

"Sheep Ridge. His shut-off valve stuck, he fussed with it and flew too close to the big trees at the wrong elevation."

Jefferson said, "Damn it, JL, you're the hell of a good man, but on this one, everything seems to be going wrong."

"I read someplace," JL said, "that Napoleon said he didn't necessarily want good generals; he wanted lucky ones. I haven't been very lucky. You want to replace me?"

"Nobody said anything about that, damn it."

"By the way," JL said, "my ankle's fine."

"Oh, for Christ's sake! Just keep me posted, is all."

JL put down the phone, pushed back his chair and stood up. Not for the world would he have betrayed by expression, words or action the heavy, deep sense of sadness and disappointment that he felt.

Another man dead, he was thinking, one of ours, another accident where accidents were immediately penalized severely. Bad planning the cause? Maybe, but analysis of cause, whatever the result, could not alter the basic fact that he, JL Harmon, the man in charge, was totally, inescapably and devastatingly responsible.

He was aware that Ben was watching, waiting for comments or orders. Still expressionless, "16:30 briefing," he said to Ben. "Let's go convey our messages of joy."


It was still light, and the sun low in the western sky had turned a copper color by the time Stacy drove home from the Inn. She paused on the County road at the end of her long drive to stare at what seemed to be a new area of fire—in the base of the finger of big trees that extended down toward her property and that of the other large holdings, as well as Bellevue Acres and Mrs. Wayne's Vista Hill estate which had been the first of them all.

It was while she sat there, studying the heavy smoke and the occasional visible burst of flame, that the green Forest Service pick-up came slowly by. Automatically, she waved, and the truck stopped. JL behind the wheel gave her his faint, inscrutable smile. "Yes, it's a new area on fire," he said, "something we could have done without."

He was bone-tired; that was Stacy's first judgement. There were lines around his eyes she had not noticed before, and his shoulders did not seem quite as erect as usual. Fresh from her talk, and early dinner, with Sophie Swift, she was, she supposed, in a softened, and sympathetic mood. "Are you off-duty?" she said.

"For a while. I was having a look along here on my way home."

"Come in," Stacy said, "and I'll give you a drink. You look as if you could use it."

As with Ken Delacorte, they sat at opposite ends of the big leather sofa, a cushion's width of distance between them. JL sipped his drink gratefully, but did nothing to start the conversation.

This, Stacy thought, seems to be my day for good works. "What happened?" she said, and listened quietly to the tale of the abortive backfire.

"So we swung and we missed," JL said in summation, "and killed a man and lost a piece of valuable equipment in the process."

"And you blame yourself."

JL shook his head. "Blame," he said, "is for hearings and investigations where they feel they have to come up with someone to hang it on. What I have is the responsibility. I'm the Fire Boss and it happened on my fire." He shrugged gently, not dismissing the matter, but, rather, acknowledging it, and filing it away in memory.

"Do you resent that?" Stacy asked curiously. "Or is that another wrong question?"

JL thought about it. "Not exactly resent," he said. "It's a different thing. I'd rather just answer for my own

269

performance. But somebody has to run the show—"
Here a faint, self-deprecating smile appeared. "—and
I'm good at it, so I'm out there leading the parade and
making the decisions." The smile changed a little in
character, and was now turned even farther inward,
mocking his own thoughts. "And I won't try to pretend
that I don't enjoy it even if things do go wrong."

"But you'd really rather be alone?"

JL studied her carefully, and found no mockery in
the question, so he answered it truthfully. "Yes."

Another loner, Stacy thought, like her father, like
herself, totally unlike Sophie Swift.

The beeper on JL's belt gave out its sudden shrill
signal. He silenced it as he stood up. "I'll use your
phone, if I may."

Stacy waved him toward the office-library and
watched him until he disappeared.

It seemed a long time, she thought, since their first
meeting that day when she had come, barefoot and still
dripping from the spa, wrapped in her terrycloth robe
to face him and ask what he wanted. She supposed that
the chip on her shoulder had been quite visible that
morning, and she had wondered then, and still wondered now, that JL's reaction had been as mild as it was.

"There's more to JL," Ken Delacorte had told her,
"than you may think on first meeting. You'll probably
find that out for yourself."

Stacy had said curiously, "You know him well?"

"I don't think anybody does. I've hunted and fished
with him, played poker with him, sat with him and
drunk probably more than was good for either of us—
well, I've even seen his paintings, but I don't know him
well."

It was the first Stacy had heard of JL's painting, and
she asked about it. "Watercolors? Folksy little scenes?
That kind of thing?"

270

"Not on your life. Oils. Big canvases. I'm no connoisseur, but I've wandered through a gallery or two and a few museums, and I've seen the hell of a lot of forest scenes hanging in them that didn't give me half the jolt in the belly that one or two of his do. His work is maybe crude, but you begin to understand that Forest out there when you see on canvas how he feels about it."

"Does he exhibit?"

"Nope. Fighting forest fires is his bag. Madge—that was his wife—didn't like his painting *or* his fire-fighting. So she left."

It was the first Stacy had heard of Madge, too, and again she asked questions.

"Why Madge?" Ken said. "Why anybody? I think a lot of guys get married for the same reason—because it seemed the thing to do. Now, don't lay your ears back. It's true."

In honesty, Stacy had to admit that probably a number of women married for the same reason—because it seemed the thing to do. "I won't argue the point," she said.

"But I'm still a male pig," Ken said. "I have the message."

Now, sitting on the sofa waiting for JL's return, hearing from time to time the low murmur of his voice on the phone, Stacy remembered that conversation with Ken quite vividly, possibly because it was so typical of their relationship.

The guy next door, Ken had called himself, and it was an apt analogy. Even back in college, when Ken had been a track and football star, big man on campus, and she, Stacy, champion cowgirl, they had been more like sister and the brother Stacy had never had, and long wanted.

Or maybe the shrinks would say, Stacy thought now,

that what she had long wanted was not a brother, but a second father to replace the one she had lost. And maybe that put a different light on things.

JL came back from the office-library. He sat down at his end of the sofa again, picked up his drink and drank deeply. He set the glass down carefully. "The front we've been expecting is moving in," he said.

"Fronts," Stacy said, "sometimes bring rain."

"This one won't. Warm, dry air, wrung out by passing over the coast range in California, the Sierra Nevada, the Arizona high country and our own mountains to the northwest. No moisture left. Just wind and pressure change."

Stacy said, "Is this my warning?"

"I wish it weren't, but I'm afraid it is." JL finished his drink and stood up. He looked down at her. "I am grateful for the little time of relaxation. And the drink."

*"De nada."*

JL shook his head in slow wonder. "Funny," he said. "We used to strike sparks, you and I. We don't seem to any more."

"I've noticed that too."

"I wonder why?"

"Maybe the fire's more important."

A nod, and the slow smile. "Maybe that's it."

"We'll just have to see," Stacy said. "And there's one more thing."

"Yes?"

"Some day will you let me see your paintings?"

"They aren't much."

"Ken says they show how you feel about your Forest. I'd like to see that."

JL hesitated. "Maybe they show too much. Somebody told me once that I'd stay here and grow moss — like the trees."

"Was that Madge?"

JL stood quite still, and silent.

"Another wrong question?" Stacy said.

JL took his time. He said at last, "It doesn't matter." He turned away then and walked out into the entrance hall. The big, carved front door opened and closed gently.


In the tower of the Forest Service airport, Andy McIlvain had listened to the latest weather forecast too. He pondered it as he went back down the stairs to the main hangar.

Jake Jarvis and the crew they had parachuted in thirty hours ago were back now, having held their sector until danger of fire spreading into that area had swept past. Then, gathering their gear and hoisting it to their shoulders—115 pounds per man—they had hiked the ten miles out over rough terrain to the nearest road passable to four-wheel-drive vehicles, where a jeep wagon had picked up the load and carried it out to the airfield, leaving the men to make their way on foot.

Under Jake's eye, they were now repacking their chutes and reloading fire boxes against the certainty of another drop. The balance of the smoke-jumping crew, fourteen men, their fire boxes already loaded into the Twin Otter, pitched pennies to a wall, pitched cards into an upside-down helmet on the floor, leafed through the worn collection of magazines—mostly *Playboy* or *Penthouse*—or read paperback books while they waited for their call.

Andy, unable to sit still any longer, called Jake to him. "The front's coming," he said. "I've seen the infrared photos so I have an idea what it'll mean, but I want to see the actual scene. I'll be gone maybe thirty-forty minutes."

Jake said, "If JL calls—?"

Andy wore his crooked grin. "Tell him I've quit and am headed for the big city fleshpots. Then get on the radio from the tower to me." He walked out to the field where his own single-engine aircraft was parked.

Airborne, he felt free and loose and easy, sharing with the soaring ravens, the eagles, the hawks and the vultures the ability to look down on the world and see it in its true, constricted dimensions.

Dominating the earthbound scene, of course, was the big mountain, still proudly thrusting its rocky peak above the smoke. Looking carefully, squinting against the glare that at this elevation was harsh, Andy could make out white shapes on the mountain moving unhurriedly across a steep talus slope. Mountain goats, their instinct, unlike that of other local animals, having driven them upward rather than horizontally away from the encroaching fire. Andy counted eight in the group—one big male, shaggy, bearded and burly but as light on his feet as any of the others; four smaller females and three kids obviously enjoying themselves as they sprang from almost non-existent ledge to precarious boulder foothold, kicking up their heels as they went.

"You'll be fine, fellows," Andy said. "Just stay up there and nothing can touch you."

In one section below timberline, even as he watched, the flames spread inexorably upward, and no firefighting crews attempted to stop, or even slow, their progress. Andy nodded approvingly. JL had obviously written off that single fringe of trees as not worth a futile effort to save them.

He flew over the cirque, the cliff in front of which he and JL had jumped, and noted, as he had expected, that the vegetation-free rocky face had been a natural barrier beyond which the fire on the mountain's flank could not pass. Right to the edge of that cliff face but not yet above it, the timber stand, mostly lodgepole pine, was blackened and charred, all green foliage burned away and the standing trunks mere shafts of charcoal testifying to the heat of the holocaust that had swept over them.

Closer to timberline, a section of trees was beginning to shrivel although open fire was not apparent. Super-heated air, Andy thought, probably without the oxygen to support actual combustion, was creeping through the trees, consuming them with invisible energy.

He took the aircraft up in a wide swinging turn until his view was from a position even above the mountain's peak, and the full extent of the fire called BACK-SLOPE was spread beneath him. He continued to circle slowly as he looked.

The total fire area was roughly elliptical in shape, its major axis extending westward from the big mountain; its minor axis running almost due north-south. Airborne estimates were mere guesses, but it looked to him as if the fire had to cover an area about fifteen miles long and perhaps ten miles deep, 150 square miles, or — he did quick mental calculations — Jesus, in the neighborhood of 96,000 acres!

Looking down on the blackened, totally devastated areas where the fire had already come and gone, smoke still rising and here and there an occasional yellow-orange flare of flames as fuel somehow left intact suddenly reached flash point, was, he thought, like looking down on a silent battlefield, or a city — pictures of wartime Hamburg, Tokyo, Hiroshima came to mind at once — bombed into smoking rubble and left for dead. Hell, he decided, must somehow resemble this.

He put that concept aside and settled down to study details.

Beyond Highway 14 to the north, where the gasoline

tanker had exploded, and the crater that was its grave still showed plain and clear, the fire had established a bulge — against which Andy could see ground crews, backed by bulldozers and ground tankers, fighting a desperate holding, and containing, action. At the moment, as Andy could see from the blowing smoke, the wind was against the ground crews, driving the open flames inexorably forward, north and northwest.

The southern line of the fire was almost straight, except for an expanding area of flames at the base of the finger of Forest that pointed toward the big houses, the Bellevue Acres development and the town beyond. Along that southern line, the wind aided the efforts at suppression, although, as Andy could clearly see from his eagle's-eye viewpoint, the crash of that helitorch had been a very near thing indeed, and only immediate action by the hotshot crew on the spot had kept the fire from spreading among the big trees out of control. So far, then, the eastern flank of Sierra Grande was secure; the fire's penetration from its starting point had not proceeded east or northeast beyond the Sheep Ridge area.

But there was one more item that caught his attention, and at this he stared long and hard and unhappily.

To the northwest there was no smoke, which was momentarily puzzling, because the fire beyond east-west Highway 14 was being pushed by wind out of the southeast, and a trail of smoke from that fire should by now have stretched north and northwest for miles over unburned territory.

There was, of course, only one explanation: the anticipated wind shift had arrived, and the smoke rising from the bulge beyond Highway 14 was being blown back upon itself, so everything was about to be reversed, and what had been secure would soon be in jeopardy as the invisible propelling force, wind, turned one hundred and eighty degrees.

Andy reached for the mike and called the tower at the field. "Can you patch me through to JL?"

The tower could. JL's voice came through loud and clear.

"I'm up here at fifteen thousand," Andy said, "and if you want to eat my ass out for leaving the field, at least wait until I report. There is no smoke, repeat, no smoke beyond the fire line in the northwest quadrant. Got it? Or shall I spell it out?"

JL's voice contained weary but instant comprehension. "I think I can work it out. A one-eighty wind shift." He added, almost to himself, "Just what we don't need."

"My beamish boy. Now tell me to haul ass back to the field."

This time there was faint amusement beneath the weariness. "Consider yourself told," JL said. "Over and out."


Frank Orwell, up on the mountain, was not lost; on the contrary, he knew all too well where he was — between a rock and a hard place. Below him, and coming closer, were flames. Above him, he could hear the voices of a fire-fighting crew cutting a break, grunting with their efforts, cursing obstacles and at times chattering among themselves like a cageful of monkeys, the sons of bitches.

And from time to time, almost as if calculated to torment him, the voice of that big bitch with the shovel sounded off, echoing through the trees and drowning out even the crackling sounds of the approaching flames.

The heat and the smoke were both increasing, and

try as he might, Orwell could stifle neither the urge to cough nor the growing terror that was gnawing at his guts.

Maybe that greaseball Vigil had been right when he had said that the crews were only interested in the fire, not in two escaped convicts who might be in the area; but whatever the case had been then, it was no longer so. He, Frank Orwell, was now instant raw meat the moment he showed himself. And it was all that big bitch's fault, her and her goddam shovel.

Orwell had his gun, of course, and there was nothing to prevent him from walking straight up the mountain to sanctuary above timberline, shooting as he went anybody who got in his way. Nothing, that was, except a hollowness in his belly whenever he thought about what had happened to the greaseball. Jesus, that bitch had swung the shovel right from her heels like Reggie Jackson swinging for the fences, and if Orwell lived to be a hundred he would never forget the sound when the shovel blade made contact, and Vigil was instantly changed from a man into something that might hang from a butcher's hook.

And so, hating himself for refusing to dare the open, he crouched like a goddam rabbit and took one cautious step backward after another in the growing darkness while the sounds of the flames came closer, and the heat and the smoke became almost unbearable.

Eloy Jaramillo, working and grunting next to Bessie's crew on the fire line, said, "Hey, big mama! I hear you clobber some dude. Is so?"

"I guess so, Eloy," Bessie said, and raised her voice in a roar. "Way to go! Skin it right down to bare dirt! Don't leave a twig for the son of a bitch to feed on!"

"What he done?" Eloy said. "I hear rape. That right? Some chick out here loose in the Forest?"

"That's about right, her and her husband."

"She not like you, huh' She like most chicks, you know, helpless?"

"Something like that."

"And her man—what about him?"

"He was hurt, Eloy."

"So you come on like John Wayne, huh?"

"That's me," Bessie said. "John Wayne." Raising her voice again. "All right, Pete, let's get the lead out. Stop playing and start using that thing you've got in your hands!"

"I think," Eloy said, "when we get to Antlers Bar, I buy the beer, okay?"

Bessie's shovel paused momentarily, and then resumed its steady, powerful progress. Her voice had altered, softened. "Why," she said, "why, that's goddam nice of you, Eloy. I appreciate it."

The sounds of the voices above and the flames below, the two pinching him into a corner; the crackling, crashing sounds too of blackened and weakened tree limbs tearing loose and spreading sparks as they fell. The choking smoke and the heat like a furnace blast. Orwell continued his step by step retreat.

He had the feeling that there was no end, no way out, all exits blocked—because of that big bitch who like an angry bear would as soon kill you as look at you.

Sooner or later, he told himself, he would reach the point of daring to stop, of advancing and showing himself, of having at least the satisfaction of putting a bullet in the big bitch's gut. Sooner or later, but not this step, nor yet the next. He wiped the sweat from his eyes with the back of his wrist. Just a little farther, and then he would make his stand.

He took one more step backward. It was his last.

Rock crumbled beneath his weight. He tried to throw himself forward, but there was no support for the thrusting leg. He felt himself falling, where and into what he had no idea. And then he was in free fall, cartwheeling into space over the cliff above the small lake. The scream he heard was his own.


Eloy, raising his head and cocking it at the sound as a hunting dog will, said, *"Qué pasa?* What the hell was that?"

Bessie shrugged. Her shovel did not miss a beat. "Some animal, probably. In the dark they sound funny sometimes."

## 23

Aaron Swift, a thoughtful man, studied the glow clearly visible on the lower slopes of Sierra Grande, and did not like what he saw. BACKSLOPE — the name was by now common knowledge in Sanrio through word of mouth and Carter Norris's TV newscasts — was not only alive and well after four full days, he decided, but with winds now out of the northwest, was obviously gaining in strength and size.

Debby said, "It's on the news. Will it come close to us, A?"

"It would have to go through town first. And that," Aaron added wryly, "would make us more of a footnote than a headline."

"You joke sometimes about funny things."

Aaron supposed he did. Basically, he was a serious man, something he did not believe Debby even suspected; serious and, he supposed, a creature of intellect as well, which Debby obviously was not.

Debby's reactions — and her life consisted largely of reactions — were visceral rather than products of ratiocination. Living, as Aaron did, in a world of reasoning, he found this refreshing. With Debby it was not necessary, or even sensible, to search behind words or actions for other than obvious motives. Debby was precisely what she appeared to be, as straightforward and unambiguous as a period at the end of a sentence.

"What if it did come this far?" Debby said. "What would we do, A?"

Aaron thought of Sophie's careful list of preparations, and shook his head. Except within his own field, the law, he was not a man of decisive action, and he knew it. "Probably end by taking something of absolutely no value like a favorite ashtray, and running," he said. "Dressed, I hope, although I'm not sure I can even guarantee that."

He shook his head again. "I knew a man," he said, "a physicist who was also an expert mountain climber. He traveled a great deal on hush-hush projects, and that meant staying in all kinds of hotels both here and abroad. He carried a hundred and fifty feet of nylon rope in his suitcase, and figured that in case of fire, he could tie it to something secure, and rappel down the outside of the hotel building to safety. A fore-thoughted man, as I am not."

"Did he ever have to do it?" Debby said.

Aaron smiled. "No. But he felt better for being prepared."

Debby said, "Our house is all on one level so you wouldn't have to do whatever you said."

Aaron nodded solemnly. "You're absolutely right. And besides, I don't know how to rappel." Refreshing, yes, he thought; but on occasion a trifle frustrating too. Never mind.

Debby said, "Shall we eat at the Club tonight?" She smiled suddenly. "You can do like you said last time, and take your fiddle with you."

Aaron nodded solemnly again. "A capital idea."

Bart Jones waited while his chauffeur-handyman took the wheelchair from the car's trunk, opened it and set it beside the open door. Then with his strong arms Bart swung himself out of the car into the chair, and began to propel himself up the walk. Before going inside the house, he paused to look at the fire area.

He had read of fires like this, and seen occasional pictures of them on TV. In wilderness areas of Canada, Australia and Mexico, he understood, fires involving literally millions of acres sometimes occurred, but rarely made headlines. Even here in the US, he would have been willing to bet, this fire called BACK-SLOPE would be receiving scant attention in the eastern media. To Easterners, the Southwest was vast beyond comprehension, and only sparsely settled, so what difference did a few tens of thousands of blackened acres make unless a known city like Santa Fe, Phoenix or Tucson were involved?

All of which musing brought Willard P. Spencer to mind. Spencer, in Bart Jones's opinion, was a pompous ass of the first water, shallow, opinionated and not too bright. It was not clear why Spencer had come to Sanrio in the first place — probably on a whim — but it was quite evident that he could not wait to leave as quickly as he could, and return to familiarity. In the meantime, as Bart had pointed out, he could be useful.

Over their second drink at the Inn, Bart had laid it right on the line. "You took a big flyer in commodities," he told Spencer, "and you took a licking the way amateurs usually do." He raised one hand to forestall objections. "I told you you're naked as a jay bird if anybody wanted to bother to look a little. I did, because I like to know as much as I can about the folks I'm likely to run into in a new place." He smiled

283

without amusement. "Some of those same folks like to know as much as they can about me, too, so that makes us pretty much even-Steven."

Spencer sat quiet, and unhappy, feeling that he had been unfairly enticed into this embarrassing situation, but feeling too in a vague way that it might well be to his advantage to hear what Jones had to say.

"You aren't going to go hungry," Bart Jones said. "There's that spendthrift trust that'll take care of your needs. But what you are lacking is walking-around money, and with the insurance lapsed on your house and this BACKSLOPE fire looking as if it might get completely out of hand, you're probably wondering just where that walking-around money is coming from. Well, sir, it's pretty comical, I'll admit, but I'm offering you a chance to earn it."

Spencer said incredulously, "In real estate?"

"Yep." Bart gestured toward the large windows and the spectacular view of Sierra Grande. "Fine country. Clean air. Lots of space. Good climate. Another Scottsdale, Tucson, Sun Valley, Vail. All it needs is the right push. By the right people."

Spencer said stiffly, "I have neither the experience nor the desire—"

"But you have friends. With money. And names. A ranch in the west. Or a getaway condo. Like discovering a new restaurant in Venice or Rome; it only takes one or two of the leaders, a few at most, and then the sheep begin to follow. Ada Loving is already here from Hollywood—"

"I am certainly not acquainted with film people."

"But she *is* an attraction. And there'll be others. Palm Springs is a good example. Or Santa Fe."

There was a short silence. "I do not understand," Spencer said, "what it is you think I might do, or for that matter, what I would gain by it."

284

It was going well, Bart Jones thought; there was already an avaricious glint in Spencer's eye. He said easily, "What you do is simple. You just entice a few well-known and well-heeled friends out here to see the beauties of the Sanrio Valley and that big mountain yonder the Apaches consider holy." He paused to let that sink in. "What you gain is also simple, a percentage of the price they pay for land *and* buildings. And with prices *beginning* at a quarter of a million or so, those percentages can add up." He picked up two menus from the table and handed one to Spencer. "Think it over," he said. "Now what shall we have to eat?"

Like shooting fish in a rain barrel, Bart Jones thought now as he rolled his chair into the house. Willard P. Spencer was well and truly hooked.

There was a telephone message on his desk, and he stared at it for a moment or two, wondering what it might mean. Miss Cummings had called? Stacy? He reached for the phone.

Stacy was direct, as usual. "I saw you and Willard Spencer leaving the Inn as I came in," she said. "You get acquainted fast."

"He's an ass," Bart said. "Other than that, no comment. Is that why you called?"

"Not exactly." Stacy hesitated. "I've had my warning. The fire may change direction."

"And you called to pass the word to me? I'm flattered. The last time you warned me, I remember, you said, quote, 'Damn it, you're soused'."

There was silence on the line. Bart broke it. "As a matter of fact, you were right, and I should have listened to you. What do you think of that?"

"I'd rather not think about it at all."

"But you did call to warn me. Strictly good neighbor?"

"Don't try to make anything of it. I've also warned my stableboy."

"That puts me almost in a class with the horses. I'm coming up in the world."

"You enjoy being a stinker, don't you? What were you and Willard Spencer putting your heads together about?"

"Why," Bart said, "I'm considering building some condos out here in God's country. Does that offend you?"

"Not if they're done right. Some developers bulldoze the land clean first."

"Makes construction easier."

Stacy said slowly, "Do you realize that some of those piñon trees are five hundred years old? And some of the junipers are even older?"

"So? Age doesn't necessarily mean anything. How old are the rocks we blast out?"

"As I said, you enjoy being a stinker."

"But you did call to warn me. Thank you for that."

"You can roast in hell for all I care." And then quickly, "Strike that. It isn't something I'd wish on anybody, and I've already done you enough damage."

Bart said slowly in a strange, different, more gentle voice, "This time I will heed your warning. Thanks."


"Here and here," JL said to Ben Hastings, indicating on the map the north and northwest sectors of the fire's perimeters, "the wind change will work to our advantage, of course, pushing the flames right back to burned-over territory where they'll die for lack of fuel. We can pull crews out of there, and bring them down here—" His finger indicated the southern fire boundary. "—where the new danger will be."

Ben said, "We'll have to run our trucks carrying the

286

crews all the way around the Wilderness and that's going to take hours."

"Under the circumstances," JL said, "I think not." His face was guileless as he looked up to see that Ben understood. Then he bent to the map again. "There's an old logging road running due south right here. It skirts the Wilderness." He looked up at Ben again, and waited for reaction. Both knew that the logging road did not skirt, but ran through, the Wilderness area. It had not been used since the Wilderness designation had been applied.

Ben said doubtfully, "If you say so."

"I'll give it to you in writing," JL said. "Now, we've asked Albuquerque to send in another helitorch, just in case."

Ben closed his eyes. He could still see that sudden fireball as the helitorch-chopper slammed into the ground and exploded. He could still hear the pilot's voice cut off in mid-sentence as it implored the chopper to lift. He said, "Another backfire?"

"If we have to." JL studied Ben carefully. "You'd rather someone else flew in the following chopper and called the shots?"

Ben shook his head. "I'll do it." He took a deep breath. "And I'll get those trucks moving crews down the old logging road." He faced JL steadily. "I won't need authorization in writing. If you're willing, I am too."

JL permitted himself the faintest hint of an approving smile. Good man, he thought, but did not say aloud. He nodded. "Get to it then. And keep me informed."

Jay Paul came up to the table as Ben left. Jay said, "I'm pretty much extra baggage around here. If you—"

"We don't keep extra baggage around," JL said. "So you're going to work. Have a look here." He tapped the map and waited until Jay bent over it reluctantly. "Sudden wind shift into the northwest," JL said then. "What will that do down here?"

Jay straightened. He faced JL squarely. "Push the fire down towards those big houses. But you've already figured on that." His voice was scornfully resentful, that of a small boy being asked the obvious.

"And over here to the east?" JL said, his expression unchanged.

Jay Paul glanced at the map. JL's finger pointed to rough wooded terrain on the big mountain's flank. "I don't know," Jay said.

"And neither do I for sure. But suppose the wind bringing sparks around into this canyon starts a fire line moving east to south? What about the crews working that southern quadrant?"

Jay Paul looked again at the map, with careful interest now. He said, "They'd be caught. They wouldn't stand a chance."

"So," JL said, "we want to see that that doesn't happen, no? You go out to the airfield. Show Andy McIlvain what we've got, and let him pick a spot in this area where he can put in a crew to guard against that kind of encirclement. You fly along with them, and once they're on the ground, give them instructions for placement from the air. Got it?"

Jay Paul took another quick glance at the map. The contour lines showed how rugged the terrain was, how steep. He looked at JL again. "They can't go in there by parachute."

"Wrong. They can, and Andy will. And when they're safe on the ground, you'll tell them how to deploy because you'll have the whole picture and they'll be down among the trees and rocks, working almost blind."

JL sat quiet for a little time after Jay Paul, still

doubtful, but now determined to try, had headed for the airfield. Jay was a good man, JL told himself, or he wouldn't have been here in the Sanrio Forest as Fire Boss of the Forest team. How good a man, they would find out. Right now, Jay was still handicapped by his experience in the flat piney woods back in the southeast, and what he had to do was become accustomed to this southwest country, much of which stood on end.

Ben, on the other hand, had no such problems. Ben was a good man all the way. Still a little young, but catching on fast.

And he, JL? For the first time in his life, he felt that he had had it; the realization came as a shock. Nothing, really, had changed, and yet, paradoxically, everything seemed to have. He was still seeing all the right things, still calling the right shots, still able to bear up under the disappointments and temporary failures. But something had gone, and he was unable to tell what, or why. You came to a time, perhaps, when you reached the point you had always aspired to—and found the view ahead flat and uninteresting. He had an idea that somebody else had said that once, and now he too was beginning to find it so.

He roused himself. The hell with it. He was tired. That was all it was. Okay, so he was tired. Whip this fire, he told himself, and then you can rest all you want. But whip it first. Make sure of that.

Bessie Wingate herded her crew into the back of the truck, giving the last man, Stinky, a helping shove on the rump that almost carried him the length of the truck bed and over the top of the cab. Then Bessie herself heaved mightily and got her bulk over the tailgate. She took a quick look around.

"We got room for a couple more!" she bawled in a

voice that carried above the sound of truck engines. She spotted a familiar face. "Come on, Eloy!" And, pointing, "And you, and you!"

She caught Eloy's arm and hoisted him bodily as by a crane. Then she hauled up the next two, and hammered with her fist on the cab's top. "Let's go! We got a full load!" The truck lurched off.

Pete, of Bessie's crew, said, "Sure as hell beats walking. But where we going?"

"Wind change, jughead," Bessie explained, "so we go down to see that those rich dudes sitting bare-ass around their swimming pools don't get singed." She noted the rutted dirt road they had taken, but said nothing about it.

It was Stinky who raised the point. "Hey!" he said, "we're going into the Wilderness. How about that?"

Eloy Jaramillo looked at Bessie and waited for explanation.

"We're the raggedy-assed ground troops," Bessie said. "Nobody tells us nothing, and we don't ask. You got that?" She looked truculently at them all.

Eloy showed his white teeth in a broad smile. When Big Mama talks, he thought, you listen. But good.


Andy McIlvain said, "Okay, let's move it. We're going out." He beckoned Jay Paul into the tiny cubicle he used for an office. "JL wants you to fly with us?" He nodded. "Good. We'll take Jake as spotter, and after we're down, you and he can work out how we deploy." He beckoned Benjie who had gone in on the previous drop. "Get Jay here some coveralls, and a chute pack." He saw the look of surprise in Jay's face. "No," Andy said, "you aren't jumping with us, but if anything happens and you have to jump, or if you fall out, you'll be happier with a canopy to let you down a little easier."

In the almost bare fuselage of the Twin Otter there was only the single wooden bench along the starboard side and the spotter's place for seating. They put Jay, in coveralls and wearing his parachute pack, on the fuselage floor next to the open doorway, and, using a cargo sling, attached him to one of the fuselage stringers. He tried not to be obvious about grabbing another stringer with his hand for support. By the time they were well airborne and reaching for altitude, Jay found that the hand holding the stringer was numb and faintly bruised from the pressure grip.

He watched Jake in the spotter's seat, and Andy McIlvain in the open doorway, as they searched the ground for a drop site. And, craning his neck, he looked down through the open doorway too and saw only treetops and rocks, and was sure that a drop was not possible.

But it was Andy, pointing, who said, "Over there! We can circle and come upwind to it! Duck soup!"

Jake nodded, and spoke into his mike, directing the pilot.

Jay Paul watched in fascination as the two sets of colored streamers were dropped. He swallowed hard as the first two jumpers, Andy and a man name Quirt, took their places at the open doorway, the static lines of their chutes carefully hooked to the vertical cable and clear of all obstructions. He found himself unable to swallow as Jake's hand tapped Andy on the shoulder and Andy launched himself from the aircraft and Quirt followed. He closed his eyes in relief when the two chutes deployed and the men began their guided descent to the chosen spot.

When, two by two, all jumpers were gone, Jay Paul watched Jake put down his headset and leave his spotter's seat to begin wrestling fire boxes toward the fuselage door, hook their static lines to the vertical cable, and, as the aircraft repeated its careful circling, push them out two at a time.

With difficulty, Jay unsnapped his cargo sling from the stringer, and, conscious of his clumsiness because of the chute pack he wore, gave Jake a hand moving the fire boxes into position for dropping.

When all boxes were gone, including the single, heavy box that did not have a parachute, the climbing irons just in case, Jake returned to the spotter's seat and replaced his headset. He stared out of the window, and Jay Paul looked cautiously out the doorway as they considered the terrain and the smoke now being blown by the wind out of the northwest around the mountain's flank. It was while they were considering the problem, because of the wind noise communicating between themselves as best they could by signs, that the two Air Force fighters appeared out of nowhere and swept past beneath them.

"We were at 1200 feet," Jake reported later to JL, "and none of us saw a thing when those two came under us like bats out of hell. I thought we'd hit something. Their turbulence bounced us like a cork in a heavy sea. I hung on to my seat. I saw Jay Paul make a grab for a stringer, miss, start to slide for the doorway, make another grab and this time catch hold and hang on so tight his hand was all bloody when we finally settled down and he could haul himself back and let go. He was scared pissless, and so was I. Just fun and games for the fighter boys."

From the ground, Andy McIlvain radioed in, "We're

down and deployed. We'll mind the back door, and if we can't hold it, we'll give you warning so you won't be caught by surprise."

"Be careful," JL radioed. "That wind can play dirty tricks."

"I hear you talking, pappy."

## 24

One night, after a number of beers at the Antlers, Bessie Wingate had delivered one of her lectures to all who would listen, which meant everybody, because her voice had carrying power. "Wind," she began. "Funny, goddam stuff. You can't see it, but you can sure as hell see what it does. And you can feel it, sometimes just like a cool hand when you're sweating, sometimes trying to snatch you baldheaded. You know what I mean?" Rhetorical question.

"I seen wind grab up a burning branch, carry it halfway to hell and gone and drop it in the middle of some area you thought was secure just like it was planned, and—bang! you've got a new fire front, just like that.

"I seen wind come out of nowhere too, just when the fire you're fighting is whipping your ass and damn near running over you, and all of a sudden it's like somebody dropped an asbestos curtain and the fire stops, tries to go back but can't and then dies down for lack of fuel.

"Some places, I've heard tell, they even got names for winds. Out in Southern California they got the Santana. Over in Europe a dude told me once, they got a wind that's spelled funny, but comes out sounding like 'fern'. In Colorado they got Chinooks, and I heard about Williwaws and Chubascos too. Seems folks have been thinking about wind for a long time. And you can't blame them.

"There's places—you ever been in the Texas Panhandle?—where the goddam wind blows all the time. There's other places, like way up north—I was up to Barrow at the top of Alaska once—where the wind don't hardly blow at all. There's just no goddam figuring, but there's one thing that's for damn sure: whenever you get wind and a fire together, you'd goddam well better watch your step every minute, or you might get your ass burned right off clean."

"We don't often get a one-eighty-degree wind shift," the meteorologist said to JL, "but we've got one this time. You want the genealogy? Okay. Now what we've been having is really the aberration, because our normal winds are west-northwest, as you know, and the wind that's been causing you all the trouble, out of the southeast, is probably caused by this tropical disturbance—it isn't a hurricane yet, and may not ever be—moving around down here in the Gulf."

The meteorologist was using a soft pencil to mark the national weather map he had spread on the table. JL watched, and listened, not, he thought, that he was going to learn much, but there was always the chance that he had overlooked something.

"If you're hoping for rain," the meteorologist said, "forget it. Near as I can see, this new air mass moving in is about as dry as you'd like to have the crackers you set out for canapés. Now, for duration, I'd say that the winds will hold steady. . . ."

All good, up-to-the-minute, state-of-the-art information, JL was thinking, and worth to him about as much as notice of last year's appliance sale at Sears. On the other hand—"What was that again?" he said sharply. "Those velocity figures, I mean?"

"Maybe twenty-five mph, gusting to as high as forty at times," the meteorologist said. He smiled. "You don't like that?"

"Not even one small little bit."

You had to see sparks and burning debris carried by forty-mile-an-hour wind gusts, JL was thinking, to realize what kind of havoc could be created.

Man was an earth-bound animal, and forest fires usually, but not always, began on the ground where man could get at them. But when winds such as the rainmaker was now talking about got into the act, fire, the enemy, could immediately leap out of reach.

In mountain terrain, currents and eddies could form without warning. Small whirlwinds which, in dry flat country you could recognize as dust devils, could snatch burning fuel a hundred feet into the air and set the tops of towering pines ablaze. Gusting winds sometimes found solid obstructions no barrier, sweeping easily around them, and by their own velocity creating negative pressures—suctions, they were sometimes called—on the lee sides, to draw in more conflagration.

Winds provided continuing, fresh supplies of oxygen, without which no combustion was possible, and in suddenly constricted areas could establish blowtorch effects, devastating in their fury.

JL had seen fires leapfrog burned-over areas hundreds of yards in width, to ignite fresh fuel in virgin forest and turn an entire stand of trees into a holocaust. He had seen fire driven by gusting wind change direction without warning or apparent cause, sweep suddenly up a ridge that had been secure, and then dive into the arroyo below, roaring, bellowing its defiance as it swept clean brush, trees, houses in its path.

"Sorry about that," the meteorologist said. "I'd hold the velocities down if I could." He smiled to show that he was joking.

"Okay," JL said. "Thanks. Leave the map, huh?"

He looked up as Jay Paul got out of his jeep and came toward the table. There was a tightness around Jay's mouth, and the kind of knowledge that came from combat deep in his eyes. His right hand was wrapped in a bloody handkerchief. "Jake gave you the poop?"

JL nodded. "Sorry your first flight was a little rough."

"Those goddam fighter jockeys," was all Jay said.

As suddenly as that, JL thought, the man had grown up. Gone were the uncertainties and the vague resentments, and in their place there was anger, deep and solid, and determination, an obvious eagerness to come to grips with problems.

"Sit down," JL said. "And simmer down a little. We'll complain to the Air Force. Through channels, of course, and probably nothing will come of it. You didn't get any aircraft serial numbers because there wasn't time. There never is." He made a small gesture of dismissal, and tapped the weather map. "The rain-maker's brought us news."

JL explained about the predicted wind velocities. "That makes Andy's job all the more important. I want you to go back to the field and see that Jake and his people, all the rest of the fire-jumping crew, are loaded and ready, with their fire boxes stowed in the aircraft."

Jay Paul nodded. "Do we send them in?"

JL shook his head. "You hold them ready, and you personally stay in contact with Andy. Stay in contact too with Ben Hastings about those crews we're moving south. Put it all together, and if it looks as if Jake and his people are needed, send them in."

Jay Paul nodded, and stood up.

"If you want to check with me first," JL said, "fine. But you don't need my okay if you think they're needed." Andy would keep him posted on what was going to happen, JL knew, but there was no point in letting Jay know that and by that much undermining his new eagerness. "On your way," he said.

The front-running gusts that heralded the wind change were mild, tentative, but nonetheless welcome to the crews still manning the fire line in the north, beyond Highway 14. The flames they faced now wavered and lessened in force and vigor; here and there they even withdrew over area already burned, there to fade for want of fresh fuel, and settle into small, scattered conflagrations.

The chief of one of the crews left on the north line laughed at the retreating flames. "Got you, you bastards! We're going to whip your asses right down to nothing at all and then stomp you dead!"

Someone blew an imitation bugle and shouted, "Charge!"

In the sky to the northwest, high, thin cirrus clouds, like the banners of an approaching army, announced the main front.

"Bring rain, damn you!" someone said audibly.

"No dice." This was the crew chief, having had weather data via radio, along with continuing eavesdropped information concerning crews on other sectors of the fire, their current and anticipated conditions. The entire BACKSLOPE operation was tied together by radio contact on various assigned frequencies. "This is a dry front. California and Arizona stole all the moisture as the weather moved toward us, but we'll whip the mother anyway."

As the high cirrus clouds approached, the wind strength picked up, steadied, and gusts became fewer and stronger. The crew chief from time to time watching the fire's behavior in trees still burning, did not like what he saw, but kept his thoughts to himself. The fire was in league with the Devil, he thought, and was calling up its reserves. "Bring on your worst," he muttered to himself. "We'll whip you anyway."

Aloft, the sudden gusts were plucking weakened, still burning branches from doomed trees and carrying them astonishing distances into the already burned-over forest. Harmless, but indicative, the crew chief thought, and what would be happening down on the southern fire front did not bear thinking about. There, gusts blowing in the same direction would be carrying sparks and burning fuel into fresh, untouched areas.

Down there — he knew the terrain well — it was not only trees, but houses as well that would be threatened. And people who built houses were sometimes such damn fools.

Cedar shake roofs, for example — pure invitation to fire from flying sparks. Heavy planting against house walls — ditto. Most houses close to the Forest were on wells, too, and the power lines carrying the electricity that ran the well pumps were always vulnerable in a large fire or a big wind. Some building sites were in natural draws or situated on ridges, architects or developers ignoring the facts of terrain where wind always blew, and in a fire, wind meant flying sparks. But house after house — he had seen surveys — once destroyed by fire, was immediately rebuilt in exactly the same spot to the same plans. One house he knew about in a Los Angeles canyon had been burned three times, and rebuilt the same way in exactly the same place. After the third time the insurance company had called it quits.

Down on the southern fire front, in short, there was going to be hell to pay and no pitch hot, and the sooner the chief and his crew could make this front secure, the better, because they were going to be needed real bad where the going was worst.

"All right," he shouted, "let's get the lead out! We're needed elsewhere!"


Ross Oliver, secure in his conviction that his deity watched over him, carried his loaded shotgun in one hand and his garden hose turned on full in the other. There was no doubt in his mind that it was the wickedness of Sanrio that had brought this fire upon them.

Young women flaunting their near-nakedness in public places, hard liquor freely dispensed at bars and retail stores, the town's Adult bookstore and the X-rated movie house (open Friday and Saturday nights), bingo games in places of worship and barbarously suggestive dancing to savage rhythms — all of these, and more in Oliver's view, were affront to decent folks, and therefore had to be even more than offensive to his stern and wrathful God. Disaster was inevitable.

But he himself, and therefore his family as well, had led the moral life, and it was not fair that they should be punished along with the wicked. And so, unafraid, he moved against the fire, hose and shotgun in hand, a plump determined little man unfaltering in the face of the raging flames that threatened.

He was beyond the boundaries of his own property and almost into the Forest itself, a magnificent stand of lodgepole pine on the edge of the wooded finger that pointed at the town, when two things happened: a sudden wind gust, stronger than any of its predecessors, tore sparks and burning fuel from the tops of flaming pines and carried them beyond Oliver and into the immediate vicinity of his house; and, the electric power choosing this moment to fail when an overheated, automatic breaker switch threw, the pump in Oliver's well stopped, and the water pressure in his stretched-to-its-limit hose line began immediately to fall.

Oliver hesitated, considered flight and rejected it.

"He was like some kind of Horatio at the bridge," Ben Hastings told JL later. "I was deploying a truckful of troops from the north line, and saw it, the whole damn thing.

"He put his thumb partly over the mouth of the hose to increase its range, but the pressure was dropping fast, and he might as well have been spitting at the fire. He waved his shotgun and shouted something, but we couldn't hear the words. Bessie Wingate roared at him like a bullhorn, 'Get out of there, you damn fool!' He didn't even look back."

Ben was silent for a moment. "A big, burning branch came out of that lodgepole stand, riding a wind gust and flying straight at him like it was remote-controlled. He threw up the shotgun and fired both barrels before the branch hit him. Then it was all over, just like that." He snapped his fingers to indicate the instantaneous end. "Civilians," he added.

JL kept his eyes, unseeing, on the map in front of him. His face was hidden from Ben, and he made no move to indicate that he had heard and understood the words, but in his mind thoughts of blame echoed like a dirge.

One more dead man, he was thinking; the list was growing steadily—the tanker-truck driver, the heli-torch pilot, now this one. Add the convict victim of Bessie's shovel, and the raped bride, and this fire of his was turning into a carnival of violence, totally out of control with no end yet in sight.

He looked up at Ben, keeping his face as expression-less as possible. "Now tell me about Sheep Ridge itself," he said, and settled in his chair to wait.

The trucks had used the logging road, reached the Sheep Ridge area, discharged their human loads and made the fast run back empty, bumping and jostling off the track when they met a loaded truck south-bound.

"We spread them thin at first," Ben told JL, "but as more and more came down, we could thicken up the line, and begin to make a solid stand. By then, the wind had swung completely around, and the fire was coming right down the ridge at us." He watched JL nod with understanding this time, and knew that he was remembering fires when he had been the one to watch the flames coming at them.

On the line, Bessie said, "You're not the only one, Eloy, who doesn't know where the hell their own crew is down here. So you stick close to us, you hear, and we'll get it all straightened out when we got this goddam fire line under control."

Eloy grinned and nodded, saving his breath for his work. You felt the hell of a lot better, he was thinking, when you had somebody like Big Mama working alongside and giving the orders.

"Get the lead out of your goddam pants!" Bessie shouted at the rest of the crew. "We're not down here on vacation!"

First, though, there had been the matter of recover-ing Ross Oliver's burned body which lay in plain sight fifty yards from them. "You, Stinky, and Pete," Bessie had ordered, "haul ass out there and see if you can get the poor little bastard without getting singed yourselves. But be careful, hear?"

To Ben Hastings, passing by on inspection, she said, "Can we get him hauled away somewhere? Guys don't like to look right at what can happen. Matter of fact, neither do I." Against the crackling roar of the flames in the trees, the deep sound of bulldozer engines and the high-pitched snarl of chain saws, Bessie had to shout to be heard. "And another thing!"

Ben moved closer to listen.

"How's about putting two, three guys in a jeep with tools and maybe a couple of pack pumps to patrol back and forth right behind us? That goddam wind throws out burning fuel till hell won't have it, and a lot of it lands back there. Makes your ass twitch to think flames might be sneaking up behind you."

Sweating and swearing and sometimes grunting like pigs from their exertions, they cut a swathe across the finger of Forest that pointed downridge toward the town. The air was filled with smoke and heat, the taste of burning pitch and the sounds of conflagration. Trees sawed through and crashing down added to the din, and the deep-throated roar of bulldozer engines along with the high-pitched beeping warnings when they were in reverse, filled the scene.

"You know what it's like," Ben said now to JL. "The fire's got the wind behind it. We've got plenty of troops to man the line. Right now, it's a stand-off."

JL nodded, hearing still that dirge of blame in his mind. "So you'd better get back there," he said, "and keep the pressure on the Division bosses. Keep me posted." He watched Ben turn away, and stopped him. "One more thing," JL said, and was silent for a few moments, setting his thoughts in logical order.

Ben stood quiet, watching, waiting. He was beginning to understand something of this man, he thought, something of the depths of his feelings as well as his abilities. Never again would he stand by quietly and listen to references to the ice water that flowed in JL's veins.

"Bellevue Acres," JL said finally. "The big places too, but Bellevue Acres in particular."

"Yes, sir." The thought had been in Ben's mind as well.

"A stand-off now, you say," JL went on, "but you could lose that line." A statement, no question, but answer was demanded.

"Yes, sir. Depends on the wind."

"I think," JL said slowly, "that you'd better start thinking about being ready to evacuate Bellevue Acres, just in case. All those kids, pets—" He shook his head. "With the big places, you tell them to get in their cars and drive off. With that development, you'll have a round-up problem on your hands. Got it?"

"Got it," Ben said.

JL nodded once again. "Good man," he said, and immediately seemed embarrassed that he had uttered such praise.


Aaron Swift, in his role as Federal Magistrate, considered the case in his office, Les Lawry standing before him, with uniformed Van Padilla, on loan from the Sanrio County Sheriff's office, standing nearby.

"The jeep in the Wilderness is yours?" Aaron said to Les Lawry.

"Well," Les said, "I guess you could say that. I mean, it was. How we got in there—"

"We'll talk about that in a moment, Mr. Lawry— how you got in, as well as why. Right now I want to establish possession, in effect, title. The license on the vehicle is Texas—" He read the number, and waited.

"I'm not very good at remembering numbers," Les

said. "I mean —"

"Fortunately," Aaron said, "the Texas Motor Vehicle Department is. They confirm that that license number and the vehicle are registered in your name."

"Well," Les said then, "I guess that kind of settles it, doesn't it?" He tried a smile. There was no response. "I don't get it," Les said. "What's the big deal?"

"Now," Aaron said, "we'll get to the how and the why." He was silent, watching Les steadily.

"Well, you see," Les began, "there was this fire. What I mean, it was really burning up a storm, and I thought, 'Les, you'd better get the family the hell out of this. You got responsibilities, boy.' So we high-tailed it away from those flames just as fast as we could, like I think anybody in his right mind would do the same. What I mean, Judge, we had just one idea and that was to get away. At a time like that, you don't pay attention to signs and things. You just bust your ass — excuse it, Judge — trying to keep your family safe. Why, there wasn't time to think about it all, you see what I mean?"

"Not quite," Aaron said quietly. "As I understand it, there was the entire night to think about it. The first night, when you made camp by the stream, well inside the Wilderness, Mr. Lawry. What about that?"

"You mean," Les said slowly, incredulously, "we were where we shouldn't of been even then? I mean, we didn't see any signs or anything —"

"The tracks of your jeep, Mr. Lawry, lead immediately past a very legible sign forbidding any kind of machinery within the Wilderness area. As a matter of fact, you had to take down part of a fence in order to drive through."

"Why, that couldn't of been me, Judge. It had to be somebody else. As a matter of fact, we saw —"

"I am not really amused, Mr. Lawry," Aaron said. "Blatant lies tend to have quite an opposite effect on

305

me, and outright perjury annoys me even more."

"Why," Les said, "you can ask Cindy Lou and Tad—"

"Would you ask them to perjure themselves too?" Aaron leaned back in his chair while the question hung unanswered in the air. "You see," Aaron said, "I can refer this entire case to a United States District Court, with recommendations. That could turn out to be a great deal more than you may have bargained for. Perjury, for example, is a criminal offense. Or I can, within limits, deal with the entire matter myself. But if you persist in lying, Mr. Lawry, I promise that I will refer the case without further ado. Do you have a preference?"

Les hesitated. "Well, now," he said at last, "I don't see why we can't work this out right here, Judge. The jeep's totaled, no good to anybody. So why don't we just leave it lay where it is, and forget the whole thing? Now wouldn't that be the sensible thing to do?"

Aaron's voice took on an edge. "No, Mr. Lawry, it would not. Totaled, as you say, or whole, your jeep is, nevertheless, a piece of machinery. It is within the Wilderness which you caused it to enter quite unlawfully. I am convinced that your actions were intentional. You will now remove the jeep, all of it."

"But, Judge, that would mean having a truck go in, and that would break the rules again, wouldn't it?" Les, having scored a debating point, was smiling now. "So why don't we—"

"No one but you mentioned a truck, Mr. Lawry, or any other powered vehicle."

Les was frowning now. "But you want the jeep out of your woods, don't you?"

"That is correct. You will remove it. At your expense."

"What am I supposed to do, carry it on my back?"

The edge in Aaron's voice was sharper now. "Precisely how you do it, Mr. Lawry, is a matter of complete indifference to me—as long as it does not involve taking more machinery into the Wilderness area. The last transgressors had their jeeps hauled out by mule team. You might do the same. That, of course, is just a suggestion."

Les said, "Hire a wagon and a mule team and enough men to pick up a jeep and load it, and then have it hauled out? Do you realize what that would cost, Judge? A bundle, a great big bundle."

Aaron took his time. "How unfortunate," he said. "You might have thought of that beforehand. You may go now, Mr. Lawry. Sheriff Padilla will accompany you."

## 25

It was one of the SWFFF crewmen, a Chiricahua Apache, who spotted the body lying on the rocks at the edge of the small lake beneath the glacial cirque. The SWFFF crew chief radioed in the information, and two men, one of them a State cop, and a packhorse worked their way through burned-over ponderosa and aspen forest to the site.

The State cop, whose name was Portilla, squatted on his heels for a close look at the body. "At a guess," he said, "I'd say we've found the second one who walked away from Los Ojas. Fellow named Orwell." He stood up and squinted at the cliff wall. "Long fall," he said. "Let's have a look around. He was supposed to be armed."

They found Orwell's handgun in shallow water at the edge of the lake, a mere ten or twelve feet from the body. "That pretty well wraps it up," Portilla said.

The other man said, "Did he fall, or was he pushed?"

"You know," Portilla said, "as far as I'm concerned he fell, and that's where I'm leaving it. Couldn't have happened to a nicer guy. Let's get him on the horse."


JL heard the news from Ben Hastings who watched closely for reactions. They were subtle, but to Ben with his new awareness of the compassionate side of JL, nonetheless plain.

There was pain behind JL's smile. "The list grows, doesn't it?"

"The tanker driver panicked," Ben said. "The chopper pilot took his eyes off what he was doing, got careless. Oliver—" He shook his head. "I think he was hearing voices. And this one walked off a cliff in the dark." He spread his hands. "None of it is our—your fault."

JL nodded slowly. "All true."

"But you don't believe it."

JL made a short, sharp gesture of dismissal. "Forget it. Fill me in on the Sheep Ridge sector."

Ben hesitated. He had come with news, and now was almost afraid to speak it. He extended both hands, fingers crossed. "I hate to say it, but I think it's under control."

"The houses are safe? Spencer's, Swift's, Cummings's, Jones's, Loving's, Holloway's, Bellevue Acres, Mrs. Wayne's?"

Ben kept his fingers crossed. He nodded.

JL said, apparent digression, "Jay Paul hasn't committed the rest of the jumpers. And Andy agrees that they aren't needed as of now."

Ben sat down slowly, his eyes steady on JL's face. "But still you're worried? Why?" It did not occur to him to wonder that their relationship had altered, that in no more than forty-eight hours he, Ben Hastings, had changed from a definite underling to a near-equal. "There's something I don't see?"

Again there was apparent digression. JL said only, "The replacement helitorch-chopper has arrived. It's out at the heliport, ready to go."

"If I'm right that the Sheep Ridge front is under control," Ben said, "we won't need it. But since you're obviously thinking about it, you must doubt that Sheep Ridge is under control." He expressed no resentment; he was merely stating a fact that, even without words, asked a question.

"The best of us see shadows sometimes," JL said, "and there's no use pretending they aren't there. I hope you're right about Sheep Ridge. But until we're cold-trailing the embers, I'm going to wait and see. And I think you'd better do the same."

It was the best he could do because there was no way to put into words, even to Ben, what he had once heard described as the anxiety of helplessness you felt in a situation like this.

Murphy's Law, that what could go wrong would, did not apply. Rather, it was that what could go wrong *might*, and the consequences if it did, and caught them unprepared, were too appalling to contemplate. It behoved him, therefore, to play it with caution, even if waste might seem to result.

It was not that he distrusted Ben's estimate of the situation, that Sheep Ridge was under control. He did not even feel an urge to go down and see for himself; Ben's word was sufficient.

But what there still might be, lurking in the shadows of the future, was what he could not know, and had to guard against. There was simply too much at stake — precious Forest to be defended, of course, but beyond that, inevitably to go if the Sheep Ridge fire line were breached, would be the houses, the large estates first, but then the crowded housing development of Bellevue Acres with its people and its kids, to many all that they had in the world, and perhaps even, in misguided efforts to save something, lives as well put in jeopardy.

Nor was that all, because beyond Bellevue Acres, with no natural barrier of any kind even to delay, let alone halt, the fire's wind-driven progress, were the outskirts of Sanrio itself, with houses and stores on tiny city lots, crowded as San Francisco's blocks had been crowded in 1906 when so much of that city was destroyed by the fire that followed the earthquake.

He was conscious that Ben was watching him, waiting for an explanation of some kind. JL shook his head. "Sorry," he said.

Ben hesitated. Slowly he nodded. "You're the boss," he said.

"Yes," JL said flatly, "I am. We wait, and watch, and hope that shadows are all I'm seeing."

Ada Loving drove a leased sky-blue Mercedes 380 SL, top down. In sandals, skin-tight slacks and a crisp white, short-sleeved blouse now instead of the G-string-and-pasties bikini, she parked behind Ken Delacorte's aged Ford and went into the real estate office.

Ken was at his desk staring at a map. He stood up to acknowledge her presence, and then sat down again as Ada sank gracefully into a visitor's chair. She was unsmiling.

"I'm scared, Ken," Ada said, the words coming out too fast. "The fire's too big and too close. And everybody else seems to be pretending it doesn't mean a thing. That's the scary part."

"Is the whole world mad?" Ken said, and smiled. "Probably."

"Be serious."

They had known each other for some time and their relationship had never been more than friendly. Now there seemed to be a sudden difference, a new seriousness. Ada's discomfort was plain.

"Did you come to have your hand held?" Ken said.

"It would be a welcome relief from the hands I usually have to contend with." Again the words came too fast, almost tumbling over themselves. "Are we safe, Ken? Can they control that—monster?"

*Monster* was the right word, Ken thought, as he knew from experience, and few did. One summer vacation from school, young, strong and active, he had worked in a fire crew, and he had seen up close, too close, the roaring, menacing spectacle of a wildland fire on the loose, an advancing furnace throwing its heat ahead of itself in a blast that could sear your skin, and your lungs, where no flames touched.

He had seen flames climb so high that they disappeared into smoke clouds of their own making, and felt the earth shake as giant trees tumbled to the ground. He had seen wild creatures, large and small, from bears and moose to tiny squirrels, fleeing blindly in panic totally unaware that they were running toward and through numbers of their greatest enemy, man.

A wildland fire was not simply a line of flame advancing evenly. It seemed to have a cohesion of its own, and both a plan and a purpose—devastation. It appeared irresistible, a primal force that had burst out of its confinement and would settle for nothing less than destruction of the world and all that was in it.

Facing it, your bowels seemed to turn to water and you wanted to turn and run and leave the thing to do its evil unopposed. But somehow you stood, and fought, sometimes retreating, sometimes managing to hold firm in the heat and the smoke and the roaring, crackling din that made verbal communication impossible, seeing the flames leaping high until they seemed sometimes to overreach you, and you found time to wonder that you survived. And you remembered.

Now, "You do have it bad, don't you, baby?"

Ada said in a slower, calmer voice that nonetheless seemed to emphasize her fright, "I was in a fire once. I was five. The volunteer fire department didn't arrive until it was too late, and I can still close my eyes and remember standing with my mother, holding my doll, the only thing I'd carried out, and watching the whole house go up—with my crippled aunt inside screaming. I've been terrified of fire ever since."

Ken was silent, vaguely shamed.

"I'm afraid to be alone," Ada said. "I want a man on the scene."

"What about Sturgis?"

"I said be serious, Ken. He isn't a man. He's a piece of typecasting. You get near enough, you can smell the sun lamp and the hair dye, and see the contact lenses."

"And the Hollywood pigeons?"

"They decided to cut their losses, and sent them back in the chartered plane."

"They?"

"Whoever backs the show. I'm hired help, not part of the management."

"But you're also a bright girl."

"I'm not supposed to be. It's the body they want, not any brains I might have."

Ken said slowly, "There's a dude in town name of Jones, goes around in an electric wheelchair. This sounds like his kind of operation."

"I've met him," Ada said. "But whether it's his bankroll or not, I don't know. I'm paid in cash for showing the flesh, and that's an end to it." The famous eyes watched Ken steadily. "And if you think it's a pretty sleazy way of making a buck, why, I agree."

Ken took his time. "What do you want me to do, tell you everything is going to be okay?"

Ada said, "Coming from you, it would help. You're real. You're not make-believe like the ones I spend my time with."

Ken shook his head almost angrily. "Don't make me out to be something I'm not. I get the same ideas about you that any male would."

"I've lived with that since I was fourteen. I'm used to it. The difference between you and the rest is that you treat me like a person, not just pieces of anatomy. Can I stay here?" She gestured around the small office. "I don't know how to type. I don't know how to file things, either, but I do know the alphabet and maybe I could figure it out."

Ken studied her carefully. "You're serious," he said.

"I told you, I'm scared spitless. I'd run, but I wouldn't know where, and besides, then I'd be alone again. Don't let the fire reach me, Ken. Please. That's all I ask."


Angela (Mrs. Willard P.) Spencer, lying in the sun beside the pool in an artfully cut one-piece swimsuit, shaded her eyes and looked over at her husband who sat beneath a multi-colored umbrella staring into space.

"Did you tell them, Will, that we think that fire is entirely too close?"

"In detail," Spencer said. "They mentioned a wind shift. I said I didn't want excuses, I wanted results."

"Then I don't understand it. And why can't we go away, as I suggested? Take that new Orient Express from London to Venice, and then maybe fly on to Greece. The Trumbulls have that place near Athens—"

"At the moment," Spencer said, "it simply is not convenient."

"What a bore." Angela lay back on her chaise and closed her eyes again, the subject apparently forgotten. Angela's attention span was short.

Spencer glanced at his wife, and then, seeing that he was unobserved, fell to studying her. She had been a stunning bride, and now, fifteen years later, was still a stunning woman, as many of the wives of his friends were not. It was small wonder that at parties Angy was always the center of a group of admiring males, laughing, teasing, in her light-hearted way flirting, innocently, of course, or so Spencer had always assumed and even now had no reason to doubt — not that it really mattered.

Angy had always been popular. For some, the gathering of guests for a party was a fearsome chore; for Angy there had never been anything to it. Angy beckoned, and guests came.

A vague thought was beginning to take shape in Spencer's mind, and, his eyes still on his wife in that swimsuit that seemed so modest and yet was so suggestive, he allowed it to grow.

For Angy, summoning houseguests from New York or Connecticut or Virginia, from any of their familiar haunts, would be easy. Keeping them here and making them interested in Sanrio and its environs, as that barbarian Bart Jones had suggested, would be something else. But the lure of Angy as a neighbor just might be attractive enough, to some of the men, anyway, that investment in land, even in a residence, might very well follow. And certainly Angy would welcome the presence of the kind of people she knew well, and liked, and would, in her own way, try hard to make them feel comfortable and at home.

Just how far Angy's neighborliness might go, was not really a matter of serious concern to Spencer. Angy would certainly know how to conduct any indiscretions in a discreet manner, which was basically what mattered.

Almost as if Angy had been reading his thoughts, she said, without opening her eyes, "I do wish we had some of our own kind of people out here, Will. It would be nice, wouldn't it?"

"Funny," Spencer said, "I was just thinking the same."

Angela's eyes opened. She shaded them as she looked at him. "How clever of you," she said. "How very clever." And then, with one of her remarkable, and inexplicable changes of subject, "Do you think the smoke is thicker, Will? Why do you think they haven't already put a stop to it?"

The doctor, an old family friend, saw Elsie and Don Edwards together in his office. "The X-rays show no fracture," he said to Don. "Concussion, of course, as you assumed, and the headaches are inevitable, but they will go away. Rest is indicated."

Elsie sat quiet. Her turn next, she thought, and wondered why it was that she felt no sense of embarrassment, let alone shame, that what had happened to her would be openly discussed. Perhaps it was that the terror she had felt on the mountain, caught between the fire and the two men, made other, lesser emotional reactions seem without importance. A strange, new concept.

"I am not a psychiatrist," the doctor said, looking now at Elsie, "but I would guess, my dear, that you are still in a moderate state of shock, which is perfectly understandable."

"There's nothing wrong with me," Elsie said.

"Physically, no. You are a very strong and healthy young woman. But certain—associations may, it seems to me, tend to—inhibit you in your future behavior." His faint smile was tinged with embarrassment. "If you see what I mean?"

She had known the doctor all her life, Elsie thought, and always he had seemed a larger-than-life figure, omniscient, and wise in his judgements beyond questioning. Now, in the light of what she felt, he seemed smaller than before, a less-than-infallible mortal going through the motions of making pronouncements not out of conviction, but merely because he felt they were expected. He was a dear, but suddenly he had become an elderly, bumbling dear, no longer to be taken too seriously.

"I don't think Don and I will have any troubles in bed," Elsie said, and saw by the doctor's expression that she had understood perfectly what he did not want to say aloud. "A bad thing happened to me," she said. "Two men raped me. I won't forget that, ever. But the same thing has happened to other women and they have survived, and I am not going to allow the experience to—unhinge me." At least, I don't think I am, she thought and did not say. "But what I may have more trouble with is watching that—man being almost chopped apart." She was silent for a moment. "Because of me," she said.

She saw Don open his mouth to protest, and was quick to forestall him. "Not my fault, I know. And they—attacked you, too, for no real reason. Still—" She shook her head, remembering the sight of Bessie bursting out of the trees like an avenging Fury in one of those Greek tragedies, a force against which neither defense nor escape was possible.

"I repeat that I am not a psychiatrist," the doctor said, speaking still directly to Elsie. "But age does have its different ways of seeing things. You, both of you, have been through an experience that could have been shattering. And in your minds it still seems enormous, and was. But—and this is the important part—you have survived it, and by this much you have put it behind you. It should diminish in importance as you go along and other experiences, not as traumatic but nonetheless disturbing, come along to occupy your attention."

Here he smiled, just as he had smiled, Elsie remembered, when he had assured her that adolescent pimples were not life-threatening, nor would they leave permanent scars. And all at once their relationship was again as it had always been. The change was strangely comforting.

"In one sense," the doctor went on, smiling still, "the process of reaching maturity seems to consist of going from one crisis to the next. I think that between you, you'll be fine."


Of the larger houses adjoining the southern boundary of the Forest, the Holloways' was the closest to the new Sheep Ridge fire line. Byron Holloway stood on the smooth green lawn off the patio, studying the Forest, the smoke, the occasional burst of visible flame, hearing the sounds of engines and chain saws punctuated by voices shouting commands.

Byron was a retired New York stockbroker who had begun his adult life as an engineer, and had never forgotten his early training. Both he and Frances, his wife, had luggage neatly packed and fitted into the trunk of Byron's car. If the fire did burst its bounds, it would take only moments to get into the cars and flee. But there were other thoughts also occupying Byron's mind.

He and Frances had been in Sanrio for ten years, having come out from Connecticut for Frances's arthritis. During those ten years, three things had happened: he and Frances had grown noticeably and admittedly older; the house which they had built, together with its grounds and garden, had become something of a burden rather than the joy it once had been; and, at the same time, the house and property had increased many times in value and was now insured, at Byron's insistence with an eye on contemporary prices, for $300,000. True, other house values had also increased, but in a temporarily sagging market, as Byron was well aware, there were splendid new smaller homes presently available at less than their listed prices; in effect, bargains.

And there was more. Byron's shrewd and experienced assessment of the financial markets convinced him that the beginnings of a major bull market were at hand. The problem was that he was currently almost fully committed, and to sell his present holdings in order to re-invest more advantageously along the lines of opportunity he foresaw, would be to incur what he considered outrageously exorbitant short-term capital gains taxes. An unhappy situation.

His eyes were still on the Forest and the smoke, the occasionally visible flames. If the fire were to burst its bounds and destroy their house, he was thinking, the spread between the insurance money and the cost of one of those splendid, new, smaller, now discounted homes would be on the order of $100,000-$150,000, cash, with no real estate broker's fees to pay, a tidy sum with which to anticipate a rising securities market.

The wind had risen, and smoke from the fire was blowing toward his house. As he watched, a wind gust plucked a burning branch from a towering pine and hurled it skyward. Byron's eyes followed it as it fell, showering sparks which in turn became windborne, and finally disappeared beyond the wall that marked the end of his property. Cedar shake roof shingles such as his house had were highly inflammable, he had read. He turned to look at the roof now, and studied it thoughtfully.

Frances came out into the patio. "Worried, dear? I think that Juan—" Their twice-a-week handyman. "—keeps the garden hose in the toolshed. We could attach it. I have heard that wetting down a roof is very good protection against sparks."

"No." Byron's voice was firm. "I will not have you on a ladder, and I don't intend to clamber about like a monkey myself."

"Your arrhythmia," Frances said, and nodded. "I quite agree, dear."

"We'll just have to take our chances," Byron said.

"Should we call the Sanrio Fire Department?"

"We're not within the city limits."

Again Frances nodded thoughtfully. Then her face brightened, "There is that Volunteer Fire Department. We contribute to it. And we have a—I believe it's called a grid number. It's on that loose page on the phone book. A nice young woman explained it to me one day."

"They certainly know by now that there's a fire. And there's no point in tying up their emergency line telling them what they already know."

"True." Frances nodded yet a third time. "I hadn't thought of that."

Byron said in sudden decision, "No point just staying here watching and waiting. It's—unnerving. Let's go to the Club for early dinner."

"Splendid dear. I'll just get my purse."

"We'd better take both cars. Just in case. You go on ahead in yours. I'll be right along."

"Of course, dear. I'll take a table in the dining room."

Frances sat at a window table for two, on this early June evening looking out over the 18th green. She had her usual glass of white wine before her. A cold, dry martini-with-twist, straight-up, was waiting at Byron's place when he arrived.

They smiled at one another as Byron sat down. "Do you know," Frances said in a conversational tone, "my first inclination was to ask if you had stayed behind at the house in order to set a fire near the shed or on the roof for all that insurance money." Her smile remained steady.

Byron stared across the table, not quite believing what he had just heard. It occurred to him to wonder suddenly if he had ever really seen his wife before. He decided that he had not, and his hand was less than steady when he picked up his martini.

"But when I thought about it," Frances went on, her voice unchanged, "I decided I really didn't want to know. So I won't ask." She touched his glass lightly with her own. "Cheers," she said.

## 26

Bart Jones's voice on the phone, Stacy thought, was hardly subdued, but there was in it a quality of restraint she had not heard before, and it was this, as much as anything he said, that piqued her curiosity. Her reactions might otherwise have been different.

"Damn short notice, I know," Bart said almost in apology which was totally out of character, "but it was just sprung on me too. Duane Semple—name mean anything?"

"It rings a very faint bell. Why?"

"Oil," Bart said, "gypsum, uranium back when it was worth something, a couple of up and coming high-tech industries, Florida Everglades development, a piece of the action in more enterprises than it's easy to count."

"What about him? And why should I be interested?"

"I'm invited for dinner," Bart said with more than a hint of diffidence, "and I'd take it kindly if you'd keep me company." His voice resumed its normal tone. "They've put out an all-clear, by the way, on the fire in the Sheep Ridge area above us. They've finally contained it. If you don't believe me, call your ranger pal."

Stacy had never known him to lie when he could easily be caught out, so she accepted the news as true. She had assumed all along, she thought, that JL would eventually bring the fire under control. He was the kind of man who accomplished what he set out to do. She said now, "Why me? Don't you know anybody else?"

Nothing changed in Bart's voice. "For one thing, Duane knew your Daddy, and liked him. So being with you puts me in good company."

"I'm flattered."

"For another, I'd still rather be with you than anybody else."

"I doubt that."

"For a third—" The voice still did not change. "—I thought you might be interested in putting in a word for Ken Delacorte's nickel-and-dime housing operation before Duane takes it over. Or I do."

Stacy was silent, thoughtful. "When is this dinner?"

"Tonight. Black tie. It's a thirty-minute drive to Duane's spread. I'll pick you up a little before seven. Of course, if you'd like to give me a drink first—" He left the sentence hanging.

"Oh, hell," Stacy said. "All right."

"That's my gracious girl."


JL studied the latest infra-red photographs while Ben Hastings sat close by, watching. The 16:30 briefing and shift change were well behind them, but JL had given no indication that he was planning any rest for himself at all.

"You had maybe two hours sleep last night," Ben said. "Are you thinking of knocking off sometime tonight? You look beat."

"I don't like it," JL said, ignoring the question, "and that's the damn truth." It was also vast understatement. The infra-red photos, in particular the one that covered the Sheep Ridge area, were setting off alarm bells in his mind that could not be ignored. The most recent weather reports were responsible.

"They call this storm in the Gulf Charley now," he said, "and it's beginning to flex its muscles. They say, but they won't guarantee, that we're probably in for another wind shift. And stronger winds." He tapped the topographic map also spread before him. "If that happens, I think we'd better buy some insurance."

Ben looked where JL's finger rested on the map. "Sheep Ridge?" He was frowning.

"Below. Between the ridge and these houses. That's our last possible defense line."

"A backfire?"

"If we get a wind shift. Not otherwise."

Ben was silent, thoughtful. He said at last, "You don't trust our Sheep Ridge fire line?"

"I don't trust anything in this whole fire."

"You're tired," Ben said. "That's—"

"Yes, I'm tired! But I'm not yet ready to turn the job of whipping BACKSLOPE over to the technicians." JL tapped the infra-red photos. "From 10,000 feet they can show us that a spot on the ground one foot square is smoldering. Fine. I'm glad to know it. But they can't tell us if it's going to become open flame, because that depends on what the air on the ground is doing, it depends on the humidity, on the kind of fuel that is heated almost, but not yet quite to combustion, and on a dozen other factors their cameras can't pick up."

Ben sat silent, listening, wondering at this sudden outburst.

"The weather reports," JL said, "can give us all kinds of data, but they can't tell us specifically if we can expect a wind change that will affect Sheep Ridge, and even if they could, they wouldn't be able to tell just how that wind change will behave when it actually hits the ridge. And we have how many hundred men down there right now depending on our judgement to stay out of trouble? You've been on fire lines, and you know what it's like with nothing between you and the flames but whatever tool you have in your hands, and the faith that somebody running the show knows what the hell he's doing and will get word to you if it's needed."

He took a deep breath. "We have ground tankers and slurry drops, helitack acres, bulldozers, smoke-jumpers, two-way radio communication, weather forecasts, these infra-red photos, ground temperature and humidity readings, computers and God knows what-all, but it finally gets down to crews on the ground with hand tools and somebody making the judgements to direct them."

He paused again for breath. "Long speech, but what it boils down to is my judgement that Sheep Ridge is too tricky in these weather conditions to take chances with—any chances. So I want you out at the heliport, and at the first sign of wind change that makes a backfire possible and feasible between the ridge and these houses, you take off and tell the helitorch where to lay its flame. Don't hesitate, just go. There's only one time to lay a backfire, and that's the moment you see it will work. Wait, and the chance is gone. Got it?"

Ben nodded silently, and stood up.

"And give the ground troops the word," JL said. "The last thing we want is somebody, anybody, caught between two fires."

Ben hesitated, looked as if he might say something and then changed his mind and, nodding, turned away again.

JL spoke to Ben's back. "Go ahead and say it," he said, "whatever it is."

Ben turned to face him reluctantly, "It's just—" He stopped and shook his head. "You're the boss," he said.

"That's right," JL said. "And I want to know what you're thinking."

"Okay." Ben drew a deep breath. "I don't like back-fires."

"Because you saw a man kill himself laying one?"

"No." Ben's head shake was emphatic. "I don't like them on principle. They're dangerous. They can work both ways, get out of hand and do the same kind of damage you're trying to prevent, only do it sooner, and maybe worse." To his surprise, he watched JL nod.

"Right," JL said. "And explosives can blow up in your face, too, instead of where and when you want them to explode. But sometimes explosives are neces-sary, and sometimes backfires are too, and then you take as much care as you can, and hope for the best. This," he said, and drew his finger across the infra-red photograph between Sheep Ridge and the houses, "is our best defensive line. It's also almost our last before we get into the housing development and then the town. I want that line held, and another wind change will give us the chance to take out that insurance I mentioned with a well-placed backfire." He paused and watched Ben's face. "Unless you have a better idea," JL said.

Ben spread his hands helplessly. "I don't, but—" He stopped.

"Go on," JL said. "But what?"

"You're playing a hunch, aren't you? That some-thing more will go wrong and we won't be able to hold the line we already have?" He expected denial. Again he was surprised.

"I am. I admit it. So I want to hedge my bet with another hundred acres deliberately sacrificed." He tapped the map again. "Right here between Sheep Ridge and the first houses. If the wind shifts, it'll be safe to set a backfire and cut a good, wide firebreak there, just in case. It may not be necessary, and it's not the kind of thing that's in the book, but neither was sending trucks down that logging road through the Wilderness, something I may have to answer for one day."

Point taken, Ben thought with something of a shock. Without the crews those trucks had brought south in time only because of the logging road shortcut, they would not have been able to establish, and hold, the fire line he was now so stoutly defending. "Okay," he said, "now I know what we're doing."

"There'll be some who won't agree," JL said. "There always are. But you don't fight a battle by committee, and this is my best judgement."

Ben nodded again, suddenly looser and easier then he had been for some time. "I'll go along," he said. "But I've got a suggestion. I'll go out to the heliport. Jay Paul is already at the airport with Jarvis and the smoke-jumpers. Let me call in Jerry Weinstock, my night man, to take over here while you go home and get some rest. We'll shout if we need you." He watched JL's hesitation, and then his slow nod of assent. "We'll whip it," Ben said. "We won't let you down."

JL drove the Forest Service pick-up slowly toward his own place along the County road past the large holdings, in his mind reeling off the names of the property owners automatically—Sophie Swift, Bart Jones, Stacy Cummings not long ago just a name on a mailbox and an impersonal plat; farther on, Willard Spencer, Byron Holloway, Mrs. Tyler Wayne, Bellevue Acres and the rest.

Be nice to live out here, like this, he thought, trying for the present to push BACKSLOPE from his mind. He wondered what the prices for property and homes might be. Ken Delacorte would know. One million? Two? When you got that high, you needed a calculator just to figure how many zeroes. Like trying to calculate the number of acres in a Forest. 80 chains to the mile. Now why had that random bit of knowledge popped up now? He was more tired than he thought. And Ben Hastings, who was a bright young one, could and would cope. Maybe it was time that the old order did indeed changeth, yielding place to the new—good God, how long was it since he had read Tennyson's *Idylls of the King* in school and been struck by that archaic kind of language?

He closed his eyes for a moment, trying to remember.

When he opened them again, he and the pick-up were upside down in the ditch by the side of the road, and blood was running up his cheeks and into his nose from a gash on his chin.

"This," Bart Jones said, as if he had said it many times before, "takes a little doing. Stand by."

He actually smiled up at Stacy as he stopped his wheelchair beside the open rear car door, set its brake and, with what appeared to be an impossible gymnastic maneuver, propelled himself by his arms alone out of the chair and into the car to a precarious perch on the edge of the rear seat. Then he lifted and turned himself to a comfortable sitting position. Stacy watched, wishing she could help, but not wanting to interfere and not knowing what, if anything, she might do anyway.

Bart smiled again. "Your turn. Come in," he said.

Stacy raised her long skirt, entered the car and seated herself. Embarrassed by what she had watched, she kept her eyes on the chauffeur as he closed the door, folded the wheelchair and carried it to the back of the car to stow it in the trunk.

"I met a fellow," Bart was saying easily, "who had been crippled by polio from the time he was a kid. He showed me some tricks about getting yourself around without legs." And, with a sensitivity Stacy had not realized he possessed, he added, "I'm used to it, but other people aren't. It makes it harder on them. Sorry."

"You can be a nice guy when you want to be," Stacy said. "I'd forgotten that."

"But I don't want to often, is that it?" Bart smiled and nodded. "Depends which side you're on. Most things do. To you, your Daddy was a great guy. You were on his side. To some, he was a stinker because he whipped them good. In your day you've whipped a few, too."

"I've stopped."

"Have you?"

They paused at the end of the long drive, and then turned on the County road. Almost immediately their headlights picked out the Forest Service pick-up, still upside-down, its lights still burning. JL was slowly and laboriously clambering out the front window. Blood dripped from his chin.

Bart said, "Well, well. I think we'd better stop." He looked at Stacy. "You want out? I'll wait."

No matter that in a long dress and heeled sandals she looked ridiculous, Stacy thought briefly, the important thing was to see how badly JL was hurt. Standing in the glare of the headlights, "You're bleeding like a stuck pig," she told him in a voice that was not quite steady. "Do you have a handkerchief?" He did. "Hold still. I'll have a look." She wiped blood away and examined the wound. "Not too bad." There was relief in her voice. "But you could use a stitch or two. Do you want a ride?"

"I've called in." JL held the handkerchief to the wound. His voice was muffled. "I closed my eyes, slept.

329

Damned foolishness."

Stacy could smile faintly then. "Don't expect argument. Otherwise are you all right? Pooped, but all right?"

"You've got it."

No shilly-shallying, Stacy thought, just the plain truth. She liked that. "Maybe butterfly tape will do. Simpler." She looked up the road at approaching headlights and a red light blinking. "Here's your rescue team."

JL glanced down at the long skirt. It was the first time he had seen her dressed up, he thought. She looked good, very good. "Go along to your party," he said. "Thanks for stopping."

Stacy hesitated. She disliked leaving him in this condition, but, she told herself, he would be in good hands. "Luck," she said. "I'll check with you when I get back." She turned reluctantly to the waiting car and got in. They drove off.

"He fell asleep," Stacy said.

Bart's voice was amused. "Not very heroic."

"Mortal men make mistakes," Stacy said sharply. "So do I. Duane Semple probably doesn't. How about you?"


On the phone in a clear, unflustered voice, "This is Byron Holloway," he said. And, reading from the loose page in the telephone book, "My grid number is A8 B6."

"Got it," the impersonal voice said. "What's the problem?"

"My roof is on fire. Those blowing sparks from the Forest —"

"Stay there. Put outside lights on so the crew can find you easily. Stay well away from the house."

"Understood," Byron said, and hung up. He looked at Frances. "They're on the way. We're to wait outside."

"The cars—"

"We'll move them clear. Come along."

From the Sanrio Volunteer Fire Department phone to the Forest Service dispatcher: "We've got a roof afire at A8er B6er. Our pumper's on the way."

"A8 B6. Roger." A very brief pause. "Holloway?"

"That's it. He called it in."

"Damn!" the dispatcher said. "That means it must have jumped our Sheep Ridge line. Much obliged, Sanrio. Your people will have company."

Jerry Weinstock took the news over the phone, sitting in JL's chair. He promptly called Ben Hastings at the heliport.

"Okay. I'll check it out. I'm closer," Ben said after listening quietly. "I'll keep in touch." As he trotted out to his jeep, two thoughts crossed his mind: the first was that JL had to be psychic; and the second was that the proposed backfire was now academic, which was a relief.

Watching in what he supposed could only be called morbid fascination, Byron Holloway was astounded at the speed and suddenness with which the fire engulfed the house. At first there were merely flames flickering along the roof; and then, all at once, the entire house went up in a great column of flame, and sparks from exploding cedar shakes landed among the piñon and juniper growth, in the trellises of Frances's garden and on the roof of the garage-shed. Almost at once, everything was ablaze.

The Sanrio Volunteer Fire Department pumper arrived, and in its wake private cars of the volunteers, some with red lights flashing. Men hurried about in seemingly haphazard, but actually carefully planned confusion, and in no time at all, a hose was leading from the swimming pool to the pumper, and a solid stream of water was dousing the house.

Frances held Byron's hand as she too watched, expressionless. Their conversation was odd in its seeming changes of subject, and the comments were widely spaced.

"It's been a happy house," Frances said after a long silence.

Byron's response was equally long in coming. "Yes."

Another long silence. Then, "I liked the Connecticut house, too."

"So did I."

"But your commute was too long."

"And the climate was not good for you."

"We could have stayed in Manhattan. There was that apartment that was going to be available."

"I think we outgrew Manhattan. We both wanted space."

With a crash, the roof collapsed and flames shot even higher into the dark sky. The shadows of the firemen seemed to cavort and dance in an eerie ballet.

Frances said after a silence even longer than those that preceded it, "Are we rootless, By? I don't believe I would like to think of myself that way." Her tone almost pleaded.

Byron's hand squeezed hers. "We have roots. We just transplant them from time to time. That's all it is."

Frances took her time thinking about it. "I'm glad you feel that way too."

JL, two blood-encrusted pieces of butterfly tape on his chin, came up out of a deep sleep to answer the phone. He discovered that it hurt to yawn. "Go on," he told Ben, and listened carefully. "The Holloway house," he said.

"Totaled. Nothing left but some of the foundations and a cracked swimming pool. And the wind has shifted again, so Jarvis is jumping in with his crew at first light to reinforce Andy McIlvain and his people."

"Your idea?"

"With Andy's agreement."

JL nodded approvingly into the darkness. "Send a car for me."

"It's on the way."

"Better swing crews around so we keep as close as we can to Andy's people. I know the terrain is rough in there, but we don't want them hopelessly beyond reach."

"Right."

"The Holloway house," JL said again. "Sparks flew that far?"

"Apparently."

JL nodded once more into the darkness. "I'll get some clothes on."

"You're okay? I heard about the pick-up."

"I'm fine."

He was not fine, but he was functional, and that was what mattered. Ideally, of course, on a project fire of any duration, you settled down to day-and-night crews, and shift changes at the established briefing hours of 04:30 and 16:30. But every so often, no matter what the book said, especially on an escaped fire of this magnitude when all bets were off, you found yourself ignoring the clock because crises arose from situations you have been aware of, and had watched carefully for days, and to try to explain all of the factors involved to your opposite on the other sift was an impossibility. Besides, in the end there could be only one commander, one man whose fire it was.

He was outside, showered, shaved and with fresh butterfly bandages on his chin before the car sent to pick him up arrived.

## 27

Ben Hastings, back at JL's table after assessing the breakout that had destroyed the Holloway house, took the call himself from the Sanrio dispatcher. He listened with growing incredulity. "You're sure you have the coordinates right? That's two, three miles beyond anything previously reported."

The dispatcher's voice was calm and unhurried, as usual. "Commercial aircraft usually know where they are. This one spotted flames and took bearings from the beacon on Sierra Grande and the ground omni beyond Brown's Corners, just to check himself. I make the spotting on Forest land."

"So do I, damn it."

"I have two men in the area."

"Send them in to check."

"Roger."

Ben sat back in his chair to stare at the area map and ponder. As he had told JL on the phone, the wind *had* shifted again. From almost dead out of the northwest, it had now swung north and then northeast, with occasional easterly gusts. In the area where the commercial aircraft had reported new fire east-by-northeast of Andy McIlvain's position—no sparks from the fire line they were already holding could possibly have blown to start fresh trouble.

On the other hand, as the dispatcher pointed out, commercial aircraft could usually be counted on to know their own positions, and their reported sightings almost invariably checked out.

Ben had the uncomfortable, and he hoped foolish, feeling that even though he didn't know the answer to the apparent riddle, he ought to be taking action anyway. It occurred to him to wonder if this was the kind of dilemma the man in ultimate command was constantly facing—to move, or not to move, and if so, in which direction? He felt a guilty sense of relief when the car he had sent for JL arrived, and JL himself, with bandages on his chin, came to pull out a chair at the table and sit down wearily.

"You were right," Ben said. "About Sheep Ridge, I mean. Somehow it did get past us to the Holloway house. We're trying to hold it there."

"It can always happen, sometimes in funny ways. How about the other houses?"

Ben pulled the map closer so they both could see. He pointed with his pencil. "So far, we're okay. But Andy's sector could cause trouble. And we've got another funny one." He explained his recent call from the dispatcher, and with his pencil indicated the area reported on fire. "Clear over here."

JL said without hesitation, "We want to hear from those two men sent in to check, just as soon as they know anything. With the humidity we have, or the lack of it, and no rain for going on seven weeks—" He shook his head. "Civilians don't begin to understand. There are too many clichés. Too many situations are described as powder kegs, or ticking time bombs or accidents waiting to happen. The Forest right now is all of those, but how do you get the point across? So somebody tosses a cigarette out of a car window, or leaves a campfire not completely dead, or some kids get hold of firecrackers because the Fourth isn't all that far away." He spread his hands. "Either I'm getting old, or I'm just plain tired of it." He produced his faint, crooked smile. It contrasted strangely with the butterfly bandages. "And maybe I'll feel different when we've got it whipped."

The phone rang, and JL indicated that Ben was to take it. He watched and listened.

Ben blinked. He said, "Wait a minute. Slow down. Shot? Who shot him? Where? Why? I know it's dark, but—"

JL could hear the slow, steady tone of the dispatcher's voice, but could not make out the words. He saw Ben's pencil touch a spot on the map, and he leaned forward to stare fixedly at it.

Something was running around in his mind, and he began to pursue it cautiously lest he drive it into hiding. Damn the gash on his chin which hurt when he smiled, and ached when he didn't; it was a distraction he could have done without. He closed his eyes and concentrated on that spot on the map Ben's pencil still touched.

It was sparse forest over there; even the ubiquitous piñon-and-juniper growth was scant. At one time the ground had probably been overgrazed, maybe by sheep which took vegetation right down to its roots, and in the way of this arid land, the area would be a long time recovering. So? It was maddening how extraneous thoughts kept intruding when you searched for a vague idea. Still he persevered, because what he was trying to pin down could be important.

"Okay," Ben said into the phone, and nodded. "There *is* a fire, and it looks like it's been set. You've sent in an initial attack crew? Good. Tell them to be careful. We'll get on to Andy McIlvain and warn him because he's downwind and it could sneak up on him. You get your

337

man patched up and send both of them over here. We'll want to talk to them." He hung up and looked at JL.

"One man shot," he said. "In the dark. They didn't hang around to see who was doing the shooting. I can't blame them."

JL opened his eyes. He thought he had it now, that elusive idea finally cornered. He said slowly, "That marijuana you showed me—remember? Where was it found?" He looked up at Ben and waited.

Ben said, "Oh, migod! That's probably it. The field was here." His pencil touched a spot just beyond the new fire area. He was watching JL closely. "How do you read it?"

It was easy enough to work out a scenario. JL said, "Cash crop, you said, heavy cash. So they want to get as much as they can before the fire gets to it, or fire crews run into it. I'm guessing, of course—"

"So they set a backfire," Ben said, picking up the idea and running with it, "to protect themselves while they harvest as much as they can. And they post guards with rifles. Why, damn it, we'll send in a crew—"

"We'll call the State cops," JL said, "and they can call in the National Guard or the Marines if they want. We fight fires, and we're more interested in this new one than in any amount of pot, because it's coming downwind at Andy's rear and if we aren't careful, he's going to be caught right in the middle." He paused reflectively. "Between a very hot rock and a damned hard place," he added. He was smiling no longer.


Andy McIlvain on the radio said, "Thanks for the good news, pappy. Somebody's playing games?" He listened while JL explained what they guessed had happened. "Better and better," Andy said then with heavy irony. "Who's writing this script, anyway?"

"Jake Jarvis and his people are planning to jump in to join you as soon as there's enough light," JL said. "You still want them?"

Andy thought about it. "No," he said at last. "If this new fire isn't too big, we can handle it. If it is, we'll just take out for timberline like big-assed birds. A dozen more men won't make that much difference, and getting them all out would be just that much more complicated."

"And if the wind shifts a little more when the sun comes up?"

"Good question. I'll bear it in mind. There *is* one thing."

Ben, watching, saw no change of expression in JL's face as he waited in silence.

"You might invent a parachute," Andy said, "that would go up as well as down."

JL nodded solemnly. "I've thought of that. A number of times. Good luck. Over and out." He pushed the microphone away and sat for a few moments in thought. Then he looked at Ben. "What's their position? Your last fix?" He watched Ben's pencil point touch the map. "And the nearest ground crew?" The pencil touched paper again.

With the first joint of his bent thumb, JL made a rough measurement between the two marks. "Well over a mile," he said, "a damned rough mile." He looked up at Ben. "Whose is the nearest crew?"

"Hotshot. Gordy Walker."

JL nodded approval. "Throw your next best crew in with them. Who would that be?"

"Big Bertha."

"Bessie Wingate?" JL smiled faintly, and nodded again. "Move her in with her crew. We want to get to Andy if we can."

"I'll tell her to whip their asses."

339

JL's smile was grim, but despite the hurt chin strangely confident. He shook his head. "You won't have to. Not with Bessie."

Ada Loving's Mercedes followed Ken's Ford into the drive of his house. Ada got out and walked with him in silence to the front door. As she watched him put his key in the lock, "Think of me as a stray that followed you home," she said, "because it had no place else to go."

"It's okay," Ken said. "I can smell the smoke too."

"But it doesn't scare you. You're a guy, a big, strong guy."

"Don't turn on the 'poor, little, helpless me' routine, honey. You've scratched and clawed your way just like the rest of us. And against bigger odds because you're female."

"You have noticed."

"Only a eunuch wouldn't. I think a drink, and then whatever we can scare up for dinner."

Ada, searching refrigerator and cupboards, found eggs and bacon, a can of chopped chiles and some onions — "Any tomatoes?" she said. There were. "Okay," she said. "You make coffee."

"There's beer."

The full, dazzling smile appeared. "A feast," Ada said. "Stand back. *Huevos rancheros*, or a reasonable facsimile coming up."

Her hands were deft and sure, and there was no hesitation in her manner.

"You know your way around a kitchen," Ken said. There was surprise in his voice.

"Where I grew up," Ada said, "there weren't any restaurants, or supermarkets with frozen foods in packages. And Mom worked all day. So did Pop. So I did the cooking. The glamor bit came later, a lot later."

Over their meal, "I taught myself to dance," Ada said, "by sitting through Ginger Rogers movies three or four times, and then practicing like mad, and trying out what I'd been practicing in front of store windows so I could watch myself. People thought I was the town nut. I stole a baton from the local high school. I gave it back eventually, but by then I was good enough to win a couple of competitions and a college scholarship. Lucky for me, baton twirling was real big then. A guy I knew at college was in dental school, and he capped my teeth for free. Well, almost for free." She smiled suddenly. "I didn't have it so tough. Not really."

"Tough enough," Ken said, and meant it.

"You got your brains beat out playing football," Ada said, "so you could make it to college, and then business school."

"I got paid for it."

"Let's say we're about even. I'll clean up these things."

"We'll both do it."

"No," Ada said. "Every night after dinner, Pop would offer to help, and Mom would say, 'No thanks.' That's the way I like it to be."

She stacked the dishes neatly and carried them into the kitchen. Ken was pushing his chair back to the table when he heard the crash. He reacted instantly, crossing the room in two long strides. In the kitchen doorway he stopped.

Ada was standing quite still, the wreckage of the dishes on the floor around her. Her eyes were wide, and seemingly unfocused. "I'm—sorry," she said in a distant, automatic voice. "I broke your dishes, and I'm sorry." She spoke the words as if they were without meaning.

"What scared you?" Ken said.

Her eyes closed, and slowly opened again, back in focus now. "Look out the window." she said.

Ken walked to the sink. Outside, it was fully dark, and against the black of the sky not-too-distant flames were plain, flaring, cavorting, destroying. "The Holloway house, I think," Ken said, and after a few silent moments turned back to Ada. "A damn shame. I thought they had it under control. But it has nothing to do with us. It's a long way off."

"I hear what you say." She gathered herself with visible effort. "I'm all right. Honest. Where's the broom? And dust pan?"

She came out of the kitchen into the living room, and sank gracefully down on the sofa. "Silly," she said. "Some people are deathly afraid of cats. Did you know that? Ailurophobes—that's what they're called."

"Yes."

"I guess I'm a pyrophobe, and I can't help it any more than they can. I'm sorry."

"Forget it."

"You know about suttee?" Ada said. "In India, Hindu women used to cremate themselves on their husbands' funeral pyres. I had nightmares for months after I learned that." She shivered, remembering, and then smiled again suddenly. "Okay. I've got that out of my system. I won't talk about it again. Promise."

"I can stand it."

"Yes," Ada said. "You can stand a lot. That's obvious. But I don't have to load my problems on you. You probably have enough of your own. Do you have it bad for the Cummings woman?"

"You've got a grasshopper mind."

Ada nodded. "It does jump around, but maybe not as far as you might think."

"What does that mean?"

"It all has to do with you."

Ken shook his head. "I don't get it. What about me? Or am I just being dense?"

"You're a nice, sweet guy," Ada said in a new, quiet voice. "I plant myself on your doorstep like a kitten nobody wants, and you take me in as if it happens all the time."

"The world is full of guys who would love to have Ada Loving knock on the door."

"But you don't make passes, either."

"Magnificent self-control, not lack of interest."

"If you'll let me," Ada said, "I'm going to stay here tonight, and maybe tomorrow night too. Maybe even — who knows? — a number of nights." Her eyes watched him steadily.

"You're welcome to stay as long as you like."

"And no nonsense," Ada said, "about you being Sir Galahad and sleeping on the sofa, either. Okay?" She stood up, and with slow deliberation pulled her blouse out of her slacks. She began to unbutton it. "I've played a lot of scenes like this in front of the camera," she said. "This is one time when I really mean it."


Bessie Wingate herded her men into position alongside Gordy Walker's hotshot crew. "All right," she told them in her normal, carrying voice, "this is where we start earning our C-rations! Let's get the lead out!" To Gordy, she said in as quiet a tone as she could manage, "What gives? All I know is we're told to get our asses up here on the double."

Bessie was half again as large as Gordy, and a woman to boot, but between them there was a strict sense of equality. Gordy explained, and Bessie listened.

"Son a bitches," Bessie said when he was done. "All they care about is their goddam pot, and it don't make no never-mind to them if they just happen to fry

343

somebody's ass off with their backfire." She was already at work with her shovel, grunting as she dug and heaved. "That Andy McIlvain's the hell of a good man. They're all damn good men."

Gordy too was hard at work. "You can say that again."

"So all we got to do is move this goddam mountain," Bessie said, "or at least this hunk of it, cut down a few trees, clear out some low growth and put out a few fires on the way, right?"

"You've got it," Gordy said. Bessie loved to exaggerate, but the funny thing was, she tended to come up with performances to match. In Gordy's book, Bessie was real pistol.

"Eloy!" Bessie shouted. "We still don't know where the hell the rest of your crew is, so you just stick with us, okay?"

Eloy grinned and nodded, conserving his breath for his labor.

"Hell of a good little man," Bessie confided to Gordy. "Kind of a mascot I guess I sort of adopted!" She raised her voice again. "All right, you lazy bastards, let's see some action! We got folks waiting for us!"


The chief of the Sanrio Volunteer Fire Department, still in rubber boots, his long coat and his fireman's hat, snapped off the lantern he carried and turned away from the smoking ruins of the Holloway house. To one of his lieutenants he said, "I don't think there's much left to burn, but we'd better have somebody eyeball it until light just in case."

The lieutenant said, "Funny only this area caught fire. All the other properties along here are safe as far as we know."

"Sparks," the chief said. "Who the hell can tell how

far they'll blow? And a shake roof just waiting to go up." He shook his head. "You'd think anybody rich enough to own a place like this would have better sense. But some of them never learn." He waved his hand. " 'Night, guys!"

In a comfortable bedroom-sitting-room suite at the Inn, Frances and Byron Holloway unpacked their suitcases and got ready for bed.

"Only for a few days, maybe a week or two," Byron said as he took off his robe and placed it neatly on a chair. He took off his slippers and placed them precisely beneath the chair. "In the morning, I'll see the insurance people, and look into those new condominiums near the Club. No sense camping out any longer than we have to."

"Of course not," Frances said. She was silent for a moment. "I'll miss my garden."

"Sorry about that."

"It can't be helped, of course. I'll plan a smaller one at the new condominium."

Byron nodded. "Sensible. Time we pulled in a little." He got into bed and reached for the light. "Goodnight."

"Goodnight, By." Frances's voice was steady and firm. "You always know what's best for us to do."

# PART III

## 28

Stacy rode home from dinner at Duane Semple's house in a thoughtful mood which, for a wonder, she thought, Bart Jones acknowledged by keeping silent until she chose to speak.

"I don't like him," Stacy said at last, and turned in her seat to study as best she could Bart's face in the dim, late evening light. "But you expected that, didn't you?"

"The dinner wasn't intended to be a lovefest, if that's what you mean. He doesn't have time for women as such."

"He's counting on me to warn Ken that he's about to lose control of Bellevue Acres. Why bother?"

"Perhaps humanitarian impulse."

"You haven't really changed, have you? You always could lie with a straight face."

Bart's lips twitched gently. "So could your Daddy. I played poker with him, with cards and chips, and for real with certified checks and deeds of trust. It's how business is played."

"But I think he knew when he was letting somebody fool himself or reach out too far and head for trouble. I'm not sure you can tell the difference between what's real and what you want it to be. Semple wants to see Ken. Why? And why try to use me?"

349

"Because Ken believes you, he might not believe me, and he doesn't know Duane." Bart wore his angry half-smile now. "You wanted a straight answer. There it is."

It had the ring of truth, and Stacy thought about it. She said after a pause, "Why does he want to see him? What shenanigans does he have in mind?"

The angry half-smile remained as Bart shook his head. "Don't make it too complicated. Duane wants to size him up. It helps to know the man you're going to tangle with."

"So he wants Ken to come to him."

"Because he doesn't get around even as well as I do."

True enough. Stacy had been shocked. Semple was an obviously sick man, getting from room to room and chair to chair in the huge house only with enormous effort. He made her think of a great, bloated spider in the center of a web, waiting for his prey. He was polite enough, even gracious as a host, she admitted, but she had been able to find no sense of warmth behind the smile and the solicitude.

"Your Daddy and Duane went around and around a couple of times," Bart said as if he were reading her mind. "It pretty much was a stand-off. I think that's why Duane liked him. He never met many he had to deal with on even terms." His voice changed. "How about it? You'll deliver Ken?"

"I'll leave it up to him."

Now she sat alone, still in her long dress, at the desk in her office-library, strangely hesitant to pick up the telephone and call Ken with this odd invitation.

She told herself that she disliked the feeling of being maneuvered into the position of—face it—Judas goat, in a sense leading Ken up the ramp to slaughter. It was, of course, a ridiculous concept because Ken was a grown man, presumably well able to fend for himself, and the more she thought about it, the less reluctant she became, and so at last, as she had probably known all along she would, she picked up the telephone and placed the call.

Ken was a long time answering, and when he did, his voice was a trifle breathless.

"I'm interrupting something?" Stacy said, and quickly added, "Strike that." None of my damn business, she told herself. Immediately another question obtruded itself into her mind: what if it had been JL coming breathless to the phone? That, she thought angrily, is nobody else's business, either. "Do you know a man named Duane Semple?" she said.

There was a short silence. "*Of* him," Ken said then. "I've never met him. He plays in the big leagues."

"He wants to meet you."

There was another silence, and this time no reply while Ken pondered this new information.

"Bart Jones took me to Semple's for dinner," Stacy said. "They want me as go-between. What they're after is—"

"Bellevue Acres," Ken said. "It figures. Milk it dry, raise the mortgage payments until the people are driven out, then tear the houses down to build their fancy condos." His voice was quiet, with anger in its depth.

"That doesn't make much sense," Stacy said.

"It does, because that land already has a variance from the local zoning, and they won't face any hassle with the City Council about whether and what they can build. That's worth quite a bit to them."

Stacy was silent, thoughtful. She said at last, "What will it do to you?"

"Personally? Nothing I can logically object to. It will put money in my pocket when they buy me out, as they'll have to. Or cut me into their project, one."

"And never mind the folks with all the kids and the

351

dogs being pushed out? I'm tempted to use one of those stable words you seem to object to."

"Honey," Ken said, "when you were sitting on that big cutting horse of yours, your rope in your hands and the piggin' strings in your teeth waiting for the calf to come busting out of the chute, did you worry about the folks who were going to come in second or third or clear out of the running, who maybe needed that prize money just to get to the next rodeo?"

Stacy forgot her careful language. "So I was a son of a bitch too, is that what you're saying?"

"You were just better than they were, and you liked to show it. What's the point of working your ass off to get good if you can't demonstrate it? But this—" Ken's voice stopped. It was a few moments before it resumed. "This," Ken said, "is taking candy from kids. Or putting razor blades in Hallowe'en apples. When does Semple want to see me?"

"Tomorrow night. Dinner. He dresses. Will you go?"

"I'll be there."

"What'll you say?"

"You'll be there too?"

Slowly Stacy nodded. "I'll go."

"You'll hear it then. Okay?"

Stacy hung up and leaned back in her chair to stare at the pictures on the far wall. I've changed, she thought, far more than I even guessed. The realization came as something of a shock, and she searched for reasons.

Her father's death—was that a turning point? Or maybe Bart's accident? Or was there no one incident but, rather, only the steady, inexorable progression of a process which could be called growing up? Simplistic thought, but then, she told herself, she had never been a deep or subtle thinker, something her father had warned her about.

"Damn few things in this world are either all black or all white, honey," he had told her once. "That's a sure-as-hell truism, but it's funny, and sad, how many folks never learn it. They think with their stomachs, not their heads." And then he had produced his crooked grin, mocking himself. "Now, there *are* times for thinking with your stomach and forgetting you even have a head—that's for damn sure—times when all you can do is let her rip and shoot the works and never mind whether in the circumstances that's the logical thing to do. You may come up with a bloody nose, probably will, but chances are the other fellow will be even worse off."

The grin disappeared. "But most times, it's the hell of a lot better to use the brains the good Lord gave you, walk all the way around a problem and try to look at it clearly before you make up your mind. Do that, and you'll be surprised how many shades of gray you'll find in just about everything."

Achilles and the tortoise and angels on the head of a pin, the kind of theoretical nonsense she remembered vaguely from a college philosophy course, Stacy thought, all of which had nothing to do with now. For a change of subject, she sat up straight, called the Forest Service switchboard and asked to be put through to JL. In very little time, he answered the phone himself.

"How's it going?" Stacy said. "You okay? Had some sleep?"

"I did, thanks. I'm alive and functioning."

"But—" Stacy began, and stopped. "Problems?" she said. "I detect overtones."

"You ride in the Forest," JL said. "You see it up close. Do you know what marijuana looks like when it's growing?"

Stacy closed her eyes in relief. Not personal problems, she thought, it was Forest problems that troubled him. "I don't even know what it looks like when it's dried and rolled into joints," she said. "I've never been into pot."

JL said, "You sound as if you have problems too. What's up?"

Stacy's smile mocked herself. She was thinking again of her father, of Ken, of Bart and Duane Semple and tomorrow's dinner. "I may be about to make a damn fool of myself is all," she said. "I'll tell you about it sometime."

There was a short silence. JL said slowly, almost in wonder, "It's beginning to look as if we're going to have a lot to talk about, you and I, when all this is done."

Stacy's smile was no longer mocking, it was suddenly warm. "You know," she said, "the same thought has been running around in my mind too." She paused. "Take care of yourself," she said, and hung up, smiling still.


The Weather Service meteorologist assigned to BACKSLOPE was named Wilson. In his weather-station-camper-truck now he studied the latest radar-enhanced photographs taken from a weather satellite in synchronous orbit 22,300 miles above the earth, and accompanying computer print-out data. It was evident that the tropical storm they had named Charley had gone well past the simple muscle-flexing stage, and now, packing winds in the 100 mph range, was definitely a full-blown hurricane.

Had Charley been a male athlete, Wilson decided, he would by now be capable of bench-pressing on the order of 400 or maybe even 500 pounds, which would not make him world-class, but would definitely establish him as someone to stay well away from in a back-alley brawl. The problem was to figure out which direction was *away*.

Tropical disturbances in general, and hurricanes in particular, made their own decisions. That was a fact of meteorological life weather forecasters like Wilson had to learn to put up with. You could punch all the data you choose into a computer—all present measurements, past performances, best estimates and pure guesses—and come up, say, with an odds-on prediction that a storm like Charley would start moving southeast. And your next report from the aircraft tracking Charley might well have him moving hellbent-for-election dead into the northwest, 180° from his predicted course, with the bit in his teeth and nothing at all to keep him from slamming into a populated coastal area you had thought was safe.

If it wasn't actually quite that bad, it sure as hell seemed that way from time to time. So direction was one variable.

Another was moisture content. Charley had been spawned out at sea. Within his gigantic, whirling, potentially devastating heat engine, then, he undoubtedly carried enough moisture to drown a good share of BACKSLOPE's flames, a large enough proportion certainly to simplify, if not completely carry to successful conclusion all of JL's desperate fire-suppression measures. But where, when and whether Charley would be obliging enough to drop all or even some of that moisture in the form of rain was anybody's guess.

Charley could decide to stay off-shore well out in the Gulf, in a sense just spinning his wheels, causing but not being any actual part of all kinds of trouble, his enormous strength causing winds far inland to back and veer in insane shifting patterns no one could predict, with which JL's people would simply have to try to cope as they happened.

Or Charley could come romping ashore at a place of

355

his own choosing, and once over land he could break up into smaller wind systems, or, perversely, hold together longer than was usual for hurricanes over land and spin off any number of atmospheric progeny to cause mischief, or relief, all on their own.

Charley, in short, was in the catbird seat, as the sportscasters put it, and there was not a single, damn thing anybody could do about it even in defense until Charley chose to make his move or moves.

Weatherman Wilson heaved himself out of his chair, ducked through the camper-body doorway and down the steps, and, satellite photos and computer print-outs in hand, headed for JL's table.

JL listened quietly, as he usually did, and when Wilson was done, all he said was, "Unpredictable beasts, aren't they?"

"They're the grizzly bears of the storm family," Wilson said. "What a hurricane decides it wants, it takes. And it can change its mind just as fast. We've got statistics you wouldn't believe, but on each new big one, we start from scratch."

"We could use rain," JL said. "That's obvious. But we're not going to count on it. We could use a dead calm, too, but we're not counting on that either."

Wilson stood up. "Ever think of another line of work?" he said.

Despite the butterfly bandages, JL smiled. "Lots of times." And recently oftener than usual, he thought, but did not say aloud. "Keep me posted as best you can." He reached for the ringing phone on his table.

It was Ben Hastings. "Our first real accident," Ben said. " A SWFFF crew man name of Eloy Jaramillo. Been working with Bessie Wingate's crew because of a mix-up in the truck lift down from the north line." His voice stopped.

JL said, "And?"

356

Ben said slowly, "He thought he'd better get back, find his own people. He got—cut off. Used his shelter and the fire went over him, but he's burned. Bad."

JL closed his eyes briefly. He nodded. "Okay," he said, carefully keeping all pain from his voice. "I want to be kept informed."

"Right." Ben's voice changed. "Bessie and Gordy Walker—they're tearing that mountain apart. That's the good news."

JL said, "There's more bad?"

"Andy McIlvain and his people. They're fighting a rearguard action uphill toward timberline—"

"If there's any doubt at all, I want them to cut and run." JL's voice was grim. ("We'll head for timberline like big-assed birds," Andy had said. Well, obviously they hadn't.) "You hear me?"

"You've got it."

"Tell Andy I said so. Tell him too, we've got a full-blown hurricane down in the Gulf, and the winds—" JL shook his head. "Just tell him. He'll get the point."

## 29

It was the last ironic twist Sophie Swift would have imagined, and confronting it with aplomb taxed her self-control to its limits. The situation was compounded by the fact that, as she had told Stacy, she liked young Debby, Aaron's wife who appeared unannounced at her door on this evening.

"A doesn't know I'm here," Debby said, "but I had to talk to someone, and you're the wisest person I know. May I come in?" Young and vulnerable and obviously over her depth.

They sat in the study where Sophie and Aaron had sat so many evenings, reading, talking or just listening to music on their fine equipment — usually Mozart, Bach, Haydn, Vivaldi, Beethoven or Dvorak, old favorites of their eclectic taste.

"I had no idea where he was," Debby said, "until he walked up to me at the Club, and said, 'Hi.' Can you imagine my shock?"

Sophie said in a kindly tone, "I'm not sure I understand the situation, Debby. Whom are we talking about?"

"Johnny Joe Ames. We went to school together. Clear through high school. He was my date for our Senior dance. He gave me a corsage." She added vaguely, "He wasn't a very good dancer."

The girl's mind, perhaps under strain, Sophie thought, jumped about as aimlessly as a cricket, but what it seemed to be revealing was anything but extraneous, and Sophie kept her face as expressionless as she could. "And after that?" she said.

"He went off to college and then joined the Navy. Men do." As if that explained all.

"And now he's here in Sanrio?"

"Well, not exactly. He just came to see me. Back home, he asked around and they told him that I — well, you know — that I was here."

"I see."

"And he just wanted to see me, he said. That isn't wrong, is it?"

"Not to my knowledge," Sophie said, as judiciously as she could.

"I mean, it isn't as if I was seeing him on the sly. It was right there at the Club with lots of folks around."

"It sounds quite innocent to me."

"I wouldn't want A to think I was going behind his back."

"Of course not."

"I mean, I *like* A. I really do. He's awful good to me. I don't always understand him, what he says, I mean, some of the funny things, but I do like him lots."

"I know," Sophie said, and was not surprised to find herself quite sure that she really did. Lawyers, as she had told Stacy, were very good at seeing others' problems and dilemmas clearly. It was when they came to try to see and understand their own that they became astigmatic, if not wholly blind.

Debby had married Aaron for the things she had never had, financial security and comfort, status, pleasant surroundings and, probably above all, the wisdom and easy sense of decision of an older man more than willing to relieve her of all responsibilities.

359

But the youthful fire had been missing, and until Johnny Joe suddenly reappeared, she had not realized how much she had missed it. It was as simple as that.

As if to underline Sophie's thoughts, Debby said, "Johnny Joe is—well—Johnny Joe, if you see what I mean."

Sophie said slowly, with care, certainly here wanting no misunderstanding, "Perhaps you'd best tell me."

Debby took a deep breath. "I'm not very good with words, but, well, you see a person you haven't seen in a long time, and all of a sudden you start remembering things you thought you'd forgotten." Her eyes clung to Sophie's face, pleading for comprehension and sympathy.

"Like the Senior dance, and the corsage?"

"You do understand, don't you? I was sure you would." Debby's face showed immediate, intense relief.

Sophie kept her own face carefully composed. Her hands were in her lap, and she willed them to remain motionless. She said, "Sometimes things, events from long ago seem more important at first remembrance than they actually are, Debby."

"I know. And I've thought about it a lot. That's why I came to you." Debby's smile was hesitant, but almost eager. "I mean, you're a lawyer."

"True."

"You represent people."

"I can't deny that, either, Debby. But what is it you think I might be able to do in this situation? If it's my advice you want—"

"No. Like I said, I've thought about it a lot. If Johnny Joe asks me to go with him—"

"Where, Debby?"

"I don't care. Anywhere. I'll go." There was finality in the words and the tone.

Sophie blinked. It was the only evidence of emotion

she allowed herself. "And what is it you want me to do, Debby?"

"Explain to A for me. I'm not good with words like he is, and you are. I—feel things, but I don't know how to talk about them."

There was silence. Out in the front hall, the grandfather clock that had belonged to Sophie's grandparents chimed the hour. Sophie listened until the last echoes had died. She said, "Did you ever hear of conflict of interest, Debby? Never mind. It's just lawyer talk."

"Then you'll do it? Talk to him, I mean?"

Sophie said gently, "Has Johnny Joe asked you to go with him, Debby?"

"No, but he will. I know it." Her smile this time was confident, brilliant. "You can tell."

I doubt if I could, Sophie thought, and found in the concept just one more indication that she was *manqué*. She said, "I would rather you asked someone else to speak for you, Debby."

"No. Please. I know you. And you know A. And I wouldn't know who else to go to."

"I could make recommendations."

"Please," Debby said. "Don't do it for me; for A. I wouldn't want to—hurt him."

Ben Hastings, mindful of JL's earlier justified scepticism, told the Division Boss, "On this one, I want to see nothing but embers before I believe we have it whipped. Another sudden wind change—" He shook his head, temporarily dismissing that potential disaster. "Gordy Walker and Big Bertha, how're they doing?"

On the radio, Wilson, BACKSLOPE's Weather

Service meteorologist, listened to a resumé of Hurricane Charley's recent antics. "He's like one of those tricky runners taking a lead off first base," he said in his customary sports-oriented way. "Is he or is he not going to try and steal second?"

"Charley has enough heft now," the voice on the radio-telephone said, "that he can do whatever he damn well pleases just about anywhere from Galveston to Brownsville. Times like this, I begin to wish I'd taken up astrology instead of meteorology. Safer."

George Jefferson, on the phone to Regional Headquarters in Albuquerque said, "Rapes, near-homicides, equipment explosions and now people setting backfires and shooting off guns to protect a field of goofy weed while a hurricane churns up winds that meet themselves coming and going—" He paused for breath. "What happened to good, old-fashioned forest fires? Don't answer that. And JL, who usually doesn't see shadows, thinks we've got a torch job on our hands as well. I just thought I'd plug you in."

"What do we know about the Byron Holloways?" JL had said with no warning at all.

And Jefferson, his mind on other matters, had replied automatically, "Why?"

"Theirs is the only house in the Sheep Ridge area to catch sparks that far from our fire line that was holding well. I have a feeling—"

"Clearly outside the Forest boundaries," Jefferson said. "None of our business. You're not usually nosey."

"It could have set off the whole damn neighborhood, all those fine big places you were so worried about. And the edge of town, Bellevue Acres, Vista Hill—"

Along with the Cummings place, JL thought, but did not mention. "Seems to me I remember something when they moved here. From Connecticut, wasn't it? Stamford, or some such place? Didn't we have some kind of warning?"

"It seems to me," Jefferson said, "that you've got plenty on your plate right now without worrying about ancient history. How are McIlvain and his people?"

"We're watching that."

"Could a chopper get in to take them out at need?"

"That's strictly foot terrain. Where they are now it's even too rough for another air drop."

"You've got ground crews working their way in?"

Despite the butterfly bandages, JL smiled faintly. "Thirty-nine men, and Bessie Wingate." Bessie could hold up the mountain, he told himself with wry humor, probably with one hand while the other put out the fires. It occurred to him to wonder if Bessie knew about Jaramillo who had been, if only temporarily, under her supervision. He had heard no report from the hospital on the man's condition.

Jefferson said, "If it'll make you feel better, I'll see if I can find out anything about Holloway in Connecticut. I know a couple of people there. Stamford, you say?"

Bessie got word of Eloy's burns by walkie-talkie, as did Gordy Walker. "Poor little bastard," was Bessie's immediate comment, and Gordy, telling about it later, swore that the stout handle of Bessie's shovel bent like a toothpick beneath the sudden force of her emotion. "Damn it, Eloy," Bessie said, "I told you to stay with us!"

"He's in the hospital," Gordy said. "You want to go see him, I'll cover for you."

"You," Bessie said almost savagely, "talk like a man

with a paper head. We got folks waiting for us over yonder. Let's stop clicking our teeth and get to them." She worked in furious silence for a little time before she spoke again. "This goddam fire," she said.

There were others who shared Bessie's opinion if less profanely. Down in Bellevue Acres the young, pregnant woman who had taken in Ross Oliver's wife—now widow—and small children was uncertain what to do as the wind shifted for what seemed the umpteenth time, and smoke thick, black and acrid, again blew down upon the development. The young woman's name was Betty Howard, and her husband drove an eighteen-wheeler on a wide-swinging route as far east as Buffalo, a round-trip that took six days. He had now been gone four.

"Fire is such a terrible thing," Betty said to Emma Oliver, "and it seems as if it's coming closer. They'll warn us, of course, at least I hope they will, if there's any real danger, but it is frightening."

"Ross always used to say it was the Lord's will," Emma said.

Above all else, Betty wanted to avoid argument. "That may be," she said as mildly as she could, "but I'd still like to have some say in the matter."

Carter Norris, TV7 newsman, did a special on BACKSLOPE that early evening. Not surprisingly, it turned out to be a polemic against Authority in general and the Forest Service in particular. If the roots of Norris's antagonism were unclear, the antipathy itself was well recognized.

"From what began as a plain, garden-variety fire caused by lightning, something that should have been handled with ease by the vast resources of the Forest Service," Norris began, "BACKSLOPE has been allowed to grow into a national symbol of bureaucratic bungling which so far has produced over thirty thousand blackened acres of prime Forest land, the destruction of private property running into the millions of dollars, inexcusable harassment of private citizens, two hospital cases, and at last count at least four deaths.

"Let me detail some of the highlights of this tragic series of events:

"Item: When the fire was discovered — considerably later than it should have been, by the way — the man ostensibly in charge of fire suppression, the Fire Management Officer of the Sanrio Forest, JL Harmon, inexplicably packed his bag and flew off to Idaho. Why? I do not know. Mr. Harmon is not available for comment.

"Item: Because, through inattention or neglect or both, fallen dead trees and brush — what the Forest Service refers to as 'fuel' — was allowed to accumulate on the floor of the Forest, the fire spread far more rapidly than it ought to have and thus gained size and strength far beyond what should have been anticipated and allowed.

"Item: The first of the four tragic deaths occurred when a Forest Service truck, tardily hurrying to block off Highway 14, an obvious danger area, took a curve too fast and forced a gasoline tanker truck off the road. The tanker crashed and exploded, killing the driver instantly. The truck hurried on without stopping.

"Item: The second death occurred when a helicopter pilot, sent on an impossible mission to set a totally unnecessary backfire, crashed into a stand of trees, and thereby spread the fire even farther.

"The third death was that of an ordinary householder trying heroically to save his house from destruction after sending his wife and small children to safety. Professional fire-fighters were on the scene, but the householder was given no support by them, and perished in the flames.

"The fourth death is a special case in which callous brutality probably played a role. Two convicts had escaped from the Los Ojos facility and taken refuge in the Forest. One, now in intensive care in the hospital, was undeniably attacked by the fire-fighters. The other either fell or was pushed from a cliff to his death on the rocks below. Admittedly, neither man was someone you would care to take home to meet mother, but neither is the treatment they received justifiable under any conceivable circumstances.

"It is not necessary to dwell on the cruel and unusual punishment decreed for an out-of-state family, tourists who ought to have been welcomed rather than persecuted, who, in the face of the fire raging out of control, blundered innocently in their jeep into territory forbidden to motor vehicles. Nor does further explanation indemnify an elderly couple, prominent members of the Sanrio community, for the inexcusable loss of their $500,000 home. But it *is* worth mentioning that a crew of heroic smoke-jumpers, sent on a near-suicide mission, is presently isolated on the mountain and in imminent danger of extermination.

"Changing winds have been mentioned as contributing to the difficulties of controlling BACKSLOPE's tragic progress. But there are always changing winds in the Sanrio area, and these ought to have been anticipated. Nor is lack of equipment or manpower any excuse; both are available in enormous quantities.

"It is leadership that is lacking, leadership and intelligent planning, and unless and until these twin weaknesses are remedied, all we can expect, I am afraid, is more of the same.

"I am Carter Norris."

"It's been a long time," Ben Hastings said, "since I walked up to a man, called him a son of a bitch to his face and hoped that he'd react physically. But as soon as I get the time, I'm going to look up Carter Norris—"

"Forget him," JL said. "You'd only make it worse. What's the latest on Andy and his people?"

"He told me to tell you it's his skin, and he'll make damn sure it doesn't get singed."

JL managed his faint smile. "That's good enough."

"And the State cops went into the cannabis patch with riot guns. It was no contest. Only thing is, they want to burn the field."

"We'll burn it," JL said, "in our own good time. What we don't need now is more fire."

Ben took a deep breath. "Carter Norris—"

"The world," JL said with sudden, unaccustomed vehemence, "is filled with sons of bitches. Leave it at that. Some folks will believe him, but they'd believe the worst anyway and nothing we can say will change their minds. What do you think public servants are for if it isn't to play whipping boy?"

Ben said slowly, "I don't think I've ever heard you sound bitter before."

"Maybe it's past time," JL said.

## 30

At 16,000 feet, well above Sierra Grande's rocky peak, the infra-red photographic plane bucked and jumped in updrafts heat-produced on the ground. "That," the pilot said, looking down on the immensity of BACKSLOPE's blackened or still flaming area, "is quite a little bonfire. Can you take it all in with your wide-angle lens?"

"Just about," the photographer said. "JL won't get the detail we usually give him—"

"Detail is the last thing JL's worried about now. He's thinking in miles, not acres. Look over yonder. Another house, one of the big ones—"

In point of fact, it was not a house that had suddenly erupted in flames, but the dressing-room-game-room cabana at the end of Ada Loving's swimming pool, its stylish wooden shake roof and extended striped awning turning instantly into a fiery mass that boiled into the sky.

"More grist for Carter Norris's mill," the pilot said, "and if the wind shifts another ten-fifteen degrees that won't be the last of them to go. In the meantime, we've got ringside seats."

Ken Delacorte got the word by phone from one of the local volunteer firemen. "Thanks," Ken said, and turning to face Ada. "Sorry, baby," he said. "Your swimming pool game room—"

"I don't care. Feed the whole house to the monster if it will help. Even if it won't, maybe it will keep some other house from going up."

"I'll go over—"

"No. *Things* aren't important. Not really. I learned that a long time ago. Only people matter."

Ken said gently, "It's okay. You're—"

"Damn it," Ada said, "I'm not being hysterical. I mean it. I've been broke. Stony. With nothing. It's uncomfortable, but it doesn't really matter. But when you lose a—friend, maybe a part of the family, somebody who counts, then you see what really is important. That's why I don't want you going near the place. It's—unlucky. It always has been, nothing but a joint on the local Strip to attract suckers for their money." She smiled suddenly, the full, brilliant smile that could make a film scene glow. "Think I could go back to baton-twirling?"

"I think," Ken said slowly, "that you could do anything you put your mind to, baby, and do it superlatively well."

Hurricane Charley seemed headed for shore in the Brownsville area, changed his mind and decided to stay a while longer off shore, his enormous strength whipping the waters of the Gulf to churning foam, sending twenty-foot waves to tear small boats from their moorings, and strip beaches of their sand to expose the underlying rocks.

Inland, winds rose in intensity and, in obedience to a sudden mixing of temperature and pressure gradients, began a kind of atmospheric tarantella in which chaos rather than order was the rule of the day.

Wilson, the BACKSLOPE meteorologist, said to JL, "You've seen one of those film clips where a loose ball behaves like it's greased and everybody is running in different directions trying to grab it? Well, trying to make sense out of what we have here in the way of wind changes is just about like trying to make sense out of that scene. I might as well curl up with a good book for all the help I can give you in the way of predictions. Sorry, chum. You're on your own."

JL studied the wide-angle infra-red photographs as soon as they were delivered, Ben Hastings standing at his shoulder. "If the rainmaker's right," JL said, "and it looks as if he is, we can have big trouble at any time anywhere on the perimeter. We can't consider any sector safe." In over twenty years of fire suppression, he could not remember another time when a statement like that had been true.

"Over here," he said, pointing with his pencil, "we get out of forest area into grazing land, sparse grass and occasional cholla. We can afford to let that go for a time if we have to. And up here —" The pencil drew a rough circle. "— above timberline on the big mountain, there's no fuel but lichen and Alpine tundra, so that's another area we don't have to worry too much about. But all the rest of the outside boundary —" He shook his head. "And especially here where the big houses are, and the Bellevue Acres development, and then the town, we need insurance bad." He leaned back in his chair and looked up at Ben. "And we need more troops to beef up the whole line."

Ben said nothing, but his expression told much.

"You're thinking," JL said, "that our friend Carter Norris will crow and say that he had to point out to us that we were under-manned." He nodded. "So he will, and we just grin and bear it."

"We could issue a release and explain—" Ben began.

"Explanations sound like bad excuses and just make things worse."

Ben had never seen the inner workings of top command as clearly as now. "How do you stand it?" he said. "No, that's the wrong question. *Why* do you stand it?"

"It goes with the territory. You do your best, and you keep your mouth shut. Those who *know*, don't need explanations. Those who don't, wouldn't believe them anyway." Add one more category, he thought suddenly, those who needed explanations, not because they *knew*, but because they *believed in him*. And he had no hesitation about including Stacy in that class, which was maybe a little presumptuous of him, but was a warm concept to cling to. "So now for that insurance," he said, and sat up straight again to stare at the photographs and the map.

"You're still thinking backfire?" Ben said. "With the wind shifting the way it is?"

JL was silent for long moments. He said at last, "You ever read about the big San Francisco fire? 1906? Following that earthquake that took out the water system? They dynamited whole blocks of buildings. Those were their firebreaks. They destroyed part of the city to save the rest. The only way."

Ben stared at the map in deep, silent thought. He said at last, "Bellevue Acres?" and looked at JL.

"130 frame-and-stucco houses," JL said. "They'd go down easy, wouldn't they?"

Ben was silent, waiting.

"Instead, we could take out that whole belt of big houses," JL said, "far more area, flatten every garage, every stable, every shed, every cabana, every garden trellis *and* every house and displace no more than twenty-thirty people all of whom could stand it. They wouldn't like it, and they'd have the clout to raise hell about it — but *after* the fact, not before, and we'd leave the town reasonably safe, no?"

Ben opened his mouth to speak, thought better of it and closed it again, still silent.

"Something to think about," JL said. "Correction: something we're damn well going to *have* to think about. And soon."


Stacy walked past the spa on the way to her bedroom suite to dress for the second dinner at Duane Semple's place. The clear, bluish-green water in the tiled tub stirred gently, indicating that the solar collectors on the roof of the house had activated the pump that circulated solar-heated water — no fuss, no muss, no bother, all as it should be.

She had not been in the tub with its soothing whirlpool action for a long time now, and it passed through her mind that the day JL had come to talk to her and interrupted the party was indeed a while ago, and much had changed, of which the fire, and to a lesser extent the spa, had become only symbols, no longer either symptoms or causes. Strange.

She had heard that Ada Loving's cabana was gone, and that the house itself was threatened, and so by that much the danger had moved closer, but somehow the menace had lost its power to shock, or even to bring panic, as, she supposed, long-continued earth rumblings to those who live on the slopes of a volcano become familiar and cease even to provoke jokes, let alone prayers.

Showered, bath-powdered, perfume lightly applied to breasts, throat, arms and flanks, she put on bikini lace panties and padded to her closet to decide which long dress to wear for this occasion. How long had it been since she had dressed two nights in a row for dinner? That, too, was somehow a symbol of change, and she could imagine how her father would have chuckled and teased her.

"When you put your mind to it, honey, you really can turn into an eastern dude. Those years in Boston weren't wasted after all. And when you try real hard, which isn't often, I'll grant, you can behave just like a lady. I'm proud of you, honey, I purely am."

"It's all because I had such a genteel example to follow in you." Always they had been able to joke together, snipe at one another without meanness.

"Pity they didn't trim off some of the thorns while they were about it," her father would have said. "Times you remind me somehow of a real pretty Doberman bitch I knew once. Every so often she'd get a gleam in her eye and you knew she was trying to decide which of your arms she was going to take off at the first bite."

"Thanks a heap."

"Who you fixing to take a chunk out of tonight, honey? That gleam shows up real plain."

And if she had wanted to explain the situation to him, as she would have, he would have listened in his smiling, quiet way, and might have said, "It's been my experience that every time I declare myself into a game where I don't really hold cards, I end up getting kicked in the belly. On the other hand, it's pretty damn hard just to sit still and watch a real bastard pick on folks who can't fight back, so I see what you might call your dilemma. Follow your instincts, honey, that's all I can say."

Well, Stacy guessed there wasn't really any better advice to be given, and the thought buoyed her spirits some. She had a pretty fair idea that Ken was going to put his concern for the folks who lived in Bellevue Acres with all the kids and all the dogs ahead of his own best interests and, in effect, spit in Duane Semple's and Bart Jones's collective eye, by his own admission stepping out of his own league into competition he couldn't really hope to match. So that left her choice pretty damn plain, didn't it? Well?

She could stay strictly on the sidelines, neutral. It was, after all, none of her concern; she bred and trained horses, nothing more.

Or she could, as her father might have said, declare herself into the game without really holding cards—and probably end up getting kicked in the belly. What that meant in this instance, of course, was that she could offer Ken financial backing he needed and didn't have, maybe, even probably, lose a bundle and come away having nothing at all to show for it, which on the face of it seemed not a very smart thing to do.

But she was beginning to get the idea that it was precisely that latter course Bart had been hoping she would follow, just to teach her a lesson and take her down a peg. Worse, she had a shrewd idea that Bart knew damn well she wouldn't sidestep the challenge, which was why he had maneuvered her into the whole affair in the first place.

The more she thought about it, and the harder she tried to be dispassionate, the more she got her dander up. Her father, she decided, might not have approved, but he sure as hell would have understood, just as he had understood that long ago day in the corral when she picked herself up out of the dust and told the foreman to keep his goddam hands off Boots who was *her* horse.

By the time Bart's car arrived, and Bart himself wheeled his fancy go-cart up the walk to her front door, Stacy was keyed-up as she always was before competition, and smiling as if she hadn't a care in the world. "We've time for a drink, I think," she said, and stood aside for the wheelchair.

Glass of wine in hand, and the smile still holding steady, "I hear," Stacy said, "that the fire got Ada Loving's place."

"So I heard. Pity." Bart's eyes watched her warily.

"Your house, wasn't it?" Stacy said. A guess, pure and simple, but, she thought, on the basis of what she knew from Ken, and what she heard last night, a good guess.

"Why do you say that?" Bart's face showed nothing.

"Part of the long-range operation, wasn't it? Famous, and sexy, movie star picks Sanrio for her hideaway. And, of course, acts as magnet to draw in potential quote-unquote investors? Willard P. Spencer, for his own reasons, ditto? Bellevue Acres with zoning variance already approved, the ideal site for new, fancy condos? You aren't going to tell me it's all coincidental. Daddy taught me a long time ago to look at a horse's teeth before I accepted his age as represented."

Bart said, "A lot of your Daddy rubbed off on you. Maybe you should have been a boy."

"I like it the way it is."

Bart sipped his drink. His eyes did not leave Stacy's face. He lowered his glass slowly. "Your Daddy had a lot of moxie. He had a lot of business sense too. You inherited the first. Did you get the second as well?"

"I've never had to find out. Things have always been pretty easy for me."

Bart smiled at that. "A few busted ribs, dislocated shoulder, broken wrist, I remember, and a leg in a cast for some weeks—"

"They don't count. It's the big things that have always been easy. For most folks they never are. They're always trying to get out from under, and never can."

"For God's sake, don't quote Thoreau at me about lives of quiet desperation. He never knew what desperation was."

"Have you?" Instantly, she wished she could recall the question, but there was nothing to do but await his reaction.

Bart wore now his crooked smile. "I've had my moments," he said. "Of wishing. And hating." He finished his drink. "We should go. If you're ready?"

Stacy stood up. She had regained her easy smile. "I only tried riding a Brahma bull once," she said. "I landed on my kiester out in the middle of the arena, and he came at me, all 2000 pounds of him. Lucky Joe Henry, the rodeo clown, was there to distract him while I shinnied up the fence." She watched Bart steadily, and there was no smile in her eyes. "So let's go out to Semple's and we'll try it again."


Ken Delacorte finished tying his black tie and turned to find Ada holding out his dinner jacket as a valet might. Smiling, he shook his head slowly. "How many men would believe this scene?"

"I not only believe it, I like it. I just don't like your going."

"You know where I'll be."

"Yes."

"And you know it's important?"

Ada helped him into the jacket and smoothed the shoulders fondly. "I've heard you say so," she said, "and I believe what you say." She waited until he had turned again to face her. Idly, she brushed a non-existent speck from his lapel. "You don't even know this Semple character, do you?"

"Only by reputation."

"I've heard of him too. Big bucks. Back a production. Take a piece of the action here or there. 'Semple says,' or, 'Semple says not.' Like that stockbroker ad, when Semple talks, people listen."

Ken said, "You're making a point. A big one?"

Ada nodded slowly. "In a funny way," she said, "I'm talking about you and me. I don't mean any ties or commitments or anything like that. There aren't any strings at all, honest. It's just that you and I are one kind of people, and, well, the Semples are another. I'm probably talking out of turn. I learned a long time ago, or I ought to have learned, that men don't like to be told what they aren't, so I'll shut up if you want."

"No. That's the last thing I want."

The blue eyes searched his face. "Okay," Ada said then and took a deep breath. "You're a nice, sweet guy. You're a lot more than that. You're a decent person, and there aren't very many of those, not nearly enough. You're not going to screw somebody, anybody, because you wouldn't want to be screwed yourself. Isn't that what the Golden Rule says? Do unto others —?"

"I guess that's one way to put it." Ken was smiling.

"Sounds funny, I know," Ada said, and smiled herself. The smile faded quickly. "But the Semples don't work that way. They figure everybody's out to screw them, so they just do it first, and hardest. That's why I say we're one kind of people and they're another. We can't compete with them in their field because the only way would be by behaving as they do. And I've stopped trying because even if I made it, I wouldn't like it, knowing all the poor jerks I had to step on to get where I wanted to go." She was silent for long moments.

"That's all."

There was a short, understanding silence between them.

"I'll remember it, baby," Ken said. "And—thanks."

## 31

It was a single, tall lodgepole pine tree clinging precariously to one of Sierra Grande's steep upper slopes, together with a flying, burning branch, that did it. Higher on the mountain, a rock slipped beneath the boot of one of Andy McIlvain's smoke-jumpers. The rock rolled, gathering loose talus into a minor slide. The slide loosened the lodgepole pine's already frail grip on the mountainside, and slowly, almost majestically, its topmost needles blazing from that almost casual contact with the flying burning branch, the tree began its fall.

By the time it crashed to the rocky ground, breaking apart as it hit, its lower branches too were ablaze, and what had been an open, if hazardous escape route for Andy and his people, was now closed.

This fresh, open flame raised the temperature to bring the ambient air, already superheated from conflagration below, to flash point, as sometimes a single match will bring embers to flame. Instantaneously the entire mountainside was ablaze.

Brush seemed to explode as if from dynamite blasts, and tall stately pine trees turned into towering torches as if by magic, sending orange-red flames two hundred feet into the sky, crackling and hissing as their pitch boiled, and throwing off clouds of smoke that twisted

379

and churned as if in pain. The sudden roar of the conflagration gathered in volume, above which Andy raised his voice in a great shout.

"Make like mountain goats!" Andy shouted. "Head for timberline! Heels and asses are all I want to see! Move it!" Already scrambling up the slope himself, he poured information into his walkie-talkie. "Tell JL we swung and we missed," he finished. "You'll find us up top with the picas. I hope. Over and out."

Gordy Walker, the hotshot crew chief, held his walkie-talkie at an angle so Bessie too could hear Ben Hastings's report.

"That area's cut off," Ben's voice said, stating the facts without haste or excitement. "Chopper observation reports Andy and his people above the fire area and for the present safe. Break off your operation as it goes now, and start establishing a north-south line to seal off that entire area where the jumpers were working. We'll let it burn itself out to timberline. Over."

Gordy looked up at Bessie's sweat-and-smoke-stained face. "Shit!" Bessie said, and shrugged in resignation.

Gordy suppressed a smile. "Roger," he said into the walkie-talkie. "North-south it is. Let her burn. Over and out." He hung the radio on his belt and looked up at Bessie again. "Now do you want to knock off and go see your mascot?"

Bessie shook her head. "I'll wait till change of shift. Way I probably look now, I'd scare him into a coma. Let's turn these raggedy-assed troops around, and get them going."

From the broad terrace of Vista Hill, Mrs. Tyler

Wayne looked out at the great mountain across her favorite grove of specimen trees so modestly begun so long ago. A black walnut had been the first planting, she remembered, a gift from a now-forgotten visitor from Nebraska. It had arrived by truck, neatly balled, and Mrs. Wayne and Tyler had discussed at length where to have it put, never guessing that it would be the beginning of what became almost a private forest of exotic plantings.

From a California nursery they discovered two of the more than three hundred species of eucalyptus that would thrive in Sanrio's climate. From Inverewe Gardens in Scotland they learned of species of tree rhododendrons, hardy almost beyond belief, that had taken to the Sanrio valley as if to a new and hospitable home. A copper beech, carefully tended, seemed determined to last the ages, and tupelo, hickory, maple, locust, ash, ginkgo, birch, cherry, dogwood, larch, elm, sycamore, poplar, oak, yew and others had delighted visitors and guests for years.

It was a pity that the development, Bellevue Acres, had been built so close to the grove, almost touching it, and Tyler would no doubt have seen to it that such a thing had not occurred, but there it was. On the other side, the finger of Forest offered protection against any encroachment. When they had made their first plantings, as Mrs. Wayne often thought, there had been only open land where Bellevue Acres now was, and who could have dreamed that such change might take place?

But it was Sierra Grande that occupied her attention now. It was probably illusion, Mrs. Wayne hoped, but the entire mountain seemed ringed with fire, and smoke rose into the otherwise clear sky almost as smoke had risen in those dreadful films she had seen of the hydrogen bomb test out in the Pacific back when one of Tyler's Committees had had to do with such matters. She remembered saying silently to herself then, as she wished she could say now, "It is only a film. It is not real." But now, as then, reality could not be avoided. There were too many reminders.

She had listened on TV to as much of Carter Norris's polemic as she could stomach, and then switched off the set, thinking with insight born of long experience that no doubt the incidents Norris spoke of had occurred, but that in the way of newsmen seeking dramatic impact, Norris had adroitly turned them inside-out and chosen to impute ignoble motives to actions that had probably been dictated by unavoidable facts.

She remembered something Tyler had once said. "The damage is done when the charge is made, and no amount of supposed retraction can alleviate it, because the charge is news and rates the front page, and the retraction is not news so it only rates a one-column two-inch piece buried among the brassiere ads. Not fair, but, then, who said that public life carried with it any guarantee of fairness?"

And so, Mrs. Wayne thought, that nice Mr. Harmon would simply have to bear his vilification as best he could. She wished there were something she could do to lessen his load.

And, as she stood on the terrace looking out at the smoke and the occasional glimpse of open flames, seeing the Forest being maimed, if not destroyed, before her very eyes, she wished too that there were something she could do about those who were facing devastation to their homes and to their lives if the fire spread farther, as it seemed determined to do.

She knew the Holloways casually, and she was aware that their home had been totally destroyed, poor dears. Now the home of that film person, such a stunning young woman, Ada Loving — could that last name really be the one she was born with? — either was gone or was about to be burned to the ground.

Where would it stop? Where could it stop? Despite all efforts, the fire seemed to be moving inexorably down that finger of the Forest, as it must also be moving in other sectors, mocking man's efforts to control it.

Again she thought of Bellevue Acres, all those people, all those children — and bicycles and dogs and scruffy untidiness — and what would they do, living, as they no doubt were, right on the edge of those recession statistics the newspapers were forever talking about, if the fire did come all the way down that finger of the Forest, and—?

She closed her eyes in sudden pain, and opened them again only with reluctance. For a long time she stood quite still, staring at reality, and knowing once again that it would not go away. At last, slowly, she turned and walked back into the big house, directly to her desk in the room that had been Tyler's library, and there she seated herself and picked up the telephone.

"This is Mrs. Tyler Wayne," she said in a steady voice to the young woman at Forest Service headquarters. "I wish to speak with Mr. JL Harmon, if you please. It is a matter of urgency. I will wait."

JL's voice on the line was polite, but there was obvious fatigue and faint impatience in its depths. He sat staring at the latest aerial photos spread before him as he said, "Yes, Mrs. Wayne?"

"I have been watching the progress of the fire down what Tyler and I always referred to as the finger of the Forest — "

"We call it that too. It abuts your land."

"Yes." Mrs. Wayne was silent for only a moment. "Can you stop that fire, Mr. Harmon? I realize that I am probably asking a question you would rather avoid, but I should like an honest answer. It is important."

"We're doing everything we can, Mrs. Wayne. But these winds—"

"The answer then is no? I was afraid it would be."

"Mrs. Wayne—"

"Please," Mrs. Wayne said. "I did not call with a plea, but rather with a suggestion. If that finger of the Forest is lost, then the grove of specimen tree plantings you have been kind enough to admire—"

"It is beautiful. And unique." And possibly priceless, JL thought sadly, but said nothing more.

"Thank you. I think so too, as did Tyler. But for the moment, that is beside the point. That grove will also be destroyed. It is inevitable."

"I'm sorry—"

"Please, Mr. Harmon. I am not finished. That grove, Mr. Harmon, as you know, abuts the development."

"Yes."

"How many houses? How many persons? If the grove is destroyed because the finger of the Forest is lost, the development is certain to go as well. Am I not correct, Mr. Harmon? No doubt you have already considered this?"

"I'm afraid we have."

There was a picture of Tyler Wayne in a silver frame on the desk. Mrs. Wayne looked at it now, expressionless. She said, "If you were to burn my grove now, Mr. Harmon, before it is in immediate danger, could you control the blaze and keep it from reaching those houses? And if you could, would you then have created a fire break across which the fire in the Forest might not travel? Could the development houses then be safe?"

JL sat unmoving. He said slowly, in a gentle voice,

"The answer to all those questions, Mrs. Wayne, is probably yes. But I can't promise."

Mrs. Wayne's eyes had not left the picture. "Then burn the grove, Mr. Harmon. You have my permission." She hung up. "I'm sorry, Tyler." It was no more than a whisper.

Ben Hastings, summoned, said, "Jesus! You mean it? When I was a student, a kid, some of us were allowed to make a field trip to that grove. There're two rhododendron trees from the Himalayas, and a specimen tree from way up the Amazon. There's—"

JL said nothing, nor had he made even a vague movement, but Ben's words ran down. "Okay," Ben said. "It's going anyway, isn't it? It's just a matter of timing."

"And with more wind it may not do the whole job, either," JL said. "But get on it, and make sure it's a good, clean burn, as successful as we can make it. That's the least we can do."

He sat on, unmoving, for long moments after Ben had driven off in his jeep. Fires, JL thought, and probably large crises of any kind brought out the best, and the worst, in people. Correction: in some people. He supposed that was a truism, but he had never pretended to be a deep or original thinker, so banality—a firm grip on the obvious, as some like to say—bothered him not in the least.

He was a watcher with feelings, and possibly because of those feelings also with some understanding of how other people thought and felt. Right now, for example, although nothing would show on the surface, Mrs. Tyler Wayne was crying inside. And when the blaze actually began, which would be momentarily, Mrs. Wayne would be standing at a window watching, compelled by the same motives that would have made her hold an old, loved dog's paw while he was being put to sleep—so he would not die alone.

And then there were the Les Lawrys, very different types indeed, and the Byron Holloways, the Carter Norrises with their inexplicable hostilities and resentments—the list was endless.

But to the great mass—this JL had learned over the years almost with a sense of incredulity—a fire, an explosion, a disaster of whatever sort meant absolutely nothing, unless and until it obtruded itself forcibly into their lives. Even now, that phenomenon still retained the power to astonish him.

He had not bothered to sound an alert or even make a call to local or State police concerning Bellevue Acres, for example, because life was still going on there, as it was in the town itself, in quite normal fashion, and why stir up hysteria prematurely?

The everything-will-be-taken-care-of syndrome was universal and deep-rooted. Fire in the Forest? Smoke and flames visible? The authorities will cope. That's what we pay taxes for, isn't it? Are you going to so-and-so's party? What will you wear?

He remembered hearing himself say to someone—was it Ben?—under what circumstances he could not now recall, "Most people don't have the sense to come in out of the rain. That's not criticism; it's just plain fact. So somebody has to think highly enough of himself to lead them. That's more fact, but there's some criticism in it too, because when you get right down to it, who the hell has the right to think so much of himself that he's sure he knows best?" And he also remembered adding, "Oh, hell, forget it. I get tired a lot easier these days than I used to, and tired makes sour. Where were we?"

Where we were, he told himself now, was facing a

fire that hadn't gone away and wasn't going to go away by itself. He looked at his watch. 16:30 briefing coming up fast, and there were a lot of questions he wanted answered. From Air Control, from Regional Dispatcher on new troop resources, from the rainmaker if there was or was not any change in Charley, from the Line Boss on perimeter conditions. . . .

"I asked you to come out here, Aaron," Sophie said, "because the office is something less than—neutral ground. Also, I knew that we would want privacy."

"Mysteriouser and mysteriouser," Aaron said. He glanced at his watch. "It is after hours. Is a drink in order?"

"Please," Sophie said. "I'd prefer that you waited."

Aaron settled back in his chair. He had again that odd feeling that he scarcely knew this woman and yet knew her well, apparent contradiction but not really so. It was as if what the mathematicians would call her parameters were quite familiar—her unyielding honesty, her sense of duty and of responsibility, her devotion to equity and justice and her willingness to fight for all of these—but that within these boundaries not infrequently she saw matters from quite a different viewpoint than his own. He waited quietly.

"I have a client, Aaron," Sophie said. "This client is not of my choosing. You must believe that. I tried to avoid the engagement, and in conscience was unable to. Have you guessed already that my client is Debby?"

"I was beginning to see the light, counselor." It was his dry, courtroom voice, agreeing to a stipulation in order that matters might proceed.

"There is a young man," Sophie said, "Johnny Joe Ames, who has turned up unexpectedly."

"Out of the past, no doubt."

"They were high-school sweethearts."

"How romantic."

"Is law school so long ago, Aaron," Sophie said quietly, "that you cannot remember how it was with us?"

"They used to call that a low blow, Soph. Now I believe the phrase is 'a cheap shot'."

Sophie's lips tightened, and there was sudden color in her cheeks, but her voice remained calm. She said, "There are considerable differences. They were young, and romantic, as once upon a time we were. We have—I suppose the phrase is, grown up, become mature. I don't believe they have. I am quite sure that Debby still retains—"

"If you're saying that in many ways Debby is immature, counselor," Aaron said, "I shall so stipulate. And the swain?"

"I haven't met him, but—" Sophie spread her hands.

Aaron forced himself to relax a trifle. He nodded. "I think we can read between the lines. Go on."

"Debby is not carrying on an affair, Aaron. She tells me that she has behaved—honorably, and I believe her. But if Johnny Joe asks her to go with him, as she is sure he will—"

"Where?"

"I asked the same question. Her answer was—anywhere."

Aaron was silent, and still. He said at last, "She wants out?"

"Just that. Nothing more."

There was more, and longer silence. In the hallway, the grandfather clock's ticking seemed overloud. "You may tell your client, counselor," Aaron said finally, with slow distinctness, "that she is welcome to an uncontested divorce. Is that satisfactory?"

Sophie closed her eyes. She opened them again and

nodded. "Thank you, Aaron." She drew a deep breath. "Now would you like that drink?"

It was as if the question had not been heard. "Jesus, Soph!" Aaron said suddenly. "Why in hell did it have to be you?"

## 32

Bessie Wingate, silent and ponderously graceful, came into the hospital room almost on tiptoe, and stood quietly looking down at Eloy motionless beneath his bandages.

Eloy's fire shelter had split as he tugged it over himself, she had heard, or he hadn't stretched it taut, or maybe some other goddam thing, but what difference did that make now? This was all that was important.

Eloy's eyes opened and came slowly into focus. What showed of his mouth began to spread in a weak smile. "Hi, big mama." It occurred to him in a dreamlike way that this was the first time he had called Bessie to her face by the name he had carried in his mind for days, but it didn't matter now. "I screwed up, didn't I?"

"You want argument?" Bessie said, and shook her head. "I'm sorry as hell, Eloy." She reached into one of her jacket pockets. "I didn't think you'd go big for flowers, or any shit like that, so I brought you a beer." She took out a can of Coor's, set it on the table beside the bed, and withdrew her hand with an odd, awkward gesture of helplessness.

Eloy's weak smile reappeared. "When I get out," he said, "and we go to the Antlers, that make three beers I buy you, okay?"

"You got a deal."

Eloy said, "Nobody tells me nothing. You get to them smoke-jumpers?"

Bessie shook her head. "But they're okay." She hoped. "They hauled ass for timberline when the wind changed again."

Eloy's eyes closed. He opened them with effort. "They shoot me full of, you know, all kind of stuff." He waggled his head gently toward the intravenous stand and the transparent tube coming down from the plastic bag and disappearing beneath a bandage of his arm. "You know?" he said.

"Sure. Makes you sleepy. That's good. So you sleep, Eloy, okay?" Bessie's big hand touched his arm with gentle care. "Hang in there. Think of those beers."

His eyes were already closed as she let herself out of the room and walked down the hallway to the nurse's station. There she stopped, and stood, large and motionless. "How about it?" she said, looking down at the seated nurse.

The nurse said, "Patient Jaramillo?"

Bessie waited in silence.

"He's doing quite well," the nurse said.

"Cut the shit." The words hung in the air like a growl.

The nurse took a deep, uneasy breath. This, she thought almost hysterically, was a situation beyond her ken. It was as if suddenly she faced a mother bear, a grizzly, maybe, asking about one of her cubs, and wanting a straight answer. *Now*; without if's or maybe's.

Bessie stood motionless, hovering at the limit of patience.

"I'm not the doctor—" the nurse began. She stopped. Wrong approach; she could see that in the storm gathering behind Bessie's eyes. "I don't know," the nurse said then. "He — may make it. Or he may not." She sat silent, all at once physically frightened.

Slowly Bessie nodded and seemed to relax in acceptance. "Okay," she said. "If that's the way it is." She nodded again. "That goddam fire," she said, and turned away. Immediately she turned back. "Thanks," she said, and turned away again to walk massively, and expressionlessly, down the corridor.


Duane Semple's property was enclosed by a well-maintained, four-strand barbed-wire fence, its posts cross-braced at intervals to keep the barbed-wire taut. Stacy had scarcely noticed last night. Tonight she studied the fence with interest. "He runs blooded cattle?" she said to Bart.

"No cattle. No horses."

And, although this she had noticed idly last night, the high, masonry wall that surrounded the house itself came almost as a shock. "If he has a coat-of-arms," Stacy said, "and when you come to think of it, he's the kind of guy who might pay to have one made up, it ought to show paranoia rampant, don't you think?"

Bart's face was only dimly lighted in the early evening glow, but the harsh, hawklike outlines Stacy had once admired were nevertheless very plain. "You've got your spurs with the big rowels on tonight, haven't you?" Bart said.

Stacy patted herself. "No gun," she said, "no knife. Just me."

"Spoiling for a fight."

"You set this up. Answer me one question. Do you need the money?"

"No."

"Then why bother? Just to flex your muscles and show how *macho* you still are?"

There was an edge in his voice now. "I told you once, a man has to have something to do."

"Then collect butterflies or write poems, but stop picking on the kind of people who think they're lucky to have a Bellevue Acres house to live in."

"They were born to be picked on. They're the bottom link in the economic chain of life, everybody's prey. That's why they exist. Your Daddy—"

"My Daddy, damn it, didn't pick on cripples." Stacy shook her head, suddenly angry with herself. "Sorry about that."

"I'm used to it, honey. I wake up with it in the morning, and go to bed with it every night. I could say that the word doesn't even bother me any more, but I'd be lying, wouldn't I?"

Stacy sat silent.

"You want to have it both ways," Bart said. "You've always wanted to be top of the heap, and you have been. But now you want to pretend that you never hurt anybody by getting there, that you wouldn't kill so much as a fly walking up your expensive adobe wall." He shook his head, and the harsh lines in his face showed again in the dwindling light. "You didn't get all those trophies and all that prize money being sweet and nice to everybody. And your Daddy didn't make his pile without stomping folks into the dirt, either. You—"

"You've made your point," Stacy said. And, she thought, it was the same point Ken had made to her as well, but in a different fashion. Time, she told herself, that she accepted facts.

The car drew smoothly to a stop at the entrance to the big house. Behind them Ken's car swung into a parking place, and Ken got out. "Okay," Stacy said, unconsciously echoing her father's words in the corral that long-ago day, "let the festivities commence."

In Bellevue Acres a small crowd gathered to stare at the fire in Mrs. Wayne's grove of specimen plantings. "Migod," one man said, "they might have warned us if it's that close. What I mean, our *houses* will be next!"

Ben Hastings drove up, braked to a stop and did not even get out of the jeep. In his yellow hard hat and his green Forest Service shirt, he was the immediate center of the small crowd's attention. "I just wanted to tell you that we've set that fire. For your protection." There was anger in his mind at the necessity of destroying the grove, but there was, he knew, no other way, and maybe even this much was not going to be enough. "A fire break," he added, perhaps unnecessarily, "to try to make you safe."

The man who had spoken up first said, "To *try* to make us safe! That's the hell of a poor reassurance. Like Carter Norris on TV7 says—"

"I know what he says," Ben said, "and I'd like to be standing next to him when he says it, but never mind. We're doing our best for all of you, but just in case—"

"Here it comes," the man said. "Jesus Christ, can't you people do anything right?"

"Just in case," Ben repeated flatly, "you might start thinking about what you'll want to take *if* we have to evacuate you. I don't think we will." Mentally, he crossed his fingers. "But, like I said, just in case. We can't control the winds."

A pregnant woman said, "Oh, no! You can't mean it! I mean, everything we have is right here! We—"

"I wish," Ben said, "that I could tell you different. But I can't. That's the way it is."

There was silence. It grew and stretched.

"For your information," Ben said then, "that grove of trees we are deliberating sacrificing to try to protect you is worth more than all your houses put together. Those are extremely rare specimen trees gathered from all over the world at enormous expense—"

"Big deal," the man who had spoken before said bitterly. "Who the hell cares? They're just trees."


Bessie drove directly to the Antlers from the hospital. To the barman, she said, "Gimme two beers. In two glasses. And if you make some funny crack, I'm going to pop you one."

In silence the barman opened two bottles of beer, poured two glasses full and set it all on the bar.

Bessie said, "You talk Spanish?" She watched the man nod. "Okay," she said, "how you say, like, 'Here's looking at you, or mud in your eye?' Like that?"

The barman thought a moment, "*Salud, amor y pesetas*," he said, "*y tiempo para gustarlos*. That's the formal way."

"What's it mean?"

" 'Health, love and money and time to enjoy them.' "

Bessie closed her eyes briefly. She shook her head. "Won't do." She took a deep breath. "Okay," she said, "we'll forget it." She lifted the two glasses, one in each hand. "Luck, Eloy, you poor little bastard," she said, and emptied both.


Duane Semple was not a big man, and he was obviously in frail health, but there was no mistaking his air of authority, and his unspoken expectation that matters would inevitably arrange themselves as he desired them. His greetings were easy and gracious.

"I am delighted to see you again, Miss Cummings, and I thank you for coming." He smiled up at Ken Delacorte. "I spent a large part of one Sunday afternoon in Texas Stadium, Mr. Delacorte, admiring your abilities on the football field. I might add that my pleasure was somewhat dampened by the fact that I was sitting in the owner's box, and the Dallas Cowboys football team does not enjoy losing."

"I didn't think anybody did," Bart Jones said from his wheelchair.

Semple's nod was almost imperceptible. "I appreciate it," he said, and nodded toward the waiting butler. "What will you have to drink? Miss Cummings?"

Her father, Stacy thought, would probably have understood the ground rules of this meeting, as Ken and Bart seemed to, and she did not. Men were supposed to be direct, economical and to the point in their talk, utterly unlike the common concept of women who were supposed to beat around the bush, approach a subject obliquely, never really say what they were actually after in clear, unmistakable terms. Somebody, she told herself, had turned conventional wisdom inside out.

Before dinner, there was talk of the Sanrio fire, the current baseball standings, the drought, the strength of the US dollar against other major currencies, New Orleans restaurants, steeplechasing versus flat racing as a spectator sport, and the coming elections. Bellevue Acres was not mentioned.

Over soup—a fine consommé—the talk turned to a new television series, the emergence of the second professional football league, national budget deficits, the likelihood of interstate banking, the Santa Fe Opera and the success of *Cats* transplanted from the London stage.

"Anyone interested in what we came here for?" Stacy asked. "Or have I just coughed in church?"

"Her Daddy didn't have much patience, either," Bart Jones said.

The main course was Beef Wellington, which the butler carved and the maid passed together with soufflé potatoes and baby green peas with pearl onions. The wine was a classic California Cabernet Sauvignon.

"Humor me, please, Miss Cummings," Semple said. "My digestion is somewhat delicate, and I try to avoid controversial subjects at mealtimes."

Stacy was aware that Ken was watching her, expressionless, and that Bart Jones wore an amused smile which annoyed her. She tried, and failed, to think of something bright to say.

It was at times like this, she had often thought, that her inadequacies showed up. And, remembering what Ken had told her, she supposed that it was a sense of those inadequacies that prompted her to resort to the shock quality of stable language as a form of defense. It was strange how clearly she was seeing matters in a new light these days.

To the very young, she had read once, all things seem within one's grasp or at least possible. It is as one grows older (grows up?), the piece had gone on, that one begins to realize one does have limitations, that perhaps brain surgery or abstract mathematics or even becoming President of the US are goals one might better leave to others. *Know thyself*—Stacy was not sure who had said that first, but it was becoming in her mind a dictum well worth remembering.

Now, "Good beef," she said, "well hung, and from first-rate stock." This, at least, she knew about. "Hard to come by these days, even here in cattle country."

Without looking directly, she saw that Bart's amused smile had faded, and that Ken wore an expression of approval. "Cross-breeding experiments," she went on, "artificial insemination, possibly even genetic engineering coming—" She shook her head. "Hard to keep up with."

Semple said, "You are against interference with nature, Miss Cummings?"

"I breed horses," Stacy said. "I go after the results I want, so the answer is, no, I am not against changing things. As long as the change benefits, instead of hurting people." She smiled suddenly. "You see, I'm really a very simple person."

"I am beginning to doubt it very much," Semple said. "A touch more wine, perhaps?"


From its synchronous orbit 22,300 miles above the earth, the weather satellite transmitted its final pictures of the day in the fading ground light. On earth the pictures were received, computer-enhanced and sent off by teleprinters across the nation.

Combined with data from the aircraft tracking Hurricane Charley, and set against ground information collected from a hundred weather stations, a comprehensive picture began to emerge.

"I'm not going to make any dogmatic predictions," the chief weatherman said. "Not with Charley, who is turning into a very willful fellow indeed. But I have more than a hunch that he's getting ready to launch his major attack, in short, shoot the works in the direction of the mainland."

"Where?"

"That," the chief meteorologist said, "is a splendid question. We'll answer it as soon as we can and warn the coastal areas that may be affected. But inland—" He shook his head. "We can already guess what's going to happen inland almost regardless of where along a two-hundred-mile stretch Charley goes ashore. With his mass and power, he's going to push winds, some of them near gale-force, as far inland as the Rockies." He looked around. "Agreed?"

There were nods, and thoughtful silence. One meteorologist said, "There's still that fire in the Sanrio Forest." He had been assigned from time to time to large fires, and was acquainted with the techniques of fighting them. "And flames driven by near-gale-force winds can jump almost any fire break you can devise."

"I am aware of it," said the chief, who was not unacquainted with fire-suppression tactics himself. "And I wish them luck."


In the large living room after dinner, with coffee, cognac for the men and for Duane Semple a cigar as well. "Now to business," Semple said once the cigar was properly lighted and drawing well. "Undoubtedly you have a price in mind, Mr. Delacorte?"

Ken wore an expression of alertness Stacy could recognize and understand, and she supposed that like Ken she herself had worn it often enough as well.

For her it would have been the expression that awaited the moment when the gate swung open and the calf came out on a dead run, or the pistol fired starting the breakneck dash around the barrels strategically placed within the arena.

For Ken, it would have been the moment before the ball was snapped and he began to run his pattern—down-and-out, or hook, or fly—so many strides, so much distance before he turned his head to see the thrown ball coming toward him, to catch, to tuck away securely, to carry as far forward as he could before the almost inevitable shock of collison.

All that might have gone before was unimportant. This was the moment when the contest began.

"A price for exactly what?" Ken said.

Semple nodded as if he had expected the question, and approved of its being asked. "For your total interest in Bellevue Acres," he said.

"The property," Ken said, "the houses, the people, including the kids and the dogs and the few flowers in the ratty little gardens? The home-built barbecues that smoke, and that funny-looking badminton court? My share of all of it?"

"Oh, for God's sake," Bart said from his wheelchair, "let's not be mawkish. This is a business proposition."

"For you, yes," Ken said. "I see it differently."

Semple said, "I think that is understandable. The project was your idea in the first place, and you worked to bring it to fruition, which involved surmounting a number of obstacles, I am sure."

"Such as getting a zoning variation," Ken said. "That's really what you're interested in, isn't it?"

"Having the zoning variation in place would be helpful," Semple said. "There is no question about that."

"Getting the people out," Ken said, "won't present much of a problem, will it? Jack up the interest rates, which means increasing the mortgage payments. Invoke the due-on-sale clauses if they try to sell, which will quash all deals. Make a few extra bucks in the process, and all of a sudden the peasants have gone and you have nice empty land where you can put up your fancy condos or town houses or whatever you call them, and the real profits begin."

Semple, wholly unperturbed, admired the long, even ash on the end of his cigar. "Your business-school studies were not in vain, Mr. Delacorte," he said at last. "You understand exactly how business is conducted. I return to my original question. Undoubtedly you have a price in mind?"

Stacy had the odd feeling that she was inside Ken's mind now, both seeing and hearing his thoughts. She could even anticipate his words.

400

"My total interest in Bellevue Acres," Ken said, "is not for sale. Neither is any part of it."

"Indeed?" Semple's tone contained no indication of surprise. "You are already skating on rather thin financial ice, Mr. Delacorte," he said. "We took the trouble to ascertain that. A few obstacles placed in your way, perhaps litigation of some sort which would involve legal expenses, or the sudden discovery that certain building codes had not been properly adhered to and extensive alterations were required — unfortunate and unforeseen expenses from matters such as these might cause that thin financial ice to collapse, might they not?"

"I don't think so," Stacy said.

Ken said sharply, "Stay out of this."

"I think freshman year was the last time you tried to tell me what to do," Stacy said. "It didn't work then, and it's not going to work now." Her glance included them all. "Daddy said that whenever he declared himself in a game where he didn't really hold cards he ended up being kicked in the belly. Okay, so be it." She did not miss the almost triumphant gleam in Bart's eyes as he watched her accept the challenge. "He also said," Stacy went on, "that it was pretty damn hard to sit by and watch a son of a bitch, in this case apparently two sons of bitches, picking on folks who couldn't fight back. I feel the same way. So —"

The butler, a cordless telephone in hand, coughed politely and said, "Excuse me, sir, but there is what is apparently an urgent call for Mr. Delacorte. The lady sounded quite upset." He held out the phone.

Semple said, "If you would rather take the call in my library, Mr. Delacorte, please feel free."

Ken merely shook his head and reached for the telephone.

It was Ada. Her voice, under tight control, came

clearly. "The fire's broken loose," she said. "I'm not being hysterical, I can see it, and it's on the radio. It's blowing like mad, and—"

"On my way," Ken said. He handed the phone back to the butler. "Sorry," he said to Semple, and looked at Stacy as he stood up.

"Right with you," Stacy said. She was already on her feet. Her eyes swept Semple and Bart Jones. "You get the message," she said. "We can pick up later where we left off."

## 33

Billy Bob Barker, Sanrio Mayor, was neither a bold nor a profane man, but he felt that crisis demanded extraordinary emphasis. "Goddamnit, George," he told the Forest Supervisor on the telephone, "I warned you about this. JL is a nice fellow and all that, but apparently he's damn well over the hill, and now we've got a real mess on our hands. Pete Trujillo's market is about to go, they tell me, and if it does, you know what's next? Do you?" His tone demanded an answer.

George Jefferson's mind was on a number of other matters. "You tell me, Billy Bob."

"The Sanrio Valley Propane Company, that's goddam what. And only two weeks ago at Kiwanis Joe Jordan from the Fire Department told us what would happen if that propane storage tank ever went up. What we'd have left of downtown would be nothing but a big hole in the ground."

The second light on Jefferson's phone was blinking. He said, "I've got another call now, Billy Bob. JL, I hope. I'll get back to you." He switched connections, and spoke his name with savage emphasis.

It was JL. He echoed the mayor's sentiments. "We've got a mess, George. No question about that. Our airport tower is measuring sixty-mile-an-hour wind gusts shifting through a forty-five-degree arc that takes

403

in a good share of the town. Whether it was torched or not, it's a good thing the Holloway house and the trees around it are gone. The Spencer house is going. We can't save it, so we're just letting it go and establishing our line beyond it. The Cummings place is probably next—"

Jefferson said, "What about that propane storage tank?"

"The city's going to have to take care of that. And the market next door. We're throwing everything we have in a curved line from Sheep Ridge and the Vista Hill specimen tree grove around to the River—"

"In the dark—"

"It isn't dark any more, George. Look out the window and you'll see. We have more light and heat to work by than we can use."

Always there was one more thing to think about. "McIlvain and his men? What about them?"

"They're safe, I think, up with the picas and the mountain goats above timberline. They'll be cold by morning, but they won't be in real trouble unless they try something foolish." It would be typical of Andy, JL thought, to try to help if he saw any conceivable opportunity. JL hoped he would stay where he and his men were—out of harm's way.

"All right," Jefferson said. "Keep at it and keep me posted. Anything you need—"

"I'll shout." There was a short pause. "And, George?"

"I'm listening."

"I haven't been what you might call lucky, and maybe that's my fault, I don't know. But if you're thinking of replacing me—"

"You keep at it. It's still your baby."

Jefferson broke the connection and sat for a few moments in thought. Obviously, JL was beginning to question himself, although despite Billy Bob's feelings in the matter, Jefferson could see no reason why JL should have any doubts at all. In battle, things happened, many of them bad and almost all of them beyond your control. And for the good ones, like JL, the temptation to blame yourself was almost irresistible. For others, the incompetents, the temptation was always to blame either circumstances or someone else.

He dialed Billy Bob's number, and the phone was answered with breathless immediacy. "It was JL," Jefferson said, "and things are not good."

"You're replacing him, George?"

"I am not. He's the best we have, and we're going with him. Now here's what you can — no, what you have to do."

Billy Bob listened, breathing hard into the phone. He said at last, "That propane tank—"

"It's a nasty situation," Jefferson said. "No argument. But we have our hands full, and your people can do the job as well as we can. We'll try to keep the fire off your back by not letting it get any closer to your city limits. We've established our line—" With his eye on the wall map, he explained the limits JL had given him.

Billy Bob said, "And if the fire jumps your line?"

Jefferson had anticipated the question. "Then," he said, "you'd better give thought to dynamiting some houses to protect the rest of the town."

"Jesus, George!"

"I know," Jefferson said. "My house is there too, remember?"


Willard P. Spencer was close to apoplexy. "The Governor will hear of this outrage," he told Ben Hastings. "Washington will hear of it! I demand that my house and property be protected, thoroughly protected! What happens to those chicken coops in that housing development is of no consequence. None! Mrs. Spencer and I are taxpayers, large taxpayers, and we demand respect!"

"Fine," Ben said. He beckoned one of the crew chiefs. "Get that hose hooked up to the swimming pool, and see that the well pump keeps running until it sucks air."

"That well," Spencer said, "cost fifteen dollars a foot to drill. The pump and related equipment are the best obtainable. If you burn out the pump—"

"Move it, amigo," the crew chief said. "We got work to do and you're in the way." He squinted through sooty eyes at Spencer's immaculate polo shirt, blazer and flannels. "Was I you, I'd be hauling the family silver and maybe Grandma as well out of the house and headed for far places. Split, buster! You hear me?"

Angela Spencer took her husband's arm and urged him to one side. "I don't think they will listen to you, Will," she said. "I believe we'd do well to take some things and move to the Inn temporarily."

"You don't understand, Angy."

"Quite possibly not. But I can't see that you are accomplishing anything by staying here. And I wouldn't put it past that man with the dirty face to turn violent."

"He wouldn't dare."

"There was that taxi driver at Kennedy Airport, Will."

"A maniac."

"That may be, but there is nothing we can do here. The house is obviously threatened, and we may lose it, insurance or not, so—"

Spencer stared down at his wife's face. "What do you know about insurance?"

"We have none. Isn't that correct?" There was no answer. Angela had expected none. "So," she said, "I

406

think we might well go to the Inn, and await results. We'll need night things, at least, and you'll want your toilet kit and shaver. We'd best get them while we can."

Sophie Swift had the station wagon packed in accordance with the list she had made. Her grandmother's silverware was already securely tied in a pillow case and sunk in the deep end of the swimming pool. With some difficulty she had hooked the horse trailer to the station wagon's trailer hitch and urged the mare Impatient up the ramp and inside. The foal had followed obediently. The other two horses were tethered behind the horse trailer, and already restive because of the gathering smoke.

Sophie had refused payment from Debby and Johnny Joe, who turned out to be a personable country boy with an overlay of worldliness from his Navy travels. Sophie hoped that he and Debby would be very happy together, and thought that they might well be. At this moment, patting the two tethered horses and trying to calm them, all she could think was that with his country-boy background, Johnny Joe was probably very good with livestock of all kinds, and she wished he were here now.

She did not consider herself an emotional female, as many were, and perhaps this was merely one more flaw in her make-up, but now, faced with the logical necessity of abandoning the house she and Aaron had built together and filled with memories as well as memorabilia, she found herself very close to tears as she had not been even after suffering that unnerving first loss in court so long ago.

She told herself that logically, despite the multitude of reassurances, she had known this moment was coming. Why else had she prepared herself? But between *knowing* and *experiencing*, between *thinking* and *feeling*, there lay a gap the vastness of which could not even be described, let alone measured.

She had told Stacy that the Aaron-Debby business had been a chastening experience. Here was another, almost equally devastating, and it was beginning to seem that the life she, Sophie Swift, had once considered so organized and well-balanced, securely built upon the rock of assurance, was now crumbling like a sand castle as the tide came in, and would in a short time disappear altogether. Despite all her erudition and experience, what then would become of her?

Inside the horse trailer the mare whinnied and stamped a nervous hoof. The two tethered geldings stirred restlessly, their ears cocked forward, their nostrils wide and their eyes rolling wildly.

"Easy, boys," Sophie said, but she too was conscious that time was running out and that the sensible thing for her to do was get into the station wagon and drive away, turning her back on all that she had once held so dear.

Still she hesitated, unwilling to make the first move toward abandonment, clinging to she knew not what forlorn hope that *something* would happen.

Through the trees at the Forest's edge, she could see the flames and hear their crackling menace, smell the smoke that rose in heavy, rolling clouds obscuring the stars overhead. And the wind, gusting powerfully and changing direction without warning, also altered its pitch, sometimes sounding a dirge through the trees, and sometimes rising to a banshee shriek as of souls in torment.

The mare in the trailer whinnied again and stamped that single hoof angrily. The tethered geldings tugged at their tie ropes.

"All right," Sohpie said at last. "You're right. Time to

go." Tears were very close.

Ken drove, pushing his aged car to its limit on the road from Duane Semple's spread. He was in dead earnest and in haste, but he was amused and smiling too. "You sure as hell did declare yourself in," he told Stacy, "even if you don't hold cards. I don't believe either Jones or Semple enjoyed being called sons of bitches."

"But they are."

"I won't argue. But the world is full of folks who resent being told what they actually are. I reckon that takes in most of us." He glanced at Stacy's face. "Just what are you fixing to do, anyhow?"

"Back you. You need financial muscle to go up against them."

"And you've got it." Ken shook his head. "Just like that."

"I didn't earn it," Stacy said. "In some ways, I haven't any right to it. Just because I was lucky enough to be Daddy's daughter, damn it, I'm the rich bitch kid who plays at breeding horse." Funny, but with Ken she could talk without shame, relaxed as she might have been with the brother she never had. "For whatever reasons," she said, "I've been taking fresh looks at myself, and I'm not sure I like much what I see."

"You're all right," Ken said. "A mite prickly, maybe, like a cholla cactus, but easy enough to get along with most times."

He sounded, Stacy thought, very much like her father, and she responded in the same way, without rancor. "Thanks a heap."

She was silent for long moments, watching the countryside rush past in the headlights' glow. Ahead, the fire area was clearly visible, expanded, menacing.

The sight brought an empty feeling in her chest. "That was Ada Loving," she said for distraction. "On the phone, I mean."

"Yes." Was there some kind of question behind the word?

"I don't know her much," Stacy said, "but I like her. For all the build-up and the glamor hype, she seems real."

"I like her too," Ken said. "And she is."

In the darkness, Stacy could smile to herself. "I guess we've settled that," she said.

"Meaning what?" His voice was suddenly sharper than usual.

"Simmer down," Stacy said. "It's me, remember? What I mean is, you don't wave your arms and start explaining the girl. Or defending her. You just say, 'Yep. She's the greatest thing since sliced bread, period.' And that says it all. I like it. I like it fine."

Ken, vaguely embarrassed, drove in silence for a time, his eyes too on the fire area. "It's jumped the reservation for sure," he said, "and it's going to raise hell before JL can stop it."

"Can he? Will he?"

"If it can be done, and maybe even if it can't. He's a man to put your money on."

"Yes," Stacy said slowly, "I've been getting around to thinking the same."

"So I've noticed," Ken said. And then, quickly, before Stacy could respond. "Where you want to go? Your house?"

"I don't care about the house," Stacy said. "No, that isn't true. I do care. A lot. There are things in there I'd hate like sin to lose, some of them Daddy's things."

"But what?"

"The horses," Stacy said. "They're what's important. They rely on me, they're my responsibility. The rest of it can go, but I won't let the horses down, damn it. No way."

Ken nodded. In a strange fashion, Stacy's priorities and Ada's were identical, and he felt a sense of pleasure that it was so. "I sort of thought it might be like that," he said.

Aaron Swift walked out of the home he and Debby had shared into the eerie near-darkness flickeringly lighted by the flames of BACKSLOPE. Overhead, he could see stars, as once in a ground blizzard in La Veta Pass, the radiator ornament of his automobile invisible in the driving snow, he had been able to look aloft and see blue sky above the ground-level storm; and it occurred to him to remember now that when he had finally topped the 9500-foot summit of the Pass, he had emerged into brilliant sunlight and a cloudless western sky.

He did not believe in omens, and he despised neat aphorisms that mentioned silver linings to storm clouds, or maintained that it was always darkest just before dawn. On the other hand, there was something to the hope, if not the belief, that when things got bad and stayed bad, the chances were that any change would almost have to be for the better.

And things had been bad. First, of course, there had been and still was the fire. Raised in this country, Aaron knew what devastation was right now being caused by those flames he could see so clearly, and knew further what an agonizingly long time it would take for the Forest to replenish itself when at last the fire had passed.

First, of course, would come erosion. Torrential late summer thunderstorm rains would soak the naked ground to its capacity in short order, and the excess

411

water would then start its inexorable downward movement unchecked by vegetation, first in trickles which, joining, would become rivulets and small streams. These in turn, combining forces, would swell in size and force, finding already carved arroyos, filling and overflowing these, and turning at last into flash floods, real gully-washers capable of tearing great chunks from the defenseless land, uncovering and setting in motion rocks and boulders, gouging new channels, tearing out highway foundations and bridge supports, catching unwary motorists in the open and tossing two-ton vehicles on their crests as ocean surf will toss a beach ball.

The Forest Service would attempt to plant replacement vegetation, sowing grass seed and setting out tiny fast-growing evergreen trees. And some of these would survive the rains and receive the autumn and winter snow cover gratefully to emerge into the spring and early summer growing season and try to survive another year. Fast-growing plants such as fireweed would spring up in burned-over areas, these two providing at least some protection against the later heavy rains.

But the resuscitation of a fire-destroyed evergreen forest was, inevitably, a long, slow and painful process, and Aaron, looking now at the brightening glow of BACKFIRE, felt a sadness of spirit that was difficult to contain.

And then, of course, there was Debby, who had already packed, wept sincerely in their farewells and gone off with her Johnny Joe. Aaron had long approved of the ease with which the laws of New Mexico allowed a husband and wife to decide jointly that they had made a mistake, and almost without further ado go their separate ways unimpeded, thereby avoiding what could so often be a long, drawn-out period of great unpleasantness and uncertain status. But now

412

that it had happened to him, and not as a result of his own decision, he saw matters in a little different light.

First and foremost, of course, Debby's leaving, her desire to leave, was a blow to his ego. He was honest enough to admit this, and to admit as well that he had done precisely the same thing to Sophie, which left him ruefully contemplating Aaron Swift as a man hoist by his own petard, a tragi-comic figure who deserved sympathy from no one, including himself.

And now, as the final blow, there was the news on the radio that BACKSLOPE was once again out of control, had already destroyed the Spencer property, and was probably closing in next on the ranch he and Sophie together had built, almost quite literally, from scratch.

Like Churchill in the wilderness years, Aaron had found solace and relaxation from the demands of his law practice in masonry. There was not a wall on the property that did not contain his handiwork; not a brick in the patio flooring he had not laid and tapped level in the carefully spread and smoothed bed of fine sand; not a polished tile throughout the new wing that contained their study-library that he had not selected, fixed with mortar and grouted into permanence.

Together, he and Sophie had spaded the garden and metamorphosed the quality of the soil from dirt capable of supporting cactus, an occasional patch of grama grass and horny toads to dark richness in which it was their truthful boast that almost anything would grow.

They had planned the bookcases that lined the study-library wall, drawn the rough design, and then, dissatisfied with the architect's renderings, taken a night course in home architectural planning at the local university branch, and produced their own working drawings.

Sophie was still at the ranch. Aaron would have been

willing to bet on that. She would be prepared for flight, but she would not yet have driven away unless the danger had become too imminent, and Aaron did not think it had quite yet.

And he was here, nursing his wounded pride, pretending to mourn the departure of a young wife whom he had teased for her shortcomings, and worrying about trees.

"You," he told himself suddenly aloud, "had damn well better put your priorities in order, counselor." And with that he walked quickly to his car and got in.


Sitting at the command center table was no longer possible. JL pushed back his chair and stood up. To Ben, "You stay here. I—" He stopped and shook his head. "Not a chance," he said. "Not even a madman would try to take a chopper into the air in these winds. But I've got to see for myself." He nodded then in decision. "Okay, jeep it is. I'll keep in touch." The butterfly bandages on his chin, grimy now from the smoke, seemed oddly out of place.

"Take somebody with you," Ben said. "You're going off-road—" He too shook his head. JL was already gone.

As he drove, still on road that wound through the trees, JL studied the map in his mind, setting against it the reports that had continued to flow in. Sheep Ridge first, he decided. He'd give a lot to be able to put Ben in charge of that sector, but Ben was needed right where he was, at the nerve center, able to make decisions for division bosses who would inevitably ask for guidance. Then who—?

He took the microphone from its bracket. "Where's Jay Paul?" And then quickly, "Never mind where he is. Find him. Tell him to get over to Sheep Ridge. I want him. Over."

Ben's voice was comfortingly calm. "Roger."

"And get your relief man, Weinstock, and give him the sector from the river right up to the town."

Again the comforting, "Roger."

"Over and out for now," JL said, hung up the mike again and concentrated on his driving.

## 34

Ken skirted the town and intersected the County road near the Holloway place. By the furious glare of the fire they could make out what was left of the skeleton of the house: two standing walls pierced by a gaping doorway and a large, ragged hole where the view window had been.

Stacy said unexpectedly, "Serves us right. All of us. Building that close to the wildland."

"JL's tub-thumping has got to you, has it?" Ken's voice was grimly amused.

"Damn it —" Stacy began automatically, and stopped. "Okay," she said in a different tone, "the answer is yes." Her tone changed again. "God, look there!"

It was the Spencer house, still in flames. And, in a scene from hell, the moving figures of fire-fighters threw enormous shadows to move jerkily against the curtain of smoke rising from the Forest trees.

"Ada was right," Ken said. "The wind—look there, that shower of sparks and burning branches!"

Fourth of July fireworks came to mind, Stacy thought, only on the Fourth you knew that it was celebratory make-believe under control. Here the monster was loose, and insatiable. "Will this thing go any faster?" she said.

Ken merely grunted and bore down harder on the accelerator. There was no noticeable change in their speed.

"Let me out at the end of my drive," Stacy said, remembering JL's dislike of the long, curving, one-way entrance. "I don't want you stuck up by the house not able to get turned around."

"Now," Ken said, "you're telling me what to do, so cut it out."

There was a sudden burst of light brighter than the rest, and a full count later the sound of an explosion.

"Toward town," Ken said. "Gasoline storage tank. Maybe propane—"

"Oh, God," Stacy said, "not that big one!"

"Nope." Ken's tone was positive. "If that one goes, we'll know it—then again, maybe we won't, maybe we won't know anything."

"That's my cheerful boy."

Ken turned to look at her. Once, he remembered, he had described her to JL: "You see her on top of that big cutting horse of hers, the piggin' strings in her teeth, waiting for the gate to open and the calf to come busting out, and you look at her face and you know that there's no give in her, none. When she puts her mind to it, she's pure rawhide all the way through." That, he thought, was the way her face looked now.

"I'm not going to try to tell you what to do or not do," Ken said, "but if it comes to a choice between you and your horses—"

"I'll take care of it."

"I know you will, but, goddamnit, what I'm trying to tell you is to take care of yourself as well, you hear?"

"I hear." Stacy's voice was unexpectedly soft. She put her hand on his arm. "Stop worrying."

"Fat chance. You're as independent as a hog on ice. You—"

He stood on the brakes as a car burst out of the entrance to Stacy's drive, swung sharply and almost rammed them. Ken could see that a woman was driving, but recognition came slowly, and Stacy was already out of the car.

"Juanita!" Stacy's voice was shrill. She reached the other car and bent to the window. *"Qué pasa?"*

"The fire!" Juanita's words, a mixture of Spanish and English, almost ran together. "And Pancho. That *chico*! He thinks of nothing but the horses, and you were not here, *señorita*, he is letting them out of their stalls—"

Stacy half-turned to wave at Ken. "Beat it! And you too, Juanita!"

She turned then and began to run up the curving drive, uncertain on the high-heeled sandals, holding the long skirt above her knees.

Here among the piñon and juniper, she realized, the smell of smoke was heavier than it had been in the car, and the sense of the fire more imminent. Because of the trees and the curving road, she could not see the house, or the stables; nor, she thought, would she have been able to see a car coming toward her until it was too close to avoid, and so JL had been right in his concern. Why did her mind keep turning in JL's direction? And what difference did that make now?

Running uphill, working hard to retain her balance on the gravel, she was breathing hard, and her legs were beginning to ache. Slow down, you fool, she told herself, or you'll be too pooped to do anything when you get there. But the urgency in her mind was in control.

Once more curve, she thought, and then one more after that—when you're looking for something it always evades you, damn it—but it has to be just around the next curve.

And at last she burst into the parking area and turn-around, took a quick glance at the house and found it still intact and then turned to run towards the corral and the horsebarns.

She saw Pancho. He was bareback on a big gray gelding named Walter, clinging like a burr to a saddle-blanket, controlling the animal with a hackamore instead of a bridle. He saw Stacy, and his face split wide in a white-toothed grin. "*Vámonos, señorita*! Let's go! There is a hackamore on Sam! And the horses are loose!" He gestured to them milling in the shadows.

Good boy, Stacy thought, and ran toward Sam who stood patiently, the hackamore rope hanging to the ground. Sam's ears were pricked forward toward Stacy, and his eyes implored her to hurry. The smoke was thick, choking, far worse than it had been coming up the drive. The milling horses whinnied in panic. The sounds of their hooves were like distant thunder.

Stacy seized the hackamore rope, and then looked down at herself, at the long dress, the long, impossible dress in disgust. "Hold it, Sam," she said and dropped the rope. "What the hell?" She said it aloud, merely for her own benefit, and with both hands tore the dress to the waist, let it drop and stepped out of it. She wore only the high-heeled sandals and the lace bikini panties.

She seized the rope again, and a handful of Sam's mane. "Move it, boy! Let's go!" And as the big horse took his first jump forward, Stacy used his momentum and the spring in her own legs to vault to his back. "Get them moving, Pancho! Let's go!" She pursed her lips and tongue, whistled shrilly and waved her free arm. "Yeeeeay!" And another whistle.

"Not the drive!" she shouted to Pancho. "Down the hill, through the trees, away from the road!" There would be cars, maybe city fire trucks, too much chance of collision. "Turn them toward the Swift property!"

419

As she rode into the firelit night, guiding Sam as much with her bare knees as with the hackamore, riding at breakneck speed through trees and brush, it occurred to her to wonder if Pancho had ever heard of Lady Godiva.

Duane Semple sat silent with his cigar for some time after Ken and Stacy had left. Occasionally, seeming about to speak, he glanced at Bart, who was also preoccupied, but changed his mind and the silence held.

It was Bart who broke it. "Under the circumstances," he said, "I'd probably better get along too. Whatever the news was, it didn't seem good."

"One moment," Semple said, and studied the ash of his cigar for another short, silent spell. When he looked at Bart again, his eyes were narrowed in a speculative frown. "Between you and Miss Cummings—" he began.

"Ancient history, Duane." The words and the tone carried a faint warning.

"I am not so sure. Whatever it was, it seems to have carried into the present. I had the impression that you were waiting for Miss Cummings to come to Delacorte's aid. Financially, that is."

"Likely."

"You intended to teach the young woman a lesson in business practices?"

"Maybe rub her nose in the dirt a little. She's been asking for it for a long time."

Almost reluctantly, Semple tapped the cigar ash into the nearby tray. He studied the gray heap briefly. "I prefer not to bring personal vendettas into financial transactions," he said at last.

"My money, Duane."

420

Semple nodded faint agreement. "So far," he said. "But you are counting on a considerable amount of my money to flesh out your project, so that gives me legitimate concern." He even smiled, a brief, passing, meaningless expression. "In Miss Cummings's picturesque phrase, I do hold cards in this game. And to carry her father's analogy further, I do not expect to be kicked in the belly. I suggest that you control your libido."

"This, damn it," Bart said, "has nothing to do with—"

"—frustrated lust? I am not so sure of that, either. What is between you and Miss Cummings—"

"I told you that was ancient history. I meant it."

"So now we are right back at our starting point, aren't we?"

Bart restrained himself with effort and said slowly, "I am surprised that at some point Stacy's daddy didn't pop you one if you baited him like this."

Semple shook his head. "Brawler though he was," he said, "I was physically quite safe with him. He didn't pick on the ill or the crippled."

Sitting rigidly quite still, Bart forced his strong hands on the arms of the wheelchair to relax. The flat muscles in his jaws showed plainly. He said at last, "I'll thank you, Duane, if you will have your man call my car." Then, switching off the electric drive, he turned the chair, spun it, actually, by hand, in the effort finding outlet for his anger. Over his shoulder he said, "Goodnight. I thank you for the dinner." He whirled the chair out into the entrance hall.

Sophie Swift opened the door of the station wagon and started to get in. In the horse trailer hitched behind, the mare whinnied loudly and stamped that

421

single hoof again. "Easy!" Sophie said automatically, but, hesitating there in the darkness and the leaping shadows cast by the flames, she too was conscious of something she could not comprehend, and she searched the trees for the cause.

It was a sound, her senses told her, but it was also a feeling, communicated she knew not how, as if the earth itself were shaking beneath her feet. Amid cavorting shadows there was sight, as well, a vague phantasmagoria of movement, bringing to mind stampedes she had read about in western literature.

And suddenly, a running horse did appear, and another, and then a bunched mass amid a thunder of hooves and the tremors of the earth. A shrill whistle cut through the sounds without warning, and a voice raised above the din shouted, or screamed, "Turn them, Pancho! Take them left toward Vista Hill!"

Sophie, only partially comprehending, could see then a big, gray gelding with a hackamore encircling his nose, and on his back, hunched forward over the withers like a jockey in his stretch run a small human shape that shouted, also in falsetto, "Aaaaiiiie! *Izquierdo, chicos! Arriba! Vámonos!*" and a thin brown arm waved a coiled rope, as the gray leaned obediently into his turn, forcing the mass of horses to the new direction. They thundered off into the darkness.

And here, on Sam, came Stacy, naked, as far as Sophie could see, and totally unconcerned about it, to rein the big horse to a sliding stop as she surveyed the situation.

"Turn the geldings loose," Stacy ordered. "I'll take care of them. You have the mare and the foal in the trailer? Good. Get going. Luck." She half-turned on Sam's back to stare at headlights coming up the drive. "Who's this? Get him out of the way, and you get going!"

Sophie too was staring at the headlights as if mesmerized. She could make out the shape of the vehicle behind the lights only dimly, but somehow she *knew*—

"Turn the geldings loose!" Stacy's voice was sharp with command, and Sophie stumbled to the rear of the horse trailer to obey.

She heard Stacy say then, "Oh, it's you! Good. About time. Get that wagon and trailer out of here! Pronto!" and again the shrill whistle sounded as the two geldings moved free, and Stacy shouted, "Move it! They're all ours, Sam!" And the thunder of these hooves too disappeared into the darkness.

Sophie hurried back to the station wagon's door. Inside the trailer box stall the mare was kicking up a stamping fuss and whinnying in terror. "We're going!" Sophie almost screamed, and into the darkness, toward the now stopped headlights, she called. "Is it you? Is it?"

"You lead," Aaron's calm voice said. "I'll follow. It's going to be all right, Soph."

"Oh, thank God!" As she scrambled into the car seat and switched on the engine, Sophie had no idea whether she had said the words aloud, or only in her mind. Not, she told herself, that it mattered. Not even a little bit. Not now. Or ever again.


From his vantage point well above timberline on the great mountain, Andy McIlvain could look down, almost as if from the cabin of his plane, with a 270-degree view of BACKSLOPE's vast area from high in the northeast all the way around into the northwest. He could watch the surging flames as wind gusts buffeted and drove them, and although the distance was too great to hear any sounds, through familiarity he could with ease imagine the tumult and the shouted orders as foot-by-foot and sometimes rod-by-rod, the crews on the fire line gave ground.

Even at this elevation, it was no longer cold; rising heated air, as from a floor radiator, overpowered the normal nighttime downslope winds, bringing vividly the odors of conflagration and massive destruction.

The war was being won; that much was clear. The earlier 180-degree windshift had driven flames back across Highway 14 into territory already burned where the flames were now expiring from lack of fuel. To the northwest the same thing had happened, and in the northeast and east, the north-south fire line Gordy's and Bessie's crews had cut was holding fast with only a few men still remaining to make sure that matters did not get out of hand again. Gordy and Bessie and their people had probably been brought down to the one remaining area of greatest danger—the Sheep-Ridge-Forest-Finger-Specimen-Grove vicinity which, together with the flames that had escaped to the east from Sheep Ridge, threatening the remaining estates, the housing development and the town itself.

It was the way these things worked, he thought; gradually you got one part of the perimeter under control, then another, and yet a third, and as these conquered territories became joined, the fire area shrank until at last, as now, you were in a position to throw everything you had into the remaining breach in your line. Then, if you were lucky, you closed the circle before too much damage had been done.

It was not really as simple as all that, of course. Even when the circle was closed, there would be occasional breakouts requiring emergency action by standby crews. A fire the size of BACKSLOPE would need cold-trailing for days lest the monster again arose from the ashes.

But right now, there was still a critical breach in the

line running through the Forest finger, and that was where the major battle would have to take place. And, he thought with a smile, that was where Bessie and Gordy's troops would be now, grunting and sweating and swearing.

His eyes still on the scene spread before him, he lifted his radio and called the dispatcher. "Patch me through to JL, if you can," he said, and waited impatiently until the familiar voice acknowledged reception. "Call me your eye in the sky," Andy said then. "I'm perched up here in mountain goat land, with a clear view of the entire battlefield. Call me if you want specifics."

JL, driving with one hand and manipulating the jeep's mike with the other, felt an immediate surge of hope. Andy, with a clear view of the entire area—nothing could be better. Were they beginning to get the breaks at last? "I'm in a jeep," he said, "trying to cover the entire line. Mrs Wayne's grove that we backfired—is it holding as a break?"

"As of now. Bellevue Acres is still intact."

"And down the finger?"

"Troops fighting a rearguard action, pappy. And I suggest that if you're thinking another backfire to protect the town, you'd better get to it quick. There's that empty parking lot by the wooden rodeo grandstands, and if you set your backfire with that lot behind you, you'll be as safe as any place I can see—"

"Got it."

"We could try to come down around the shoulder of the mountain—"

"You stay right where you are. And keep your people with you."

"Aye, aye, sir."

"And call me soonest if you see anything else I need to know."

"Luck, good buddy. Over and out."

Andy switched off and beckoned to one of his men. "You and Joey scurry around to the far side of the pinnacle," he said. "Better go above that talus slope rather than across it. It's a long way down to the bottom. And if you see anything that might affect them down below, get back here with it."

"Right." The man, whose name was Quirt, paused momentarily to look down toward the town and the massive spread of flames. "Jesus, did you ever see a sight like that?"

"Only in nightmares," Andy said, and meant it.


Ada was waiting in front of the house when Ken drove up. She wore an unsteady welcoming smile, and she took his arm in both of hers and held it tight against herself for reassurance as they walked to the door. "I'm sorry," she said. "I—"

"You did just right. It's bad."

"What do we do now?"

"I get out of this soup-and-fish and into jeans and go over to Bellevue Acres."

Her reaction was immediate and vigorous. "To do what? And why? That's closer to the fire line. I've heard on the radio, and on TV, that they don't know where they can stop it, so why do you—?"

"Slow down, baby. Those are my houses." He was thinking of Stacy's declared responsibility for her horses. "Damn it, in a sense, they're my people too, and—"

"But what can you do?"

Ken was taking off his dinner jacket, undoing his tie. He stopped and looked at Ada. "Nothing," he said. "Not a thing—except be there."

There was silence. Ada closed her eyes and shook

426

her head gently as if to drive a bad dream away. Presently her eyes opened again. "Okay," she said, and the smile she produced had lost its unsteadiness. "I go too."

"Now, look—"

"You look," Ada said, and her voice was firm. "I know the place. It's full of kids. Kids worry. I'm good with kids." The smile spread, lighting the entire room. "I used to be one. Maybe I still am. Where you go, buster, I'm tagging right along."

Driving back, alone in the rear seat of the big car, Bart Jones was annoyed with himself for having risen to Semple's innuendoes. Damn it, his libido had absolutely nothing to do with his attitude toward Stacy, nothing; frustrated lust did not even enter the equation. Once, perhaps, it might have, but that was back when he was still a whole man, filled with strength and pride, confident that he was able to compete on better than even terms with anyone.

After an accident such as his, what you had to learn—and this was perhaps the hardest lesson of all—was to accept the fact, and the implications, of your condition, thereby automatically setting limits to what you could even aspire to doing. And that meant putting aside forever even ideas such as the domination of Stacy Cummings that had been kept on the back burner because there was ample time to get around to them.

Stacy needed to be taught a lesson; that much was unchanged. She was, she always had been, too damn headstrong and willful, like one of her more spirited horses, in need of being shown that she was not top of the ultimate heap. But beyond that, his interest in Stacy was little more than academic, and it was probable that Semple knew it, which made Bart all the more annoyed with himself that he had risen to Semple's baiting.

To take his mind off the matter, he switched on the radio, tuned to the local station, and immediately wished he hadn't, but, instead of switching it off again, found himself listening in morbid fascination.

". . . and while it is not yet known how many thousands of acres the fire has consumed," an announcer's voice said breathlessly, "it is nonetheless apparent that now the town of Sanrio itself is threatened, and desperate measures are being taken in the town's defense."

Desperate measures unspecified, Bart thought, and then did switch off the sound. He doubted if he would get any coherent account until one of the more responsible newspapers came out with the full story, and in any event, he was about to see for himself just how serious the problem had become.

In the front seat the driver reacted as if the thoughts had been spoken aloud. Without turning his head he said, "Do you think it's safe, sir? To drive to the house, I mean?" It was a mistake.

"I wouldn't know," Bart said. "We'll find out, won't we?" Always he reacted instantly at the first hint of a challenge. He sensed hesitation in the front seat. "Just keep driving," he said, his voice hardening. "I'll tell you when or if we're going to stop."

## 35

JL braked the jeep to a sliding stop on the dirt road that overlooked the finger of the Forest. It was, he decided, a scene far beyond man's puny talents to depict on canvas or even on wide-screen film.

Wind-driven flames, deep, dirty orange to yellow in color, flung themselves high into the evening sky, backlighting as they destroyed massive ponderosa pine trees as a furnace consumes soft coal. The air was filled with flying sparks and ash and bitter, choking smoke, and the roar of the conflagration was as the thunderous sounds of mighty engines of destruction, rising and falling in pitch and magnitude as madmen maneuvered the controls.

Against the backdrop of the flames, the men on the fire line seemed tiny, insignificant, wielding tools like children on a beach trying with their toy shovels to hold back the thundering surf. They retreated slowly, stubbornly, grunting and sweating and swearing as with brush hooks, shovels, Pulaskis, axes, chain saws and McClouds they robbed the advancing fire of as much fuel as they could and bellowing bulldozers pushed it away. But the results, JL thought, were inevitable, and disastrous.

He surveyed the area swiftly but carefully, wanting no oversight to turn into a mistake because memory or present scrutiny missed a salient point.

There was the parking area, acres in extent, that Andy had mentioned, bare dirt and patches of grama grass which would amount to nothing as supporting fuel for a fire as voracious as BACKSLOPE.

In the center of the parking area was the rodeo grandstands, wooden, ancient, used these days only twice a year, for the annual rodeo itself, and on Fourth of July as a place to perch uncomfortably and watch the town's fireworks display.

Beyond the parking area, the town itself began, only scattered houses and an occasional convenience store at first, but further on, close, too close, more houses crowded together, divided by narrow streets as old as Sanrio itself. Once flames reached those houses, there would then be no stopping the conflagration short of the river. On the other hand, JL thought, if they could hold it here, it just might spell the beginning of the end for his voracious enemy.

He plucked the microphone from its bracket and sent out a call for Jay Paul, heard gratefully the almost immediate response, and identified his own position. "Here on the double," he ordered, and hung up.

While he waited, he reviewed the situation in his mind, again wanting no mistake in reasoning to come back later to haunt him. He had no panacea, he thought; indeed, with the winds what they were and were likely to continue to be, he was not even sure that a possible solution existed, but the alternative was simply turning your back and walking away, and that was unthinkable. Quit? Never.

He found himself thinking of what Ken had said

once about Stacy. "There's no give in her, none. She's pure rawhide all the way through."

JL liked that. Stacy would never quit, either. He was even smiling as Jay Paul drove up, got out of his own jeep and came over. Immediately JL was all business again.

He pointed back at the finger of the Forest. "We're fighting a loseing battle there. All we're doing is slowing the fire's progress. But we *are* doing that, ands that gives us a little time."

Jay Paul listened in silence. Since that flight experience, JL thought, Jay had matured. It was strange how quickly it could happen. No matter. He pointed again, in the direction of the town this time. "Those two parallel dirt roads," he said, "a quarter, three-eights of a mile apart, piñon and juniper between, thick growth." He watched Jay Paul follow his pointing finger, and nod slowly.

"Below the lower road," JL went on, "there's that parking area, and the grandstand." He paused. "Then the town begins." He paused again. "And it's all downwind." He waited. Ben would have seen it instantly. He wondered if Jay would need it spelled out.

Jay did not. "We burn out the piñon and juniper between the roads," he said. "If we do it fast enough, it will give us a fire break, burned-over area, no fuel, as wide as the space between the roads, *plus* the park area to protect the town." He nodded. "And the grandstand?"

"Explosives," JL said. "Take it right down flat. Lumber lying on the ground we can handle if it starts to burn. Flying sparks from a standing grandstand structure can go right over our heads and start setting roofs afire in town." He waited again.

Jay Paul thought about it briefly before he nodded. JL liked that moment of contemplation instead of blind

431

obedience. "Makes sense," Jay said.

"You're in charge," JL said. "I want to see the rest of the line firsthand. You can reach me on the radio."

Ken was surrounded as soon as he got out of his car at Bellevue Acres. He stood head and shoulders above the group, easy, friendly, in the face of what looked like incipient hysteria. "How's it going? Okay?"

The man who had spoken up to Ben Hastings previously said now, "Hell no, it's not okay! The Forest Service clown said that by burning that funny looking grove of trees we'd be okay, but just in case, we'd better get ready to run. Now what the hell kind of assurance is that?" He gestured broadly. "Look at all those goddam burning branches flying around! You call that okay?"

Behind him, two or three men had their garden hoses out, and were spraying the roofs of their houses. "I think," Ken said in a voice that had altered subtly, "that you'd better get off your ass, mister, and hitch up your hose and fall to with the rest of them. Let the women pack up, just in case."

"And just how in hell will we know when we ought to run? Tell me that!" There was a murmur of assent around him.

"I think you'd better rely on the Forest Service people to get the word to you," Ken said.

"I wouldn't trust those clowns to do anything. That's—"

"Mister," Ken said, and his voice was very quiet now, "I'm trying to be friendly, but you're making it very hard. If you keep stirring these people up, you're going to have real trouble on your hands—starting with me." He paused. "Is that clear?" He waited. "I asked a question," he said then, totally relaxed, but very large

432

and formidable. "I want an answer."

The man hesitated. Slowly he nodded and his eyes fell from Ken's. "Okay," he said and turned away. To the woman behind him, "Where's the goddam hose?"

Ken looked around at the group. "Any more questions?" There were none. "Then," he said, friendly again, "if I can use a phone, I'll see what I can do about getting someone here to keep an eye on things for you while you pack up, just in case."

Ada, standing a small distance from the dispersing group, took a deep breath. To a nearby nine-year-old boy she said, "Hi. What's your name? Jimmy? Okay, Jimmy, how's to get a bucket. Fill it with water. Got it? Then get a couple of tin cans, and you and I will set up an auxiliary fire brigade. How about that?"

"You nuts, or something? What can we do?"

"What we can do," Ada said as if she had been hoping the question would be asked, "is keep our eyes open for burning twigs — like that one over there — that are blown here. And when we see one, we dip up water in our tin can and douse the twig, but good. Then it can't cause any trouble. We'll leave the grown-ups with hoses to take care of the roofs. Okay?" She saw indecision in the boy's face. "Now scoot and get that bucket and the tin cans, huh?"

"Where'll you be?"

Ada tried to keep her eyes from the flames in the finger of the Forest beyond Mrs. Wayne's blackened grove. It was imagination, of course, but in the sudden wind gusts, she thought that even this far away she could feel the heat of the fire. (A little girl, holding her doll, watched the flames like these, and heard her crippled aunt screaming inside the house.) "I," she said, "will be right here, Jimmy. If you hurry." She took another deep breath. "Promise," she said.

433

Jimmy, breathless, raced back to fill his tin can again, and then scampered off to douse another small, burning branch that had landed on the lawn. "Ten!" he shouted in triumph, and bathed himself in Ada's approving smile.

Two other small boys watched, and approached Ada. "Can we help?"

"Sure thing. Get tin cans. But one thing," she added as they started to turn away, "Jimmy's auxiliary fire chief, okay?"

"Hey! He's only nine!"

"That may be," Ada said, "but he's had more fire-fighting experience, and that's what counts."


Pancho and her own herd of horses were well ahead, Stacy figured, probably too far to catch by straight pursuit. She guided Sam by the pressure of her knees and her shifting weight as well as by the hackamore, her balance as delicate as that of a downhill ski-racer on a perilous mountain course.

"We'll take these down toward the road, Sam. Short-cut," she said, neither knowing nor caring whether she spoke the words aloud or only in her mind.

After all those months, years of working together, Sam understood her body movement, if not the words. He changed direction subtly, anticipated the panicked move of the nearest Swift gelding and without seeming effort increased the length of his stride to block the gelding's escape. They tore through the trees, into the night. Stacy's shrill whistle kept the geldings at full gallop, and the flames nearby added panic to their pace.

Naked, except for the tiny panties, she was not unscathed. Twigs and small branches scratched her

434

bare arms and shoulders. She saw just in time a leafy aspen branch hanging too low, and she flattened herself against Sam's strong neck, her face pressed into his mane, and felt the leaves and branch ends scrape her back as they swept beneath. At least they were not in brush — this passed through her mind and was gone — she with bare legs and no chaps for protection. No matter. The horses were on their way to safety, and that was what counted.

Bessie Wingate was back on the fire line, working side by side with Gordy's hotshot crew, grunting and sweating and performing prodigies of work with her round-point shovel.

Gordy said, speaking of Eloy, "Tough. Will he make it?"

"A toss-up, I guess. They got him pumped full of pain-killer."

"I never had to use one of those fire shelters," Gordy said, "and I don't aim to get in a fix where I have to."

"Nor me."

Overhead a pine branch burst suddenly into flame with a roaring, crackling sound, and sparks came showering down. "Son a bitch is trying to crown," Bessie said. "This wind and all." She brushed a live spark from the back of her hand, and shook the hand vigorously. "Goddam!" Her shovel resumed its steady pace. "You think they'll try backfire?"

"That," Gordy said, "or let the whole damn town go, one."

In her peripheral vision, Bessie watched a burning branch break free and, windblown, go flying through the air. "No helitorch this time if they try it," she said. "No chopper can operate in this wind."

"Yeah," Gordy's tone was uncharacteristically grim.

"We'll do her by hand, on the ground." He glanced at Bessie and grinned suddenly. "Fun, huh?"

On the map in his mind, JL visualized the actively threatening fire line as beginning somewhere in the Forest above Stacy's section of land and stretching east-southeast through a part of the Swifts' property, dipping down to include the Holloways' and Mrs. Wayne's specimen grove, then rising northeast across the finger and above the County road almost to the access road that led into Forest Service Headquarters.

"Give or take a half mile," he said it aloud to himself, "or maybe by now even more." As he drove away from Jay Paul he called for Andy McIlvain on the jeep radio. Line-of-sight to the mountain peak, no sweat, and Andy's voice came in loud and clear.

"Your end position is in the upper part of that El Rancho Costa Mucha place — and I'll bet it did, too — and then, you're right, it runs pretty much the way you thought, staying above the County road. On the western end, they've got a job on their hands, but it looks as if they may contain it. With luck."

"I'll have a look-see," JL said. "Over and out." He headed the jeep westward.

The road was no more than a deer path, but in low transmission and four-wheel drive the jeep bounced and jostled and hammered its way through still-standing low brush. A State policeman materialized in an open spot and following orders gestured JL to stop, but the jeep did not even pause in its crashing progress.

From time to time JL bent his head to take whipping branches on his hard hat, but occasionally one caught him by surprise and banged against his shoulder or scratched hard against his face. No matter.

And suddenly there was the end of the fire line, dug

436

in, ground crews at work with hand tools, two bulldozers marching off pushing loose, cut debris out of
the fire's way, the acrid smoke and the heat and the
roaring, bellowing fury of the fire filling the air.

JL stopped and got out for his own close look.

Wind aloft, he saw; no slackening there; as he
watched, a flaming treetop, green and whole, broke
loose and went flying out of sight behind them. Sparks
and burning branches flew everywhere. Men, sweating
and grunting and manning the line, did not even look
up as he passed, and once he had to jump quickly aside
to miss being flattened by a bulldozer blade rolling
inexorably in its straight-ahead way.

He saw Jerry Weinstock whom he had told Ben to
put in charge of this sector, and he made his way
toward him.

Jerry was tall, cadaverous, all whipcord and spring
steel, with bony knees and sharp elbows, now filthy,
smoke-grimed, and obviously near exhaustion. But he
waited quietly in his reserved way, his eyes steady on
JL's face.

"Hand tools and bulldozers," JL said. "Doing it the
hard way." He nodded in understanding approval.

"Sometimes," Jerry said, "that's the way it goes."

JL looked around. As far as he could see into the
smoky murk and dust, men, almost shoulder to shoulder, were cutting their fire break, clean and sharp and
good, bare ground the enemy could not cross. Behind
them, he knew, would be back-up troops, and in the
more open ground, more equipment able to maneuver,
a defense in depth, solid yet flexible, and strong. He
looked again at Jerry. "Can you hold it?"

"We'll hold it." No hesitation, no doubt.

Slowly JL nodded. "I think you're right. Keep at it."
He turned away then and with no further words made
his way back to his jeep. The radio was crackling as he

437

got in. He picked it up, and spoke his name.

"Jay Paul here." There was anger in the voice, controlled anger beneath the words. "The Mayor objects to the backfire. And to blowing the grandstand."

A new voice came on the radio. "How does this damn thing work?" The mayor's voice was also angry. "Okay. Damn it, JL, you're trying to ruin good, saleable land. You know how long it takes a piñon to grow? Or a juniper? And that grandstand—"

JL pressed his microphone switch, pressed it again, shutting off reception. He pressed it yet a third time and said, "Jay? Over."

"Jay here." JL could picture the mike suddenly plucked from the mayor's hand.

"Carry on with that backfire," JL said. "I'm on my way." He started up the jeep's engine with a roar. Cursing civilians for their interference was an exercise in foolish futility, but there were times, like now, when the temptation was irresistable. Pushing the jeep as fast as it would go through the brush and among trees too large to knock down, he thought of all kinds of things he might say to His Honor the Mayor—and knew that he would say none of them because they would accomplish nothing.

And then, all at once in his headlights, in the dimness of the Forest growth, he saw what he could not for an instant really believe—Stacy, apparently naked, bent low on Sam's withers, dodging through the trees herding two other horses ahead of her and running straight toward what JL knew was an area aflame.

He blew the jeep's horn and shouted, but the apparition was already gone into the gathering gloom, disappearing as if it had never really existed.

JL reacted automatically, spun the wheel, bore down hard on the throttle and set off in pursuit. Damn the mayor. And the backfire. Both would have to wait unless Jay Paul could sort it out himself.


The horses saw, or sensed, the flames ahead before Stacy did, and without warning one of the Swift geldings screamed, turned so suddenly as almost to snap a leg bone and ran headlong into and through a solid mass of piñon and juniper branches without slowing. The other gelding followed.

Sam at full gallop spun as only a cutting horse can, and tore off in a new direction ninety degrees from his previous course.

Stacy had no saddle for support and no saddlehorn to grab, so she settled for a firm handful of Sam's mane which she almost pulled out by its roots as she struggled to retain her precarious balance on the big horse's back.

"Sam!" It was almost a scream, and it went unnoticed. "Ho, boy!" That, too, was wasted breath. With no bit in Sam's mouth to control his flight she was helpless, suddenly an unwilling passenger clinging as best she could as they crashed through low branches, an unexpected clump of brush and down and across the bottom of a dry arroyo.

Up the far side without slowing the mad pace, and there, in the darkness, at first invisible but suddenly looming, impossible to avoid, a low, solid pine branch scraped Stacy from Sam's back as cleanly as one scrapes snow from a boot sole.

She hit the ground and rolling limply, arms flying loose, fetched up against a dumped pile of debris by the side of the dirt road. She lay motionless as Sam thundered off into the night.


A State policeman flagged down and stopped Bart's

car. "Sorry," he said, leaning in the lowered rear window. "It isn't safe to go on."

"I live there."

"Maybe you did," the State cop said, "but it's a fair bet there isn't anything left to live in now."

"That I'll see for myself. And I'll take full responsibility."

"Look, mister," the State cop said, "my orders are to—"

The radio in the police car across the road came alive with a hollow sound and a voice spoke in police-radio jargon Bart could only hear faintly. The State cop turned away and walked quickly to the vehicle.

"Let's go!" Bart said, and when the driver hesitated, "You heard me, damn it!"

The big car rolled down the County road.

It was a scene of desolation, and even Bart, not customarily sensitive to his surroundings, was shocked by the blackened and smoking destruction of what had been a green, living forest. Here and there small flames still survived, feeding hungrily on last morsels of fuel; and the odor of charred wood hung in the air like the stench of death.

"*Madre de Dios*" the driver muttered and crossed himself hastily as in a graveyard. "*Señor*—" His voice, unconsciously dropping into Spanish, held an imploring note.

"Just keep going," Bart said. "If it's gone, it's gone, but I want to see."

They rounded a broad curve and, astonishingly, came upon a stand of tall, still living trees, flames now attacking their helpless perimeter. Wind gusts rocked the tree tops, and a burning branch flew across the road and narrowly missed the car. The driver winced visibly. Ahead, rising smoke marked other areas where the fire was still very much alive.

"*Señor*—" the driver said again, still in that imploring note.

"Shut up, damn it!" Automatic response. And then, in a louder, far more urgent tone, "Stop! Stop this goddam car, hear?"

The white, almost naked body by the side of the road showed clearly in the headlights.

"Jesus Christ!" Bart said. And then, "Don't just sit there, damn it! Get out and fetch her here! Jump!"

The driver set the brake and opened the door. Hesitantly, fearful at leaving the comparative safety of the big automobile, he stepped out. The woman looked dead, he told himself; and he had no desire to touch the dead body. Around him the wind wailed and shrieked with the sounds of souls in torment and the air seemed filled with ashes and small burning branches. Hellfire come real.

From the car, Bart's voice bellowed, "Goddam it, get going!"

One careful step, and then another, trying to look in all directions at once—and so it was that the driver saw, and, ducking, avoided the large, burning branch that flew towards him and crashed into the car, starring the windshield as if from a hammer blow. Suddenly the car was engulfed in flames.

Without even looking back, the driver turned and fled the scene.


It was George Jefferson's practice to maintain a hands-off policy toward the conduct of fighting a fire. As Supervisor of the Sanrio Forest, he considered, rightly, that his position was administrative rather than technically active, and in JL he believed that he had the best Fire Boss in the Service, so the trick was to give the man the job and let him do it.

But BACKSLOPE, Jefferson was coming to believe, was the kind of fire that ignored all the rules, and when one of those came along, all bets were off.

June, for example, was really too early for hurricanes, but there Charley was on the weather maps, flexing his muscles and raising havoc even this far inland. Over six weeks in summer was too long for no precipitation at all, but Jefferson could testify from his own knowledge that there had not been a drop of rain on this side of the great mountain.

The plain fact was, of course, that weather never behaved exactly as it was supposed to, as the sometimes wild variations among any comparisons of yearly weather charts would show.

El Niño did this or that and no one knew why; the jet stream meandered; Arctic air moved unobstructed down from Canada, or warm, moist air moved up from the Gulf, or sometimes both happened at once and suddenly tornadoes blossomed on the weather maps.

JL then, although he would not for the world have admitted it to anyone, much less to Jefferson, who understood all too well, was really pretty much in the position of a man blindfolded in a dark room trying to fight an enemy of unknown size, strength and numbers. BACKSLOPE was that kind of situation. So Jefferson decided that he would have a look-see for himself.

Down by the finger of the Forest where the greatest threat to the town was posed, Jefferson found Billy Bob Barker the mayor and Jay Paul in confrontation. "Where's JL?" was Jefferson's first question.

"He's on his way," Jay Paul said. "In the meantime—"

"In the meantime," Billy Bob Barker said. "Look!" He threw his arm in a dramatic gesture toward the piñon and juniper area upwind between the two parallel roads.

The trees were burning briskly, and two crews, Gordy's hotshots, minus Gordy himself and Terry Young, and Bessie's flock, were shepherding the conflagration, making sure that it did not get entirely out of hand and yet accomplished its scorched-earth mission.

"And," Billy Bob said, "that isn't all. They're setting charges under the rodeo grandstand, and they're going to blow it all to hell. So how do we stage a rodeo this year? Answer me that. All that tourist trade and traffic, let alone all that good, saleable, piñon and juniper land they're ruining." He was breathing hard.

Jefferson said, "JL's idea?" He was looking at Jay Paul.

"He doesn't think we can hold the finger, and if that goes, and there's no fire break between it and the town—"

Jefferson studied the towering flames in the big trees of the finger. Changing shadows and reflections hid his expression. "Judgement call," he said, looking now at Billy Bob. "And I trust JL's judgement." Because I have to, he thought.

A burning piñon branch, wind-driven, flew suddenly over their heads. Jefferson and Billy Bob ducked, pure reflex action. Jay Paul flinched, but turned to follow the flight of the burning branch. It landed only feet from the wooden grandstand in the center of the parking area. "That's what JL's afraid of," he said, his voice not quite steady. "If that grandstand catches—"

Jefferson said, "You've got men under there setting charges? Then you'd better get them out before they're trapped. And where the hell is JL?"

In rough, wooded country, a jeep was no match for a western-bred horse, and JL, having lost the trail, was pursuing the apparition he had glimpsed merely by guesswork now, driven by a compulsion against which there was no defense.

Stacy was a stubborn, damn fool. That much was clear. She had no business running around, clothes or no clothes, in the middle of a forest fire. As a matter of fact, neither did he, but at the moment that was unimportant.

Damn the woman, anyway, with her quick smile and her quicker wit and all the rest. He had the chance of a snowball in hell of finding her now, and the only sensible thing for him to do was to get out of this danger zone himself, but he plunged on, ignoring the brush and the small branches that caught against the windshield and then snapped against his body and his face as the jeep charged past.

There was fire to the right of him, he could see, and, yes, fire ahead as well, close, too damn close; he was beginning to feel its heat. He came to the dry arroyo Stacy had crossed, took its steep bank at an angle that almost overturned the jeep, and, all four wheels churning, scrambled up the far side. Brush ahead suddenly burst into flame, and he floored the accelerator and hoped that what was beyond was clear.

For a moment the heat of the flames seemed to sear his flesh, but the moment passed, and he was through and clear, bouncing out on to the road where the burning automobile stood, almost consumed. He stopped then, jumped out and ran as close as he could.

Bart had managed to get the rear door open despite the weight of the large flaming branch. Now, dragging himself by his hands, his clothing already afire, he was making his tortured way toward the verge of the road. He saw JL, and instantly his expression of grim determination changed to that of triumph, and with one hand he pointed.

"Get her!" His words came out as a croaking scream. "Goddam it, get her out of here! Never mind me!"

JL glanced toward the side of the road, and then looked again, stunned. Stacy's body lay motionless, seemingly without life. At that moment, he thought, something died within him, and movement was impossible. He looked blankly at the man on the ground.

"Goddam it! Will you do as I say? Get her out of here!" The tortured tone of the voice could not be ignored.

JL roused himself. He moved toward the body, slowly at first, and then broke into a trot. He scooped her up, finding her limp, helpless, unresponsive in his arms as he trotted back to the jeep and laid her gently in the front bucket seat. Then he turned back to Bart.

Bart's head was down, but it came up again, still wearing that expression of triumph. "Now get the hell out of here!" The words were almost impossible to understand, but the sudden arm gesture was not. "Look!" Bart said, pointing again with effort at the trees.

The flames had reached the near edge of the grove now, and a stately pine, aflame from trunk to top, was beginning its slow, inexorable death fall toward the road.

"Goddam it," Bart croaked, "will you go?" His head collapsed on the dirt.

JL ran to the jeep and jumped in. A few yards to a safer spot, he told himself, and then he could go back for the man. He put the jeep in gear, let out the clutch, and was starting away when a crackling, tearing sound announced that the last of the big tree's restraining roots had torn loose. In the jeep's mirror JL could see the tree itself, gathering speed as it fell.

He floored the accelerator, and even at the resulting, surging speed felt the heat of the burning branches as they crashed across the road behind them. He looked in the mirror again, and saw no Bart, no car, only the rising flames of a funeral pyre filling the road.

He drove on, his mind numb.


Bessie Wingate, peremptorily summoned to the jeep by JL's waving arm, her shovel still in her hand, stared at the naked, limp white body in the front seat. She stared then at JL's stricken expression. She nodded decisively.

"You got it," she said, and tossed the shovel into the rear seat as she squeezed herself massively beneath the jeep's steering wheel. "I'll take care of her. You tend to your goddam backfire." And she added angrily. "Will this fucking slaughter ever stop?"

The jeep roared off into the night.

## 36

JL moved like a man in a dream toward the spot where Jefferson, Mayor Billy Bob Barker and Jay Paul still stood. On his way he noticed automatically that the backfire had been set and was burning briskly between the two parallel roads upwind from the parking area and the grandstand, and that the towering fire in the finger of the Forest had progressed, driving back the crews that were fighting it. These facts impressed themselves on his consciousness as if from a distance.

The trouble, he thought, was that only a part of his attention was here, and that meant that his mind, instead of being in sharp focus, was wandering in directions and areas where it had no business being now, or perhaps ever.

The sight of Bart Jones driving himself to drag crippled body across the road toward Stacy, his clothing already ablaze and his body suffering God only knew what torment as the flesh was seared—this was not something you put out of your mind easily. Nor the helpless weight of Stacy's body — especially that — as he, JL, had carried her to the jeep and fled from that crashing, burning tree. And Bessie's last, muttered words, a defiant demand that the carnage stop—

"We're wiring charges under the grandstand," Jay Paul said.

"Good." His own voice, JL thought, spoke in its normal, calm tones as if they were discussing the weather or the baseball pennant races. Incredible. He was aware that Jefferson was studying him carefully.

"You okay?" Jefferson said. "You look skinned up, and maybe burned a bit. What happened?"

JL made a short, sharp gesture of dismissal indicating that what had gone before was unimportant. The hell it was. Bessie and Stacy, he thought; if anything could be done, Bessie would see to it. "Jerry Weinstock has his end anchored, secure. This is what we have to worry about." His broad gesture included the finger, the burning backfire, the town. He looked at Jay Paul. "Who's setting the charges?"

"Gordy Walker and Terry Young."

Jefferson watched another burning branch flying through the air in the direction of the grandstand. "Better get them out of there."

JL held out his hand for Jay's walkie-talkie. He pressed the mike button. "JL here. Come in, Gordy. Over."

It was Terry's voice that answered, irrepressible. "Hi, boss. How's every little thing?"

"How much longer?" JL said.

"It's nice in here," Terry said. "Cozy." In the background Gordy's voice said, "Tell the man, bigmouth. Ten minutes. Maybe a little more. Over."

JL said, "You're catching sparks. That dry wood and

448

all that paint can go up easy."

"You ain't seen nothing yet." Terry's voice again. "When we blow her, she's going to go WHOOOOMP!" And again Gordy's voice broke in. "Ten minutes. We want a complete job."

JL closed his eyes and nodded. "You got it." He handed the walkie-talkie back to Jay Paul. "Ten men," he said, "with pack pumps. Douse whatever lands on or near the structure." He turned to Billy Bob. "Get your city firemen on the job. A pumper at the far edge of the parking area. When she blows, there'll be sparks flying—"

"I'm against this whole thing," the mayor said. "I want to go on record—"

"Noted," JL said. "So now get your pumper in place." He was thinking again of Stacy.

The resident on duty in the hospital emergency room opened his mouth to protest as Bessie pushed the door open with one shoulder and walked in carrying Stacy in her arms as if she were a small child.

"Which table you want her on?" Bessie said. "This one?" She laid the limp body down with vast gentleness, and turned, huge and grimy, yellow hard hat jammed down on her ears, her eyes peering out through the smudges on her face like burned holes in a blanket, to glare at the startled doctor.

"Well?" she demanded. "Get going, goddamnit! You're a medic, aren't you? She's breathing, so you got a handle to grab. Let's see you move your ass and get on it!"

She walked to a nearby uncluttered wall space, leaned against the wall, crossed her booted ankles and folded her massive arms. "I'll wait," she said, and watched with approval as two nurses appeared and the doctor came out of shock and began to stir himself.

From his mountain perch, looking down upon the entire semi-circular spread of the fire, Andy McIlvain studied the situation with experienced eyes. At last he raised his walkie-talkie and called for JL.

"It's blowing merry hell up here," Andy reported, "and I imagine it is down there too. Your west flank is holding. Whoever's in charge there—"

"Jerry Weinstock," JL said.

"Good man. He looks in fair shape. Bellevue Acres at the moment looks reasonably safe too. Along the center, you're going to lose at least one more of those big places. Take that as read. The backfire by the parking area—"

"That's where I am."

Andy's voice took on a new, warning note. "Figured. There's more wind coming at you, pappy. I can see the smoke north of you lying out flat. That grandstand—"

"We're going to blow it."

"Then you'd better do it quick because the wind that's coming is going to be tossing burning branches around like pine needles, and that old structure will go up in a hurry if it catches. It's pure timber, and it'll damn near explode if it isn't flat on the ground."

"Got it," JL said. "Over and out." He handed Jay Paul the radio and looked at Jefferson. "You heard? Okay." No hesitation or lack of clarity now. He jerked his head sideways at Mayor Bill Bob Barker, but spoke still to Jefferson in a tone of command. "Kick his ass if you have to, but get that town pumper in position at the far end of the parking area. Those houses are going to need all the protection they can get." He turned away.

Jefferson said, "You—" But JL was gone at a brisk trot, headed for the grandstand. Bending low, he ran in beneath it.

One of the emergency nurses, working with quick, deft, gentle movements to tend to the cuts and contusions on Stacy's naked body, said, "There was a wild story on the radio about a nude woman herding a bunch of horses. Do you think—"

"Nonsense," the doctor said, "somebody made that up. We want an X-ray of this shoulder, and I think her skull as well. I don't know where she's been, but she's taken a beating." He glanced up at Bessie still leaning against the wall. "You still here? There are chairs in the hall outside." It was a less than gentle hint. It was also wasted breath.

Bessie had pushed her yellow hard hat a little back on her forehead, exposing a line of clean skin. Other than that, she was as she had been when she walked in. "I'll wait right here," she said in a tone of finality.

She had no idea who it was lying limp and helpless on the table, but JL had spoken of her with more than respect, with obvious affection, and Bessie trusted JL's judgement, and that was all there was to it.

From puberty Bessie had envied females who looked like Stacy, normal-sized, shaped the way God meant females to be shaped, usually pretty damn helpless, but that was okay too, given what they had to work with.

But when a man like JL spoke of one of those normal-type females, it wasn't usually with the kind of feeling that had been in his voice when he spoke of Stacy, so that made this one something special who'd probably done something out of the ordinary to get

451

herself banged up like this. Eloy Jaramillo came strangely to mind, poor little bastard.

Bessie shifted her position, and re-crossed her ankles. "You're doing fine, doc," she said. "Just keep at it."


Beneath the grandstand, JL switched on his helmet light and made his way as quickly as he could among the X-braces toward the lights farther in that marked Gordy's and Terry Young's location. Reaching them, "How we doing?" JL said.

It was the irrepressible Terry who answered, "Ginger-peachy." He was wiring a charge to one of the grandstand uprights.

Gordy said, "We'll bring her down, not blow her up. Take out these supports and she'll collapse like a house of cards."

JL nodded approval. "How long?"

The question was echoed by one of Gordy's hotshot crewmen, scrambling in toward them. "Bernie says how long?" He was panting. "The wind's blowing harder and those piñons are going up like bombs! Bernie says—"

JL said, "Are we clear overhead? The structure hasn't caught yet?"

"It's going to," the crewman said. "Pack pumps won't hold what's flying around. I mean, that wind is *blowing!*"

Gordy moved quickly to the next grandstand upright and began wiring his charge. He talked as he worked. "I told Bernie I'd kick his ass up between his shoulder blades if he didn't hold that backfire under control. Tell him I meant it. Tell him that." He merely glanced at the crewman. "And you get the hell out of here."

JL said, "You've got a reel of wire? Good. You,

452

Terry, take it on out and hook it up. We'll hook to it here when we've got the charges set."

Terry said in protest, "Hey!"

"You heard me," JL said. "Beat it!"

And then JL and Gordy were alone, working with careful haste. Gordy said, "Old guy I knew once drove a nitroglycerine truck in the oil fields back in the Thirties. Got a dollar a mile, big wages then, depression times. Got paid every night. Spent it every night too. Man has to be crazy to take a job like that, no?" He threw a quick glance at JL, and in the light of his helmet lamp, his face showed a faint smile. "Let's not answer that, huh?"

Jefferson said to Billy Bob, "I'm not going to tell you again before I do what JL suggested and start kicking your ass. Get that pumper in place!" He watched a burning juniper branch fly through the air and land almost lazily among the darkened grandstand seats. He waited, but no flames appeared. "You hear me?" he said without looking at Billy Bob.

Billy Bob said, "We can post more men in the grandstand, can't we? I mean, to put out any fires that could start? Then we wouldn't have to—"

"We could not!" Jefferson's voice was sharp now. "If that fire trap even begins to go, we don't want anybody anywhere near it. It—" He stopped, his eyes still fixed on the spot where the juniper branch had disappeared. "Christ!" he said softly. "There she goes!"

One moment there was a small column of smoke rising. Incredibly, the smoke turned on the instant into flame that ran along a wooden seat, reached a cross-brace, climbed to the seat back and jumped to the next row. Within moments an entire section of seats was

453

ablaze.

There were running footsteps in the parking lot gravel behind them, and as Jefferson turned, he saw a yellow-hard-hatted man with a walkie-talkie at his mouth, saying urgently, "Gordy, come in! Come in, damn it, Gordy!"

"Give me that!" Jefferson said, and taking the radio to his own mouth, pressed the microphone button. "Jefferson here," he said. "The stands are on fire. Get out. Repeat, get out! Acknowledge!"

Terry, on his knees nearby attaching the detonator to the wire he had carried out, said, "Stop clicking your teeth. They'll come as fast as they can."

"Damn it—" Jefferson began.

And here came Gordy on a dead run to slide to a stop in the gravel and hunker down to inspect Terry's connections. "Okay." He nodded judiciously. "That ought to do her." He glanced up at Jefferson. "JL'll be along directly."

"He'd damn well better be." Jefferson's eyes were on the grandstand, which was now a mass of flames.

"Here comes old JL," Terry said. "For an old man, he motors pretty good."

JL was running, limping slightly, Jefferson noticed, and holding one arm with the other hand. He whistled, a shrill, piercing sound, and his voice raised a shout that reached them clearly. "All set! Blow it!"

Terry pressed the detonator handle. There was a dull, *harrumphing* sound, hollow as a door closing on a gigantic distant closet. For a moment nothing happened, and then the whole, flaming grandstand structure seemed to shudder as if from pain, and with slow dignity collapsed inward upon itself in a fiery mass that flung sparks high into the air. All that remained when the mass had settled was a low-lying pile of shattered lumber burning as a fire burns in a grate.

"Told you," Terry said in triumph, "busted wood and rusty nails. Now maybe we can get some comfortable seats when we watch the rodeo."

JL arrived, breathing deeply, but not hard. Jefferson's eyes were on the burning debris. "Town pumper on the way," he said. "It can handle that." He looked then at JL. "What happened to your arm?"

JL made a sharp gesture, dismissing the question, and turned to survey the entire scene. The burned-over area between the two roads was still glowing, still throwing wind-driven sparks and burning branches into the air, but with the grandstand no longer there the threat was gone. Beyond the upper road, trees in the finger of the Forest burned on, the force and fury of the fire slowly diminishing for want of fresh fuel. The town pumper arrived clanging noisily, and firemen set about subduing what was left of the burning grandstand.

Billy Bob Barker said, "A bond issue! Migod, do you know what that's going to mean politically?"

"Shut up, Billy Bob," Jefferson said without taking his eyes from JL who was still holding his arm as he walked to a nearby jeep. "Just shut up!" Jefferson repeated, and turned to Gordy Walker. "What's wrong with his arm?"

"A timber burned loose and fell on his shoulder as we were wrapping it up."

Jefferson blinked, remembering the grandstand flames. "It was that close?"

Gordy's face and voice were expressionless. "Let's say we didn't have the hell of a lot of leeway."

Reaching into the jeep with his good hand, JL switched on the radio and took up the mike. "Patch me through to Jerry Weinstock," he told the dispatcher.

455

And when the connection was made, "Still holding?"

No hesitation, no uncertainty. "We'll hold it," Weinstock said.

"Good man." JL's voice held its customary calm. "Now get me Ben Hastings," he told the dispatcher, and then, quickly, "No. Make that Andy McIlvain up on the mountain." And while he waited, he had a final look at the collapsed grandstand, and at the burned-over area between the two roads.

It was not over yet, he thought, not quite, but despite Charley and all the rest, they had the upper hand now, and unless Andy had bad news, the outcome was no longer in doubt. His face remained expressionless.

Andy's voice said, "That was quite a cliff-hang, but never mind, you pulled it off. The town looks good from here."

"And the rest of the way around?"

"You're under control from that north-south line to the northeast Big Bessie and that hotshot crew established, through the north quadrant where what's left of the fire is down below the highway, through the west where they've contained it, and as far as the estate area where Jerry Weinstock says he's holding. Little flare-ups here and there, but, what the hell, you're going to have those to contend with for days."

True enough. But it was still victory. "Over and out," JL said, and called the dispatcher. "Now Ben Hastings," he said. And when Ben's voice came on, "How are we over at the development? Bellevue Acres?"

"They're packed up, ready to get out if they have to, while the men are spraying the roofs with garden hoses. So far, okay." Ben hesitated. "Your friend Ken whatever-his-name-is wants somebody official there to tell them when to evacuate if it becomes necessary, but—"

"Yes," JL said in sudden understanding. In the end, he thought, it all came down to people, individuals, not forests or trees or paintings on canvas, individual persons. Like—Stacy. It was a new concept. "I'll go," he said. "You can reach me there."

Gordy Walker said, deadpan, "All the same to you, me and Terry'll come along to carry your walkie-talkie." He walked toward the jeep. "Come on, loudmouth."

Ken Delacorte was easily visible, towering above the householders, directing hoses here and there, encouraging, praising, urging where necessary. He saw the jeep pull up, and he walked quickly toward it. He studied JL briefly and showed the hint of a smile. "They sent a boy on a man's errand, I see," he said.

"Something like that." JL's eyes caught Ada Loving, totally occupied with the kids who scurried to and fro at her direction. He smiled up at Ken. "Breaking her to harness?"

"That'll be the day." Ken's smile disappeared. His eyes studied JL's face intently. "What's the word?"

He could savor the moment. Once again, they had fought the beast and whipped it. They had had luck, most of it bad, and they had lost a great deal, some of it irreplaceable, but they had learned some things too, and in the process blooded some good young ones like Ben Hastings and Jay Paul to take over. So it was no stand-off; it was victory, and he could say it with pride. "You're safe. We've got it whipped." Only for this time, of course, because there would be others, but never mind. "You can tell them that."

Ken said, "I think you'd better tell them yourself. They'll listen to you." He watched JL nod slowly, and

457

take a deep breath as he heaved himself wearily out of the jeep.

"Better make it short," Gordy Walker said. "Next stop the hospital to have that shoulder looked at."

"You hear the man, bwana?" Terry said.

# POSTSCRIPT

Bessie Wingate, cramped into store clothes and scrubbed until she shone, was coming out of the hospital room as JL, his arm in a sling, came down the corridor. Bessie stopped. "What happened to you?" She shook her head. "Never mind. You look like you'll live."

JL was smiling faintly. "I expect to."

"Somebody," Bessie said, "said they heard you were quitting. I said, 'That's a lot of crap.' You get a taste for smoke, and like a drunk, you can't give it up." She flipped one large hand in a parting gesture. "See you at the next one," she said, and rolled off down the corridor in her uniquely ponderous but light way.

JL, expressionless, watched her go. Bessie was about as subtle as a fist in the mouth, and her view of the world was pure black-and-white, no shades of gray allowed. Nothing on God's green earth was going to change her, ever. You could depend on that, just as you could depend on her, and there were damn few of whom you could say the same. He was about to see another of those few.

He glanced up at the number of the room Bessie had been visiting, knocked on the partially opened door and went in, expressionless still.

Stacy was propped up in bed. Her left arm was in a cast, but that was the only bandage that showed. Her face reflected no pain, and her eyes watched him steadily.

JL looked around the room at the vases of flowers. "I guess I ought to have brought something."

"You know better. You're the reason I'm here at all."

"Your friend is. Was. Jones."

Stacy shook her head gently as if to drive that thought away. JL felt the same himself. "I just wanted to see how you were," he said. He felt ill at ease, and yet strangely comfortable too, as if words were not really necessary in order to say a great deal of what was in his mind.

Stacy was smiling faintly, almost certainly reading his thoughts. "You whipped it," she said. "I knew you would."

"We were lucky."

"Yes." The faint smile was gone, but amusement remained in her eyes, amusement, and something else that had no name. "The harder you fight," she said, "the luckier you get. I've noticed that too. Shall we add that to the list of things we have to talk about?" She paused. "When you show me your paintings?"

"That list," JL said, "is getting pretty long." He took a deep breath. "What I mean is—"

"That it's going to keep on growing," Stacy said. "Yes. I've been thinking that too. It's going to take a very long time to talk our way through it."

From sparks that had flown between them as freely as from a blacksmith's hammer, JL thought suddenly, to—this. He shook his head in wonder. Hard to believe. But also more pleasant to think about than he would have thought possible. It produced the kind of feeling that warmed a man clear down to his toes. He said slowly, but not tentatively, "Maybe we won't ever reach the end of it."

Stacy's faint smile had returned, but its amusement was replaced by pure warmth. "We'll have fun finding out," she said. "Together."

# CONTEMPORARY FICTION
## From Zebra Books

**ASK FOR NOTHING MORE**                    (1643, $3.95)
by James Elward
Mary Conroy never intended to become the Other Woman, but suddenly she belonged to a world of exotic hideaways ecstasy filled nights. . . . and lonely Sunday mornings. A world where desire and desperation, love and betrayal, were separated only by a plain band of gold.

**JADE**                                    (1744, $3.95)
by Nancie MacCullough-Weir
Inside the all-white interior of Ivan and Igor's Spa, Manhattan's very rich and pampered women worked their already beautiful bodies into perfect shape. Jade Green was one of these women. She had everything except the love she craved.

**SOMEBODY PLEASE LOVE ME**                 (1604, $3.95)
by Aviva Hellman
Beautiful high-fashion model Cat Willingham became a vulnerable, sensuous woman in Clay Whitfield's arms. But she wondered if her independence was too great a price to pay for passion.

**WHAT THE HEART KEEPS**                     (1810, $3.95)
by Rosalind Laker
When Lisa met Peter she instantly knew he was the man she had been waiting for. But before she surrendered to the fires of desire, Lisa had to choose between saving herself for a distant wedding night or having one night of unforgettable sensuality to cherish for the rest of her days.

**WINTER JASMINE**                           (1658, $3.50)
by Pamela Townley
From the instant they met in the crowded park that steamy morning, Beth knew that Danny Galloway was the man she wanted. Tired of life in the fast lane, Danny was ready for someone like Beth. Nothing would stop him from making her his own!

# TALES OF TERROR AND POSSESSION

**MAMA** (1247, $3.50)
by Ruby Jean Jensen
Once upon a time there lived a sweet little dolly, but her one beaded glass eye gleamed with mischief and evil. If Dorrie could have read her dolly's thoughts, she would have run for her life—for her dear little dolly only had killing on her mind.

**JACK-IN-THE-BOX** (1892, $3.95)
by William W. Johnstone
Any other little girl would have cringed in horror at the sight of the clown with the insane eyes. But as Nora's wide eyes mirrored the grotesque wooden face her pink lips were curving into the same malicious smile.

**ROCKABYE BABY** (1470, $3.50)
by Stephen Gresham
Mr. Macready—such a nice old man—knew all about the children of Granite Heights: their names, houses, even the nights their parents were away. And when he put on his white nurse's uniform and smeared his lips with blood-red lipstick, they were happy to let him through the door—although they always stared a bit at his clear plastic gloves.

**TWICE BLESSED** (1766, $3.75)
by Patricia Wallace
Side by side, isolated from human contact, Kerri and Galen thrived. Soon their innocent eyes became twin mirrors of evil. And their souls became one—in their dark powers of destruction and death . . .

**HOME SWEET HOME** (1571, $3.50)
by Ruby Jean Jensen
Two weeks in the mountains would be the perfect vacation for a little boy. But Timmy didn't think so. The other children stared at him with a terror all their own, until Timmy realized there was no escaping the deadly welcome of . . . *Home Sweet Home.*

*Available wherever paperbacks are sold, or order direct from the Publisher. Send cover price plus 50¢ per copy for mailing and handling to Zebra Books, Dept. 2041, 475 Park Avenue South, New York, N.Y. 10016. Residents of New York, New Jersey and Pennsylvania must include sales tax. DO NOT SEND CASH.*